Sharper Mind
Darker Dreams
A Novel

LEONARD SEET

Excelsior Publishing

Washington, DC

Published in the United States by Excelsior Publishing

ISBN-10: 0-967-49376-5
ISBN-13: 978-0-967-49376-3

Seet, Leonard

Sharper Mind Darker Dreams / Leonard Seet.

p. cm

1.   Sharper Mind

2.   Darker Dreams

3.   Leonard Seet

First Edition

Library of Congress Control Number: 2019920057

Praise for *Magnolias in Paradise*

"Leonard Seet brings his intelligence and wit and gifts as a writer to a broader audience in *Magnolias in Paradise* in a gritty, realistic novel. Seet has reinvented himself as a writer in his evolution from his deeply rich, engaging and inspirational books about spirituality to the rough ride on the mean streets of *Magnolias in Paradise*. ...you'll definitely be engaged by this novel."

- David Lentz, author *Bloomsday: the Bostoniad*

"The book is immensely readable and is packed with fast paced actions, and cliff hanging chapter endings."
- Ashok Shenolikar, author What Did You Say Your Name Was?

Praise for *Meditation on Space-Time*

"Meditation on Space-Time is a strong pick for those seeking a metaphysical twist..."

- Midwest Book Review

"Great lyrical novel... A rich, intricately plotted story."
- Mike Bresner, author *All I Want for Christmas*

"Literary, Metaphysical, Thought-provoking."

- Mallory Heart Review

Acknowledgement

I would like to thank my wife for her support.

CONTENTS

CHAPTER 1 - X

September 5 (1)

Woke up from a nightmare. Pounding headache. My mind empty. Lying on a mattress with floral sheets. Bandages around my arms and legs. My eyes focused, but I recognized nothing, not the closet, not the paperback on the side table, not the damn fog outside the window. The walls almost as blank as my mind. No calendar, no clock, no posters, not even a TV. Only a surveillance camera under the ceiling, a lens gazing at me. Outside the bay window, a chestnut tree emerged from the lifting fog.

I pinched my left palm with my right thumb and index finger. Pain stirred my mind, but my head spun and sweat soaked my back.

Where am I? How did I get here? And who in Descartes' name am I?

***

My heart pulsed. My nerves tingled. Ocular migraine. A vacuum in my stomach. I sat up. Gripped the pillow to steady myself, but shoved it over the bed. Pushed the side table and almost knocked it over. I panted. I sweated. Scintillating scotoma. Migraine in my right temporal lobe. I shut my eyes. Hoping to dispel the pain. Hoping to return to my own world. Opening them again, I faced the same coffee table, the same ceiling fan, the same fog, and the same damn migraine.

Is this my bedroom? Is this my house? Is this I?

The book on the side table, Descartes' *Discourse on Meditation*, I seized it. Was going to read it, but found the word "NFTU" across the inside front cover.

The sheets I flung off, and tried to infer the season, the month, the time of day. Ignoring the bandages, I struggled down the bed. My hand crashed against the bed railing and dented it. My hand neither bled nor bruised. Steel-hard like a robot's claws, these fingers I couldn't relate to. Not only this hand, but also my pupils, my eardrums, my cerebrum, and my atria and ventricles. All alien. Where could mine have gone?

In an oversized gown I reeled to the closet, my slippers squeaking. In the mirror, a stranger, a man lost in time, alien to this earth and sky, gazed at me across the boundary between illusion and dream. The face an abstraction, a representation of a person, not myself, but a generic *he*, whom I couldn't relate to or empathize with. I should sing or sigh or roar or moan, but fear expanded in my stomach. I sensed a self, distinct from the mirror, the pillow, and the book. A consciousness trapped inside a body. My skin formed the boundary separating me from not-me. I am myself, not the nitrogen atoms in the air.

The self before the mirror—that is, the self somewhere in the front of my head—was examining the *he* in the mirror. I observed myself studying the stranger in the mirror and not recognizing the observer.

***

Focused for twenty-eight minutes. Except for the headache, my mind blank, as if I had just sprung into this world. Reviewing my journal entry's first lines, I couldn't recall my sensations and mental states. Had I dreamed? Maybe, still recovering. I took my pulse and blood pressure. Tracked a bug zigzagging outside the window. Finished a Soduku in four minutes. Solved a second-order partial differential equation. Played a familiar tune with a piece of paper. While balancing the laptop on my index finger.

Beyond the bay window, chestnuts dropped from the tree and reality shifted under my feet. At first, the chestnuts fell faster than they should. Perhaps losing my memory had skewed my perception. After a while, by hocus-pocus, they fell slower, yes, slower.

The void spread in my stomach, turning into a chill through my arms and legs. I remembered—maybe from the part of my mind still working—objects, ignoring air drag, should fall at the same rate regardless of mass and size. Was the gravitational constant changing before my eyes? Or my mind warping? I waited for the chestnuts to fall faster again, but the system seemed to have rested. Or, universal constants had stopped taunting me, for now.

If only I could reach out to my kinsmen, to my friends, if only I could reach out to my past, my identity. At time's edge, my present self must confront the future, those possibilities, without the knowledge, the wisdom, the camaraderie of my past self. To trek across the desert, to step onto the sand, to face the dunes, this stranger in time, a baby who must construct his past with each passing moment.

I have no name; I have no past; I have no memory. Only the word "NFTU," a clue that means nothing to me.

I turned from the chestnut tree and read *Discourse on Meditation*. After contemplating the existence of my left ventricle and dorsolateral pre-frontal cortex, I ate the apple and tried the doorknob to find myself a prisoner.

CHAPTER 2 - FRANCISCO

August 22, 2011 (1)

I'm Francisco Guzman. I'm not sick. I'm not spiteful. I'm not unattractive. And no, I'm not X, that amnesiac in my dream. Remember you're relishing my story, not his, as you sop up my words and my syllables. So, never mind that nameless ameba.

As a wise guy once said, it is a universal truth that if you assert some nonsense as if it were God's Word, everyone including yourself will sooner or later accept it as Scripture. Amen.

Well, this morning, I woke up from my dream to find Ms. Redhead gone without leaving her phone number and Twitter handle. Not even lipstick on my cheek. Talk about being cold. For half an hour, I sat in bed trying to replace the nightmare with memories of her lips, her skin, her hair. But the dream's aftertaste, dull and dreary, still lingered in my mouth.

Outside, the fog had hidden the George Washington Bridge and the roses I'd bought my neighbor two days ago, they looked pale in the vase on her kitchen table. The *horn concerto* in Amsterdam Avenue blasted through the mist and heralded another New York stick-it-in-your-face morning. What a lovely city.

In the kitchen that reeked of onion and garlic, I cleaned the dishes in the sink, and made French toasts and scramble eggs that'd shame a chef into early retirement, if not hara-kiri.

Though the nightmare still plagued me, I'd fill my belly before calling my sidekick Clint a.k.a. Mr. OCD to have him buy a bouquet for

4

Wednesday's funeral, but before I could step into the dining room to enjoy the gourmet, my phone crooned. I held the coffeepot for five seconds, deciding between breakfast and spat, before opting for a pick-me-up to begin the day. The spat, not the coffee. Lovely, make my day. Pushing aside my soiled striped socks, which my previous girlfriend Holly had bought me, I picked up the iPhone on the counter, ready to curse the dunce for disturbing my morning sacrament, breakfast.

A monotone, as if the maggot had just awoken from a trance, droned, "Tell me again. How'd you transcend good and evil?"

"Ahem, you said you're from Pluto? Well, since it's no longer considered a planet, I've decided not to gyp anyone there. You know, no more Most Favorite Planet treaty." The marketer was probably trying to sell a cure for baldness or impotence, both of which, as you know, I didn't and wouldn't need. Then again, the knucklehead might be talking in his sleep.

"Keep in mind, it's life and death, yours. So don't put off finding the answer like those dolts who focus on the urgent rather than the important stuffs. Remember, last time we talked about the amnesiac in your dream—"

"I remember kicking the butt of a butt-face who'd tried to bully me. Maybe yours. Don't recall. Don't care. Not interested in fortune telling, horoscope or witchcraft. So buzz off." How did he know about my dream? Did this maggot peep into my diary? I hung up and expected the loser of a loser to call again, but the phone didn't whine the rest of the morning.

I would've gone back to bed if I had dreamed of Ms. Redhead or even if I hadn't dreamed. In last night's dream, I awoke in a hospital bed and found a journal in a laptop. No password, no encryption, the file exposed on the screen. I peeked and scanned a few lines:

I have no name; I have no past; I have no memory. Only the word "NFTU," a clue that means nothing to me.

This dream self, not related to me, is a John Doe Nobody, a.k.a. Jodono, a stranger without a birthday or a birthplace. A shadow in a dream, living in some God-forsaken Hilbert Space. Fine, let the amnesiac search for his past and let me live my life.

For several nights, I'd returned to the same dream, the same bed, the same room, the same fog and chestnut tree in the hospital courtyard. I'd met the same doctor, the same painting, the same puzzle. If only the amnesiac would stop harassing my butt.

Throughout last week, I drank whiskey, I bungee-jumped, and I hacked into databases, but still couldn't exorcise Jodono. Never fear, I'll find the spell to purge the demon. That amnesiac, trying to dump his neurosis onto my psyche. Unlike him, I have a life. And a damn decent one, too.

I didn't allow a shrink to toy with my mind though. Not this mind, on par with those of Einstein and Hawkins, not to mention Gauss and Fermat, and Euclid and Pythagoras. I would've proven Fermat's Last Theorem, if I'd been born a few years earlier. Well, life isn't fair.

While I crunched toast and buttered the coffee, the mysterious caller's question slithered through my mind, mainly my neo-cortex, and I reflected on the yin and yang of good and evil and surveyed the philosophers and theologians who'd formulated *definitive theories*, which sooner or later succumbed to other *definitive theories*. Amen.

After breakfast, I turned on the TV and navigated through the living room's laundry to the sofa and rummaged through beer cans and programming language manuals until I located my copy of Dostoevsky's *Notes from the Underground*. I scanned through the parchment for the underground man's wisdom—wish we have such wisdom nowadays—but even that masterpiece couldn't enlighten me. And as I mulled over the dialectics between good and evil, the caller's hissing disturbed me more than the question. I could imagine his tongue sticking out at every syllable, searching for prey.

I was watching the news of a CEO who just received a ten-million-dollar bonus for laying-off a quarter of the staff to turn his company profitable when the doorbell crooned "Praises to Fransuccesco." Lovely tune. Did Ms. Redhead return to set up our next date? No, a sweet voice called from the hallway, "Francisco Guzman?"

When I opened the door to a lady holding a photo and glancing at it and then at me and again at it, my knees trembled and my mouth dried. Don't laugh. She'd bring me joy and pain and more joy. And, more pain. And these emotions traveled back in time to sweeten my heart. What could I do when la dolce vita seized me? Except to surrender.

CHAPTER 3 – X

September 5 (2)

I should have stayed in my prison and not left the *bedroom*. So I could keep my illusion and peace of mind. When the door didn't open, I twisted the knob and broke the handle. Just like that. I hesitated, unsure whether shotguns were pointing at the door. No voices and no footfalls in the hallway. Just fluorescent lights buzzing and instruments humming.

Several minutes later, maybe two or three, I pushed away the door with Descartes' book. Stepped into a corridor smelling of anesthesia. Several gurneys stood on both sides of the wall. A nurse station at the end of the passage.

A hospital, not a house or an apartment.

Had a Dr. Frankenstein inserted a microchip in my neocortex? Was a Jack the Ripper preparing to cut me up?

I tiptoed along the corridor, glancing back once every nine and a half seconds, searching for doctors, nurses, or human guinea pigs. Determined to find out by hook or by crook where I was and why I was there.

Then I heard it.

Breathing. Someone was breathing.

I turned around. A security guard chewing gum or tobacco approached, swiveling a baton. Where had I seen that ogre in the past?

Into the room next to my bedroom I peeked to search for a bat or a pipe, or just a hatchet, unaware of the paperback in my hand. Inside the room, a lean doctor with aquiline nose and penetrating eyes, a shadow

7

even during the day, he gestured for me to enter. Behind him, another bay window facing the fog and the chestnut tree.

How could I wake up from this nightmare?

"Never mind him," the doctor said.

With the guard two feet away, I entered the room and shut the door. After putting the book on a tray table next to an apple, I sat beside a white-sheeted bed opposite the stranger.

"Who are you?" I said.

He flipped through my book and asked about Descartes' rubbish.

I picked apart the philosopher's arguments, focusing on those after he had arrived at *Cogito Ergo Sum*. Rejecting his argument for the existence of the bed, the tray table, the chestnut tree, I could only affirm my own flesh and blood, maybe just my mind.

Okay, thinking is sufficient but not necessary for existing, so if "Cogito" implies a thinking self, I could restrict it to the brain or even to the neo-cortex. But who am I? Just a neo-cortex? For Descartes not only did his body, brain and sense of self exist, but also his history and future. Yet, even as I write this entry, I have less than a day in my past and no vision of the future. Sure, my brain can analyze and debunk Descartes' arguments. So what?

"So who the hell am I?" I said.

He showed me photos of a car accident. The crumbled sedan, the brick buildings, the cement sidewalks, the gesturing bystanders in the photos, they intrigued me, especially the blue-nosed clown in a three-piece pinstripe suit, but they didn't bring back any memories.

A miracle that I survived the accident. But I don't believe in miracles. Only in conspiracies.

"I want to know the truth," I said.

"Even at the cost of freedom? Even at the cost of your future?"

"Are you here to help me? Or to experiment on me?"

"You'll need courage and strength and often callousness and resignation to enter the desert, to face the sand dunes, to confront the sandstorms."

"I know nothing about sandstorms, much less courage and strength. I only know I have to find me. Without me, what am I?" I had to choose between history and destiny, between the caterpillar and the butterfly, between DNA and synaptic pulses, between what I was and what I could be.

"Are you callous enough? Are you totally resigned? You'll face sandstorms and they won't care about your courage and strength."

"Fear," I said. "I fear losing my self. I fear losing my past. I fear existing but not living. Fear. That's what I have plenty of. That's what'll force me forward. Not courage or strength, not callousness or resignation. Just pure and sanctified fear. To step into the wasteland, to risk finding some ghoul, some gargoyle, some slimy leviathan. And face them with my fear."

I will dig up the records buried among the neural labyrinths in my cortexes. I will rediscover me, the companion for the past decades. And if I grind my teeth and enter the swamp, I will succeed. Somehow. What sludge, what scum, what toxins will I reveal? Sure, I will enter the desert, driven by a horde of bandits, but will I exchange a quick death for the slow decay? I won't allow the past to dictate my future just as I won't forsake my past.

The doctor seemed deep in thought, maybe mulling over an autumn afternoon when his Juliet had bade farewell, or a winter night when, in his lab, he had stumbled upon a cure for cancer or AIDS. Without my own past, I could only delight in picturing his recollections, in savoring his joy and pain as a wife in longing for the distant husband through his photo. Still, as a sage once said, imagining the irreal can never replace the perception of the real. Whatever that means.

"Who are you? What're you really doing here? And where is here?"

Dr. Tang, who turned out to be a psychologist and a neuroscientist, had begun, after graduation, to combine Freudian, Jungian, and Minskyan concepts of consciousness to cook up new theories. "They're classified and I can't disclose them. But they created interests among neuroscientists."

"Sure, I'll believe you when I see your monster, Dr. Tangenstein."

"The excitement bubbling through my veins, as if my blood had turned into champagne. As if I had stepped into a new world, with sweeter air and bluer skies and brooks murmuring more melodious tunes. The prospect of solving a problem, of conquering a natural law, of inventing a new reality and ushering a new future. Perhaps the prospect of creating a new heaven and a new earth." He paced from bed to window, but after gazing at the tree sway in the fog, opened the door and waved away the guard.

A Frankenstein, to be sure.

"Oh, I can imagine that. A scientist seeking for omnipotence. Nothing new." My eyes traced his footsteps, his oxfords tapping on the linoleum floor. I tried to sense the same heartbeats, the same adrenaline rush, the same breath of fresh air on a mountaintop. No luck.

"Every cell in my body was stirring with life, fighting for a new chance to taste this Zen-like drunkenness. Alive, alive to DNA intertwining into a double-helix, alive to a cell dividing in two, alive to the air molecules jitterbugging, alive to a neuron's dendrite firing its signal and tickling another neuron, alive to the Poisson process and the Law of Large Numbers."

"Maybe you really are Tangenstein. Maybe I don't want you toying with my gray matter."

"Before my eyes order growing from chaos and I almost, yes almost, believed humanity is evolving toward the Omega point."

"Are you trying to make me jealous? Are you trying to make me sad? Well, forget it. Not with your mumble-jumble DNA, mitosis, dendrite and Omega point." I bit into the apple and savored the juice and closing my eyes, imagined eating the fruit as a boy in the school cafeteria, as a college student sitting under an oak, as a young professional driving through rush hour traffic. But my mind rebelled and returned to the hospital room and the chestnut tree.

"And at that time, alive, excited, with zest, with a clear vision of the future. The Rainier Tang who was in ecstasy, who seemed to have surpassed mortality. Yet, not only the self at that instant, but also the one at a previous instant and the one at a future instant, all unique yet integrated into a continuous self, who swims through continuous time, this amorphous medium, this ether of existence. No longer fragmented time, sampled at specific instances, but integrated, with an integral function, into a continuous personal history."

"Are you sure you aren't a patient? Should I call for a real doctor?" I finished my apple while he savored his delusion of grandeur. Maybe I should ask for another doctor, a sane doctor.

"The studying and learning in the past and the developing and testing in the future, enriching the research and analysis in the present. My mind sped through time." He circled the bed waving my book, his sleeve swiveling in the air. "I was enlightened. Not only my history and my memories, but also the vision and the rainbow dangling before my mind's eyes, they create my present moments, the instantaneous now. Just as at every instant, I create the past by reshaping memories, so too I create the future by manipulating matter and energy."

"Easy for you to say when you have memory to play with. And a future to look forward to."

"The vision of men and women free from past suffering and evil, free to choose a sunnier tomorrow, pushed me to continue my work and energized me to live, just to live. And so I was living." Dr Tang handed me the book. "And so will you. You'll find your past. You'll create your future. And you'll integrate them with your present."

"Maybe I should create my past. Once I have that, I'm sure I'd find my future. That seems more sensible. Less magic, less hocus-pocus, you know." His lecture on the integration of past, present and future gave me a headache. I would worry about integration if I should find my past. One step at a time.

"So, let's begin our journey," Dr. Tang said, "I'll need to hypnotize you." He took out his wallet and while pulling out a card with a twirling pattern, dropped a photo.

A lady's portrait, blonde hair, blue eyes, pointed nose, seductive collarbones. She sported a rifle on her left shoulder and dangled a rabbit by both ears in her right hand. And squinted into the camera as if daring a lecher to seduce her. I didn't recognize the face and yet, as Pavlov's dogs would salivate to the jingles, grief swelled through my chest. I tried to associate her with a color, a scent, a texture, but my mind stared back, as if reproving me for disturbing its slumber sacred and mystical. I knew her, I was sure.

"Who is she?"

"Happiness in a previous life." Dr. Tang picked up the photo. Dolly, his girlfriend, had left him five years ago. They had dated for about two years when she broke up with him. "She seemed sad to leave, but was willing to sacrifice love for something more important." He inserted the photo into the wallet.

"Tell me about her." Her background might trigger my memory and lead to my past. If I could get a phone number, I would call her and she might reveal my identity and my past.

"So, you've taken a liking to her."

I share my sensations at seeing her photo. "I trust my intuition, flimsy as it is. Any odds of recovering my memory, of regaining my past, I'll pursue the lead, even to Antarctica and the North Pole. Right now, besides the cryptic word in the book, I only have this lead. So, come on, Doc. Tell me more."

"Look here." He raised the card and the pattern seemed to rotate and expand.

From across the desert, his voice echoed in my ears, in my mind and in my heart, and it beckoned me to follow. When he hypnotized me, I dreamed of being a data-thief named Francisco Guzman, who considered everyone else a loser, when he excelled in being one. Couldn't I dream of someone less crude and less narcissistic and less self-deluded, someone like this Tangenstein? Wouldn't mind being a world-famous neuroscientist, mapping out the brain's neural pathways and searching for the mystery of consciousness. Maybe.

CHAPTER 4 - FRANCISCO

August 22, 2011 (2)

I'm too humble to believe in Houdini and too wise to believe in Cinderella. Still, on a day like today, when heaven's gate opened and an angel descended to bless my life, then the hell with quirks like humility and wisdom.

My brother used to say that if you could find your Great Commission you'd tap into the Fount of Life. Sure, he was referring to his whim of finding Father, who'd gone poof seventeen years ago. But as the angel in navy-blue dress-suit, after descending from heaven, greeted me, I drank upon that fountain, the elixir, the ambrosia, through Baptism an epiphany I'd assigned to fools. Maybe, I'd become a fool. I'd found my Great Commission. Amen and praises to fools.

The lady continued to scan my face and my photo with my name at the bottom.

"Well, lady, this is your lucky day. I'm the man you're looking for. No need to roam the continents anymore. Have you been looking long? But it's worth the effort, right?" I invited her to enter my abode, slipping a peppermint into my mouth. "Normally, I'd prefer an appointment, but in your case, I'll make an exception. In fact, I'm giving you carte blanche to visit me anytime. Of course, if you call, I'd get champagne and caviar."

"Hmm, you don't look like a computer genius." She checked my face again. "Will have to trust my client since she specified you. You're probably used to breaking codes, but this assignment should challenge you because there aren't much information. Then again, your job is to find it." In the doorway, she stared at the *Eat Your Durian Pie* T-shirt on the shelf, as if expecting it to leap at her.

"I'd break any code for you. I'd break an arm for you. And I'd get a better mug shot for you. That picture doesn't bring out my best features." I kicked aside the T-shirt and socks to open a way. So they wouldn't scare her away.

"One thousand now and five more when you finish the job. And the client doesn't want to show her face." She stepped into the apartment, turning sideways to avoid my Harley Davidson leather jacket on the clothes rack.

"Let's sit down and break the ice before we talk dollars and deliverables. I don't know anything about you. Like your name, your address, your birthday. Not to mention your favorite food and fragrance. Oh, no need to give me your social security number. I run a legit outfit; no identity theft." I cleared a path to the sofa and invited her to sit down. I couldn't find the laundry basket to hide the socks' crumpled faces. Maybe I didn't have one.

"You have to find the code word to open a file. She called it the Guzman code, to honor you. I guess that's a motivation to work on it. She suggested looking into your diary for clues because someone called Fernando created the file and the password." She declined to sit and pulled out a mailer from her handbag.

After dropping the socks and underwear onto the floor, I picked up the Willie Mays baseball card Fernando had given me for my birthday. I had to unmask this client and find out how she'd gotten hold of his file. My brother didn't even have a girlfriend.

"And she said that includes the diary in your dream. Oh, you have to solve it by October 26, or something bad will happen to someone you love."

"Don't worry. I won't let anything happen to you." If she'd known me longer, she'd pooh-pooh the threat and rely on Fransuccesco. "But wasn't nice of her to rattle her tongue like that. Of course, I've worked with lobsters who like to mob, I mean mop, advice left and right. You know, to encourage me. They should update their cerebral software, these dinosaurs."

"Any questions? If you accept, please read and sign the contract and I'll hand you a check."

"Yeah, I got some questions. First off, what's your favorite restaurant? And what time will you get off work tonight? You still haven't told me your name." I put down the baseball card and picked up my coffee, the cup clattering against the plate as if sneering at me. "And have you been looking into my diary and studying my dreams? Not that I mind. I'd like you to know me better. But your client—"

"I know nothing about your diary or your dreams. Or how she knows about them. I'm only a messenger, a middleman. I get my commission for relaying the message because she prefers to stay in the background. If for this reason you can't take the job, I'll let her know."

"I always have these clients who'd want to remain incognito." I entered the kitchen and took a slice of cheesecake from the refrigerator. "But at the end of the case, I'd know them, and not just their names either." I grabbed a fork and handed her the cheesecake. "So, never mind your client trying to stay in the dark. I'd know enough about her very soon. I promise with all sincerity and honor." I'd stick to my rule and review her client's passport and social security card sooner or later. Whatever game this Madam No-face was playing, I'd turn a knight into a queen to checkmate her before she could find out all my pieces, except the king, had changed into queens. You see, I can play chess, real chess.

The lady declined the cheesecake and handed me the contract. "So, you're taking this assignment, then? I appreciate it since I'd get my commission."

"Oh, I wouldn't want you to miss out on your daily dough. Making a living is tough these days." Since this project involves Fernando, I'd take it even without payment. "Here's the deal. You can help me with this assignment, and we'd split the eight thousand. What do you say? You'd be working with a winner, not one of those two-time losers." I put down the cheesecake and took the contract and I waited for her to accept my offer.

"Very attractive. But I have to pass. I don't have the expertise and I got work waiting. A promise is a promise, you know."

"Oh, well. I tried." I wanted to ask her name again, but decided to find out myself—to enjoy the chase and to impress her. I'd meet her again and we'd be drinking champagne to celebrate our future together. Unlike my dream self, the poor sap, knowing zilch and daring nada.

She gave me a pen and glanced at the laundry on my coffee table. "Does the clue make any sense to you? Because it doesn't to me. How'd she know you have a diary and what's in it?" When her glance landed on a piece of durian pie, she stepped back and turned toward the doorway.

"Never mind the diary. I'll crack the code. And when I find out what kind of a game she's playing, I'll let you know. Promise." I signed the contract. She handed me the check and a storage device with the file, and left without revealing her name or phone number.

I skipped work to celebrate the day. Had a haircut before lunching in a Midtown sushi bar. In the afternoon, I drove to the Eternal Happiness Cemetery to visit my brother's grave, this time without bringing Clint. Ever since Fernando had died five years ago, my sidekick and I would visit the grave on the anniversaries of his burial. Every time Clint stood in front of the grave, he'd wail and wet the headstone. So, this time, without him, I looked forward to trimming the weeds beside the grave and checking other headstone inscriptions. For wisdom and enlightenment. The fog had lifted, but the clouds lingered overhead, as if about to wet the gravestone on Clint's behalf.

Fernando had vowed to join the police even as a teenager and I couldn't deter him. When he took a bullet in the arm catching a bank robber, Clint and I tried to persuade him to get a desk job. He laughed at us and said he's no coward. In the end, he died in the line of duty, chasing after an apple thief. That evening, I had dinner with my girlfriend Holly after helping the FBI nab a Ponzi schemer who'd cheated investors out of a billion dollars. She'd just left my apartment for a red-eye flight to DC when I received the call. My brother should've joined me to decipher codes, to solve puzzles, to hack into intelligence agency databases around the world. And have job satisfaction.

When I reached his grave, a rose lay beside trimmed weeds. I hadn't noticed any flowers during previous visits even though some of Fernando's police-buddies had come by during the first two years. As far as I know, he didn't have a girlfriend. Several times, Clint and I had dropped by his apartment to surprise him, but I'd never smelled any perfume or found any bras or panties. So now, I picked up the rose and wondered about his secret life. He didn't have to hide anyone from me, even if his girlfriend was a man.

Hey, brother, what kinds of secrets have you been keeping from me? You should've confided in me. Well, I'll find out soon enough, including what's in that file of yours. Anyway, Suzie is doing fine. You should see her. She's grown. And I'm taking good care of her. So don't you worry about her. As you know, failure isn't in my genes.

Below the cemetery's edge where a wired fence stood ten feet tall, cars sped through the highway and spewed carbon monoxide and related toxins. Honks greeted other honks while coupes cut off sedans. Beyond the highway, the local park's browning trees waved their branches. I'd considered reserving a spot by the fence and, as the wind whispered around me, I surveyed the empty lots. Decent view.

In the calmness, a twig cracked. A shadow darted into the woods at the other end of the graveyard. After hesitating for a moment to collect my thoughts, I zigzagged through the headstones. Chasing after it. *Come, show your ugly face.* I kicked a headstone on the side and almost fell. But recovered and leaped over the next one. By the time I reached the woods, the coward had vanished. Only an all-star baseball card lay on the ground beside two sets of footprints.

Fernando's favorite baseball card. Which he'd treasured since third grade and which I'd tried but failed to locate after his death.

CHAPTER 5 - X

September 9 (1)

The male nurse read my charts, shoved the thermometer into my mouth and left with the tray. Shutting the door behind him. Leaving me in the room.

I treaded across the cold tiles to check my charts and read my name.

I am X: a symbol pointing to a body, a mind, an organism without a past. Through this label, I emerged from a womb into the world, to breathe the air and taste the dew. Taking out the thermometer, I shouted my name, the echoes bouncing off the walls.

What's in a name? I might as well be called Y or Z or Omega. Just not Francisco.

The bed and the chair, I wondered about their names. If they had been called alpha, beta, gamma, their colors, their hardness, their functions, their molecular structures wouldn't have changed. Still, after calling a bed by its name, as if evoking a spell, I grasped it. The male nurse might call it "dud" or "apple." But he couldn't eat his apple anymore than I could sleep on mine. While his apple would evoke sleep, mine would make my mouth water.

The fog shifted to reveal the Queensboro Bridge beyond the buildings. The familiar East River, its water murky and the debris floating, didn't revive any memories. I tried to open the window. Locked. So, I shouted my name through the glass to the drivers rushing to work.

In the courtyard, a homeless man directed a doctor and a policeman to arrange several benches along the walkway, but after glancing at me, took out his iPhone and pressed several buttons. Probably reporting this lunatic to the security guard or the attending Frankenstein.

This hospital, this room, this bed, might just be part of my dream. A nightmare without ogres and goblins. I wouldn't mind the fog, the anti-septic and even the bandages around my arms and my legs if I could ground myself in my father's face, in my mother's voice, or in a proper name. As hard as I tried, I couldn't penetrate that cloud, my mind.

A rose by any other name would smell as sweet. If only. If only a rose is a rose and nothing but a rose.

When the male nurse returned with my breakfast—cinnamon oat-meal, orange juice and an apple—and took the thermometer, I grabbed his sleeve and said, "I demand to know—"

He patted me on my shoulder. "Cheer up, my man. Such a dandy day. Ever seen such a super-duper fog?" Offered me the apple and checked the thermometer.

"Hey, where'd this spring breeze come from? Did someone just died?"

He scribbled on the chart and changed my pillow cover. Stepped into the bathroom to clean the sink and the toilet.

"Aren't you the grumpy nurse? Why are you scrubbing the toilet?"

"Rick's the nurse. I'm just an orderly but I help out a bit."

How'd *Groucho* morphed into *Skippy?* Split personalities? Just great, a psychotic nurse-orderly. Whatever prank, whatever intrigue, I didn't care.

Alone again, I ate the oatmeal and drank the orange juice and when food didn't revive any memories, I leaned toward the chair to grab the laptop, my new companion. Reviewed the previous journal entries. Hoping to recover the initial emotions and trigger my memories. Had I written those words and sensed those emotions? More likely, someone forged the entries as stale as science fiction.

In the hospital archive, a news article described my accident, which resulted from a car chase, but didn't mention any names. Only that no one could've survived such a disaster. The police didn't find an ID on the victim. The officers must have checked my fingerprints and DNA, so either they weren't in the government databases or the police withheld my identity.

Who'd been chasing me? And why? Having survived what some might call a miracle, I had to dig up the skeletons. I got the local police station's phone number from the phone directory, and planned to get the accident report, which some officer might have created to replace the facts. After putting on my slippers and tightening the sash over my gown,

I stepped into the hallway (no one bothered to fix the broken doorknob), where two gurneys were parked against the wall and a patient on intravenous tried to pick up a raisin from the floor. Hadn't he entered my room as a doctor yesterday and checked my charts? Perhaps my mind was still mixing facts from fiction.

I picked up the morsel for the patient-doctor and was about to talk to him, when two nurses rushed a bloodstained gurney past me. The man on it didn't move; only his head bobbed sideways. The gardener who was trimming the bushes in the courtyard two days ago. Before I could follow the gurney, *Groucho* stepped through a door and blocked my path, requesting that I return to my room. When I asked for the phone, he quoted hospital policy forbidding patients from using it.

"Am I in prison, or something? What kind of a hospital wouldn't allow patients to use the phone?" Perhaps these *doctors* had inserted microchips in my head to tune my mind.

CHAPTER 6 - FRANCISCO

August 23, 2011 (1)

The day began with a grocer declaring I was dead and ended with a bullet rushing at my head. In other words, a ho-hum day. The grocer might be trying to fulfill his fortune telling and switch job, at my expense.

After all night trying to figure out who might've stolen Fernando's baseball card, this morning I left my apartment recalling the times my brother and I hiked the Catskill trails under autumn foliages. On Amsterdam Avenue, I inhaled the New York air and arrived at the bodega to get a pack of dark chocolate and a slice of durian pie. I also had to pick up the printed photos of a TV evangelist having sex with his secretary in his Malibu mansion. I had to deliver them to my client later in the day. Behind the counter, the grocer, who looked like the security guard in my dream, pointed at a graphic novel and said, "You forgot to pick up the new issue. Must've had a bad dream last night. Saw your old man?" And after swiping the credit card, he said, "Sorry, won't go through. Can't use this card."

"This game was fun the first time you used it on me, like ten years ago. Now, the trick's a bit lame. Should use your brain and come up with new tricks to entertain me." Even as I pooh-poohed his Vanderbilt act, I sensed more dung in my path. Everything went downhill after yesterday's *Third Heaven.*

The grocer called the credit-card company to check the problem and said, "It seems your friend stopped the card for you. You're supposed to be dead. They're waiting for the death certificate to confirm it. You know. They worry no one will pay a dead man's bill. Understandable."

"Maybe this is hell. Feels like it. Of course, my death certificate might cheer me up." I grabbed the credit card and paid with cash. A rascal had probably stolen my identity and intended to ruin my credit score. He might've opened accounts on pornographic websites with my name, to smear me, or applied for credit cards with my social security number, to e-shop nonstop. I didn't need those adventures. I'd find the loser who was messing with me, gather the stolen social security numbers—especially those of the police chiefs and district attorneys—and turn the information over to the police. Thank you for messing with Francisco Guzman. Sayonara.

Before going to the office, I took my suits to the dry cleaner and visited Suzie in the hospital. When I stepped into her room, the nurse had just finished massaging her. Her calm face reminded me of the life she had missed. Seven years ago, when she was five, her father, after losing custody, killed her mother and kidnapped her. He was fleeing from the city when the police located his SUV. Fernando chased him along Hutchinson Parkway determined to stop him. The father swirled the car and smashed it into a tree. He died. Suzie went into a coma. Since she didn't have any other relatives, Fernando, before he died, would visit her once a week and talk to her, hoping she'd wake up one day. After his death, I visited on his behalf. I even talked to her. Fernando would want it. Whenever tears flowed out of Suzie's eyes, I'd want to hug her and comfort her. If it weren't for my brother, I'd never have visited a coma patient and I'd never have cared about a little girl. Because of him, I gained some compassion, some patience, some humanity. Well, just a little. Not enough to hurt me.

***

In the office, I found the newspaper outside the front door, not on the hallway counter. So, indeed a storm was coming.

Everyday, for more than ten years, Clint would come to the office and pick up the newspaper. He'd separate the sports section from the rest and put the two parts next to each other on the hallway counter. He'd enter his room and check his emails. Then come out, take the newspaper, toss the sports section into the recycle bin and bring me the rest. Rain or shine. September 11 or Oklahoma Bombing. On an April Fool's Day, in the interest of science, I put the sports section back with the rest of the newspaper while Clint was checking his emails. Sure enough, when he came out, he separated the newspaper and returned to check his email. I tried again and he repeated the task. Would you believe we played hide-and-seek for two hours until I got bored? Not even once did he flinch. That's Mr. OCD for you.

He also followed standard operating procedures for making love. Once, I found the step-by-step instructions in his drawer. Disgusting. Of course, I didn't shred the note to pieces and ruin his sex life.

This morning, when the newspaper blocked my way into the office, I thought he'd at last forgotten his routine. I called him from the hallway. When no one greeted me, I called a contractor to remove Clint's nametag from his office door by this evening. Should he return, he'd find the door as blank as his mind and he'd search the entire floor, the entire building and the entire block for his office.

Last night, I'd drafted a plan and a schedule to hunt down the missing diamonds for the latest client VE—Very Enterprise. This morning, I'd planned to go over Clint's assignments and the daily schedules including the milestones, so we could recover the diamonds by week's end and collect the fee. If he should spoil my plan to buy a condo overlooking Central Park and to vacation in the Maldives for Christmas, I'd deduct my losses plus interest and penalty from his paychecks.

I phoned him, but he didn't answer.

Clint, a one-dimensional mind, could run errands like no other sidekicks. And of course, praise me like no other lackeys. *The smartest, sexist, funniest guy around*, as he discerned. As my foot soldier, he'd executed my strategies and helped me win quite a few battles. I'd miss him if he'd perished.

In the years I'd employed him—and there were quite a few—he'd never been late, not once, not even when he caught the flu. Sure, every Sunday evening, he'd glue his butt to the couch for the football games, but he'd turn in at ten o'clock, never getting drunk on knock-off beer. And sure, he equated Sunday with football and vice versa to the extent that, more than a dozen times, I'd failed to recondition him to associate Sunday with sleep or picnic or church, neither hypnosis nor subliminal projection could rewire his neural connections. But, he'd always show up at 6:59 a.m. on Mondays.

Mr. OCD had shopped in the same supermarket for more than ten years, though the fish stunk and vegetables perspired. And when the store shut its doors several months ago, he checked into the mental hospital for a month. I showed him the salmon and spinach from a warehouse-type supermarket around the corner, but he continued to mourn the loss. Perhaps, this time he also had checked into a mental hospital.

After failing to locate him in several hospitals, I checked for signs of foul play in his office. The chair stood six inches behind the desk and the computer screen faced the door at 45°. Just as Clint had left them.

I confiscated the fountain pen, the picture frame, and the MP3 player. I would've tossed away the photo of Fernando and him at the beach, but spared his treasure, more for Fernando than for him. Somehow, Clint looked like the ruffian in my dream, sans the red eyes. I put his candies and baseball cards into a bag, went to the window and called the beggars lying along the alley. I threw them the bag for an early Christmas present.

I sagged into his chair and imitated his expression during my brother's funeral. The droopy eyes, the slanted nose, the loose lips, the hanging jaw, the unshaved cheeks. All right, I shaved. I was plunging into an abyss, my heart throbbing, my skin sweating, my nerves reacting to the breeze. As the vacuum expanded in my chest and in my mind, I slapped my face to wake up from the stupor. A few seconds more and I might've decayed into the sap. Even during that instant, I'd sensed trouble. I must find him before his body floated along the East River.

I contacted the bank manager and informed him I was helping VE recover the diamonds stolen from his branch. I requested a copy of the security camera videos. We also arranged to have drinks in his favorite bar next Friday evening. Whether Clint had abandoned me or not, I'd locate the diamonds and go to the Maldives for Christmas.

At ten o'clock, in my office, I adjusted my diploma from Columbia University, the Worldwide Award from the International Society of Code Breakers, the ten certificates of Exceptional Achievement from The Society of American Problem Solvers (SOAPS) and the copy of the million-dollar check from an Indian tycoon. That service's details: top secret. I polished the SOAPS Lifetime Achievement Award, a golden statuette in the trophy case, until it sparkled under the fluorescent light.

Clients would scan through my certificates and awards to confirm my credentials and ask about the achievements behind each, and I'd sum up how I assisted the FBI in busting a drug trafficking network, or helped a Russian tycoon recover his kidnapped son. I'd dwell on cracking an unbreakable code, solving an unsolvable puzzle, outsmarting the cleverest masterminds. In the end, these clients would write out checks and I'd deliver the results. Happy endings.

At noon, I removed Clint's nametag from his desk, changed the front door's combination, and called my ex-girlfriend Holly to locate the numbskull—she'd helped him with legal issues a few weeks ago. No answer from her either. Must be the national Leave-the-Phones-Ringing Day. Lovely. I called her office and according to her secretary, she had gone to court this morning, but still hadn't returned. I called the court to confirm the session had ended and she'd left the building. Holly would usually return to the office after the proceedings to have the secretary file the paperwork. Today, she didn't. I called her again but she still didn't answer the phone. So I headed for her apartment. With no idea what I'd find.

CHAPTER 7 - X

September 9 (2)

I waited for the chance to make the call. Reclining on my bed, I typed today's journal entry, hoping *Groucho* would soon change to *Skippy*, so I could coax him. Then again, I could always sneak out of my room at night and find a phone.

Later, when the psychiatrist, Dr. Svensson—I prefer to call her Ingrid—walked into the room to counsel me, I studied a lock of hair curving around her temple and behind her left ear. Her face calmed my mind. Her eyes warmed me though the fog had again descended over the courtyard. Time suspended, no length, no width, no thickness. An eternal point. When the hour session that seemed like a minute ended, I understood how inhabited time could differ from the clock's ticking, according to joys and sorrows.

I listened to her voice. Followed her eyes' movements. Felt the air's vibrations. Since waking up after the accident, I had tried to avoid the nurses, the orderlies, the janitors and whoever invaded my room—except *Skippy*—by pretending to be sleeping. Withdrawing into my mind. After meeting Ingrid, I despised my hideout and longed to attend to her every syllable, every breath, every movement of her index fingers. Like sunshine drawing me from slumber and dream. A new dawn, a new dawn of swallowtails and orioles, where dreams disperse under a stream of shapes and notes.

I would share with Ingrid this infant self who was searching for clues, who was growing through every byte of memory. She'd understand me.

When she left…

When she left, I returned to the hideout I enjoyed and despised. Avoiding the orderlies, the janitor, and whenever possible the sounds in the hallway. But listening for her footsteps, the beats that I recognize.

Whenever footsteps approached, whenever the door opened, I would put down my laptop or bowl and turn my head, but too often, only the orderly, the janitor, or the other doctor visited me. When she did come and talk, time flashed away and afterward, unable to recall the precise sensations, I craved a glass of Merlot. But I only had orange juice.

Noticing my feelings toward her—the energy in my muscles and the tension in my stomach—I stood before a mirror and tried to examine this person who'd taken a liking to her. Was he the stranger before or behind the mirror? Was he the man observing the two strangers or the one questioning that observer and mediating internal turmoil and analyzing external chaos? What should I do with these selves, these voices in my head? Voices in the head, a bad sign, according to the lean doctor. I wouldn't object to sharing my mind with these other voices, since like them I was also a stranger in that wasteland. Would these other selves feel the same toward Ingrid? Or would one like while another hate and still another envy her? I could only sense an attraction toward that lock of blonde hair curling under her earlobe.

Who was the judge evaluating the self? Who owned the voice that liked Ingrid? Might this higher self, aloof and observing, envy the other selves for loving and hating, for sensing the sun's warmth and the jasmine's fragrance? However, for every judge, a higher judge; for every observer, a more distant observer. Ad infinitum.

If I couldn't integrate these voices, would I become fragmented? Maybe, I'd been and the amnesia just revealed the disease's symptom. Maybe this self, who'd been born into that collective a few days ago, was getting acquainted with the other, wiser and riper, selves.

According to her, we had several sessions, but I couldn't recall them or find them in my journal. I wouldn't have forgotten her face if I had met her before. However, I couldn't trust my memory, or my diary.

This morning, Ingrid strolled through the courtyard with Dr. Tang. She was talking, sighing, grimacing. Then smiling. Before I could study her lips' contours, to memorize their movements, they walked into the fog. I put my face against the windowpane. I squinted. I couldn't see them. When the fog dispersed, they'd disappeared. Just like my memories.

***

After reading my chart, I scoured for junk food in the cafeteria. Though past lunchtime, doctors, nurses and patients, who had taken up most of the tables, were eating, talking and joking and their voices waxed and ebbed amid the aroma of spices and grilled meat. Stalls for hamburgers, pizzas, and Mexican and Japanese food lined the back wall. The pizza's aroma triggered a craving for sashimi and I remembered having tasted sashimi pizza with extra wasabi. The doctor had said food could trigger memory and I decided to test his claim. When I walked up to the pizza stall and ordered two slices of salmon pizza, requesting double the wasabi, the cashier forced a smile and took my order. After several minutes in the back, she returned and asked me to wait for thirty minutes. I didn't complain about the wait since the chef must be ordering the salmon from a warehouse instead of borrowing from the Japanese food stall. I should appreciate his effort.

I was walking toward the Mexican food stall to check the salsa and refried beans when into the cafeteria walked *Skippy*. Turning around, I slipped behind a woman ordering a beef burrito but before I could hide among several nurses around the Japanese stall, his smile reached me. I greeted him, apologized for my comment when I first met him, but he just talked about his father's funeral arrangements. I urged him to order his food and when he talked to the lady behind the hamburger stall, I picked up the pizza and left the cafeteria.

Back in my room, I bit into the pizza chewing the salmon, and tried to recall the times I had enjoyed this dish. The wasabi cleared my sinuses and I closed my eyes to await images of friends, associates and local pizzerias. The door opened and an odor entered the room.

"Greetings, my son."

No privacy. No knocking before entering. I might only be X, an unknown variable in a second-order partial differential equation, but still wanted dignity.

When I opened my eyes, a chubby middle-aged man with a Bible flaunted his teeth.

I swallowed the food and prepared to complain about his manners, his voice and his teeth but I only said, "Have you turned the wrong corner? I'm not about to enter eternity. Not that I'd complain. Wouldn't want to swipe someone else's earned service. When my time comes, the hospital can just buy me pizza."

"Terrible weather, ain't it?" The folding chair squealed under him as he took out a flask of vodka and drank a draft.

Not interested in the weather report. So I ate my pizza and focus on my memory.

"Real grand manners them receptionists," the chaplain said, raising a thumb. "Mighty friendly, mighty efficient, mighty informative. And this here place," he glanced around and continued, "squeaky clean. Couldn't of imagined some places I've gone. Littered hallways, cracked doors, rats. And the commodes. There even drug addicts at the bottom of the stairs rotting away. They generally always scared me, and almost given me heart attacks." He shuddered and sipped his drink. "Real glad I visit with you, sure a clean coop. Pretty place you got here. Ought to make the best of it and sweeten your stay. Like the cafeteria…"

His rasp scraped my eardrums and I couldn't concentrate. According to the laptop's clock, the minister talked for twenty-eight seconds before taking a breath.

After sipping the vodka, he continued, "As a boy I played with my dog, Fifo, in the backyard. Did name him Fifo, first-in-first-out. Sounded mighty grand." He scratched his cheek with the flask. "Anyway, those were the golden days, playing with him everyday. Not a care nowhere. Waking up, nibbling breakfast, playing with Fifo, having lunch, taking an afternoon nap, falling in with them neighbors. Well, anyway, didn't get no sweat nor toil. But this job here." He wiped away the vodka on his lips with his palm. "You couldn't of imagined how tough it be. Oh, I'm used to those coons, what else would you hope for. But damn it, some days they turned on me and on top of it all I hate it being chunked out the door." He sighed and sipped his vodka.

"When the apostle John borrowed the word *logos* to refer to the Word of God, was he contradicting the Greek concept of a detached truth that filled the universe, like a background to the physical world?" I couldn't recall ever studying Greek or the Book of John, yet asked the question as if saying, "What's your name?"

The minister rolled his eyes, showing the whites around his irises. Sighed and said, "Oh, I could be a dang good salesman. Never doubt it."

No doubt he would excel as a used car salesman. What attracted him to his job? Maybe the benefits. *Please give me peace and quiet.*

"I would of liked working in a hospital fulltime. Well, don't mean here, another one, you know. Of course, here they got nice apple pies. Going to taste another piece. Well, anyway, talking about hospitals in general. They got mighty decent cafeterias. During lunchtime, I could take a break and nibble some there, instead of running around town hunting down dirty rice. Got an ulcer on account of this and spent almost a month in the hospital. Lately, been getting these headaches. Who knows, might have a heart attack one of these days. But, oh, yeah. You listen here, we should talk about you. A nice courtyard you have here. You ought to make the best of it. Of course, weather ain't been pretty for the past month. But you just wait, when the sun comes out, you ought to feel you're in heaven. So, don't worry about nothing. God taken care of everything. Oh, I'm Pastor McCoy. You can call me MC."

The more his teeth leered at me, the more I wanted to glue his lips. Would rather eat goat cheese or pickled tofu than listen to his voice. His job might've been to talk about the weather, the football game, or the best apple pie in town, but please just eat in the cafeteria—dirty rice or dirty bread or whatever—and I would sign a statement to confirm his *comforting* visit. He went on and on reviewing apple pies from New Hampshire to Iowa to Washington. The lean doctor, Dr. Tang, had taught me a way to dispel noise and focus my attention, so I centered on an image: Ingrid and I walking by a stream, the water gurgling, the wind whistling, the warbler singing. Soon, peace descended and, taking her hand, time stopped and the world vanished.

A hand on my shoulder woke me and the minister's teeth almost touched my face and his breath heated my cheeks and stung my nostrils. My right fist reached for the minister's abdomen but my left hand grasped my right wrist.

Before I could throw the man through the window, a second self reined my hands. Two selves with distinct desires, rivaling, bargaining, coexisting, each trying to outfox the other. No, I prefer an *integrated self*: one mind, one heart, one soul.

"Listen here, son. You trust in God." Pastor McCoy handed me a tract. "And he sure going to heal you and get you outta this shit hole."

"Next time you visit, could you bring me a crossword—"

The next second, I stood beside a vending machine holding a bag of potato chips. Still in the hospital. Still in the same gown. Still chewing the pizza. Just a few feet from my room's doorway. Down the hallway, Pastor McCoy leaned against the wall, gulping vodka and scratching his balding head. According to the clock above him, five minutes had passed.

I wasn't dreaming. No such luck. I could've fainted, but then I shouldn't be standing or holding a bag of potato chips. I could've sleep-walked, but I wasn't sleeping. I might be losing my mind but if I were, I wouldn't admit it. I closed my eyes. Computed the square-root of 121. Thought about mitosis. Defined post-modernism. My brain still worked.

"Did I tunnel through space or travel through time?" Maybe the accident had damaged part of my brain and Dr. Tang failed to diagnose it.

"Darn it. You gone blank like a zombie, or a sleepwalker. Went from this room. Eyes weren't blinking none, no sir. Didn't bump into the walls. Slipped the coin in the slot no problem. You must of been possessed by a demon. Of course, I don't believe in none of them hocus-pocus."

"Why potato chips?"

"I would of gone for cheese puff. My favorite. But then, it be me. Each his own. Well, got to go. Next time, I bring an exorcist. But FYI, most of them but con artists out to eke a living." He bade farewell and, carrying his tote bag, fled down the hallway. I didn't blame him. If I could, I also would flee from myself.

Back in my room, after finishing the pizza without triggering any memory, I couldn't find my laptop.

CHAPTER 8 – FRANCISCO

August 23, 2011 (2)

Though Holly and I'd broken up several months ago, we remained friends and would eat out once a month to console each other on the most recent breakups. We'd joke and cry over them to heal our broken hearts. Sometimes, but just once in a sapphire-blue moon only, I'd even wonder whether we could begin anew, but as friends we'd be more intimate. And heaven knows I don't have enough friends. After Fernando had passed away, I only had Clint as a semi-buddy. Depressing.

Had Holly pissed off a low-life in a trial? I'd told her, time and time again, to switch to malpractice lawsuits and reap more greenbacks. She spat at the idea, true to her character, too indignant to scour the sewage for diamonds.

Her mom couldn't stand without emotional crutches and drifted from one loser to the next, sometimes landing in the hospital with bleeding lips and broken ribs. So, Holly learned to fend for herself and became her mom's antipode: tough, cold, and aloof. (Can we ever flee from our damned pasts? Must the past always damn the future?) She kicked butts including mean asses in the courtroom and had harvested as many enemies as friends. The iron lady that she is, she still suffered after each breakup and yearned for friends. She'd stayed with me even after my affair with a waitress. But when… well, never mind. I cared about her and would mutilate any low-life licking his tongue at her.

When I arrived at her apartment, a midtown high-rise condo facing the Empire State Building, I rang her doorbell, which hummed the notes of "You Light Up My Life." No one answered. As expected. The concierge said she hadn't return. With the spare key I opened the door and the apartment greeted me with a lavender scent. The cat approached and rubbed its head against my legs. The magazines and remote controllers lay parallel on the coffee table. The flowerpots with orchids and mums sat on the ledges beneath the LED TV. Two Teddy bears leaned against each other on the sofa. In the kitchen, a rack of knives sat on the left side of the sink and the bread machine and the oven toaster on the right. A knife, a fork and two plates were drying in the sink. Pictures of naked men, Holly's former boyfriends, most of them losers, still decorated the refrigerator door. No bullet holes in the cabinets. No splinters on the kitchen tiles. No bloodstains on the living room carpet.

In her study, paper pads piled on the left side of her desk and beside them the pens stood in the holder. A picture of her father, the Governor, stood near the right corner. Flyers for her October 19 fundraiser to help battered women and rape victims lay next to the picture. No laptop. Yes, she'd left for work like any other dullsday. Still, someone had staged the scene. Trying to fool anyone who might come into the apartment. Besides me, who else would dare to enter her sanctuary? She'd broken up with her latest boyfriend, an ordinary Joe, about a month ago and hadn't been dating since. As far as I know. Every time she broke up with a boyfriend, she'd change her lock and phone number. I got the new key just three days ago.

In the upper drawer, a scrap of paper with the message: *You'll find Holly's body in the East River if you can't find the password by October 26. As a bonus, starting yesterday, for every two weeks you waste, someone you care about will get hurt.* Not too creative. I didn't appreciate the threat. I only cared about a few people and I'd prevent any jackass from hurting them.

I called my friend at a security firm and hired two guards to protect Suzie. I'd break the neck of any reptile that would hurt her. Besides Holly and Suzie, no one else I'd care about. Clint might've disappeared for the same reason. In a sense, I cared about him also, kind of.

I got the crime scene kit from my car, a gift from a client. Collected fingerprints on the desk, hair in the bathroom, a wineglass on the kitchen table and the scrap of paper. I could check the fingerprints at home, but would have to send the hair to the lab for DNA test.

When I returned to my apartment, the door reclined three feet from the entrance and the smashed plasma TV blocked my path. Inside, my laundries were drowning in gin, scotch and whiskey and the loud speakers donned bulldog faces. Each surveillance monitor suffered a single blow. One section of the massage chair had flattened my hi-fi system and the other pierced into the wine cabinet. The air reeked of alcohol and I couldn't decipher the graffiti on my leather sofa. The black brush strokes over my impressionist paintings showed the intruder lacked aesthetic taste or artistic skills. Was a maggot hinting I should replace my furniture, upgrade my entertainment system, and modernize my art collection? My old diary's pages lay on the bedroom floor. The maggot even splattered on the kitchen floor the leftover caviar from last night's dinner and prevented me from enjoying it tonight. And my *pate de foie gras*, gone, all ten cans. What a greedy bastard. Fortunately, I'd kept my certificates and awards in the office. But on any given day, how much spittle could a decent man take?

I was going to check my hidden wine collection when the bay window shattered and a bullet charged at me. Murphy's Law. Lovely.

CHAPTER 9 - X

September 12

Toward noon, I woke up strapped to a gurney, a shaggy-haired ruf-fian—red veined eyes, stubble-filled face and blue-veined forearms—tightening the buckles. Might've seen his picture on the FBI's most-wanted list.

"C'mon, we getting the hell outta here." He wedged a tote bag be-tween my ankles and swiveled the gurney but it banged against the bed and he cussed.

"Who're you?"

"Never you mind."

"Strange name. But a name is a name is just a name. They call me X. Now, Mr. Mind, what're you doing?"

"Ya gone the hell cuckoo with yer accident, or what? Can't under-stand nada. Speak English, por favor." He snatched a chocolate chip cookie and munched it. "C'mon, we gotta get the stuff to the client by November 9, or we're dead meat." Pulling back the gurney to avoid the bed.

Before I could reply, *Skippy* entered with a trash bin, whistling his fa-vorite jingle. "You know, should really wait until visiting hours. And visitors aren't allowed to play doctors. But if you keep quiet, I'll make an exception. You know, the head-trauma patient next door's trying to get some sleep after the surgery."

Stubble stuffed the cookie into his mouth and kicked the bin into the air, grabbed *Skippy*'s uniform and flung him against the wall. Denting the drywall.

The orderly landed on the trash bin and struggled to get up but fell again, his jaw hitting the tile. After standing up and wiping the blood from his lips, he said, "That isn't nice, hurting people in the hospital. Cheer up. What's eating you, man? Look in the mirror, seems like you're turning into the wolf-man or something."

Stubble pulled a machete from the tote bag and swung in an arc, breaking the chair's back. *Skippy*'s sleeve spotted with blood.

I broke the straps around my arms, stepped off the bed to look for a kitchen knife, but *Skippy* had removed the utensils, leaving only an apple and several cookies on the tray.

"Hey man, careful with that steak knife. Put it away until dinnertime, will you? Okay, okay, I won't disturb you two." *Skippy* tossed me a granola bar. "Don't worry. Hang in there and finish your snack. I'll check the hospital's policy on visitors and be right back." He retreated through the door, humming a different melody.

"The accident. Were you at the scene? What happened?" I grabbed the trash bin and swung at the intruder before he could turn around. Smashing his head and knocking the machete out of his hand.

"Hey, we're buddies, partners, amigos." He staggered and cowered against the wall, raising his arm to protect his head.

I believed him, though my reasoning warned me against his stubble and shaggy hair, which annoyed me. Even when this hobo Joe's face first appeared before my eyes, I had sniffed a scheme behind the leathery cheeks, the striated skin, and the bloodshot eyes. Yet, I didn't mind dealing with such a Me-Before-You. I would tickle his desires with baits and leverage his passions. Better than self-righteous saints, who would sneer at my bait and jump over the ledge for the rainbow.

"Tell me everything about Dolly. If I detect a single lie—"

His pupils dilated. He retreated along the wall. Stepped on the tote bag. Staggered but grabbed a chair to steady himself. Was Dolly his lover?

"I know her from somewhere. Where? Tell me." I seized his jacket. I had to squeeze an anecdote out of the mush inside his skull. Even as I shook his body... A spring morning, a school campus, teenagers hurrying from one class to another while others stole kisses behind the bushes. He and Dolly holding hands and strolling through the yard as Frisbees and footballs crisscrossed in front of and behind them. Sure enough, they had been dating since high school and I had studied with them. I couldn't recall the high school or my GPA, but the birches leading to the student center, the Ionic columns in front of the buildings, they shimmered in my mind. Then, their wedding on May 31. The sun scorching my face as the captain married them at sea. And, a week before the wedding, she and I had an affair, for one week. I could still hear her laughter and feel her lips.

Stubble tried to loosen my grip but my hands twisted his lapel and the veins on his forehead bulged and wriggled. Must've been training my muscles before the accident—though half his size, I tossed him against the wall as he had the orderly.

He tumbled onto the floor, groaning and whining. Got up and wiped the gypsum from his face and hair. "Alright, alright, no need to get rough. We're buddies, remember. I'm gonna tell ya everything." He opened his mouth to talk but turned to the bay window.

Outside, the security guard I met several days ago emerged from the fog, pointed at the unshaven face and slid his index finger across his throat. After taking out his pocket watch to check the time, he disappeared down the path. But not before I snapped his picture with my new laptop. When and where had I seen the face before? Perhaps from a dream. Did I recognize his eyes or chin? If only I could wipe away this amnesia.

Stubble grabbed the tote bag and tried to pick up the machete but his hands trembled and he dropped the package. "Hey, amigo, get the hell outta here. This hospital ain't what ya think it is. It's—"

Before he could finish, a dented bat smashed into his temple. He flopped onto the tray table and flipped onto the floor, the juice splashing onto his face and the cookies somersaulting onto the sheets. Blood dripping down his bruised left temple.

Groucho, brows knitting into a "V," raised the bat behind his right shoulder. "Hey, what's this bullshit I heard. You the lowlife threatening people with a knife? Want to become tonight's meatloaf, do you? I got no time and no energy to deal with this crap. As if my old man dying wasn't enough, now I've got to deal with wolf-man here. Well, I'm telling you, I'm drawing a line in the sand. I had enough. So, make my day."

Stubble kicked aside the tray table, staggered through the door, and sprinted down the corridor. The male nurse ran after him. At the doorway, he whistled and pointed in Stubble's direction.

A shout. Then a shot. Pistol in hand, the head-trauma patient next door rushed through the doorway, flinging away his bandages.

"That'll show him. Trying to make trouble in my place." *Groucho*, shaking his head, returned to the room. "Damn it, this mess."

"Would you please tell me, that is if you don't mind, how a patient was able to bring a pistol into the hospital?" I stepped into the hallway as the head-trauma patient turned a corner and pulled the trigger again. "Or are you employing him for part-time work? Probably paying him minimum wages, too."

"That wolf-man's one of the lunatics in this hospital, obsessed with all kinds of conspiracies. He believes the government's experimenting on him and monitoring his every move. Believes his food has LSD. And his headaches are from a microchip inside his head. The staff tries to humor him, but I'm here to maintain law and order. As long as he doesn't bother anybody, he can yap all he wants. But when he—"

"Tell me about these microchips. What can they do? Erase memory? Control the mind? And how do you insert them into the brain?" No, he wasn't just *maintaining law and order* when he tried to crack the intruder's skull.

He might be preventing Stubble—though possibly delusional—from revealing a secret, perhaps a conspiracy or mind-control experiment. Maybe the doctors had inserted a microchip into the intruder's head and were monitoring his chemical levels and neural activities. By chasing away the intruder, he prevented me from learning about it. I didn't care about the government inserting microchips into citizens' heads, but the secret might relate to my amnesia.

The male nurse lifted the table, picked up the tray and left with the bat.

I would locate Stubble and find out everything he knows about my past, including the accident.

Sure, I couldn't trust him, not if I still had my wits, but I would heed his warning about the hospital, whatever he was trying to reveal. But not trusting Dr. Tang and Ingrid? I had been holding onto them while drifting in the sea of amnesia.

With pictures of Stubble and the *guard*, I would identify them if I could find a government database. First, a phone.

CHAPTER 10 - FRANCISCO

August 24, 2011 (1)

I don't want to disappoint, but I didn't die. Not yet. Not that way. If I have to go, I'll die a hero's death, maybe a martyr's. And I'll take a hundred and one scumbags to hell. Of course, I'll be their hell.

The bullet didn't pierce my heart or tunnel through my brain. It only kissed my ear. The lousy shot. I dropped onto the floor while blood dripped from my earlobe and stained the carpet. As I crawled toward the bathroom to check my ear, a red light pointed at the refrigerator door above my head and moved to and fro. I decided to salvage my life rather than my look, not that I'd give away an ear. I rolled to the sink and from under it took out a dummy (an effigy rather than flesh and blood sans brain). I crawled toward the living room, dragging the effigy. Near the counter, I threw it toward the bedroom entrance and dived toward the coffee table.

A windowpane shattered. The effigy's left forearm flew into the kitchen and wads of cotton swirled in the air. A bullet pierced the shopping list on the refrigerator door. So much for my errands. I didn't have the luxury to curse at the vandal, not until I could salvage my body, especially my mouth.

From the coffee table I grabbed the book I'd need to solve the caller's riddle. I pulled away the book just as the laser pointed at the back of my hand. The red dot waited near the doorway, dancing left and right as if daring me to dash through the doorway. I found the remote controller under my underwear and pressed a button to lower the window

39

shades. The red dot wavered on the carpet, retreating back into the living room as the shade descended. A shot cracked the coffee table, the bullet piercing the carpet three inches from my nose. I spat at the bullet and crawled toward the doorway while the shade blocked the view. A volley of bullets ripped through the shade, tearing it to shreds. At the moment the shots stopped, I rolled through the doorway. Close call.

I left the apartment building through the back entrance and had Kung Pao chicken for dinner in a Chinese restaurant. I wasn't about to let a few bullets or a killer ruin my appetite.

With the bullets, the storm arrived, and I'd have to analyze every step and every word to dig out each day's clues. And, of course, to itemize my losses and charge the vandal. So, unlike previous journal entries, for the next months I'd detail my adventures. Maybe, one day I'd publish it. Who knows, I might decide to become a writer.

***

Last night, I returned to my office to check the fingerprints from Holly's desk and as expected found only hers. The glass and the scrap of paper had no prints. I searched through the FBI's database for a match with the note's handwriting. Image-processing algorithms had advanced through the years, but I'd be break-dancing if I could find a match in a week. I also sent the hair, probably just Holly's, to the lab for DNA analysis. Anyway, she disappeared because of the Guzman Code. How do I know? I know. Q.E.D.

This morning, I'd awaken in the hotel room with heartburn, probably from the shock of losing my *pate de foie gras*. The antacid calmed my stomach, but not my heart. Since Clint and Holly hadn't shown up this morning, I had to find them and ferret out those rats harassing my behind, but I must first locate the diamonds and deliver them to the client. To keep up my reputation. I'd have to interlace the clues among these mysteries. Find the correlation among the mishaps and reveal the intrigues behind them.

Despite the workload, I dragged myself to the funeral home in Chinatown's outskirts for The Usual Café owner's big farewell. After savoring my first slice of durian pie in his café, I'd think of durian whenever someone mentioned pie. So when my brother served apple pies during my visits, I might as well be eating pickle in ice cream or drinking coffee with wasabi. What is pie without durian? Whiskey without alcohol, that's what. So when Fernando visited me seven years ago, I bought a durian and made my own pie. Heavenly. My neighbors complained about the stench. So I had to return to The Usual Café for my weekly catharsis, a slice to refresh my soul. On top of that, the owner would praise my achievements—a treat as nourishing as the pie. Never tired of his praises and never tired of tipping him.

A shame that heart attack had taken the owner. I'd miss his praises as much as his cooking. I shook the son's hand and comforted him. I urged him to carry on his father's torch and continue to delight the connoisseurs.

The undertaker, who'd call every month and try to buy my client list, wanted to hire me to check on a banker promising twenty-percent return. I advised dodging the con artist before losing his funeral money. He thanked me and guaranteed a fifty-percent discount on any service. I sure wouldn't want to need it anytime soon.

The son brought durian pies for the reception, but several mourners didn't relish the aroma and had to leave. I indulged my appetite with their shares. The skinny waiter who served me looked familiar, not a Professor Moriarty from my dreams, maybe a Benedict Arnold from my youth. He didn't praise the Great Francisco Guzman, so I nodded and tipped him a penny. Simple as that.

After I had one bite, the Governor, as if he didn't have any meetings to attend, called and interrogated me about Holly. He'd received a threat, a note left on his pillow while he slept. I filled him in on my adventures and he pressured me to find the password. As if pressuring Francisco Guzman had ever helped anyone. Of course, his henchmen would be watching me.

While I crooned the lyrics of "Praise to Fransuccesco," a gift from a client songwriter to honor me and glorify my feats, I examined the dream diary's September 5 entry, where the amnesiac had scribbled his feelings and impressions when first awoken. I was studying the fragmented thoughts and sensations and pitying him when a paw reached for my laptop.

Had a skunk drunk too much New York sewage and turned into Skunkzilla? No, a man had donned a skunk costume. "Do you always crash funeral receptions in a skunk suit?" I grabbed the laptop and poured coffee on the paw.

His bat landed on the table and smashed it into three sections. The durian pie somersaulted in the air and when it landed on his head, I grabbed my backpack and walked out of the funeral home and into the rush-hour Manhattan streets.

The cars greeted pedestrians with their honks and the pedestrians replied with their middle fingers. Someone elbowed me and pushed me off the sidewalk and I stepped on chewing gum. I love New York. Clouds covered the midtown sky and the mist hid the skyscrapers' upper sections. A bicyclist, while texting, slammed into the hydrant. A policeman, munching donut, issued a parking ticket to a limousine. I zigzagged through the crowd avoiding elbows and handbags and reached the policeman just after he had slipped the ticket under the windshield wiper and was sipping his coffee to wash down the jelly donut.

"Officer, a giant skunk's trying to grab my laptop. Isn't it against the law for skunks to enter New York?"

The policeman, who looked like Clint but with a puffy face and full head of red hair, locked his sleepwalker pupils on the laptop for a moment before grasping it with his left hand. "Step back. I'll take that."

"Hey, do you have a license to rob?" I pulled away the laptop and struck his hand with it. Clint, Holly, my apartment, the shots, the waiter, the skunk, the zombie cop, pieces of the jigsaw puzzle, waiting to fit into a picture. And the laptop, at the center. Even in the dream, the chaplain had stolen the amnesiac's laptop. Of course, the zombie cop wouldn't get mine. Not while I had it.

I merged into the Manhattan rush-hour crowd. The men and women rushing to work were kind enough to block the zombie cop's way and I flowed with the black suits while he had to shove them aside. *Thank you ladies and gentlemen.* In the distance, the skunk's tail bobbed above a sea of heads. Probably looking for Fransuccesco.

CHAPTER 11 - X

September 16

Evening, I was reading *Notes from the Underground* when Dr. Tang, carrying a book-size painting, entered and said, "Tell me about E=MC^2."

"For a photon, without rest mass, E = CP." Should've asked for his phone at that moment. But this CP, it disturbed my amnesia. Not the symbols for the speed of light and momentum, it referred to... a lost memory, the contour of darkness, the pitch of silence, the life of nonbeing...

"Okay, so the cerebral damage is localized."

In a few days he would hypnotize me again, so I requested another dream, another alter-ego. However, the doctor reminded me the dream reflected my subconscious thoughts and might reveal my past. If I were this Francisco, I wouldn't want to recover my past.

I should ask about his conversation with Ingrid in the courtyard. The words that made her smile—a smile I hadn't seen before. Instead, I put the unfinished rhubarb pie on the tray and said, "Sure, I can finish a Soduku within five minutes. So my brain is working normally. So what? My memory, my past. I want them back."

"Fortunately, the accident only slightly affected your right prefrontal cortex and medial temporal cortex. The rest of your neocortex is fine. I need to recheck your hippocampus, just to be sure. Anyway, there're procedures for helping you recover your memory, your past—what we call the autobiographical memory."

"Do you have to sound so much like an expert?" Those jargons, I understood. Maybe I'd been a world-famous neuroscientist. But Dr. Tang confirmed I didn't look like any of his rivals, though I could have had plastic surgery.

When I mentioned the minister stealing my laptop, he said the hospital didn't have a chaplain.

"Hallucination? Now, you can officially declare me insane." Why would someone disguise as a chaplain and sneak into the hospital to steal the laptop with only my journal entries?

Dr. Tang suggested posting a guard outside my door. I objected to the nuisance, a guard hindering what little freedom I had. When he gave in and urged me to report future disturbances, I agreed but didn't mention the fake guard.

I discussed my conflicting selves without linking them to Ingrid. Aside from her, I could only open my heart to him, to reveal the conflicts within. His title and knowledge didn't impress me, but his eyes and voice conveyed wisdom and insight.

"All of us, occasionally have conflicting emotions, desires, even temperaments. Love versus hate. Pleasure versus power. Mind versus heart. The usual. I'm no exception. So I understand the feeling."

"Care to share, Doc?" Was he thinking of Ingrid?

"That's why we feel uncertain. That's why we can't make decisions. But most of us will choose some dominant traits, for better or for worse." He pushed the painting toward me. "Take a look at this. What comes to mind? May be important." The fluorescent light cast his shadow fuzzy on the wall while he checked my chart. What was he hiding behind that expert facade?

"Fine, I'm an outlier, a statistical deviant, a black swan. I don't have a unified personality. I don't have an integrated self. Nothing surprising. Tell me something new. Like I'm the Omega point in evolution. That'd make my day." I didn't look at the painting, not realizing the sensations and images it would trigger.

"You want me to tell you that since your habits and biases weren't strong enough to choose and favor one self over the others, that you can't integrate those selves?"

"That I'm not Nietzsche's superman. That my prefrontal cortex can't lord over the other cortexes. That I'm a Jekyll and Hyde. I feel the strain of having several individuals vying for control over my body and mind. Like a country without a leader, the chieftains striving to dominate."

"That you have multiple personalities?"

"That I should tyrannize myself and squash those other personalities. That I should exercise my will power."

"You lost your memory. So different alternatives popped up. So you have to rebuild a new historical self." Dr. Tang shuffled the Rubik's Cube and handed it to me. "However, since you still have your inclinations and preferences, though unaware of them, maybe you won't have to choose. After a while, a dominant self may emerge. Anyway, by all indications, you're sane."

"Hey, Doc, you didn't have to waste all those sentences and nice-sounding words to get to the last syllable. A simple 'sane' would've been fine." I solved the Rubik's Cube in a minute and returned it. Outside the window, the chestnut tree's shadow swayed under the streetlight. Would this phantom self ever return home?

"Bad habit."

"And what if I want to have more than one personality? Can I have unity in diversity? Can I have a dialogue among the selves without a dominant one? Must I choose efficiency over equality?"

"But it's about survival. The will to power, the will to live. Not about equality."

"But I'd like to rise above the laws of nature. Through my self, my consciousness, my conscience. Beyond survival, beyond the laws of physics."

"As I said, you're quite sane." Dr. Tang picked up Dostoevsky's book and said, "But I couldn't guarantee it after you've finished this book." Handing me the painting. "Let's see if you can locate your dominant self after looking at this."

"Sane enough to choose insanity. But would you, Doc, consider such a possibility?" I took the book from him, then the painting.

"On what basis do you assume I'm sane?"

"I thought only psychiatrists question their own sanity. Usually, you guys study loonies, not treat them, right?"

"If you're trying to belittle me, it isn't working. Try picking on my eyebrows or my hair."

"I like your hair. In fact, I like everyone's hair. Any kind of hair is better than no hair." I ran my hand through my hair. My reasoning urged me to suspect this stranger, to bolt the windows to my soul. Should I let Rumi or Descartes dominate my being? Or let my instinct pick and choose? Roll a die?

After mulling over the interplay of emotions, reasoning and instincts, I studied the painting the police had retrieved after the accident. A rising sun shone on lilacs sprinkled across a meadow. Beside the sun, clouds streaked above the dawning horizon. To the right, an oriole on a spruce branch raised its beak as if to salute the sun. To the left, beyond the meadow, a stream sparkled under the sunlight.

I didn't recall such a painting, but the sun, the clouds, the meadow, the flowers, the stream, the tree, the bird, they nauseated me and my head spun. I paced around the bed, but my limbs weakened and my thoughts launched into space. I shut my eyes, only to sense myself gyrating down an abyss. As if the shades of purple among lighted and shadowed lilacs, the fuzzy contours between land and sky, the respective sizes between sun and bird were trying to transport me to the day, the hour, the minute when I first saw this painting. I squinted, I watched, I tried to discern the contours between gray and black amid a sea of shadows, but couldn't mark out in my mind a building, a signpost or a face.

The dance between sun and clouds, the discourse between meadow and flowers, I knew, and even the imagined sonata of stream and bird had touched a memory too drowsy to rise to consciousness. A memory the shade of night almost resurfaced upon my mind; the sensation of breeze almost linked to the isolated neuron clusters. I embraced that nausea and tried to nourish it, hoping it would mature into a newborn image, an episode in my personal history, a defining symbol of my self. If only I could reach deeper into that emotion, link the neurons between my amygdala and my prefrontal cortex, I might touch my forgotten self. If only I could connect with the previous self, these eyes might find lost memories. Maybe my mother had abandoned me among those lilacs; maybe I had left my lover for the battlefield that morning. I could recount my grief, my anger, my sense of loss beside the stream, but the images didn't surface and I opened my eyes to stare at the fluorescent-lighted ceiling, the doctor rushing to help me up from the floor.

"Do you remember anything? Your name? Your parents? Your wife or girlfriend?"

"Doc, sorry to disappoint you. No pretty ladies, or mean gunslingers. No paparazzi-worthy news. " The harder I studied the details, the quicker the nausea fled.

When Dr. Tang suggested taking a break, I said, "You still haven't told me about Dolly."

"Get some food from the cafeteria. The aromas and tastes may trigger some memories. As long as you don't try the salmon sashimi. Yesterday, a doctor had diarrhea after eating it."

"Now you tell me. But I think—"

Dr. Tang picked up the apple. "An apple in my mind is not an apple but a representation of an apple, an abstraction, a symbol. There's no such a thing as 'an apple.'"

"You could've fooled me. Or maybe I'm still delusional. But what's this got to do with Dolly?" Even while laughing at Dr. Tang's words, I recalled my experience before the mirror when I had first awoken.

"This object in my mind is an instance of a class we call apple." He put down the apple and picked up a towel. "The softness becomes an abstraction in my mind to represent some fabric: cotton, wool, or poly-ester. But this, this is an instance of the abstraction *cotton towel*."

"I see." I poked his shoulder. "So you are only an abstraction in my mind, maybe just an illusion. Like Dolly? But, I still want to know about her. What're you trying to avoid?" I grabbed the towel from him and wiped my forehead.

Dr. Tang took the apple and said, "Let's do an experiment. Don't move your eyes; examine me for five minutes. Stare right here for five minutes." He bit into the apple, walked toward the door and continued, "Don't move your eyes. Keep looking as if I were still sitting on the chair and find some unique features."

He stepped out and shut the door.

Silence. I stared at the space above the chair, pretending to examine Dr. Tang. Imagining he still sat there holding the apple or the towel. Damn, I forgot to borrow his phone. After a minute, when he didn't re-turn to have a good laugh, I fidgeted and wanted to end the game. Then... My eyes hadn't been looking. But now... My mind could see without my eyes interfering. I saw him without his face, or rather his nose, blocking my view. And realized Dr. Tang had never smiled; his voice had never sounded agitated; his aquiline nose had been too serious.

Before I could examine Ingrid's profile, pain cut through my abdo-men. I groaned. Doubled over. Dropped onto the floor. The floor, an abstraction according to Dr. Tang, pained my jaw. I searched beyond the window for the chestnut tree but the fog had shielded it. Then, darkness. Yet, darkness didn't purge the pain.

I hoped to awake from this dream. To sunshine. Instead, I stepped on a stage where every performer, except me, knew his or her part.

CHAPTER 12 - FRANCISCO

August 24, 2011 (2)

Near Canal Street, I lost the skunk but several blocks away the zombie cop blew the whistle to alert his comrades. I gave my jacket to a beggar and had him stroll toward the Manhattan Bridge. After crossing Canal Street, I bought a barbecue pork bun from Lucky Man. A cop exited the subway station and greeted another coming down Canal Street. I swiveled around, passed them and continued toward City Hall, hoping they'd take a donut and coffee break, but before I reached the street corner, one cop shouted while the other blew the whistle. I was about to offer them my barbecue pork bun when a gust slapped my left side and a shadow sped down the block and around the corner. The skunk. The two cops chased after him. I whistled and strolled down the street, pretending not to have noticed either fugitive or pursuers. Just a New Yorker minding my own business.

Near City Hall, the fog had descended onto the Brooklyn Bridge, and I could cross unseen, but I didn't want to stand in the middle of the bridge while cops on both sides squeezed me into the East River. I didn't want to bathe in that sludge. I didn't want to mutate into Franciscozilla. At the corner of Chambers and Centre Street, as I was about to slip into a café to avoid the zombie cop, the skunk ran into the City Hall station.

In the subway station, where the attendant was talking on the phone, I couldn't find the skunk and decided to take the subway to the office. After passing through the turnstile, I took off my shirt and wore it inside out. Blue turned into beige. I put my laptop into the backpack and waited on the platform for the Lexington Avenue trains, hoping one would arrive before the zombie reached the platform. I missed the graffiti that used to adorn the walls and inspire me. At least the station no longer reeked of urine.

When the uptown express arrived, I stepped into the train and took a seat at one end of the coach. I'd get off at Grand Central and take a cab to my office. While I read a "Teenager Against Government Corruption" ad, a homeless man came to solicit money. According to him, a fat cop was showing my image on the phone and offering a reward to catch me. I gave beggar ten dollars to block the way. When he left zigzagging between the poles, I went to the next carriage where a young man in three-piece suit slept across a row of seats and two teenagers played five-card stud poker. In the previous carriage, the homeless man dallied with the cop. I exited the carriage at the other end and the wind whisked my hair into the air. I was about to enter the next carriage when I realized that'd be the last one. The zombie thrust aside a student playing "Candy Crush" on his iPhone and approached me. I checked the downtown express track and measured the time between the pillars while the wind flapped my shirt. After a downtown express had passed, I jumped onto the opposite track and missed a pillar by a second. Close call, as usual. I landed an inch from the third rail and waited for the train to pass before getting up. Then jogged into the tunnel, avoiding the third rail so I wouldn't become barbecue pork. I'd passed this area in May to locate an underground man and I recognized the passages near the Bleecker Street station. The labyrinth had evolved but Clint updated the underground maps every month so I could zigzag through the maze as if strolling through my apartment. Still, I could never foresee the wanderers I'd meet. Some underground-dwellers would attack and pillage passersby.

While I was ambling along the tunnel past a control box, the whistle again haunted me. The zombie must've jumped off the train also. What did he want with my laptop? I hadn't worked on the VE case, so he couldn't be after the diamonds. Instead of chasing me, the numskull should tract me until I could find the treasure. Of course, he might be trying to burn off his fat.

I opened a side door and slipped into a small passage. I drank whiskey to replenish my adrenaline, took out my flashlight and check the underground map in my phone. At Washington Square, I could take the uptown train to Penn Station. After passing a few niches where the inhabitants were eating leftover pizzas or hawking driver's licenses and passports, I jumped down a narrow ditch. The rats fled from me as if I'd slaughter them.

The smell of sludge nauseated me and after several hundred yards into the ditch, I stepped on air and tumbled down a tunnel onto muddy ground. Though my shoulder and legs ached, I thanked my guardian angel for not having fallen into a cesspool. While surveying these tunnels, Clint had returned smelling like the East River.

Once I regained my balance and picked up my flashlight, I discovered I'd ventured into alien territory. Since the GPS receiver couldn't acquire satellites and my phone didn't pick up any signals in this section of the underground, I must rely on my instinct. I would've enjoyed the breeze against my face if I knew my latitude and longitude, but now it harassed me. I sidestepped the dripping water and opened a door to the left and entered a passage, where nearby dwellers had etched messages on the wall. Amid drips, a voice echoed through the passage, a light at the other end. I followed the voice toward the light, expecting to crash the underground comrades' convention, a lecture or maybe a workshop.

I didn't want to socialize and turned to retrace my steps, but the zombie's monotone pushed me forward. The confined space amplified his shriek. Annoying gnat. According to Clint, only two or three *roamers* besides him could stroll through these tunnels blindfolded. So a traitor must be helping the cop, probably for a pack of cigarettes.

Light and voice seeped out of a worship hall. The hawker at the entrance urged me to buy a knock-off habit while he still had a few so I could crash the service. I didn't care to take communion but the cop's footfalls drove me to buy the entire stock and I urged the entrepreneur to start a new venture elsewhere. Before leaving, he warned me not to show my face if I valued my life. The worshippers would offer intruders as burnt offerings.

I put on the habit and pulled the hood over my head. Then entered the lighted room, where the heat stifled me. I threw the extra habits into the trashcan. Frescos decorated the concrete ceiling and walls: a nineteenth century Russian reading, writing and thinking. I couldn't recall the familiar face. About a hundred hooded figures stood in ten rows on the flagstone floor. In the front, a marble altar. On the podium, a robed man, who looked like *Groucho* and *Skippy*, recited from Dostoevsky's *Notes from the Underground* the passage where the underground man informed the readers he'd been lying since page one. The front of his robe displayed the words "High Priest." I'd expected a cult, not lunatics. Could the amnesiac be dreaming of me, Francisco, in this hellhole? I stepped behind a hood man and folded my hand. Only when the cop stood at the entrance, did I recall the streets of New York, but I might've also hallucinated about the zombie.

The High Priest paused and stared at the cop. The worshippers turned around and focused on him. I munched a piece of dark chocolate and searched for an exit. I perspired under the heat and body odor irritated my nostrils.

In the silence, the cop fell onto the ground. Four worshippers approached and tied his hands and feet, and they carried him to the altar, where the High Priest nodded and pointed to the table to his left.

The High Priest thanked the mighty Dostoevsky for providing the sacrifice and asked that He help recover the holiest text, then continued to read the gibberish, while several fanatics started a fire at the altar and prepared to offer the cop as burnt offering.

The guards shut the door to avoid further intrusions, and incense filled the room and irritated my throat. I suppressed the urge to cough. The others swung to the cadence of the Priest's words.

Someone farted.

The High Priest ended the liturgy with prayer to the almighty Dostoevsky, requesting that he bless the worshippers and damn the infidels. The worshippers approached the altar to receive blessing. The Priest would mutter gibberish and lay his hand on each head. The worshipper would bow and reply some nonsense. I tried to sneak out, preferring to skip the blessing, but couldn't find an exit. As I approached Ricky the High Priest, I prepared to take him hostage. The worshippers wouldn't want the Chief Fanatic harmed.

I reached Ricky and was pulling out my Swiss knife when the cop threw away the ropes and jabbed a pen into a guard's ribs. The commotion would've given me the chance to slip away. But the Priest waved his hand and only about ten worshippers moved toward the altar to surround the cop. The rest remained in place, enjoying the sideshow.

The Priest grabbed my head and muttered gibberish, but before he uttered the last syllable...

I charged at the Priest with my knife, only to realize that two worshippers had grasped my arms. They twisted them backward and after the blade dropped onto the floor, they thrust my face toward the Priest.

"Who're you?" the Priest said, his eyes piercing into mine.

"I'm me." What other answer should I give when nitwits ask such a question? Maybe, just for once, I should say, "I'm you," to mess with this non-brain, not that I'd find much inside the cranium. Sometimes, when I observed myself kicking butts, I wondered who was watching while I was flexing my muscles. I always answered: I was watching myself kick butts. Yet, whenever I tried to distinguish among I, me and myself, my head would spin.

"Well, Me, you're trespassing. And as you can see from the remains on the altar, I don't like trespassers, even if you're *Me*."

"Hey, Ricky, you've got to make an exception, even in your cult. Maybe if you interpret your other holy books, maybe *Crime and Punishment*, you'd find loopholes. Try revisionist or deconstructionist or other postmodern hermeneutics."

A captor pulled away my hood, and the other said, "Oh, Great Priest, it's him. The coward we're looking for."

"Seize his laptop."

CHAPTER 13 - X

September 18

I didn't die. Should rejoice like Francisco, but didn't. I recovered from the food poisoning, my stomach having purged the E-Coli virus, which, according to Dr. Tang, could've taken my life. The fake chaplain might've poisoned me so again he wanted a guard outside my room. No, bullets would stress me and chase away my memories.

When Ingrid entered the room to counsel me, I finished the pilaf with lamb, adjusted the pillow to support my back and asked for a date. I couldn't leave the hospital, so we would walk around the campus.

I had imaged walking alongside her through the hospital's courtyard and caressing her silky hair while passing the chestnut tree. Her she-ness, like charge and spin, would saturate my molecules and atoms. Ingrid is Ingrid is Ingrid, and by any other name would be Ingrid. Sure, without her entering this room, and therefore walking into my life, her she-ness would've meant nothing to me. But, she had entered my conscious field. And I had noticed her while ignoring others—orderlies, nurses, and other doctors—though they had also walked into this room, also entered my consciousness. These feelings, sun mixing with rain, this attitude, longing to the point of vomiting, how different from those toward the others, defined her place in my heart.

She exists, at least for me, through these feelings and attitudes. Through her and through the delight and pain she has roused, I exist. I am. I rediscovered the self that should exist apart from the sky, the land

and the sea, by bridging to her, Ingrid who is Ingrid. And by any other name, I am I, who was and am and will be.

When she agreed to the date, I pinched my lap and the pain confirmed I wasn't dreaming. My mind wandered through space and time and I couldn't focus during the session and she had to end it. My excitement lasted throughout the day and even now I couldn't sleep. I asked Dr. Tang for money to buy a shirt, a pant and a jacket and though the boutique downstairs had a small selection, I picked out my outfit. All the time wondering how he had charmed her.

My life is sprouting again. I am building a self, one to mature, to journey beside me, to share my excitement and frustration, to direct my paths, to console me. With Ingrid and with this budding self, loneliness will flee. But I still want to find the lost past, the lost self, the older and more mature one. Only now, a melody, like that in the second movement of Dvorak's Symphony No. 9, attends me.

September 20 (1)

After finishing Joseph Conrad's *Heart of Darkness*, I doubled over with a headache for several minutes, waiting for the bangs to recede. The pains around the body didn't bother me, but these headaches, just killers. I dragged myself up and put on the new shirt, pants and jacket. The headache wouldn't ruin the most important day of my new life. I didn't have a tie or a new pair of shoes, but the stranger in the mirror looked as if he had won the Nobel Prize.

Last night, I hacked into the hospital's database through my laptop and, as expected, didn't find the *guard*. An imposter, like the chaplain. I must find out whether he was spying on me or on Stubble. I wanted no part in their mess, but if the *guard* was toying with me, I must unveil the scheme inside his head.

After I had finished dressing, I paced around the room, picked up *Heart of Darkness* but couldn't focus on the words and the sentences, though I had read it a moment ago. Outside the window the fog lingered and I waited for the rain. My muscles twitched and any sound outside the door drew my eyes toward it. An inmate waiting for execution, hoping, begging, praying to shorten the wait. I checked my pulse: 140 beats per minute. I didn't dare to check my blood pressure.

When the doorknob turned, I tripped over the chair and fell onto the ground. The orderly entered and said, "Oh, no need to prostrate and kowtow. Just make sure you don't drip your urine around the toilet bowl and I'd appreciate it very much." He pushed the bucket and mop into the bathroom.

I paced in front of the bay window, glancing at the chestnut tree, and imagined walking beside Ingrid under it. I tried to plan my words, my gaits and even my breaths but the din within the bathroom distracted me and I couldn't organize my thoughts.

So spending such is, lovely thank with I. Day you time you am for. Happy a look great me this.

I gave up rearranging the words into a thought, threw the book into the bathroom hitting the orderly, turned to leave the room, and at the doorway stood Ingrid.

CHAPTER 14 - FRANCISCO

August 25, 2011

Well, didn't become the burnt offering. Tough luck for the Almighty Dostoevsky, but he'd probably prefer roasted lamb anyway. And for the record, I certainly didn't hand over the laptop to the lunatics.

When the Priest raised his arms and chanted in gibberish as if possessed by the Almighty Dostoevsky, I knelt, not to worship the ancient Russian, but to pull out my nunchuks, in which my skill excelled Bruce Lee's. If I'd been born earlier, I could've costarred with him in *Enter the Two Dragons*.

Darkness overtook the room. Even the fire at the altar went out. Silence. The cop screamed. The fanatics chanted. The commotion mingling with the heat and sweat. I slipped out of my shirt and escaped my captors, and was tiptoeing behind the altar when the floor gave way and I fell through a hole. My foot hit a step and I rolled down the steps into mud. Lovely.

I was rubbing my head and shoulders when a squeal beckoned me to follow. A splotch of light zigzagged on the wall and retreated along the passage. I called after the light but it moved away. I followed. After the worship hall's body heat, the moist air in the tunnel cooled my sweat and refreshed me. I took out my flashlight and followed the footsteps, the light no longer visible.

"Where are you?"

"Here."

The echoes masked the source. At a junction, I took a left turn, and after a hundred yards, smashed into a skeleton minus a femur. Dead-end. I retraced my steps, and at the junction, continued down the path. I stepped on mush and dispersed the flies, but didn't stop to examine my soles.

"Where're you?"

No reply. I continued down the passage, looking for a place where my phone could pick up a signal. At the end of the passage, I opened a gothic door with a "HYMN1" sign overhead, and stepped on air.

***

Night had fallen and I lay on a stage in Central Park. I inhaled the night air while the wind whispered through the foliages. As couples strolled past the stage hand-in-hand, I recalled my trysts in this section of the park but perhaps I'd dreamed of the skunk, the cop and the fanatics.

"Was I dreaming?" I caressed the lump on my head.

"Lucky you landed on your head," the man next to me said. Though the low clouds blocked the stars, the stage lights shone on his face, the contours sharp against the darkness.

The skinny waiter, who'd served me durian pie in the funeral and whom I didn't tip, rubbed his nose. He must've been tailing me. "Are you a waiter nobody during the day and a superhero by night? If you have super power, we can profit from it. Great idea. Easy money. I just want twenty-percent, gross sales, that is. Agent's fee, you know."

"I'm here to help you. Here is the proof. I was told you'll understand when I show it." He handed me a painting, the same one the neuroscientist had given the amnesiac. The sun, the meadow, the stream, the lilac, everything the same. The painting shouldn't have appeared in my dream before I saw it in real life. I'd never believed in crystal balls or Ouija boards and wasn't about to. Must be a coincident, a random event where the minute probability had projected into certainty. Some crap like that. Maybe, I'd seen the painting while passing a gallery on a summer afternoon and the image had clung onto my unconscious mind and in dreaming, my mind had borrowed it, as in plagiarism. Maybe, I'd agreed with an associate to use this painting as an ID card. Who knows? Just that I wouldn't embrace intuition, much less premonition.

Was I still dreaming? How would I discern dream from reality?

As I studied the waiter's tan face, I recalled walking down M.I.T.'s Infinite Corridor with him while sipping an orange soda, or maybe lemonade. We stopped at the Building 10 lobby and leaning against the tables discussed private key encryption. Outside the building, several students played Frisbee while the sun smiled on them, and farther away, beyond Memorial drive, sails on Charles River danced in the wind. In between the technical discussions, we reminisced on how in graduate school, we'd hacked into several multinational corporations' databases and retrieved their product designs and how after changing these designs, we'd received patents for several products and used the royalties to get through graduate school. By late afternoon, we developed a new 128-bit encryption algorithm and hurried back to our offices to scribble the details. At that time, wireless communications used the Napoleon 128-bit encryption and even children would associate the French emperor with encryption rather than Waterloo as they once had. But soon, the Guzman-Sengupta encryption would kick its butt from New York to Tokyo. The meadow painting revived that day's images, sounds, and smells, and I could almost taste the soda in my mouth and hear my arguments. But how had we parted way and where had we gone after our collaboration?

"Are you still working in M.I.T.?"

"Even if you're Francisco Guzman, there's a line you can't cross, not even you."

"Then why did you dislocate my front door, punch out my surveillance cameras, ruin my carpet, steal my *pate de foie gras*? That wasn't a nice introduction. I would've preferred a handshake or a beer." I rubbed my soles against the stage to remove the dung underneath.

"Since you're still drunk, maybe you can have another drink at the bar and we can start another time. I'm not used to working with Bowery bums." He squeezed his nose, which dominated his face. "I'm making an exception only because my amour asked me. You can imagine how I hate your skunk odor."

"Also trying to steal my laptop to get my trade secrets. Disguising as a zombie cop is a cheap trick. If you couldn't do your own sleuthing, burn your license and work as an itchy finger. Then you can legitimately steal all you want."

"I see. You're delusional and paranoid also. In that case, I have to check whether to take you on this project. A delusional, paranoid drunkard as an apprentice could ruin the project, plus my reputation. And in my business, reputation is everything."

"Nothing would stop me from solving these mysteries and identifying those scheming bastards who're playing these games." I rubbed my hands. "Since you're going to help me, that is, be my sidekick, you'd better be up to it. The more potholes in the ground, the more I'm psyched to dance around them to locate the pot of gold on the other side. You get my drift? OK, so who's the pretty lady who approached me for this job?"

"I don't care if you drift into the pothole in your mouth. I'm here to crack the code and only need your diary, which seem to be the key and the weakest link. I hope you've taken good notes for the past year or so. If you scrawl like the wino that you're, nothing I can do however brilliant I am."

"Hey, look here, does this look like chicken scratch. This is penmanship, this is calligraphy. By the way, I received the Exceptional Achievement certificate from SOAPS for the past ten years. And just got the lifetime award. What have you got to show for yourself? And, I'm used to people praising me to the sky. So, you can start practicing now." I took out my notepad to show him my writing, but the sewage had smeared the words.

"I don't care for penmanship when the words look like a breeze has scattered them across the page. And I don't care much for soap certificates or coupons. A fool can always find a greater fool to admire him, or her. I'd want to check those flatterers' IQs." He stepped off the stage and whispered to a couple passing by. They glanced at me and backed away, squeezing their noses.

"I don't like your attitude. And I don't need your help to break that code. I can do it blindfolded. If you're going to work for me, you've got to tune down. You know what I mean? I'm used to someone who says 'A' when I say 'A.'" I jumped off the stage onto the ground and bowed to a passerby.

"I've no qualm with you saying 'A' when I say 'A,' even though I'm for freedom of thought and expression. As long as you don't impinge on my freedom, you can obey me all you want. So now, I'm saying, 'let's go.'" He beckoned me to follow.

I must ditch my new Clint. I didn't want him to buzz in my ears or drag my leg. As dawn approached and the fog thickened, I went down the walkway to shake him loose. Somehow, we exited the park and walked together for several blocks along Central Park South. I ignored him and bought my coffee and blueberry muffin. But when I stepped out of the bodega, his shadow blocked my side view. Annoying.

I had my daily massage while he guarded the spa entrance. I flirted with the masseuse and got her phone number. When I ordered him to buy a chicken salad, he pretended to be deaf. What a lazy sidekick. Clint would've sprinted down the street dodging pedestrians and bikes to return with the meal before I stepped outside. This time, I greeted the New York air without my lunch. First time for everything, even in New York.

On my way to the Rockefeller Center the Governor's assistant tapped my shoulder and asked about my progress. I refused to work for a corporation so I wouldn't have to write progress reports and waste time on meetings. So, why'd I report my progress to this non-boos? Before I could jeer at the assistant, he bought me a burrito so I mumbled something about a lead. My sidekick Ganesh hissed but I ignored him. After talking to the assistant for several minutes, I realized Holly had dated him several months ago. She'd shown me a picture of him naked, but he looked different with clothes on, especially with a three-piece pinstripe suit. From the way he pleaded with me to locate Holly, he wasn't just doing his work but still cared about her.

After the Naked Man took his leave, I picked up my mail at the post office and my sidekick attended me. A package awaited me. Why'd someone send me a tattered book? Dostoevsky's *Notes from the Underground*, in Russian. Probably the scroll the Priest and his fanatics were looking for. Lucky me.

CHAPTER 15 -X

September 20 (2)

I opened my mouth to praise Ingrid but no syllables came out. Clatters from the bathroom filled the silence. While I searched for the right word, she beckoned me to leave.

"Did you notice Dr. Tang's always very solemn? We should try to make him smile a bit." Ingrid led the way through two rows of gurneys and, after the automatic doors slid open, stepped into the front yard, where doctors and patients strolled in the fog.

How did Dr. Tang step between Ingrid and me just as we began our date? We should talk about us. I should find out her favorite color and food, her past romances. My heart ached as I passed a row of daffodils. She had smiled at Dr. Tang.

"I can sense his struggle, his suffering, his yearning to create from these feelings a new tomorrow." She nodded to another doctor. "They gave him three weeks to help you regain your memory. Beginning with when you woke up. So, this is the last week."

We avoided the crowds and noises, and admire the trees in the courtyard's southwest corner. She passed a row of flowering dogwoods beside the walkway and stepped into the fog that covered the treetops.

I followed, afraid to lose her in the fog, afraid to lose the way in the courtyard. "Why do you eat alone in the cafeteria, not mingling with the other doctors, not developing a network to advance your career?" More than once she sat at a table in the cafeteria's rear left-hand corner, by the window, eating a chicken sandwich or a tuna salad and watching the fog against the windowpane, while around her doctors, nurses, and patients joked and laughed. I didn't have the courage to approach and chat with her. I just wondered about her thoughts as she stared at the fog. I just wondered about my feelings as I stared at her.

She helped an old lady sit on the bench facing a bed of tulips. Then walked along the path beside a row of benches that faced the cherry trees. Near a lamppost, she picked up a soda can and threw it into the recycling bin. Warblers chirped somewhere in the fog.

"I don't know anything about you."

"There's something I want you to know." She stopped under an American elm. Looking straight ahead as if searching for a light in the fog. "Don't forget it." She picked up an empty bottle and tossed it into the trashcan.

I would help her through her struggles, whatever burden she had to unload. "I'll memorize every word you say. You can test me every time we take a walk together." I greeted a doctor who looked like the schizophrenic talking to himself in the yard yesterday.

"First, I could never forgive you."

"Why?"

She had lost her brother as a child. "When I was thinking about crossing the rainbow, when I couldn't distinguish among ache, pain, tingle soreness, and tenderness." They cared for each other after their parents had died in a robbery, and his death shattered her world. "As if a breaker had capsized my rowboat and I was hurled into the Atlantic Ocean." In her foster homes, she beat up bullies to protect younger children.

What did I have to do with her brother?

I walked up a flight of steps and stopped under an oak tree. I couldn't look at her. The traffic outside continued its symphony, but her voice chanted an elegy and silenced the other tunes. Would my memories also bring grief?

"Yes, I would like you to absorb every word," she said. "If I hadn't believed pain would mold me into a wiser, stronger and more mature person, I would've perished long ago."

"Tell me what I've done?"

"Yes, I believed, not sure whether that belief was fantasy or maxim or both. And I survived, not dwelling on the scars and pains, but seeking and creating my own meaning, and directing and authoring my own destiny. How else could I live?"

"I'm listening. Every word, every syllable, every note." I should take her hand, I should embrace her, but I only watched her profile against the fog.

She passed an oak tree and a bench and stopped to pick up an acorn beside a lamppost.

Her words gnawed at my stomach. Her angelic face, serene as a still lake, had shielded the thorns and thistles of days, months and years. For the first time since waking up from the accident, I feared my past, though I still had to retrieve it. I couldn't say a word. I couldn't even utter a sound. I just admired her strength, praise her wisdom.

"*The Heart of Darkness* you were reading. The evil in this world. You'll find it in your soul once you recover your memory." She tossed the acorn over the bench and it landed on the grass.

I couldn't digest those words, however hard I tried. She knew an incident in my past, maybe from her research. "Tell me—"

"I wish you're someone else." Ingrid sidestepped the oak tree and stopped beside another bench as a squirrel sniffed the acorn.

"Who do you want me to be? Just say it. I'll do everything within my power to change. Since I don't have a past, it'd make the job easier. Pick any Washington, any Lincoln, any Einstein, any Gandhi." I shooed away the squirrel and picked up the acorn and dropped it into my pocket.

She walked down the flight of steps and retraced the path, marching past a row of American elms and disappearing into the fog. I followed her almost tripping over the steps and as I walked along the path, the squirrel tailed me but I refused to return the acorn.

"Sometimes, I'd also wish I hadn't come to this place. But no, I'm glad I came. I couldn't imagine happier moments." Under the chestnut tree she gazed at a second floor window. "But what'll happen when the truth comes out? I must come clean. I must." She bent down and picked up a chestnut.

"Tell me everything. I'd understand. Life can be very difficult." I should comfort her and persuade her to reveal the secret, but before I could, she ran toward the building. I picked up a chestnut and threw it at the squirrel and it scurried up a cherry tree.

Outside the gate, pedestrians rushed along the sidewalk and cars sped down the street. I envied them for having a past. Though the streets outside the hospital bustled with men and women, five blocks away no pedestrians or cars ventured. A face seemed familiar. Was I regaining my memory? But a minute ago that woman walked in the opposite direction. Was she rushing back and forth? The vendor never sold any hot dogs.

The cop still stood next to the same meter writing a ticket. I panicked for a few seconds. My mind must be playing tricks on me. Some variation of déjà vu.

After the walk, in my room, I dreamed of a life with Ingrid. The chestnut tree outside the window was shedding leaves and I had to tell her how much I loved her and how much I wanted to spend the rest of my life with her, but I also feared the future. I feared her rejection. I feared never recovering my memory, my identity. How could I love her if I was less than whole? Still, whoever I might be, I could still create a future with her. Of course, I also feared she wouldn't forgive me. That dream of walking down a sunny beach with Ingrid, like the fog outside the window, might disperse any moment. Hope, like the leaves, fell to the ground.

I would like to build a house on the hillside, facing a canyon. I could imagine waking up to the maples and the warblers. I could imagine making pancakes and scramble eggs. I could imagine life. But life, like cherry blossoms, might shed during its bloom. The fog outside descended to cover my dream and reminded me to search for the lost I, the self who had strayed. The past must not destroy my future. I would build the past as I would the future. I would call the police station to find out more about the accident. I must also find out why Ingrid couldn't forgive me.

CHAPTER 16 – FRANCISCO

September 4, 2011

Last month, with only one case, I went to the bar every night to kill time. Now, I must juggle three cases and cross-pollinate among the solutions and I wouldn't tell Ganesh about the missing diamonds or the mysterious caller. I learned to keep a few aces, and wild cards, in my pocket. I might have to trump someone, friend or enemy, supplier or client. Even myself.

During the past several days I hadn't advanced a centimeter in cracking the code. With my software I searched through possible passwords, but after three tries, the file would lock up and I'd have to wait a day to try again. A safeguard Fernando would've used. I couldn't find a cipher or a code word among the journal entries involving him. If I had to dissect every sentence and every word, it'd take me another two to three weeks.

The note from Holly's apartment didn't shed any light either. As expected, the image recognition software couldn't match the handwriting with any in the FBI databases.

After wasting a whole morning parsing several paragraphs, I had a slice of durian pie in The Usual Café. The usual customers continued to patronize the place. The son continued the tradition of praising me. Still, without the previous owner, the atmosphere had changed. Like the passing of an era.

With tomorrow as the first deadline, I called the security firm to assign two more guards to protect Suzie at all times. My beggar associates still couldn't locate Holly or Clint. They might've left New York. Of course, if Clint had hidden in the underground tunnels, no one would be able to find him.

I read the first pages of the copy of Nietzche's *Beyond Good and Evil* I'd grabbed from my apartment. The mysterious caller must be referring to this book. Was the title, the author, the content, or the cover design the clue? I had no interest in Nietzche's rants against nineteenth century morality and after three pages, yawned and dozed and struggled to stay awake. While I flipped through the pages to check for notes, two newspaper clippings tumbled out of the book.

I picked up a clipping.

December 24, 1994. SUBURBAN FAMILY MAN DISAPPEARED INTO THIN AIR.

The article described how Mr. Guzman, a father of two, disappeared on April 14 that year. Mrs. Guzman and her two sons last saw him that morning when he left the house for work. He never returned. After eight months' investigation, the police still had zero leads, but suspected Mrs. Guzman killed him before he could skip town with his mistress to a South Pacific island.

***

For months, the police harassed my mom, asking for the coolant she'd bought to kill her husband and for the young men she'd flirted with and invited for the murder. At one time, while we accompanied her to the police station, Fernando almost punched an officer in the snout. I poured adhesive into several guns while they were having donut and coffee. Probably jammed at least one.

The police also questioned Fernando and me but I couldn't recall the questions or the answers. I couldn't recall my thoughts and feelings during that time. I couldn't recall that day's events. I might've been playing with my friends after school, maybe. My mind must've blurred those memories to lessen the pain. Before this article hit the newsstands, Mom had checked into a mental hospital and would never leave. She committed suicide three years later. I'd never believed she killed Dad but the police hadn't found any trace of him. After Mom had died, I seldom thought about Dad, except when Fernando mentioned him. I didn't despise the old man; I just didn't know much about him and didn't want to.

Now, through the mysterious caller, from this parchment, the forgotten memory resurrected to haunt me. I hadn't put the clippings between that parchment's pages. A joker was helping me recall the event, either to taunt me, or to rebuke me for forgetting Dad. If Fernando

66

hadn't died, he might've played such a prank. I could trace the call, but the caller probably used a disposable phone. Still, I'd locate the joker and kick his butt. I promise.

While I ate the durian pie and hummed "Praise to Fransuccesco," I flipped through several entries to refresh my memory and look for clues.

April 14, 2000

This morning, Fernando and I hiked along a Catskill trail, which at first seemed unfamiliar, but soon I recognized the brook parallel to our path. The currents, the reef near the bank, the willows leaning into the water all reminded me of a distant date, but I couldn't recall the occasion.

When we came to an open space, Fernando pointed to the area near the bank and said, "In the fall, the white chrysanthemums will bloom along the river, while those spruces will shed their leaves. The sound of the river will mingle with the leaves hissing and the crickets chirping. Symphony of the fall."

"When have we been here before? How come I don't remember?" I seemed to recall planting those chrysanthemums on another April 14 morning.

"In a dream, a dream almost as real as reality. Almost, but not quite." He sat near the bank and read his book.

"Stop pulling my leg, or I'll kick your butt. I only allow pretty girls in my dreams. Like last night—"

"You never dreamed of me, not even as your sidekick? Come on, you afraid I might steal your dream girls?"

During high school, while I was rotating through about Abigail and Betty and Candice, as well as Linda and Margo and Nina, he didn't have any Winnie or Yvette. If he weren't my brother, I would've suspected he was gay.

"Alright, little brother," I said, "I'll introduce a Jenny to you. But you got to promise not to be St. Fernando of Bayside or Pope Fernando I. If you embarrass me once, I'll never help you again." Of course, I would've helped him again and again. He was blood. He was my Fernando. I sat on a rock next to him and said, "You seemed to be reading this book since eternity. When did you start it?"

"November 7, 1994. Remember that day? How could you not? We became orphans, not that we depended on any Tammy, Daisy or Harriet even before then." He closed the book, picked up a piece of malachite and threw it into the stream, like he used to.

How could I forget that day? I'd recorded my thoughts and feelings, somewhere among these notes. I should input these entries into the computer.

November 7, 1994

Took Mom to the ER after she tried to kill herself last night. Found her in the bathroom bleeding, her wrist cut. Fernando was crying and I had to comfort him while we waited for the ambulance. Things hadn't been good this year. Those damn cops always harassing Mom.

I finished Kafka's *The Trial* while waiting in the hospital. Felt like the poor loser in the story. Condemned without knowing my crime. But I'm smart enough to sort everything out. One day, I'd even amend the law "Thou shall not kill."

When we left the ER, Fernando said, "Reserve January 19, 2003, will you? We'll celebrate. One of these days, I'll become a cop. I promise by that date, we'll have something to celebrate."

He wanted to be a cop. Sure, he'd have to work hard to make it in a little over eight years. But why not? Like me, he didn't have failure in his genes. Still, I don't want him to take that career path. Not in New York.

Ever since Dad disappeared, we'd learned to depend on each other, while Mom dealt with her depression. In the playground, we'd fought Brat and Bully together and bled together. We'd washed Toyotas and Fords together. We'd delivered New York Times together. We'd shared a Big Mouth Burger together. I couldn't imagine life without him. I'd rather not ever date again than lose him. If I could prevent him from being Sergeant Guzman of NYPD, I would. No, he'd never give up this dream.

September 6, 2011 (1)

Last night, after reading the previous two journal entries I drank myself to sleep. Whiskey, not milk. I missed Fernando. I missed his voice. I missed our trips to the Catskill Mountains. After these years, I still longed for his jokes about Clint.

I dreamed of playground fights, two against four, kicking the butts of Steel Fist and Iron Dome and Devil's Horn and Double Blade, woke up an hour before sunrise and the first deadline had passed.

CHAPTER 17 - X

September 20 (3)

Toward noon, Dr. Tang came with the painting. So, Pastor McCoy was spying for the Russians and probably wanted the data in the laptop. I waved aside the thief cum spy and invited the doctor to chess. I had to beat him just to show I could. While opening the chess game with the king's pawn, I recounted the falling chestnut incident.

"Don't worry," Dr. Tang said, "your brain was readjusting."

"Not only my brain. My stomach is adjusting to the food. And I'd like some sunshine, if that's not too much to ask."

"Your perceptual interval, the time between two events, was probably a bit longer than normal when you woke up," he pontificated, while setting up his *Sicilian Defense*, "so events appeared faster. After a while, your brain got used to the surrounding. The interval reduced and returned to normal."

"Oh, is that all? And I was like traveling close to the speed of light. Or seeing abstractions." I grabbed the apple and gave it to him. "Here, eat this abstraction."

"Since you're able to detect the difference, you might have heightened visual perception. If you see illusions or objects get distorted, let me know." He took the apple and bit into it.

"Sure. If I see an evil spirit, I'll call you. But you'll have to purge it. That's the deal." I inquired about the Jekyll and Hyde nurse-orderly.

"No one is suffering from split personality. They are clones." He tapped his rook.

"Where am I? Isn't this the Big Apple? Or should I ask, what year is this?" His words jostled me. I couldn't focus. I couldn't sort my thoughts. The ground giving way. Falling, falling, falling into the pit. "OK, I'm probably the one suffering from delusion." Had some hospital, research center, or government agency dabbled with human genes? When I couldn't use the phone, I had suspected a conspiracy but not a sci-fi nightmare.

"Rick's the angry bird and as you can guess, he suffers from resentment. Nasty disease, incurable."

"Don't tell me the jester's disease is curable. He's incurably jolly, very annoying." I pushed my knight to B5 to prepare for a simultaneous king and rook attack, double-kill.

"Nick's hypothalamus has malfunctioned." Dr Tang pushed his rook to C8 to block my attack. "So sadness isn't one of his core emotions. Some people envy him. Scientists are working to modify the hypothalamus and eliminate sadness."

"As if we don't have enough clowns already." I pinched my lap. It hurt. I wasn't dreaming. Maybe, I had traveled to the future, where Frankensteins created their own pets. I picked up the bishop, unsure where to land it.

"Such a sad life, unable to be sad." He worried that without sadness to warn them, to defend them, the new breed couldn't spot or avoid dangers. "I can think of sadists, or psychopaths taking advantage of the social order. Like another Hitler or Stalin." He finished the apple and said, "I hope they fail."

"They'd probably throw you into Alcatraz before engineering a new social order. Just my two cents: keep your mouth shut. That way, you'd survive longer and I'd enjoy your company longer. You see, Doc, even without my memory, what you always call episodic memory, I still know a thing or two." I pushed my bishop to F4, accepting cerebral engineering as I had the other nonsense. Having lost my memory, I no longer worshipped F = Ma even though I continued to believe in gravity and admire Newton.

"And the nanodroid operating on the brain might slip and the patient could lose core consciousness. She'd lose all sense of the self. Not a pretty business. Even though you've lost your memory, you're still aware of a *you* doing things. That's a lot."

"Blissfully unaware of myself. Sounds like enlightenment, nirvana, mystical union. Aren't many people searching for that?"

Dr. Tang refocused on the chess game, but I asked about his court-ship with Dolly, whose path must've intertwined with mine.

"Yes, you do like her."

"If that'd make you talk, fine, I like her. What'd I care if I like her? I want to know more about her." I grabbed his arm. "Don't run from the past, even if it may open wounds. Please help me. I need the informa-tion." If he still loved her, then he wasn't thinking of Ingrid.

"I met her in New Jersey."

"Could be worse."

"I was minding my own business."

"Now you know better, I guess. I was probably also minding my own business when the other car struck me. Only fools mind their own busi-ness."

"Grief was always hanging at the corners of her mouth as if about to fall off. Maybe her sadness, like a mist hanging over an aquamarine lake, attracted me." He picked up the queen but put it back in the same square.

"Glad you're still in love with her. I'll help you however I can, to bring her back."

"She could be tough, as when she karate-chopped a six-foot mugger. But she could also be gentle, as when she listened to my frustrated ram-blings during one of my mental blocks. I returned to the convention center where I met her. Only a few weeks ago. When I first met her, we just chatted. She asked about my research, only a theory then. That after-noon, sunlight passed through the café's window and the chatter droned around us." He got up, walked into the bathroom and rinsed his face.

"Well, those memories are worth something, right? I don't even have them. So consider yourself lucky. Cherish them and don't ever forget them." Yes, he remembered her, he longed for her, and he grieved over losing springs and summers in the abyss of time. He must look for her. And I'd help.

Nick came to clean the bathroom, but I asked him to return later. And he obliged. I grasped Dr. Tang's concern for *Skippy*.

Dr. Tang emerged from the bathroom. "But when I returned to the café, to the same seat, I didn't feel that warm afternoon anymore. The memory, obscured by a screen, the screen of time, only revealed the date, the place, the event and the words we had spoken." He moved his queen for an attack. "And the first dinner together, I'd been nervous. I hadn't known what to say. I'd even spilled the wine. But when I returned to the same restaurant around the same time of the year and ate the same entrée, this time alone, nothing. None of the feelings. Time had shaded my memory, and my mind relived those experiences as through a polarized filter. The nuances had disappeared."

"Hmm, maybe you've moved on. But maybe, you have to return to those places a few more times." He couldn't give up. He must regain those feelings. "Tell you what. I'll come along, just to support you. Don't worry. I won't get in the way." I patted him on the shoulder and moved my rook to check.

"I'd like to re-experience the first candlelight dinner's quiet joy or the camaraderie from that lakeside discussion. Or the pain from the break up, on that hilltop, in that evening, under the setting sun. I went there, too. The hilltop. But the same thing. Nothing." Dr. Tang rubbed his chin and stared at the chessboard. Moving his knight to block my rook. "Had time, this ether that fills life, eroded the link between the hilltop and my emotions?"

"Thank you for comforting me. But not a chance. I still want to know where I had dinner two years ago or whom I dated in high school, even if returning to those places wouldn't evoke the tingling sensations." I rubbed my chin and glanced at the chestnut tree. I sensed pain and nostalgia, probably the same emotions that had surfaced in the doctor's guts. Not only that, I could imagine the hilltop, the setting, the shadows of spruces, Dolly's contorted lips, yes, even her lashes fluttering. Like a general, after losing a battle, gathering the wounded and accounting for the dead. I could almost sense her soft skin.

"No, no, you should locate your past in those neural clusters. Though my memory is decaying exponentially, time actually had sharpened the happiness, anguish and pain from our times together. So every time I recalled our breakup, though the details had faded, the memory triggered a sharper pain. As if the sights and sounds and smells didn't matter and a symbol or a sign pointed to those neural clusters, which are evolving. No, nostalgia hadn't just created and imposed new neural activities on those events."

"Hey, Doc. Forget about neural clusters. Forget about symbols and signs and pointers. Forget about exponential decays. Focus on your feelings and those images in your head. Tell yourself how much you still love Dolly."

"The Rainier who had kissed Dolly, the Rainier who had shed tears for her, I tried to understand his happiness, his grief, his anguish, his hubris. Not as a legend, like Freud or Jung, but as a pal whose past carries along the related emotions." He took out the meadow painting. "Whenever I read newspapers, journals, conference notes, I'd wonder who this Rainier Tang could be. Clothed in journalistic adjectives and adverbs, this man either a Houdini or a Charlie Chaplan. But I looked for the personal Rainier Tang, not some Merlin of Camelot. My memory of the past, however imperfect, how distorted, will reconstruct this lost man."

When Dr. Tang was with Dolly, he must've been inhaling the spring air even during the winter solstice. He must've been rejoicing life even as the cherry blossoms shed into the Tidal Basin. He and Dolly would be walking along the Maui beach while the sun descended below the horizon, thousands of diamonds sparkling in the water. And he would proclaim, "Life!" What joy, what peace, what destiny. In those moments, while he kissed Dolly with all life, he met the personal Rainier Tang, I'm sure. As he shared his thoughts, he must've retrieved those sensations, stored deep in his emotional memory, and recreated the sun, the breeze, the lips. I could almost see the colored sky, feel the caressing air, taste the saline lips, and I stored those pseudo-sensations in my memory. What happiness. After regaining my memory, I'd go to New Jersey, where they had met, to experience those sensations. Preferably, with Ingrid.

"When I woke up without any memory, a terrible feeling, a fleeting fear spread throughout my body, tingling through my nerves toward my fingers and toes. And slithering away when I tried to grasp it, to isolate the organ where it began. I feared the unknown, the uncertainty, the dangers. Of course, I also feared not knowing my identity and past, the ignorance paralyzing me." I opened the file to check the early journal entries and tried to experience those feelings. I wouldn't wait any longer. I would sneak out at night to call the police station and request the report. Maybe, I should hack into the police database, which might also show Dolly's background and the identities of Stubble and the fake guard.

"But you have the courage and the strength." Dr. Tang unlocked the painting from the frame.

"Not only fear, but also loneliness. Waking up to an unknown world without friends and relatives, without myself, that past self, that is. Not even a familiar object, not this painting or anything else." I pointed at the painting he had removed from the frame. "I must walk down the road alone. But I wish I have a friend, or even a trinket to accompany me."

"Life is a lonely path in a desolate world and we must have courage to walk that path. But you'll find your old self. For now, you have us."

"Ok, please, no adages, no maxims, no esoteric rubbish." I liked the sound of *us*, which included Ingrid also. With her by my side, I would fear nothing. And with him leading, I would head in the right direction and soon embrace my memory and my past. "But eventually I must walk alone, right? You didn't say it so you wouldn't alarm me." Sure, he would experiment on me, this guinea pig, and extract as much data as possible. But if he could help me regain my memory, then peace. I didn't expect to get a free lunch. I preferred working with self-interested individuals and I could accept his agenda.

"Checkmate."

"Would they fire you if you couldn't recover my memory in a few days?"

I hadn't checked his king with my queen, though he had moved his knight as expected. I should have won. I didn't have a reason to lose, except fear. I feared winning, succeeding, stepping into the unknown.

"You should worry about yourself. The longer you couldn't regain the memory, the less chance you would." His smile reminded me of Ingrid's eyes, sad and distant. He flipped over the painting. "This painting may help us, after all."

I mustn't associate him with Ingrid or vice versa. I must break that link in my mind. I must associate Dr. Tang with Dolly and Ingrid with myself.

This afternoon, he again walked with Ingrid in the courtyard through the mist, but this time her arms had wrapped around his right arm, as if grasping a tree during a storm. My head hurt from that sight. I doubled over and rubbed my solar plexus, trying to ease the nausea, but my stomach couldn't relax and I was going to vomit. Only after inhaling and exhaling for two minutes did the nausea ease, but my head continued to burn a fever for several hours.

What had they talked about? How could he always make her smile?

Before I could ask, Dr. Tang revealed the clue, or rather a puzzle on the back of the painting. It had to relate to my memory loss.

CHAPTER 18 - FRANCISCO

September 6, 2011 (2)

I called the hospital. No creep had bothered Suzie. Just as I was worrying about Holly, she texted me—as she'd promised five years ago. *Review everything that'd happened on August 23 for clues to rescue her*. She should've asked for help earlier. At least she'd managed to send the message. Sure, she could survive any challenge. Still, I worried.

I'd met Holly in Washington, D.C. almost eight years ago while helping the FBI crack the coded messages between a cult and a drug cartel and stop them from trafficking cocaine into the U.S. I was lunching in Georgetown, a Mediterranean café along M Street, and reading a graphic novel when she approached and asked for direction to a law firm in McPherson Square. Well, she wasn't hitting on me; she had to interview for a junior partner position. I couldn't forget her and stayed awake through the night, gazing out the hotel window at the Potomac and wondering whether she had left the city. When I returned to the same restaurant for dinner the next day—perhaps hoping to meet her—she returned, this time to buy me dinner. She'd received an offer from the law firm. After graduating from New York University, she'd taken a local job to work on criminal law, but recently had decided to expand her repertoire and try her hand elsewhere. After dinner, we made love in my place. When she returned to New York, she broke up with her boyfriend. Two weeks later, she moved to D.C. and stayed at my apartment until finding a Rosslyn condo facing the Potomac and the Pentagon. I dated her while in Washington and even considered marrying her. She turned heads when we walked down the street. She could deliver a joke's punch line just as she could her legal spiel. When I finished my assignment and returned to the Big Apple, we kept in touch and once a month, either I'd visit her or she'd come to New York. We even traveled to the Mediterranean one spring. After three years, she moved back to New York and opened her own law firm and we lived together in a midtown Manhattan condo overlooking the East River and the Williamsburg Bridge. We'd climbed Mt. Everest, skydived in Bangkok and snorkeled in Hawaii. But we'd also argued about buying a Porsche—she wanted red while I wanted black. In the end, we bought both. Two years ago, after discovering I'd cheated on her with her best friend, she broke up with me. But because she'd also cheated on me with several clients, we decided to remain friends. During this period, both she and I had slipped through half a dozen romances and non-romances and we'd talk about them over dinner. And I'd come to value her friendship.

***

This morning, I took the ferry to the Statue of Liberty and checked Holly's hideout below the souvenir shop, a.k.a. Liberty Lair. I didn't find her there, but she'd left me a message: *Dream.* In her leather chair I studied the poster of Descartes to ponder the word. My nightmares should reveal clues, but I wouldn't believe Freudian babbles. Still, after reading her message, I decided to scrutinize the dream diary. In her desk drawers were only pictures of her former boyfriends, not her laptop.

Two hours later, I took the ferry back to Manhattan. On the upper deck I had a filet mignon burger for lunch. While I was studying my August 23 journal entry, Ganesh sat down next to me sipping his colada. I had no idea he'd also gone to the Statue of Liberty and was on the same ferry. He must've been tailing me. I asked for the secret that the coded file would reveal, and he said, "Perhaps, a tycoon's affair with a young girl. Or a movie star's drug addiction. Whatever. As long the code is challenging enough, I'll put in my all to crack it. By the way, care to share some of the proteins and fats you're consuming? I wouldn't mind helping you absorb the cholesterol."

"Who's that lady who handles the interaction between us and the mysterious client?" I finished the steak burger and after downing it with beer licked my lips.

"The middleman, or middle-woman, if you prefer. You seem interested in her. Well, forget it, she's taken." He stared at the empty wrapper, sucking air through the straw and twirling his glass.

"Did I ask your opinion? I love her, nothing else matters. Simple as that." From my tote bag I took out the SOAPS Lifetime Achievement

Award I'd brought to enter Holly's hideout. I put it on the table. In case he hadn't seen it.

"You're the typical problem solver, simplifying a problem to make it manageable. Make linear a non-linear system and use the familiar tools," he said, taking the statuette to scratch his back. "Well, watch out, one of these days the black swan will get you. On top of that, when you try to make linear interpersonal relationships, you distort the problem because the second-order terms are as important as the first-order ones. So, your neat and closed solution solves the problem you created, not the original one. Sure, you can find as many solutions as the problems you created, but not the ones that count. Just remember, she chooses her lover." He took out a walnut and cracked it with the statuette.

"What's this abstract crap? What do I care about linear and non-linear systems? What do I care about black and white swans? I want that lady to be my lover. Plain and simple. You abstract and complicate simple problems when the solution is so obvious. A is A is always A." I pulled the statuette from his hand and checked for damages. "Let me tell you buddy," I said, pointing the statuette at his nose. "In this line of work, if you try to abstract the problems, you'll end up with a hundred pages of equations. But in the end, you only want that single word or number, that solution. So, don't try to explain the crappy theories behind every algorithm and don't ever try to derive any one of them. I just want to use those damn things."

"Ah yes, you're a simple man with a simple mind looking for a simple world. In that case, those algorithms you worship without questioning, they'll always lead you into the alligator pit." He ate the walnut and swept the shells over the rail into the water.

"So, you're interested in her. Well, chum, don't even try. She's way out of your league." I wiped the statuette and put it back into the bag. Like they say about swine and pearls and all that crap.

We should part company, or I'd fall into his trap and flatten his nose. We're as different as yin and yang, or matter and antimatter. He could keep his paycheck without any contributions (not that he had any so far) as long as he didn't harass me with his esoteric obscure pseudo-rational rubbish. Indeed, I'd prefer taking all the credit (as I usually do) for cracking the code rather than sharing my trophy with this egghead. But, his damn ego probably would prevent him from taking the check and lazing around. Then again, maybe not.

When the steward came to check the tickets, I reported Ganesh had littered into the water, but the pimple face smiled and left. What happened to public good and all that crap?

When Ganesh suggested working on the assignment, I pulled out my scheduler and said, "Have you made an appointment to talk to me? Where's your name?" But since he head to learn about my work habits, I made a 1:30 PM appointment to brainstorm.

After we'd gotten off the ferry, I went to the spa for massage and sauna while he worked on an unrelated project—minimizing distribution costs in a multi-node supply chain. During my massage, I studied a photo of Fernando's baseball card and pondered who might've stolen it. The all-star player's picture only recalled the times we played softball in Flushing Meadow Park.

Since I didn't need Ganesh's help, I'd hoped he'd be upset enough about having to schedule an appointment to quit his duty. Or lazy enough to skip the work. But, no such luck. At 1:30 PM., his nose and his laptop showed up at the abandoned apartment reeking of marijuana and blood. He even braved the streets of South Bronx to get there. He panted while putting his laptop on the table my associates had set up. A Dance Fever dealer must've chased him through the tenements. Lovely.

My associates had spotted the Underground Temple fanatics loafing around these premises, probably looking for their holy text. In this unit, behind the heater, I found a skunk tail, that is, a fake one. So Skunkman must be a fanatic. Figures.

"This'll be easier than changing motor oil." He sent the supply chain solution to his client and asked for my diary. "Supply chain, that's the key to this code also."

"I'd never learned to change motor oil. Just not good with those mechanical stuff. Like they say, don't have the genes for muscle work." I closed his laptop and pushed it to the edge of the table, two feet from the broken windowpane.

"Sure, I've heard those lame excuses all my life. I've made them myself often enough, like I couldn't cook hardboiled eggs. But you know what, that's just laziness, unadulterated crystal-clear sloth." He wagged his finger like a lunatic.

"Just great, a loafer proselytizing about the virtue of hard work. What'd you care whether I can change motor oil? Like I said, I don't need your brain, so you might as well toss it in a soccer field and make use of it." On the street below, my five associates guarded the building entrance. Once every fifteen minutes, one or two would cuss to signal everything shipshape.

"As if I care. Me, I keep my nose where it belongs."

"And what'd I care about your crooked nose, unless it can help me break this code? If it can sniff out the solution, then stop wasting time and get to work. If I don't wrap this up by October 26, my friend would be a goner and my reputation would gurgle down the ditch."

"So, you have friends?"

"You know, when I put my mind to it, I can break any code, natural or manmade. Like I used to say, 'Once a winner, always a winner.'" I pointed at the statuette.

"If you spend less acoustic waves promoting your ego and more mental frequencies solving the problem, you might actually succeed once in a blue moon. In information theory, the code's entropy indicates its efficiency. Have you heard of the Sengupta Encryption?"

I reminded the geek-head of my contribution in the Guzman-Sengupta Encryption, and flung the diary on the table. The pages spilled out and the cover reeked of alcohol. I still used it until a few solstices ago, but had scanned the entries into the laptop. "Well, who's that pretty lady? And I don't mind the client's name also." A pop startled me and a window behind Ganesh cracked. I eased myself against the wall next to the window. My associates on the street crouched behind cars and trash-cans.

"Hmm, a scroll from the Stone Age, the pages coming off. It belongs in a museum." He ducked under the table and flipped through my diary and scattered the loose pages on the floor.

"I've got the dates clearly written, so you have the info you need. Not that it'd help a sham pretending to be Einstein."

"Did you beautify your old entries, throwing away the old ones with the ugly truth? Or did a novelist create the entries for you? They look more like fables than daily events." He flicked away a dead bug and examined an entry while crouching on his knees.

"Why, thank you very much. My life is as adventurous, as heroic, as epic, as the best novels." I dropped onto the floor and picked up the pages. "Did you expect my life to be like yours, scrambling to work, sweating through meetings, stooping to your boss, dining in the office, dozing in front of the TV set, and somehow dropping into bed? Well, that's you, not me. My life will become a blockbuster movie." Another shot echoed outside the window. And after several shouts, a volley of shots drummed the air. Annoying. The fanatics might've come back to retrieve the skunk tail.

"Yes, one of those horror movies." Ganesh closed the diary and held it up. "Now, what's so special about the diary?"

"Well, because it's my diary, my story, my adventures, my life." I yanked it out of his hand.

"Wrong answer. Hint, the competitive dynamics of the diary industry. Bad enough that the e-diary as a substitute competes with the traditional diary. Now, we have social media and everyone's putting their daily entries online—"

"Hey, I didn't come for your dribbles." I opened the diary and inserted the loose pages back in place. "What'd I care about the competitive advantage of the diary? I came to crack the code. Anything peripheral like assessing the strengths, weaknesses, opportunities and threats of this obsolete industry wastes time. So, you've been studying too much and don't have much hands-on experience. Like I said, I don't care how it works, just show me the results."

"I was more interested in the value chain of the traditional diary, not the value added at the different stages of development, but the locations."

"You're skirting around the problem, hoping it would collapse like the walls of Jericho. At best, you're trying to showoff your ignorance on an unrelated problem. What'd I care about value chains and supply chains when I'm only interested in solutions? Listen, theories and concepts are for people who can't deal with reality. I've met enough people like you to know you'll never solve the problem. Piling barriers to entry over operational efficiency over conjoint analysis until the gibberish prevents the designer from talking to the marketer from talking to the operations engineer. In the end, they always get depressed and many had to check into mental hospitals." I found a page without a date. So I inserted it behind the last page.

"This diary was designed in Helsinki. The paper made in York and the spine in Manila. The final product was assembled and packaged in Nanjing. Then, shipped to One Distribution Center (1-DC) in California, ready to arrive in retail stores. So, what do we have?"

"Lunacy to the nth order, that's what we have. Why must I always work with delusional egomaniacs?" I blew away the dead bug on the last page.

"Don't call yourself a delusional egomaniac, even if you are. I humbly refuse to acknowledge the sarcasm though you might enjoy deriding yourself." Ganesh took out a pen and a pad. "So, we have Helsinki, York, Manila, Nanjing, and 1-DC."

"You're one step away from the loony house. So watch out." I decided to review an old entry: January 19, 2003 while the gunfight continued in the street below. Fernando had promised me a gift for tomorrow. Would he keep his promise even in death?

"I'm one step to the solution. So, stop trying to derail me. Like I said, I can solve any code if I put my mind to it. And when I work on something, I don't give up." The lunatic scribbled on his pad. "The first character of each location: H, Y, M, N, 1. There, HYMN1. Voila!"

I shut my laptop and was ready to leave the lunatic when my beggar associate stepped through the door and said bounty hunters were looking for the Russian manuscript I'd received, the Underground Temple's holy text. They'd killed a private investigator and a bookstore owner. The police arrested the culprits but that wouldn't stop the fanatics. Lovely, just lovely.

January 19, 2003

Fernando had become lieutenant two weeks ago, so Clint and I went over to his place to celebrate. Clint still wasn't speaking to me because a week ago, after a thief shot him in the arm, I called the ambulance and left him in the alley. I had to chase after the scoundrel to get the last clue and decrypt a code. If I hadn't gone after the clue, I wouldn't have retrieved the data from a Russian hacker playing Robin Hood. As I was decrypting the data, he was erasing it—a list of defaulters who owed my tycoon client money. In the end, I retrieved more than eighty-percent of the data and my client took those defaulters to court and sent them to jail. Happy ending.

When we arrived at Fernando's sty and stepped into the warm air, before I could brush off the snow from my head and shoulders, Clint was washing the dishes. He spent three hours cleaning up the mess while Fernando relayed his adventures patrolling New York's night streets. That day, he rushed into an abandoned building in South Bronx to nab drug dealers. He was waving his hands and pointing his fingers, but I worried about him. I should be protecting him. And yet, he wanted to protect others.

When Fernando boasted about having kept his promise—to have something worthwhile to celebrate on that day—I pulled out my journal entry to remind him I'd always keep track of his promises. He said he would always keep his promises. He poured two glasses of champagne and we toasted to promises and our health.

I pulled out a ten-thousand-dollar check a former client had sent me for Christmas and detailed my achievement but he rebuked me for helping the millionaire seize a plot that the man later developed into a multi-million dollar shopping center. He believed the community would've benefited more from a medical center. Well, this is America, the land of opportunities.

While Fernando talked about rising through the ranks and I persuaded him to join me, Clint cooked dinner. He steamed the lobster tails and mixed the butter sauce. He mashed the meat from Snow Crab legs and baked crab cakes. He grilled red peppers and portabello mushrooms. He mixed a chocolate batter and removed the cherry pits to make a Black Forest cake.

I ate two lobster tails and four crab cakes. I drank half a bottle of Chardonnay. I had two slices of the cake. I enjoyed food and wine so much more with Fernando around, as if he revealed life's joy.

After drinking three glasses of Chardonnay, Fernando said, "Mark this date. September 7, 2011. I'll reveal a secret to you."

Clint was sipping champagne and dropped his glass onto the floor. His face flushed, then paled. His hands trembled.

"Are you drunk or have you hidden a mistress?" I rebuked Clint for messing up the dining room. I'd never caught him on a date, not in high school, not in college, and not at work. Of course, he should hide his girlfriends from me, especially a pretty and lovable one. I wouldn't mind finding out his covert lover but preferred a juicier secret.

"Hey, don't worry. I won't share your secrets." Fernando finished his glass of wine and dug into the Black Forest cake. "No, something different. A dark secret."

"Well, I'm writing this down to make sure you keep your promise. When you promise me something, I won't forget it. And I expect you to keep it, no matter what." I tapped Fernando's shoulder with my fork. "What about Clint's dark secret? What have you two been doing behind my back? How come you know his secret and I don't?"

"Don't be jealous. You have a long-distance girlfriend, don't you? Tell me how the relationship is coming along. How come I never see her?" Fernando patted me on the back, as Clint rushed to the study, knocking down a chair on the way. I didn't see my sidekick again that night.

"I couldn't remember that day's details," I said, "you know, the day our old man disappeared. In the beginning, I tried hard to forget. Now, just a hole around that time." We'd never talked about that day or about Dad's disappearance, as if we'd dreamed the whole episode.

"When memories begin to enslave us, we must shed them to regain freedom. One of these days, I'll do something for you, something special, to set you free of your memories."

I comforted him when Mom died. I protected him when ruffians bullied him. I tutored him in calculus before the final exam. But he comforted me, not by words, not by deeds, but by his presence. As long as he stood by me, nothing could stop me. So, he'd given me all I needed. Still, I craved for his gifts.

I pressed him to reveal his gift, but he just marked the date in his e-calendar. I didn't want to wait nine years. Give me a break. What if I should die before then? That wouldn't be fair.

CHAPTER 19 -X

September 23 (1)

Was I sleeping in the hospital bed twenty-four hours ago? Did I dream it? I wouldn't be able to return to that room or smell the antiseptics, the hospital and New York having ceased to exist. Only this prison yard with the guards watching from the tower, their rifles ready to fire. Where am I? Someone played a trick on me. Everything flipped upside down, except I still don't know who I am.

Sure, in a probabilistic universe, an event, however strange or unlikely, could happen. Yet, I may be dreaming or hallucinating, reality tunneling away and disappearing into the void, as my memory had.

So, Stubble had meant this charade.

***

Two days ago, I studied the list of elements Dr. Tang had found behind the meadow painting, a clue that had to reveal how and why I lost my memory.

Tin

Uranium

Sodium

Lithium

Iodine

Gallium

Mercury

Titanium

As I searched through the periodic table of elements, Ganesh's revelation—HYMN1—popped into my mind and reminded me of the woods: the boulder, the ferns, the red maples and sunlight sparkling through the foliages. And a melody, perhaps from my childhood. In my mind, the elements and the woods overlapped but they crossed on different planes and I couldn't integrate them into a theme.

Would I have to work with Francisco to decode the puzzle? I hoped against odds that the list wasn't related to the Guzman Code, but deep in my mind, they entangled.

I paced up and down the hallway, checking on every room's patient. Perhaps their faces might link to a smell or a taste and trigger my memory. Yet, I only remembered the vendors and pedestrians on the street.

When my head ached, I read Douglas R. Hofstadter's *Godel, Escher, Bach* to relieve the tension. The chapter "Brains and Thoughts," revealed how the brain abstracts images and maps them into symbols, where a symbol could be a thought or an emotion. And how symbols link with each other. So, the meadow painting or Dolly's photo revived my nausea and grief. And the word "HYMN1" pointed to the woods and the melody. One symbol linking another through the neural pathways.

While I was reading the section on procedural and declarative knowledge and mulling over how I had lost none of the former and some of latter, outside the bay window Ingrid hurried across the courtyard toward the hospital entrance. From her half-clenched fists and jumbled paces, I sensed the turmoil inside her and dropped the book onto the floor.

When Nick came to chitchat, I thanked him for cleaning my room and borrowed his ID card, uniform, and baseball cap. I didn't consider how much I risked his life by leaving the compound with his ID and uniform. He probably didn't either. After putting on the uniform and ID, I rushed into the hallway, hoping Rick wouldn't spot me. The previous day, when *Skippy* came whistling the familiar tune and yapped about the *prophet* in the mental ward having another vision, this time God revealing the world would end on October 26, I ignored his rhapsody and continued to read my book. Yet he continued to laugh and joke. In that moment, I envied him. But as I exited the building, I wondered how he would protect himself.

Ingrid picked up a daffodil at the hospital entrance and turned right on the sidewalk. I also picked up a daffodil and imitated the way she bit her lips. Right away, sensing and grasping the grief draping over her heart. She was thinking of Dr. Tang, I was sure. I detested him, at the same time, wishing to become him, to take on his voice, his thoughts, his emotions, his total being. I hid my face from the surveillance camera overhead and waved the ID over the scanner. The gate opened and I followed Ingrid down the sidewalk as my skin itched with jealousy and my legs faltered at every step. If I could regain my memory, I would surpass Dr. Tang. During the short time in the hospital, I had learned about not only my amnesia, but also the working of the brain and the intricacies of consciousness. In time, I would learn everything about neurobiology, psychology, and philosophy. I could even compete in the Olympics, in swimming, having broken the hospital's indoor pool record.

Grasping the daffodil, I hurried after Ingrid, but she was getting farther and farther away and, as I was sure, closer and closer to Dr. Tang. The loiterers' faces—the pedestrians just stood around and sometimes glanced at me—the buildings' silhouettes, the fog's fragrance, they recalled a dream. Not sure when, but I'd had a dream. If only I could recount the locations, the players, the dialogues.

I had to overtake Ingrid and reveal my love. Yet, I must also find out whether she was meeting Dr. Tang.

A businessman in three-piece suit passed me, his face familiar. Had I met him before my accident? I stopped to greet him, but to avoid losing Ingrid, continued down the street without waiting for a response. The traffic cop was still writing a parking ticket. Damn it, the businessman, he was the lunatic in the hospital's cafeteria. Was my brain playing tricks on me again? Could I have met him in another hospital, before the accident? How could that lunatic turn into a businessman? I turned around but couldn't spot him in the crowd. I studied the other faces. The cashier in the Mexican food stall became a beggar. An ICU doctor became a street vendor. A schizophrenia patient became a violinist. My head swirled. I hurried after Ingrid, trying to forget the other faces. Not caring whether I was dreaming or hallucinating.

Soon, I would find out the truth, that the businessman was indeed the lunatic and the gardener the patient on the gurney. I would have preferred to live in a dream, in an illusion.

At that moment, Ingrid's longing for Dr. Tang wrenched my heart. I tasted her bitter despair and sour jealousy, and I felt the waves tossing her about the sea. I had to rescue her, and at the same time rescue myself from my storm.

She zigzagged down 63rd Street as if waves tossed her from side to side. I extended my hand to reach her but my feet hesitated to trek across that twenty feet. The pain, the anguish, the frustration, pounding on the left and thrashing on the right. I shared her emotions and her thoughts but we seemed to walk down divergent paths. On Lexington Avenue, she turned a corner and I rushed forward so as not to lose her. I couldn't lose her.

Something was wrong. No honking or cussing. No urine or trash. No chewing gum or paper cup on the sidewalk.

At the corner, I pushed aside a beggar's hands, but Ingrid had disappeared. A few pedestrians wandered along Lexington Avenue and a few cars crawled down the street as if they were in Smallville, USA. The hubbub outside the hospital had disappeared several blocks away. How could the streets of New York ever be so empty? Of course, I didn't care; I had to find Ingrid. In front of the corner bodega, I peeped inside. No one, not even the owner. I tried the office building next door, but the gate was locked. Across the street were a confectionery, a toy store and a Shakespeare Theater. I crossed the street and glanced through the confectionery's display window at the madeleines, macarons, and mochis. No staff or customers inside.

Behind the theater's front door, a green-nosed clown stared at me for a moment and spoke into his phone. When I opened the door to enter, he blocked my path.

"What're you doing here?" he said.

I asked to look around for Ingrid, but the clown wouldn't let me through, insisting that the theater had been closed for months and no one had gotten past him.

I raised my fist to punch his face but stopped in midair and squeezed his nose. I must confront Ingrid about Dr. Tang. But I never saw her again. I never saw Dr. Tang again. I was so upset that I didn't even inquire into the missing rush hour traffic.

At the street corner I almost crashed into Nick.

"They're looking for you," he said.

"Are you in trouble?" *They* must be *Groucho*.

I didn't want to get Nick into trouble so I followed him into the 59th Street subway station. No attendant. No passengers. No trains. Before I could ask, Nick opened a side door beside a nook and beckoned me. I stepped through the door into a dim passage, which reminded me of the underground tunnels in my dream. I didn't smell sewage. I didn't hear rats. After I returned Nick's ID, uniform and cap, we walked to the end of the passage where a ladder led upward.

"No surveillance cameras?" I said.

"Drug dealers built this tunnel," Nick said.

I climbed the ladder and pushed away the manhole cover, hoping I wouldn't enter the Underground Temple. I emerged in a dim corner behind a data storage unit the size of several refrigerators. After I replaced the cover in the manhole, Nick and I walked around the storage unit into a lit basement, pipes and surveillance cameras overhead and monitors and panels on the walls. We traveled to the end of the passage to the stairwell. Only when we walked up to the main floor did I realize we had returned to the hospital. Nick had shown me the secret passage, which I could and would use it to sneak in and out of the hospital.

Groucho and several guards waited for us as we came out of the stairwell on the main floor.

"Where the hell were you?" Rick stood akimbo like an angry mother scolding her children for stealing from the cookie jar.

"I was meditating in the basement," I said, "near a monitor that seemed familiar, trying to recall when and where I had seen it."

"What'd you remember?" For the first time, Rick seemed excited, but mixed with exasperation, of course.

"Nothing, since *Skippy* came and disturbed me."

That evening, I didn't eat dinner but sat in Ingrid's seat in the cafeteria. Glancing at the evening fog and trying to discern her vision, but thinking of Dr. Tang. A thud startled me. At the next table, a boy about seven years old, who was drinking orange juice, fell onto the table, spilling the juice onto the floor. The stalls had closed and everyone else left the cafeteria. I shook him, but he didn't respond. He might be dying. I flung away my grief and anger and frustration and carried him to the nearest nurse station. As I walked down the deserted hallway, I regained my strength. I shouldn't wallow in misery while patients were losing their lives. After dropping the boy at the nurse station, I returned to my room and finished the apple from dinner.

At midnight, I sneaked out of the room and walked down the hallway, looking for a phone. Snoring shook the gurney as I passed the next doorway. I covered my ears. When the snoring faded, the instrument beeped from a double-bedded room. The smell of urine nauseated me. Through the swinging doors, I reached an empty nurse station where the computer monitor displayed a spreadsheet. Looked around for the nurse, before stepping behind the station. The nurse had left her sweater on the chair's back and her lipstick next to the phone. I tried to call the police station, but the phone didn't have a dial tone and wasn't connected to a phone jack. No wonder Rick didn't let me use the phone. I was searching the computer for memos when footsteps alerted me. I escaped through the swinging doors in time to avoid the nurse.

Why the fake phones? Maybe I will wake up from this nightmare and return to Francisco's world. I hope not.

Back in my room, I couldn't sleep. I feared losing my sanity. Feared reality turning into a dream. Feared having lived in an illusion and tomorrow waking up to another one. I tried to separate Ingrid and Dr. Tang in my mind. Tried to soothe my headache and heartache. I needed sleeping pills.

***

The next day, Nick said Ingrid had left last night and wouldn't return. I dropped onto the floor and fainted.

Waking up, I pushed aside the attending doctor who looked like the patient on the gurney, almost knocking off his eyeglasses. I asked for Dr. Tang. But he'd no longer treat me. I opened my mouth to shout. I raised my hand to break the tray table and the bay window, and to fling everyone out of the room, but from the eyes of the new doctor, the new nurse, and even Rick and Nick, I sensed conspiracy. So I remained calm. Tightened my fist and ground my teeth.

And planned my escape.

After finding the fake phone, I didn't trust the doctors, the nurses, the orderlies, or the patients. I was going to discuss with Dr. Tang my distrust toward almost everyone in this hospital. Now, after he and Ingrid had left, I lost my bearing. I had entered another nightmare. I must leave.

With the photos of Dolly, Stubble and the guard, I'd search for my identity alone. And succeed. But without Dr. Tang, I'd have to rebuild my memory one image at a time, from news, anecdotes and gossips. A part of the past would never return from the abyss.

During breakfast, I asked about the boy's condition. After finding out he had recovered and was sleeping, I left him a pack of chocolate peanut-butter cups at the nurse station. I couldn't delay my escape to visit him.

Toward noon, I put on my new shirt, pants and jacket. Took a pair of gloves, the first aid kit, leftover pizza and sandwiches, half a bottle of whiskey. And the acorn. When the clone, not sure Rick or Nick, entered with Dolly's photo and a note from Dr. Tang, I thanked him and knocked him out. Taking the note and his ID and cash card.

After sneaking out of the hospital through the secret passage, I emerged from the subway station on Lexington Avenue. I was walking toward 63rd Street trying to retrace Ingrid's footsteps when footsteps thundered nearby. I leaned against the building and peeped around the corner. Down 63rd Street, Rick and the hospital staff rushed toward Lexington Avenue, waving their semiautomatic handguns, assault rifles, and maybe laser guns. The surveillance cameras must've shown me leaving the hospital.

I retraced my steps on Lexington Avenue and tried the door of a boutique but it was locked. I passed an empty travel agency.

Near the subway station, I entered a Mexican restaurant where men in suits, women in dresses, boys in shirts and girls in skirts celebrated an infant's birthday. Four men at the bar drank champagne and argued about the last night's football game. In the lounge, women on the couches talked about the latest advances face lifts and breast implants. Three boys were getting tacos and burritos at the food bar. Two girls played video games near the window. I dropped into a seat near the kitchen, my back facing the front door. As I glanced around for a back door, a shadow draped over me. The front door hadn't opened after I came in, so it wasn't the hospital goons.

"Just a glass of water."

The waitress sat down opposite me and said, "Do you remember me?"

Dolly. The same hairstyle, the same facial contour, and even the same clothing as in Dr. Tang's photo.

I showed her Stubble's photo and pointed at the face. "Did you marry him at sea?"

"Are you starting to remember something?"

She stared into my eyes as if trying to hypnotize me. Even as I studied that elongated face, my mind remained blank. I had recalled images when I first saw her photo, but looking at her face didn't bring back any scenes. Something was wrong.

"We used to work together as secret agents," she said.

"Tell me everything."

"Try harder to remember."

"Why can't you tell me?"

"I'm trying to help you."

She didn't have that face sharp as a blade, or those eyes piercing into my blank soul, as had the lady in the photo. I was about to take out Dolly's photo when the zombie cop from my dream appeared beside the table, stretched out his hand toward my backpack and said, "I'll take that." A waiter came to seat him at another table, but the cop threw him across the room onto the food bar, preventing the boys from taking the food.

Something was wrong. How could a dream figure appear in the real world? Had I seen this cop before and dreamed of him? I didn't have time to figure out. Just repeated to myself that I was sane. But I didn't convince myself.

"Do you know him?" the woman said.

I compared her face with my mental picture of Dolly. Sure enough, an imposter.

"Who are you?"

The front door opened and as I turned around, *Groucho* and his goons entered the dining hall. I left the seat and ran toward the kitchen while Rick shouted. At that moment, a boy, the boy who had fainted in the cafeteria, opened a side door and waved to me. I hesitated for a moment, but followed him and stepped into a playground. He jammed the door with an iron bar. Beyond the slide and swings, cars drove along Queens Boulevard. Had a transporter taken us from Manhattan to Queens? The boy gestured and rushed down sidewalk. I followed him and asked about his health and he thanked me for the candy bar. A few pedestrians loitered on the sidewalk but no cars drove down the street. When they saw me, one spoke into his phone while the others came after me. The boy and I ran down Queens Boulevard as a man at the ATM machine charged out to tackle me. I shoved him back into the foyer and followed the boy into Queens Center and he pointed to the door in the back and said, "The Shakespeare Theater." Before I could question him, he left the shopping mall and ran down the street.

I exited through the back door and returned to the hospital basement. I didn't understand. Nothing made sense. The hospital was empty. None of the phones worked. None of the computers worked. My patient record was gone. The other patients' records were blanks. Props, the whole charade, including the fake Dolly, just to fool me. Whoever they were, they were going to retrieve my memory. My head hurt from the questions that gushed forth and the images of Ingrid and Dr. Tang, and of Dolly and Stubble and the hospital staff. I must retrieve my memories and examine them to dig out the secrets and conspiracies.

CHAPTER 20 - FRANCISCO

September 7, 2011 (1)

Would you believe it? Last night, I had a dream within a dream. I was in the woods among red maples chasing after a tune, a melody the orderly in my dream was whistling. The sun sparkled through the foliages and dispensed golden rays on the earth. I recognized the path, the boulder, the ferns, the downed tree, but not the location. A shadow flitted among the tree trunks and I chased after it, but a piece of paper among fallen leaves distracted me. I picked it up and read the message: "Meet me at noon, The Usual Place." No date, no name, no signature. But I seemed to recall *The Usual Place*.

I pursued the melody, which had begun to sadden me. The path, after cutting through the lilacs, led to a brook, where the air chilled my skin. As I approached the water, sobs mingled with the stream's murmur. A blue-dress girl age about twelve, whose shoulders were shaking and whose left cheek looked familiar from behind, knelt beside the brook. In front of her, near the bank, the grass had obscured an object. I approached to find out why she was sobbing, but tripped on a stone and fell to the ground. I fainted.

I woke up in bed, as Francisco, not the amnesiac.

Since for almost a month I'd only dreamed of the amnesiac, my unconscious mind must've been roaming through a mental loop, trying to resolve an issue. Might concern the mysterious caller, the unknown client, and ultimately the Guzman code. Anyway, I'd resolve the issue. I'd untie these knots soon enough. Still, I must *shake-a-leg*. Now, this dream in the woods, so different from the others, seemed like another piece of the puzzle that didn't fit anywhere. Yet, through this dream my unconscious mind must've revealed the pivotal clue.

I think, therefore I am.

I'm Francisco Guzman, who dreamed the dream within a dream, who analyzed that dream, who is mulling over Descartes' wisdom. If the amnesiac thought *he is*, so much more could I claim *I am*. I am Fransuccesco, not Clint the Robot. The Francisco who leaps over hurdles and collects trophies.

This morning, I woke up in the luxury suite inside an abandoned mental hospital, not the amnesiac's Hollywood studio, but Ganesh's temporary office. The clouds white and oblong drifted above the skylight while a breeze seeped through the open window. After showering, I entered the kitchen and made coffee and durian pie, while the loafer snored in the next suite. Eating the pie, I tried to identify the blue-dress girl. Not Suzie. Not the young Holly. After breakfast, I took out the second newspaper clipping that'd fallen out of Nietzche's book.

August 13, 2006. AMBULANCE STRUCK COP CHASING APPLE THIEF.

The article described Police Officer Fernando Guzman chasing a thief who had swiped a honey crisp apple from a fruit vendor. When the cop called after the thief and crossed Canal Street, an ambulance carrying a gunshot-wound victim to the hospital hit him. On the way to the hospital, Fernando passed away. The apple thief disappeared into the crowd and escaped justice.

August 13, 2006

Holly visited me today. Picked her up at LaGuardia Airport. She'd be quitting her job in Washington by Thanksgiving and moving back to New York to open her law firm. I suggested dinner to celebrate her move and drove eastward on the Long Island Expressway rather than into Manhattan. I didn't realize the error until reaching Flushing. She probably didn't care where I drove her.

We had sushi for dinner. I ate and ate: salmon, tuna, mackerel, clam, abalone, salmon roe. I drank cup after cup of sake and bought a bottle of champagne to go. By the time we left the restaurant, I staggered on the sidewalk but still decided to walk home instead of taking the taxi. I took Holly's hand while drinking in the warm air.

"I met a weird dude the other day," she said, pulling me to her side to avoid a homeless man.

He can't be as romantic as I'm." I kissed her on the cheek. "Or are you dumping me?"

"Do you know your Guardian?"

"My uncle and aunt? They're swell. Let me stay out late to make out with girls. As long as I get good grades and can support myself. You know, laissez-faire. Works great for Fernando and me."

"Guardian, with a capital G."

"You mean, Freddie the mob boss? I try to stay away from him, though sometimes we scratch each other's backs. Would never trust him. Or, do you mean Guardian Angel? Don't tell me you bought into that stuff or I'd be very disappointed in you. You're a lawyer, an intellectual." I stepped on a cat's tail and it almost clawed my ankle.

"This man I met claimed to be a Guardian of Memory."

"That's a creative way of hitting on women. So, does that make him sexier? Maybe I should tell you I'm the guardian of your soul." We reached the apartment building but I kept entering the wrong code. After five minutes, I raised my hands and gave up.

"Don't you think that's a strange man?" Holly entered the code and I stepped into the lobby to check my mailbox.

"Well, I guess it works. You're still thinking about him. I'll add it to my repertoire."

"I won't mind thinking about him if it'll make you jealous."

"Don't need a guardian for my memories. Everything I need, I have down on files. The rest, don't mind forgetting." Over the years, I'd learned to forget pieces of the past and rewrite others, a skill I appreciate more each day.

"What about those you accidentally deleted?"

"Then I won't know I need them."

When we arrived at my place, we drank champagne in the balcony to celebrate our new lives. She talked about how she'd kick asses in the courtroom and we drank to that also. I called Fernando to have him come meet Holly, but couldn't reach him. When we finished the champagne, she gave me a sequence and insisted I remember it. "Keep it for the future. You'll regret it if you don't remember it."

VZNRYAFGDBJUSEHMWLOIPKXCTQ

A cipher, naturally. Though that cipher-text meant nothing out of context, I recorded it, just in case.

While we talked in bed, her law firm partner called and requested that she return to Washington tomorrow to deal with unexpected client issues. She called to arrange a red-eye, and insisted on taking a taxi to the airport.

"Give me a call when you arrive, will you?"

"Better yet, I'll send you a message on September 6, 2001. Don't delete it, or I'll never talk to you again." She kissed me and left the apartment.

I look forward to her moving into the city, even though it'd mean no more picking up ladies at the bars. Life is good. I'll call Fernando tomorrow and share the news. And he'll get to meet her.

***

I got a call that Fernando is in the hospital. In critical condition. I knew it'd happen sooner or later. Damn it.

September 7, 2011 (2)

When I reached the hospital, Fernando had died and I had to identify his body. Clint had been rummaging through the trashcans for a phone number. When he arrived, ketchup and soy sauce staining his jacket and mayonnaise and salsa smearing his face, he handed me a piece of scrap paper and broke down in the waiting area. The nurse had to sedate him with tranquilizer.

After Dad had disappeared, Fernando would look for lost cats, dogs, basketballs, and key chains, day in and day out. When old enough, he joined the police academy and became an officer patrolling New York's mean streets. If he'd become a soldier, I wouldn't have to worry about his safety. Yeah, he was searching for Dad in his own way. Whenever I probed this obsession, which had swelled through the years, he'd accused me of searching for Dad through my profession. In the end, I accepted his quirk as I had Clint's obsessive-compulsive disorder.

That night, after leaving the hospital I went to the bar. The next morning, I woke up in an alley next to a homeless man. I vomited into the trashcan for half a minute before dropping onto the ground. The wind slapped my face but I didn't want to get up. After half an hour, I walked from the Bowery to Central Park South.

By the time I reached Central Park, I swallowed Fernando's death just as I'd Mom's suicide. Only from now on, no one would share my success. Not Clint. Not Holly. Not a future lover.

I passed the street musician and as usual gave her changes. I greeted the concierge as usual in Fernando's apartment building. But when I stepped into the apartment, my brother didn't greet me and he'd never again. I faced the divan as if looking at him. I recalled his face and his voice. But the August wind knocked on the window as if trying to wake me from a dream. I tried to ignore the calls, but the beats continued through the afternoon. I searched for Fernando's favorite baseball card but couldn't find it.

That day, I didn't eat. Only drinking whiskey. In the next few days, I arranged the funeral while Clint stayed in the hospital.

***

I burned the newspaper clipping in an empty trashcan. What had Fernando meant that night, when he promised to reveal a secret? Today. He would've fulfilled his promise today, if he were alive. I didn't care about the secret, but his smile and his voice. My intuition, which I tried to stamp out, kept hinting it might concern Dad's disappearance.

The mysterious caller, by resurrecting these memories, intended to torment me. Probably among the dozens of losers trying to stab me with a paper knife, more a reflex than a strategy. Anyway, I'd record his voice next time, and check it against the profiles in the FBI database. I'd find him and I'd kick his butt across the Atlantic.

Ganesh left his room in the afternoon and we lunched while walking across the Queensboro Bridge and admiring the Manhattan skyline. I ate my grilled salmon sandwich and downed it with beer while inhaling the moist air that'd lingered for weeks. Although the wind uncovered the Empire State Building's upper section, I couldn't discern its outer contour, which seemed to merge with the fog. Two patrol boats sped down the East River toward the Williamsburg Bridge, which also had lost its edges in the haze. A sparrow flew past and landed on a cable, probably waiting for some salmon. Ganesh sipped his colada and ducked to avoid the spittle from an oncoming car.

"I met you on August 24 and now sixteen days have passed. What have you contributed? Show me some results. Not that useless HYMN1 crap. I entered it to open the file. Well, it didn't work." I couldn't finish the assignment before the two-week deadline. Now, the mobster might harm Holly. "I'm counting the days until you give me real results. I don't care about stacked-up superlatives to hyperbolize your non-skills. I want results, the concrete measures of competency. And everyday that passes, my skepticism in you magnifies, exponentially." I raised the can to toast his failure and spilled beer on my sandwich. He'd worked day and night on his tablet PC and even when I woke up at night for whiskey, light still seeped under his bedroom door. And he'd be flipping through five or six books on coding, every minute scanning from one tome to the next. But, no results. Zilch.

"You've got to use more of your pupils and irises and less of your tongue and larynx if you want to learn something from me. I know this gas-bag who can't stop praising himself as if the world would end without him. Can you imagine such a loser?" He pinched a piece of salmon from my sandwich and tossed it into his orifice.

"Okay, five bucks, and I only take…"

Something happened. Something I couldn't explain. Something from another dimension. Did I finish the sentence? Did Ganesh pay me five dollars? Just lovely, I lost several minutes, as if aliens had abducted me.

CHAPTER 21 - X

September 23 (2)

Outside the hospital, the pedestrians had disappeared from the street, probably hunting for me, the amnesiac. I ran down the empty street to Lexington Avenue, where several men and women patrolled, each holding a shotgun. I doubted they would kill me and destroy my brain, but they might torture me to teach me a lesson.

I waited behind a bulletin board across the street, and when they had passed, I crossed the street to the Shakespeare Theater. The clown had gone but the front door was locked. Beside the lock the scanner light blinked. I opened the door with Rick's or Nick's ID card and slipped into a lobby with hardwood floor, across which stood a merry-go-round. No other doors in the lobby, or any stairs. I whispered Ingrid's name but no one answered. I scanned the wooden horse but didn't find buttons in its eyes or a knob on its nose. Its head wouldn't turn. I pressed a red button on the control panel and the merry-go-round turned under a lullaby. Pressed the green button and kaleidoscopic lights flashed around the lobby.

"What the hell?" The clown entered through the front door but I hid behind the controls.

While he rushed toward the merry-go-round, I pressed the blue button and a door next to me opened to reveal a cubicle.

"Who the hell's playing in here? If the assistant director finds out, you'd be in deep shit." The clown had stepped onto the merry-go-round and was running toward the control panels.

I slipped into the cubicle to hide from the clown. Steps and shouts approached. The door shut just as the clown's neon hand appeared. I waited in the cubicle, wide enough to fit four people, but without handles or buttons, only four walls. It moved. Hums. I clenched my fists, ready to box the clown's green nose. Several minutes later, the door still didn't open.

I paced around the cubicle, fidgeting my fingers. Maybe it wouldn't open by itself and I would have to break down the door. The hums stopped. The door opened to a room with three other doors. About a dozen pairs of eyes gazed at me. The homeless children extended their hands. I gave them the pizza and sandwiches. A door on the left opened and the boy who'd helped me escape Rick beckoned me.

"Tell me what's going on," I said. "Where am I?"

He didn't answer, just pushed me through the door, and said, "Go, quickly. Look for my father."

I stepped into a hallway and, before I could ask about his father, the door closed behind me. A speaker above my head announced, "Welcome to HYMN1."

What could be the link between Ganesh's code word and this funhouse? Fragments of dream and reality were seeping across the boundary, a semi-permeable membrane. My nightmare had invaded my world.

In the hallway, I reached four doors, red, yellow, green and blue. The same monotone said, "Choose a door."

"Why should I?" I didn't expect a reply, and the speaker repeated the request. What lay behind the doors? I refused to play the game but when I turned around, down the hallway a blank wall had replaced the door.

I was about to kick down a door when the red one opened. I hesitated but Ingrid's voice sounded in my mind and I rushed through the door, which closed behind me.

Children in a playground laughed and played on the slide and swings, the playground I had just left. Leaves from a nearby tree tumbled through the air and I could smell autumn's fragrance. A little girl in a blue dress grabbed my hand and pulled me toward the entrance. "Come on, let's get out of here."

"Are we attending a wedding, a funeral, a party, an execution? Shouldn't I dress for the occasion? I hate dressing for the wrong occasion."

The girl looked like Suzie, but she was from another dream. A dream that I had trouble recalling.

"We just have to go several blocks and we'll be there."

"I know. Queens Center. The exit. But we're going in circles."

Sure enough, we walked down Queens Boulevard heading toward Queens Center. On the sidewalk, pedestrians brushed by. Clouds drifted in the azure sky and cars sped down the street. The blue was too blue, the noise too uniform and the girl's hand too warm.

We crossed Broadway. A man break-danced near the subway entrance. The head trauma patient. I walked toward him but the girl pulled me away. More cars sped down the street—the same colors, the same models, the same license plates. We passed the same buildings, the same signs, the same pedestrians. Everything had remained the same. We walked but got nowhere. And even when we reached Queens Center, we returned to Lexington Avenue, back to the hospital.

"Come on, let's get out of here."

The same pitch and the same volume. Was I holding a robot's hand? The clouds, they didn't move, even though wind patted my face. We crossed Broadway. The patient was still break-dancing. By this time, I had become so familiar with the dreamland I almost didn't care. But I stopped and released the girl's hand.

"Do you remember something?" the girl said.

I picked up a rock and threw it into the distance.

Glass shattered. The sky cracked and the pieces collapsed into darkness. The girl had gone. More props. More illusions. More trickery.

Before me, a neon rectangle enclosed a door.

I hesitated. Should I step into another illusion? How to escape from this nightmare? I closed my eyes and tried to remember the image before waking up in the hospital. Dolly's face appeared. I tried to grasp onto it but it faded into the darkness.

I opened my eyes hoping to wake up, but the same door confronted me. I opened the door and entered the room. An office suite. At the foyer I poured a cup of coffee. Checked the copier for paper while drinking the coffee. Inserted a folder into the shredder. Walked down the hallway toward the two offices. I could still remember Francisco's office.

I entered his office. The trophy in the case and the certificates on the walls, just as in my dream. I couldn't believe my eyes. The SOAPS certificates were as I had described them in the diary. I opened the desk drawers and found several documents. Maybe, I wasn't dreaming but was recalling past events.

Maybe I was, and am, Francisco Guzman. I prayed for a miracle.

A janitor stepped into the office and yelled, "Hey, who ya? What da hell ya doing here?" He picked up the trash bin near the desk.

"I'm Francisco Guzman." I stood akimbo.

"So? What'd I care? Get da hell outa here. Ya don't belong here." He dumped the trash into the trashcan and returned the bin to its spot. "Nosy body. Just do yer job. Don't poke yer nose nowhere." He left the office.

I checked the certificates on the wall: SOAPS awards for Francisco Guzman. The janitor might've just started working here and didn't know his employer.

The wall beside the leather chair didn't have the drawing of a naked lady. I didn't record it in the diary. The carpet under the chair didn't have a stain. So, just a duplicate. Whatever I hadn't recorded, didn't appear here. Someone had read my diary and recreated the office from the details. Must be the *chaplain*.

I left the room to look for the janitor but he had disappeared. On the lounge sofa, Rick sat cross-legged. Behind him stood the new doctor.

"Do you remember anything?" the doctor said.

"Did the chaplain tell you my dreams?"

"Never mind that," Rick said. "We're trying to help you regain your memory."

"What's in it that's so valuable to you?"

"Not to us," the doctor said, "to you."

"I want Dr. Tang."

"Never mind him," Rick said, "he's fired."

"And you fired him, I presume."

"He was doing a lousy job. I don't have time for incompetent fools."

Rick wasn't just a nurse. He and the rest posed as patients and staffs to dupe me.

"Tell me, what's in my memory. What're you looking for?"

Of course, he didn't answer and I would have to find the truth elsewhere. A door behind the copier opened and the boy waved to me and disappeared behind it. I put down the cup and left the office, ignoring Rick's shouts. I locked the door behind me.

I stepped into a theater with about twenty rows of seats. On the screen, rebels launched rockets at a police station. I was about to leave when a patient standing in the aisle said, "Damn bastards. This unit killed my partner. Almost got me too, if I hadn't fled quick enough."

I slipped into a seat towards the back, where the balcony blocked the dim lights. Around twenty men and women watched the film, sitting, standing or chatting. A few faces looked familiar. The cashier in the Mexican stall. The nurse who left the lipstick next to the phone. The patient who shot at the intruder. The hotdog vendor in the street. I held my head wondering what was going on.

"Be glad you're on an easy assignment. Just playing a loony," the hotdog vendor sitting near the aisle said.

"What the hell we're doing here when they need us fighting those damn rebels?" the patient said.

"From what I heard, this assignment's more important than fighting those scumbags."

"If they think acting like a schizo takes higher priority, they're more qualified to play the maniacs."

I couldn't recall any rebels bombing police stations and government buildings but wasn't surprised someone was trying to destroy New York. Of course, they might be playacting.

The door opened and a homeless man said, "Hey, move your asses. He's disappeared again. Gotta find him quick. Else, we're in deep shit."

The men and women filed out grumbling and cussing. They were probably looking for me. But who were *they*? I ducked under the seat, and after they had left, I walked toward the screen and slipped through the back door into a prison yard.

A fence enclosed the *city* and surveillance cameras on watchtowers guarded the premise.

No pedestrians, no cars, no streets, no buildings, not even sidewalks.

I had left the funhouse, but couldn't escape my nightmare. I closed my eyes, hoping to awake from this dream. Reopening them, I couldn't find Broadway or the Brooklyn Bridge. Only the fence, the gray sky and the low clouds. I turned around and touched the door. At least, it hadn't deserted me. Above and on both sides of it, a wall about fifty feet high stretched miles to the left and right.

New York City is a prison.

I hid behind a parapet and grabbed a rock. Smashed the wall, as if it were Dr. Tang's face. I smashed again. And again. After studying the scratches on the wall, smashed once more. Then wiped my forehead and smashed the wall one last time and sat against it.

***

Alone without a name, without an identity, without a past, and without resources. But alone where? What land? What planet? What age?

I trusted Dr. Tang, but he betrayed me. I befriended Ingrid, but she deceived me. Every doctor, nurse, orderly, patient schemed to con me. And Stubble may be my only friend, but he is probably escaping from the government agents.

Beyond the fence, scattered trees extend to the horizon toward the gray hills.

Ingrid spat at my trust and feelings, but her lips and her cheeks will still warm and comfort me, as I wander and search for my identity. The rock onto which I'll grasp to brave the storm, that image in my medial temporal cortex or whatever, against the fear of never recalling the names, locales, and events I once knew. Sure, warmth and peace will abandon me as they had kings and paupers in the past. But I have nothing else to hold onto except those feelings.

With my back against the wall, I took out the acorn she had tossed away and I lifted my arm and aimed for a tree beyond the fence. I swung my arm in an arc but I didn't release it. I couldn't release it. Just as I couldn't my past and my identity. I gripped the acorn, almost crushing it.

My dream of living by the hillside, facing the canyon. My dream of a life with Ingrid. Locked in the dreamland they sprouted from, unable to find turf in this wasteland called reality. But I won't stop hoping, dreaming, fantasizing, especially under these dark clouds. Not if I want to remain sane.

The hospital room, the bed, the chair, the fluorescent lights, the bay window, and the chestnut tree, their images have become surreal, their colors unnatural, their contours ethereal. And the scent of the hospital, artificial. Yet, I miss them. I can still step through the door and return to the streets, to the hospital, to the room, to the bed. And pretend. But the place has vaporized, not because a bomb destroyed it, but because it never existed. In finding the truth, I got rid of reality. As my mind drifts from reality to illusion and from illusion to illusion, I begin to doubt the breaths and voices of Dr. Tang and Ingrid. They must exist. But who are they? Deceivers, schemers, con artists.

What I have discovered about myself, I also doubt, as if in this world I can only grasp doubt. As Ingrid's image only represents the present her, the woman who deceived me, so this body standing in the prison yard only represents the present me, a man without a name, without a past, in a foreign land, in an alien time. My sole purpose: to discover myself, to search for *I*. Or return to my dream and live as Francisco whom, though only a phantom and my distortion, I have grown to despise. Worse, my lost self is fading, retreating, disappearing. Not only my past, but also the world around me, has scattered in the wind.

Could I have imagined the wall, the rocks, the trees, the clouds? My mind's artistry? But I feel the wall's texture. I shut my eyes and order the prison to turn into a beach, but when I open my eyes, the wall still blocks my path and the clouds still pave the sky. Maybe, I have drowned in my illusion and even enlightenment can't rescue me.

Still, as when I stood before the mirror and realized the self within, distinct from the toilet paper, so now I also sense the same self, different from the wall, the sky, the plains, the prison. I am not the sand or the thistle on the ground. I am this dunce, this sucker standing next to the wall and staring into the endless plains. I will and must recover my memory and regain my identity, and I will succeed, even though along the way, I must overcome thorns and thistles and cliffs and pits.

The desire to vanquish betrayal and deceit. The need to conquer the unknown future. They energize me, propel me forward. Even without Dr. Tang and the hospital, I must regain my memory before it disintegrates.

Voices clamor behind the door. The door will topple in a minute or two and the hospital staff will emerge with automatic handguns. On the watchtower in front of the door, the surveillance camera continues to swivel but no guard mans the station. He may be hiding under the balustrade, his rifle aiming at me, but I'll have to ignore the hidden threat and go for that manhole beside the fence. The underground tunnels may lead me out of the prison, maybe even to the Underground Temple.

CHAPTER 22 - FRANCISCO

September 7, 2011 (3)

One minute I was eating a grilled salmon sandwich on Queensboro Bridge and requesting money from Ganesh, the next I was humming a jingle and urinating in a public toilet. The homeless man beside me mumbled gibberish while urinating and missing the urinal. I couldn't remember when and how I'd walked into the toilet. But perfect aim, no dripping to the side. I could've fainted and was relieving myself in the dream, but I recognized this toilet, familiar quotes decorating the walls. Dreaming of amnesia and fake hospital and conspiracy had disturbed my days and nights. I didn't need multiple personality to spice up my life. Maybe a crack in the space-time continuum had created the temporal leap. I'd seen enough sci-fi films to understand the concept. Better the universe ending than my going nuts. Amen.

Ganesh was waiting outside the toilet beside the Queensboro Bridge access, still sipping his colada.

"Did I miss something?" I scratched my head, hoping the guru could enlighten me.

"Only yourself. Do you always stop in the middle of a conversation and go for a leak? A bit impolite, though I wasn't offended. Just FYI. By the way, since you didn't finish your grilled salmon, I finished it for you. No need to thank me."

I'd never before lost my consciousness while going about my daily chores. I remembered the amnesiac's episode with the chaplain. Had he sent the virus across the barrier between dream and reality? "You have something strong, like one of your traditional concoction to drive out the evil wind?" I shook my head but didn't have a headache. I rubbed my eyes but I could see the skyline across the river.

"Evil wind? I'm a scientist, not a medicine man. Of course, I've nothing against any religion, as long as the followers can tolerate others and don't bother me. I got something to get rid of headaches. Very strong stuff." Ganesh led me to a water fountain while finishing the co-lada. "But sad to say it doesn't cure impoliteness and arrogance. Oh, well." He poured powder in the cup and filled it with water. The potion's stench cleared my sinuses but gave me a headache.

"Hey, you said this stuff's used to get rid of headaches."

"Ah, but the more you suffer, the more alert you'd be, and so the less likely you'd lose yourself again. The way you walked into the toilet, side-stepping the lamppost and fire hydrant and kicking the door open as you entered, I say your senses, coordination and even knowledge of this place are intact. But that zombie expression scared me. By the way, I've video-taped it with my phone so you can enjoy it during bedtime." He handed me the cup.

After drinking the mud-like potion, my stomach churned and almost expelled the filth but in the end I didn't have the strength to vomit. I'd rather suffer a thug or an illness than savor the sense of void I'd first be-friended under anesthesia. I could meet any enemy eyes wide open, but during the instant between consciousness and unconsciousness, I faced nada and I could fight zilch.

Ganesh returned to the mental hospital while I decontaminated my stomach in my office. As I munched chocolate and checked my emails, the mailman delivered a package Fernando had mailed in 2003 but requested to be delivered today. I didn't even know the post office had such service. My brother had died but he'd kept his promise. He'd never change, not even after his death. I opened the package and found a safety deposit box key and a note specifying the bank and box number. He'd left another puzzle for me to solve, so I'd continue to feel his presence. I felt much better.

I was examining the key when Ganesh called and said he'd received a hand.

He'd fainted when he opened the package and found a man's right hand, reeking of blood. He must've been sleeping with a mobster's girl-friend. No, the first deadline. I hung up and again called the hospital to check on Suzie. She was fine. I worried even more about Holly. Had the culprit chopped off Clint's hand?

Around noon, seven donut-bellied cops invited themselves into my office and dumped their butts onto the lounge sofa. The captain asked for a drink. I took out a bottle of whiskey and poured seven glasses and we toasted to our health, the Big Apple, and good old NYPD. Sure, they didn't come to drink but I didn't inquire about their visit. After the drink, the captain showed me the warrant and asked to search the office. Had Ganesh hidden drugs inside the copier? No, the officers were looking for a manuscript. *Notes from the Underground*, in Russian.

Would they recognize it if they should come across it? The captain, leaning against the sofa, sighed and sipped the whiskey. He'd rather be getting a cat off the tree. I showed them the statuette and the certificates, but they had to finish the job and get coffee and donuts.

I ordered coffee and donuts so they could take their time. They decided not to thrash the office, only searching through the usual nooks. I also shared my chocolate and while enjoying the snack, they complained about the long hours and low pay. After they had coffee and donuts, they left their business cards, in case I should need help. My friendships with about a dozen sergeants, detectives, and district attorneys had reaped results on previous projects and I expected these associates to contribute also.

After the police had left, I opened the safe behind my certificates to examine Dostoevsky's manuscript, perhaps the holy text. Of course, the book had vanished. One day it appeared in my postal box and another it hitched a ride to nowhere. Either it grew legs or some itchy fingers took it. I was going to ask the Priest for several million dollars, but someone probably had the same idea and seized the day. I admired this rascal. Ganesh, since he was my new sidekick. I'd always suspected Clint whenever a code word or a document strolled out of the office. He had the opportunity and the motive.

I contacted my source at the police station to track down the snitcher who'd would've sent me to jail. The same worm must've sent the manuscript. Fortunately, a rat had stolen it to free me of police trouble. The cosmic law of balance and order.

A few minutes after I'd hung up, the Governor called and said an assailant had chopped off his assistant's hand. He warned me that if anything happened to Holly, my ass would sizzle. As if it wasn't browning already. I protested that the attack on the Naked Man shouldn't involve me since I didn't care about him, but the assailant had left a message with the victim, demanding I speed up my work. I promised to get those mobsters, but after this incident I worried more about Holly.

CHAPTER 23 - X

October 3 (1)

I woke up on a bed of hay in a barn. An incandescent light bulb dangled from the ceiling while darkness seeped through the doorway and the windows. For a second, I thought I was Francisco, but I wasn't in New York since the horn concerto had vanished and the crickets chirped outside and the smells of lilacs and manure wafted in the air. Was I the amnesiac called X? But I wasn't in the mental hospital or the fake New York or the prison yard.

Who could I be? Y? Z?

While I studied the stall to tickle my memory, a middle-aged man in a straw hat entered the barn with an iPad and said, "You left this while we had dinner."

I took the iPad and apologized for forgetting his name.

Farmer Jones.

"You lost your memory again, didn't you?"

Earlier in the evening, I knocked on his front door and asked to stay in the barn for a night. I didn't know my name or my past or how I had gotten on the road, but looked like an inmate who had escaped from prison. After having dinner with Farmer Jones, I came to the barn.

Couldn't remember arriving at the farm or having dinner with him. However, I remembered Francisco and his misdeeds, to the last details. I asked my whereabouts.

"Purgatory."

The place sounded familiar. The government conducted experiments there to crush its enemies. What awaited me out there? I asked for the nearest airport. The transport depot was a day's drive away.

He handed me the iPad and bade me goodnight.

According to X's diary in the iPad, I should be in the prison yard. What happened, if I am X, after I had gone into the manhole? Did the underground tunnels lead to this place? However, the entries in the iPad might be fiction, a story imitating a journal.

I might not be X. I couldn't find Nick's or Rock's ID, but felt a microchip under the skin of my right forearm. Probably an RF ID chip. In the iPad, photos of three men and a woman. According to the diary, I didn't take the picture of Rick/Nick, but now I had it.

I was feeling the microchip when a crushed stone rolled in the distance, probably at the farm entrance. Footsteps. Faint but distinct. Not Farmer Jones, unless he went to the mailbox to get his mail. No, he had gone back into the house. I could imagine the intruder tiptoeing into the farm. I grabbed the pitchfork near the stalls, tiptoed toward the window to survey the grounds near the entrance. A shadow approached the house and slid along the wall and the intruder peeped into a lighted window. I was about to leave the barn when he left the house and tiptoed toward me. I appreciated not having to walk there. Pitchfork in hand, I leaned against the wall beside the entrance.

Footsteps approached. Clumsy for a thief. Perhaps a vagrant.

He stepped into the barn and glancing left and right panted beside his shadow. I flipped a switch to turn on the light and said, "Welcome."

The man bounced away and fell onto the ground near the sty. "Hey, man, you scared me."

Rick or Nick, according to the photo in the iPad. I bent down, grabbed his jacket and lifted him toward my face. "You were probably looking for me. Well, it's your lucky day." I asked about the charade.

"Chill out and let me down, will you?" He dangled under my hand. "Just in case you're interested, we've got no time to fool around."

I shook him and his left shoe fell off.

"My friend, I've been let go. And on account of helping you run away. Shouldn't you be celebrating?" He grabbed my arm and kicked his legs in the air.

"So you're not going to clean my toilet anymore? Are you Nick? Or are you Rick pretending to be Nick?" I dropped him onto the ground.

"Sorry, never cleaned your toilet, or anyone else's. Nice fantasy though. Then, Rick couldn't pretend to be me. No way, man. Not with his brows and his lips." He put on his shoe and scrambling onto his feet. "And finally, if I were Rick, you'd be a goner by now. He's damn angry you escaped."

Yeah, he had to be Nick.

"For your information, he's the CIO, Chief Interrogation Officer, in that prison. One of those big shots in the Intelligence Agency. Section Chief, or something like that. Of course, titles don't mean much." Nick straightened out his hair and jacket.

"So that fake New York was a military prison?"

"New York? Boy, your brain must still be sizzling. Nah, no such luck, no New York, real or fake. I wish there were. I must say, you have nice pipe dreams. Must feel groovy waking up in a strange world, right? No, you were in prison, behind bars, with the rats sniffing you. Well, almost as good as in New York, right?"

"But the mental hospital with the fake doctors and patients?"

"Hmm, maybe you're the Chief Insanity Officer. Boy, this should be fun."

Nick never heard of Dr. Tang. Though several doctors oversaw the torture, he didn't go into the dungeons or inquire about the prison personnel.

"Ingrid?"

"Maybe we can chat about your fantasies while we're driving. In case you care about your life, my car's behind a hill down the road. Should we get going?" He handed me an ID. "Take it. Rick's. You may need it."

I didn't believe him. I took the ID that should be in my pocket, not sure how he had filched it. Somehow, he had replaced *Groucho*'s photo with mine. I asked about my escape from the prison, but he said, "If I were you, I'd scramble out of here. Then again, I'm not you." He shrugged and whistled the familiar tune.

I grabbed the pitchfork and threatened to harm him unless he spilled the truth.

"Hmm, maybe I shouldn't have helped you. Maybe I should put this task in my 'Thou shall not' list."

A rumble broke the silence. Crushed stones rolled and tires scratched the road. Screeches. Shouts. Footsteps. Marching into the farm.

"Well, looks like it's too late. Might as well wait for Rick to come." Nick scratched his head and looked out the window.

"Hey, you can't run away anymore. You're surrounded." A man who sounded like the playhouse clown shouted. I still remembered his voice so I had been in the mental hospital, not the jail cell.

Nick had tricked me, probably signaling the agents while we talked.

"Nice job. Your friends are here. But you'll fall first when they march in."

"What? What're you talking about?" He scratched his head. Either a fool or a mastermind.

As I was looking for a whip in the stall where a horse munched hay, Nick left the barn and said, "Hey, it's me, Nick." I picked up a sling and several stones beside the stall. Good enough. I could test my power, slings against submachine guns. I huddled behind the stall with line-of-sight to the doorway. To test the sling, I sent a rock into the sty. Then waited. Footsteps circled the barn while Nick talked to the clown. I would have to flee from the authorities and I would have to watch every shadow and listen for each footstep. Maybe even now, a surveillance camera was monitoring me.

I took out the acorn and caressed it. I had met Ingrid and I still cared about her. I tried but failed to bring her face to mind but the longing rose in my bosom. As I was yearning for Ingrid, footsteps approached the doorway. I picked up a rock and locked it into the sling and waited for the unlucky man or woman.

Nick walked into the barn and looked around. I aimed for his forehead ready to release the rock. He didn't have a gun, only a smile. Could I kill a man armed with a smile?

"Hey, man, where're you? No need to hide." Nick whistled the familiar tune.

I hesitated. The footsteps marched away. The car doors slammed and the vehicles sped away.

"Hey, man, they're gone. Are you still here?" Nick walked up to the sty. "Are you in the mud? You can get out now."

I stepped out, still aiming the stone at him.

"Looks like a nice toy. May I take a look?" He approached and took the sling and stone. "They left looking for you."

"Why?"

"They thought you left after having dinner with the old man." He shot the rock through the doorway. "Someone saw you getting into the farm and reported it."

"Why?"

"Why did they see you? How should I know? Probably not careful enough, man. There's a lesson to be learned" He picked up another rock and shot it through the open window.

"Why didn't you turn me in?" I took the pitchfork and left the barn.

"You didn't ask me to." He followed me. "Yeah, we should check on the old man."

The front door was ajar and the light spilled onto the porch steps. I hesitated for a moment before opening the door. The scent of blood drifted into my nose. Noise drifted from the living room. A sitcom was on TV. Farmer Jones reclined sideways on the sofa, his leg dangling over the edge and blood dripping onto the carpet. A bullet through his temple. Cause and effect. He died because of me. The newscasters would announce his death tomorrow. To inform me why he had died. To isolate me from the others. To turn the others against me. I picked up a warm pipe. Farmer Jones was smoking it when the agents shot him.

"Oops, should we call for help?"

I put the pipe on the end table and picked up the fishing rod that had fallen onto the clothes rack, its hook hanging onto the raincoat pocket. How could the ranch exist in this nightmare when it belonged in someone's reverie? What is life worth in this land?

I would bury Farmer Jones, though the agents might return and find me still around. Nick and I carried the body to the backyard and I took out a shovel and a spade from the shack.

The clouds still covered the sky. In the distance, crickets chirped a chord to go with Nick's tune. As we dug, a breeze wafted through the backyard and tossed the scent of blood drifted into my nostrils.

"Do the police, military and secret services usually kill on sight?"

Nick stopped humming his ditty. "About twenty years ago, they abolished trial by jury."

"Then they abolished trials. Right?"

Nick shrugged his shoulders and continued to hum.

"How can you stand this place?"

"It isn't so bad once you get used to it."

How could anyone get used to a nightmare? I was going to take Farmer Jones's truck, but decided for Nick's sake to hitch a ride in his car to the bus station. He didn't understand. I didn't explain.

I would search for Dolly in New Jersey. In looking for X's past, I might find mine. Writing my journal entries and reviewing the previous ones, I sensed a new *me* emerging from darkness, through a new personal history that would continue to grow each day.

We drove through the night without words. By daybreak, we stopped at a diner to have sausage, bacon and scramble eggs. We arrived at the transport depot a little after noon. I didn't reveal my destination. For my safety and for his safety. After his car disappeared into the horizon, I check the destinations, but couldn't find New York. I asked for directions to New Jersey, unsure whether Dr. Tang had invented or imagined the place. When the stationmaster pointed to Fermat's Last Stand (Felast), I bought the ticket at the dispenser, but even as I stepped into the Underground coach, I hesitated about searching for Dolly.

The passengers standing in the aisle, what were their stories, their memories and their pasts? What were they thinking and feeling about the government? Were they watching over their shoulders for men in black suits? Would a police officer board the train in the next station and shoot one of them? What awaited me in Felast?

CHAPTER 24 - FRANCISCO

September 19, 2011 (1)

The fist landed on my stomach and woke me from the dream before the amnesiac, X or Y or Z, arrived at Felast. My solar plexus numbed and I curled up, vomiting gastric juices onto the sand. Fortunately, I didn't have lobster for dinner last night, just burger and fries. If the coward hadn't caught me napping, my nunchuks would be drumming his head. I'd expected trouble when someone pinched my nose and lifted me. The six-footer grasped the sides of my cheeks and forced my lips into a pout. The Governor worried about his daughter and the man's anxiety meant pain for me. Well, he demonstrated it with my guts and reserved my other body parts for the next meeting. I didn't like the Governor's new assistant and preferred dealing with the Naked Man.

Yesterday, with Fernando's key, I opened the deposit box, then took out the note and read it.

Too late. Tough luck, buddy.

Not Fernando's handwriting. Some itchy fingers had stolen my brother's gift to me. I smashed the box against the counter denting the box and cracking the wood. The bank manager wouldn't reveal who had accessed the deposit box recently.

Outside the bank, I kicked the dog trying to sniff me. The D train took me to Coney Island, where Fernando and I had visited every summer. At our favorite spot I ate a hot dog for dinner. The waves crashed against the beach just as they had during our visits but Fernando no longer sat beside me. Those summer days' laughter, those sensations, like memory, seemed to have faded over the years. A similar evening, the fog had smudged the horizon. What had we gossiped about that night?

I stayed on the beach after everyone had left. The waves crashed against the shore and the wind rubbed against the sand. As the sky darkened, I drifted into dreamland. If I'd known the Governor's new assistant was looking for me, I would've pretended to sleep and prepared my greeting.

When the thug had tired of practicing on my stomach and was having a beer and complaining about his wife, the messenger from VE, who looked like Dr. Tang's replacement, sneaked up behind him, holding a camcorder. "Hey, nitwit, might want to check with your boss before taking another punch. He mightn't want these pictures in the evening news. Especially when everyone knows you're his new lapdog."

The thug cussed and dropped the beer. Before he could turn around, the Messenger jabbed a bamboo stick at his kidney and said, "You may want to walk straight ahead until you can't go further. Then turn right and continue walking. Just to let you know, I don't miss. But of course, I usually shoot from a thousand yards away."

The Messenger strapped the camcorder across his shoulder and popped a piece of ginseng into his mouth and he chewed while pressing the bamboo stick against the thug. I tried to laugh but pain ripped through my abdomen when I contracted the muscles. After about ten seconds, the thug grunted and walked straight ahead without turning his head.

The Messenger plopped onto the sand next to me as if I'd invited him for a picnic. He hadn't made an appointment and he didn't praise me. What's more, he tainted the air with his ginseng-breath. I couldn't complain about a client's breath or manner, but I'd ask for another gofer for the next assignment. I'd prefer a more courteous lackey.

After the thug had walked into the fog, I still prostrated on the sand and faced the ocean for ten more minutes as if worshipping the new dawn before I could sit up. When I breathed, pain choked me. The Messenger watched the waves cresting and ebbing while the fog dispersed and light filled the sky. As if I didn't exist.

I didn't need the thug's fist to motivate me. I wanted to save Holly as much as the Governor. Just that my nightmares had been taxing my acumen and I needed to drop Ganesh and eliminate the distraction.

"Don't die on me before finishing your job. If I have to find someone else to finish the project, I mightn't meet my deadline and get my bonus." He spat the ginseng onto the sand. "And Boss would be real mad—"

"Don't tell me you want the diamonds now. I'm a genius, not a magician. These things take time. Give me one more month and I'll get the stuff. I'm onto something." I didn't like the Messenger pressuring me just as I didn't like the Governor doing so. I received the bank's security tapes but had to process those images to extract the getaway car's license plate. The computer was still processing the blurred pictures with the image recognition algorithms to identify the numbers on the plate. Really, videotapes like other dinosaurs should rest in peace. "Don't worry. You can trust me. See this Lifetime Award from SOAPS? Well, so far, they've only awarded it to seventeen people, out of thousands and thousands of candidates. Of course, most of them can't even solve partial differential equations or design a Viterbi decoder, so what'd you expect. But, I'm the genuine article."

"Chill out. Don't get so paranoid. Don't get so defensive. No one's questioning any of your inability. Why does everything have to revolve around you? What happened when you were growing up? Jeez, I'm just here to advise you not to trust your partner even though he might look honest." The Messenger greeted the food stall's owner, who'd just arrived, and ordered a chocolate milkshake with marshmallow.

After ordering French fries, I said, "What'd you know about Clint? Don't tell me he's gay or a woman. He might be a compulsive gambler, or an alcoholic. Anyway, we've been working for more than ten years. So, don't claim expertise where you're just an amateur." I despise con artists who claim they could cure individual, social, national and international neurosis. And baldness.

While I munched on the fries, my police contact called to update his research on the anonymous call that'd brought the police to my office. He located the payphone and, along with the calling time, would identify the snitch as soon as he received the surveillance video. If I had time, I could fetch the tape before he finished dallying with the red tapes. But I couldn't waste time on the snitch.

After I'd hung up, the Messenger sipped his milkshake and said, "I mean your new partner, Ganesh, or whatever his name is. You know he surfaced only a month ago? Just popped out of nowhere. Boss had him checked out. But, no driver's license, no social security number, no federal tax returns, no nada."

"You mean you're spying on him because you don't have confidence in me? Or maybe you don't trust me. In that case, take your job and shove it. On any given day, I have more jobs to fill my plate than I have time for and diamonds don't interest me much. If you have too much time, show off your ignorance somewhere else. I'm not yet impressed by your imbecility." I thrust my nose into his cheek and he flinched away. I didn't trust Ganesh either and would dig up my new sidekick's identity and expose his slime but I didn't like the Messenger sticking that flattened nose into my affairs. Naturally, he had his agenda, or maybe the company's, but, Francisco Guzman, the modern day King Solomon, wouldn't play into his hands. I'd change the game's rules behind his back.

"Like I said, chill out. Nobody's not having no confidence in you. Just don't want you to put your head through a noose, that's all. Jeez, never met someone so touchy. Come on, don't take yourself so seriously. You're not that important. Here, if you need anything, go to St. Paul's Nightclub and show this to the bartender." He handed me a card.

"Tell your boss to come if he has a problem." I took the card and scraped the ketchup from my lips with it. "Since you're so smart, who is Ganesh's boss? Is it the pretty lady?" I handed him back the business card.

"What do you think I am, your personal database?" He dumped the card on the beach. "If you want to get information, break into the FBI databases. Stop asking me to do your job. We're paying you big bucks and we expect results, steel-hard result. Comprende?"

"Since we're talking about money. Here's how much you owe me." I handed him the bill I'd prepared along with the monthly fee. "For thrashing my place and stealing my *pate de foie gras*. And for trying to steal my laptop. Next time you want to perform due diligence, do it discreetly and at your own expense, please. When I check out someone's bank accounts, I don't leave any e-fingerprints. When I eavesdrop on someone's dream talks, I don't leave any hamburger wrappers or foam cups. Do your work without interfering with other people's lives."

"That old piece of junk you called a laptop? We have better tablet PC's than your clunker. Come on, you miser, buy yourself better equipment. After all, you live and die by it. And we didn't thrash your cozy place or eat your liver paste. So, don't pin it on us. We'd only shot at you, that's all. Not to kill you, or to injure you, or to frighten you. Nothing to do with you, so don't take it personally."

"Do I look like I'm taking it personally? I certainly won't *after* I shoot you. You know, an eye for an eye. Nothing personal though, as you said, nothing to do with you. Only to maintain the age-old wisdom." I wiped my mouth after finishing the fries. Then pulled out a gun, loaded it with a bullet and pointed the barrel at him. "As you can see, I'm not holding a bamboo stick."

"Take that away before you get hurt. That shooting in your apartment was for show, like Broadway or Hollywood. You'd probably understand. We're after the big fish, much more important than you." He stood up and stepped back, careful not to spill the milkshake.

"And I'll kick your butt for show only." I didn't want to see him until I'd received my reimbursement and an apology. The amount included my apartment's renovation and ten cans of *pate de foie gras*. When he hesitated, I waved my gun to motivate him. He walked to the food stall to get a chilidog before leaving the beach.

Though I didn't trust the Messenger, I couldn't ignore his revelations about Ganesh, who might be orchestrating the nonsense. After I bought a chilidog and returned to the mental hospital to tape a bug to the inner pocket of my sidekick's jacket, I waited in the pizzeria across the street to give him a chance to sneak out. While waiting for the double-crosser to make his move, I checked the image recognition software's progress. When I noticed a man in black suit and dark glasses watching from the café across the street, I bought a carton of milk and had my beggar associate to deliver it. After receiving the milk, the man threw the carton on the ground and stepped on it, squeezing the milk onto the sidewalk.

At four o'clock, Ganesh hopped onto the sidewalk and took a cab. I grabbed my pizza and beer and tailed him in another cab. The cabdriver, who turned out to be my friend the grocer and looked like that security guard in my dream, noted the other cab's license plate and contacted the dispatcher to have the car's location forwarded into his GPS receiver. He even promised me a discount if I'd relate the back-story. When I asked him to lose the black suit tailing us, he steered the cab into a side street, passed several vendors and exited onto another street. After cutting through several side streets, we lost the black suit. He checked the GPS and continued to follow Ganesh's cab. He recounted his adventure last month, driving a private eye to tail an out-of-state politician and his mistress from apartment to restaurant to nightclub to hotel. He enjoyed the tip, the chase and the photos the detective had shown him. I ignored his hint for extra tips and recounted the achievements that'd earned me the SOAPS awards. He ignored the anecdotes and continued to relate his other adventures. I talked about the fat cop and the Underground Temple's High Priest. We parallel-talked, like two bosom buddies, and he had so much fun he almost passed the other cab when Ganesh stopped by a florist to buy roses. So, my sidekick didn't marry his job and still had romances. Guess you shouldn't go by looks.

Ganesh got off outside a Yonkers housing complex and went into a brick-front condo. After paying the cabdriver to distract the concierge, I entered through the front door using my universal ID card. I greeted the watchman by his first name and strolled to the mailboxes, pretending to check for mail. When the cabdriver knocked on the front door and the concierge spoke to him, I stepped behind the desk to survey the security monitors. Ganesh exited the elevator on the twentieth floor and strolled to unit C and knocked three times.

I rushed to the elevator and thrust my hand between the closing doors to reopen them. I pressed the button, ignoring the two men and the woman who scrutinized me. When I got off the elevator, the woman followed me down the hallway. I pretended to have left my keys at the lobby and walked back to the elevator. After she'd entered her apartment, I passed unit C and exited onto the stairwell. I set up my equipment, adjusting the parameters for noise and echo canceling and other signal processing algorithms until Ganesh enunciated every syllable in my ears. I should ask my contact in the FBI to get a few more of those state-of-the-art bugs.

Ganesh complained about me but the lady, Faith, repeated how much she loved him until they just moaned. As a pro I recorded every sound. Somehow, I recognized the lady's voice. Boy, I should buy the lottery. After they'd talked about buying a mid-Manhattan apartment, they decided to have an early dinner.

While cooking T-bone steak with sauté onion and mushroom, Ganesh bragged about finalizing a nonlinear code for a client and soon collecting a fat check. I should charge in and scold him for thieving project time on side jobs. As unethical as charging more than one client for the same solution. I should report him to SOAPS and have his license revoked.

While they had steak and cabernet for dinner, I munched my pepperoni pizza and downed every bite with beer. The melody of Liszt's "Liebestraum" seeped through the speaker and strummed my heartstring. I fantasized about replacing Ganesh, eating the steak, drinking the wine, caressing the lady's cheeks but the beer dulled my taste buds and my imagination. When a man from the floor above came out to smoke, I covered the equipment and pretended to talk on the phone.

After dinner, they had New York cheesecake topped with blueberry sauce while I munched my dark chocolate and stared at the empty stairs.

Usually, I enjoyed spying on men and women having affairs, but that night, I couldn't concentrate. I wanted whiskey. Still, as a professional who'd earned the SOAPS awards time and time and time again, I must prove my worth. So, I listened.

While they made love, I stared at the spider spinning multi-threaded webs. Someone exited the elevator but walked to the other end. The drizzle outside spotted the windowpane and blurred the lights and buildings across the street. A perfect night to meet the mysterious lady again.

The shadow client had threatened to harm someone I love but took Holly, instead of the mysterious lady. After locating this client, I'd complain about the quarter-hearted due-diligence and take her to the Governor.

After what seemed like hours...

Ganesh asked to stay for the night, but the lady urged him to return and quell my suspicion. How considerate. I would've thought he'd picked up a girl from the bar and stayed at her place. Nothing more.

They kissed on and off for ten minutes before the final good-bye.

I'd surprise Ganesh. Tomorrow, he'd return to find me eating his steak, drinking his cabernet, and kissing his lover. Happy ending.

After Ganesh had left, I finished my dark chocolate and packed my equipment. Then stepped into the hallway and rang the doorbell. Footsteps. Then a hum. The camera above the door, which I hadn't noticed, focused on me.

"It's me. Francisco Guzman, code breaker. I'm Ganesh's boss." I smiled into the camera.

"Oh, you. Yes, I recognize your voice. But what are you doing here? Wait a second."

"Where did you recognize my voice from? On TV? On the radio? On my book signing tour? Were you at the SOAPS ceremony when they awarded me—"

In T-shirt and jeans, the mysterious lady who'd delivered the Guzman code opened the door, put my picture on the counter and said, "Come in. I was expecting you, but not so soon. More like when you've cracked the code."

CHAPTER 25 - X

October 3 (2)

After the Felast Underground had left the plains and tunneled through the mountains, I examined the backside of the meadow painting, the same list of elements Dr. Tang had revealed to X. I must assume that I am X. Perhaps Nick tried to trick me with an alternate story. Perhaps I met Rick, not Nick. Of course, the *diary* might be fiction.

The elements must relate to my past and might even help me recover my memory. What could be the link? The atomic numbers and weights didn't reveal any patterns. Their compounds and relevant isotopes: nothing either. I tried variations of the electron orbits: no help there.

If only Dr. Tang, this man who may not exist, if only he could brainstorm with me. Yet, only an empty seat escorted me. Images of the hospital still clogged my neural pathways and stifled insights.

When my headache spread from the top to the side of my head, I slipped the painting into my bag and watched the news. Armageddon had arrived. Rebels bombed a hospital in QCD, killing one hundred and wounding several hundreds, mostly patients but also doctors and nurses. Since QCD is only a hundred miles from Felast, I could have met these barbarian-saboteurs on the way. Well, nothing would stop me from finding my identity, not the rebels and not the government agents. I didn't cared about the details and tried to switch to another channel—sports, weather or music, but I couldn't find any buttons or knobs. My ears and my brain must bear with the junk.

Ever since reading about the hospital and the surrounding streets as a movie set to con X into divulging his secret, I wondered about this world's citizens and their political, social and cultural structures. Farmer Jones's death revealed a corner of the totalitarian wasteland. The news filled in the details. The Underground at any second might hit a landmine and I would shatter into pieces. However, I couldn't remember having lived in this war zone.

So, the rebels had taken over a cold-fusion reactor and threatened to blow it up. Several cold-fusion formulas flashed across my mind: hydrogen atoms, specifically a deuterium and a tritium, combining to form helium. And a face: Dr. Fujimoto. We had worked together, I was sure, at Fermi Lab. Far away. Like a dream. My office, the formulas written on the chalkboard, the books on string theory and quantum chromodynamics. I had invented cold-fusion. On a summer afternoon, Dr. Fujimoto and I discussed an efficient way to reduce the nuclear reaction's temperature. Then, the dark nights conducting experiments next to slices of sashimi pizza. Frustrated and defeated when the input energy exceeded the output energy. On a winter morning, Dr. Fujimoto and I argued about a new approach he had proposed. We decided to part ways. I had beaten him to the finish line, by one day, only one day, but the scientific community accepted both our results. In the end, we reconciled. We had invented cold-fusion. We had saved humanity and civilization.

Images of my office, the campus, the days calculating, the nights experimenting, the pizzas, the many slices of sashimi pizza for dinner. The frustration, the pain, the despair, then the joy, the exhilaration. The sensation again flooded my cortexes and I held my head in pain, expecting it to explode.

The Underground stopped at a depot and the police boarded to check the passengers' ID cards. I gave a policeman in olive uniform Rick's ID without looking at him. He saluted me. Handed the card back with both hands and scurried to the next seat. Soon, the policemen left the coach, taking two young men and a middle-aged woman with them. The other passengers watched through the window, whispered to their neighbors, or went to the dining car.

***

After several days, the coach emerged from the ground and the Felast skylines cold and ethereal loomed before me. The steel-gray skyscrapers and the patrols hovering over them melted into the fog. Only the red and green blinking lights animated the stillness.

At the transport depot, a loud speaker reminded the passengers that slandering the government would guarantee execution. Passengers alighted based on caste. Since Rick's ID indicated caste A, I passed the

123

lower caste passengers and followed the privileged ones to line up along the platform, which displayed posters such as "New America Prevails," "Long Live the President," "Execute the Rebels," and "Report Suspicious Characters." After reading a passenger's ID, electronic customs officer would issue a black pamphlet.

When I inserted the card into the slot, grunting and knitting my brows, the machine saluted me with a tune, probably the national anthem. The captain with a Charlie Chaplain mustache rushed forward and saluted me. Pushing aside the bystanders and opening a way. A row of policemen lined the terminal and saluted as I passed them grunting and hissing. Rick must've inspired fear in the law enforcement community without showing his face. When I requested a pamphlet to inspect its content, the captain twitched his mustache and hesitated for a few seconds before handing me a copy. He said the local propaganda team had followed the federal regulations. The captain led me through the lobby, where a policeman shoved a teenager into a windowless room. Before I could inquire, the captain informed me the saboteur tampered with the TV in the coach.

As I left the depot and bid my escort farewell, a shot boomed through the lobby. The captain smiled, probably waiting for a compliment. I grunted and fled from the execution. I didn't belong here. I could never live in such a place. I might fight against the regime but I despised the rebels as much as the government forces for their violence. After recovering my memory, I would leave this purgatory and look for an island. An island without natives. I wouldn't want to infect them and their world.

On Cheesecake Boulevard, I imagined the policemen opening champagne to celebrate the execution. Crowds hustled and bustled in the cheesecake shops where customers must check in with their ID cards. An efficient system to monitor citizens' whereabouts. I hesitated but entered a shop. A clerk behind the counter smiled and gave me samples. I tasted them. They tasted like sawdust, but other customers relished every morsel. I probably wouldn't enjoy any food and I resigned to taking the standard vitamin rations from the vending machines. When I shared my view with the clerk, she smiled and urged me to buy the strawberry cheesecake. She probably would sound the same syllables whatever my words.

After passing a drugstore and retraining school, I arrived at New Jersey, the five-star hotel and convention center where Dr. Tang had first met Dolly. The monitor listed the penalties for violating the rules and regulations. I inserted my ID card and entered the lobby where a seven-foot TV broadcast the news: the police had bombed a bar and killed two rebels. To the right, a row of vending machines sold snacks, health supplements and meditation soundtracks. About ten to fifteen people lined up in front of each machine. I showed Dolly's photo to the attendants behind the front desk, but they shook their heads. When I offered a hundred dollars for leads, they fought for the photo to examine the face. Everyone had seen her. When I requested the surveillance video files to confirm their statements, they returned to work. I thrust the photo at every bellhop and housemaid around the lobby, but they only squinted, pretending to study the photo, and shook their heads.

I intruded upon visitors and hotel employees for two hours, but my jaw and tongue still didn't ache. I had tea at the café. While listening to the background music, I read James Joyce's *Ulysses* to trigger my thoughts, but the stream-of-consciousness prose triggered a headache. I didn't care about Leopold Bloom's uncensored thoughts. For no reason, I wanted fish oil. I put down the book and stood up, and realized a subliminal message in the music was saying, "I want potato chips. I crave potato chips. I must have potato chips." About fifty people converged on the vending machines. Each bought a bag of potato chips. Only I remained in the café, until the customers returned with their junk foods. I concentrated and the music couldn't affect me, but my head pounded.

After reading about a hundred pages, I couldn't bear my headache. Several buzzes annoyed my ears and I was going to swat the fly, but a man was just trying to get my attention. I still should swat.

"You were showing that picture around. Maybe, I can help," he said, sitting down and thrusting me a business card.

Dr. Tang's replacement in the fake hospital. Somehow, I recognized the voice. Was my memory returning?

"Aren't you just a second-rated actor taking on odd jobs, like imitating a neuroscientist?" I took the card and ripped it and returned it.

"Have to make a living, take any dirty job to pay the bills. Sing, dance, joke, impersonate, hack into computer systems. I'm a jack-of-all-trade." He took the scraps and handed me another card.

"I don't need a professional con man. I need a private investigator. Maybe you can tell me why the fake hospital."

"You mean the fake prison. Sorry, don't have the clearance level. I'm only a contractor. Was asked to play doctor for a few days until they can find another neuroscientist to replace that fugitive."

"Then, why is your face still in front of me? Get lost before I get rid of it myself. I don't need a con man."

"I'm not just a con man. I'm Conman, Jack Conman. FYI, I've really got a medical license." He slipped the business card between my fingers and ordered a glass of orange juice. "And I can help you access useful databases, like the one in the Intelligence Agency. You know, they have lots of info and I'm sure you can find what you want."

"Don't overestimate yourself. You're just a con man."

"Naturally, with a user ID and password, real time password, that is."

"Why should I trust you? Got any references."

"As a matter of fact, I do. You know those rebels, those anarchists, those terrorists? Well, almost half of my income came from them. When it comes to paying suppliers and subcontractors, they're pretty reliable. If you ask, they'd vouch for me. Very satisfied customers." He took off his jacket and threw it into the trashcan. "To show good faith, I'm letting you have a piece of info that'd interest you."

"All right. Who am I?"

"If I knew that, I'd have retired in Dubai."

"If you still haven't conned enough money to retire, you've flopped and I don't need a failure's help."

"But I want to have my own island in Dubai before retiring." He glanced around and waited until the bellhop had pushed the luggage down the hallway before continuing, "You only had a fake ID on you when they pulled you out of the car. Believe me, I tried to find out your identity. But no match with your face and fingerprints. You probably had plastic surgery. No DNA match either. Probably not in the system. Nice job hiding your identity."

So, I had a car accident, if I could trust this Conman. "Someone had to know who I am." I must've been a double agent or an international crime boss, to hide my identity through plastic surgery. No wonder the charade to deceive me. I might know a military secret. "Tell me about the fake prison."

Jack Conman waited for a maid to push the cart past us before whispering, "I haven't been able to hack into the Intelligence Agency's top secret database. I'd probably find something there. But, only a guess."

"OK, so where's Dr. Tang?"

"The famous neuroscientist? How should I know? You want him to reprogram your brain, or something like that?"

"But in that hospital, you replaced him to dissect me."

"I have to find out who I replaced in the prison, not the hospital. But whoever he is, if he's lucky, a stray bullet probably killed him. The Agency was hunting for him. Of course, the guy who killed him would be in deep shit." Conman ran his finger across his throat. "Dolly. Aren't you interested in finding out more about her? If not, you wouldn't be showing that photo around like you're her lover."

That doctor had to be Dr. Tang. Why was he fleeing from the authorities? The con man probably had no idea. "Why should I care about your fake information? I'm sure your other client has laid a trap. However, I'd like his name."

"Oh, but this, you can verify easily. Dolly used to be General Manager at the Cyber-Clone Factory nearby. The government closed it when they turned to androids. They cost less and they work harder. You can check the business licenses with the local government." He picked up the glass of orange juice, leaned back and whistled to a maid.

I reached across the table and grabbed his tie, pulling him forward. He spilled orange juice onto his sleeve. I examined his pupils. A poker face, like the usual con man. "Where am I?"

He didn't answer. I released his tie and checked Felast's public records for the clone factory and confirmed Dolly had worked as General Manager for three years before the factory closed. "How much for access to all government databases, including the local police?" I ordered him a cup of coffee.

"Good, good. I like to deal with knowledgeable customers. Simplifies my job." He took out the calculator and pretended to tally the fee but that piece of junk probably didn't even work. "Well, since you're a new customer and I'm feeling generous, I'll give a discount. Only twenty-thousand dollars."

"So, you're a stand-up comic also." I took his calculator. "Thank you for being so generous. Unfortunately, your service is too high-end. I'm only a mass consumer looking for run-of-the-mill passwords to hack into databases." I showed him the stolen money. "Can't afford such a luxury service. Not even close." I could charge it on Rick's ID card, but I didn't trust Conman.

He drank the coffee and said, "This is your lucky day."

"So, you're giving me ninety-nine percent discount. Because even with a ninety percent discount, I couldn't afford it."

"Even better, your patron's willing to cover the entire fee. A blank check for whatever you want. That's why I'm talking to you. Quite generous. Must be a good friend."

I requested my benefactor's identity, but he said, "No can do. Confidentiality. Once I rat out on my customer, I'd lose my trustworthiness."

"What does a con artist want with trustworthiness? You lie, you cheat, you swindle; your forte conflicts with trustworthiness."

"Well, never mind contradictions. They exist only when we impose logic on existence."

"I don't care if you work as a Zen master on the side. I'm not interested in your wisdom. I just want—"

"Take things one at a time. First, get your memory back. Then locate your guardian angel." He wrote down the user ID, whispered the password, and gave me an electronic device. He showed me how to use the electronic key when accessing a database. "Now, after I've hacked into the secret files, if I find some juicy information on you, I'll let you have the first chance to buy it. See, sometimes I can be a real nice guy."

"Thank you for allowing me to finance your retirement." I waved the electronic device. "We'll see if I can use this to earn enough money."

October 12

This morning, I woke up in a hotel room unsure how I got there or who I was. In my dream, I was in a prison cell and a neuroscientist tried to recover my memory. Rick, perhaps a secret agent, pressured the scientist to shock my brain and stimulate the neural connections, but the latter refused. In the end, Rick dismissed him and ordered the guards to hook me up to the machine. He shocked me several times and I loss consciousness each time but couldn't recall anything. When I woke up, I was in the hotel room. An iPad and two ID cards on the night table.

After reading the diary in the iPad beside me, I questioned whether I had been in the hospital or the prison. X or Y? According to my dream, it should be the prison. However, I didn't trust the dream anymore than I trust the *diary*, whose entries contradict one another. Of course, I have no choice but to continue writing it, since I'll probably lose my memories again.

Later, a rookie policewoman came into my room to check my ID. After reading the card with her tablet PC, she saluted and apologized for interrupting my rest. I asked about Farmer Jones's death in Purgatory, but when she checked the local sheriff's office, the officer didn't have a report on the incident. With the help of the officer, she contacted Farmer Jones at his premise. The dead man had resurrected and greeted us through the video screen. He didn't recognize me. I had never been to his farm. He must be a clone and the government was hiding the murder. Perhaps to confuse and drive me insane. I wouldn't fall into the trap.

Afterward, I asked for the closest defense contractor that could access the government databases and she gave me directions to If So, Inc. After she had left, I checked the Internet to get the firm's address. The ID Conman gave me should help me pass the firm's security checkpoint but I didn't trust him and didn't want to walk into a trap. I would have to double-check the ID before using it.

After breakfast, I inquired about Dolly in Pythagorean Triangle. I rechecked local records on the clone factory. She was GM of the Tristar Clone Factory, rather than the Cyber-Clone Factory. The clone factory, a concrete windowless building inside a rusted barb-wired fence, slumped among thatched cottages. The graffiti on the wall revealed the rebels' ideology.

The vagrants' eyes tracked me and the flies circled me. When I drew near a window, a girl in the cottage took off her clothes and said three hundred dollars. I declined and she reduced the price. I walked from the cottages to the fence, where a few vagrants bartered leftover tuna, ground beef, and vegetable soups while the flies ignored personal property rights and sampled the food. I showed the tramps Dolly's picture and they directed me to the church at the Triangle's southern edge. For a dollar, of course.

Along the fence, I passed a collapsed storefront where several children played in the dirt. Several years ago, when the factory cloned technicians and soldiers on the assembly lines by the thousands, at lunchtime this store's proprietor sold hamburgers, hot dogs and soda by the hundreds. The workers would sit on the benches nearby and chat about a movie, a football game or the latest fashion. Dolly would eat her meal in the office and check the morning's production status. Now, graffiti covered the walls, vagrants bartered, and children played in the dirt. Why did I feel sad?

During breakfast in the hotel room, I had ignored the news broadcast and read William James's *The Variety of Religious Experiences*. His model of an experience, particularly his "sense of self to whom the attitude belongs," revealed that even without my memory, I could still sense my self as separate from the surrounding. Yet, without a history, I couldn't grasp and explain my attitudes. Like flowers severed from their stems, without roots to draw nutrients, waiting to wither away.

Long before I reached the church, its spire white and lance-like, greeted me. The red wall stretched across the building's length, only interrupted by the white paneled door. Behind the apse, a car sped down the dirt road before I could identify the driver, lifting a trail of dust. Had the minister seen me and fled? Why? I quickened my pace. At the front entrance, a vulture landed on the eave to greet me. Through the side window I saw no one. I rang the bell even though the door was ajar. Two minutes later, I entered the foyer, where the donation box blocked the path. The corridors extended to the right and the left but I walked into the sanctuary, where a cross hung on the opposite wall. The melody of "Amazing Grace" seeped out of the loud speakers onstage. Beyond the aisle and the pews, in front of the pulpit, a man lay facedown on the floor, his hand grasping a bag of cheese puff, a pool of blood around his buttock. Rats gnawed at the beam above and flies buzzed along the aisle. No breathing, not from the man on the floor or anyone else.

I approached. Knelt down. Turned him over to check his features. No one special, just the chaplain who came to the fake hospital and stole my laptop. Shot between the legs. Must be personal. Maybe an ex-wife.

Was I in the hospital room rather than the prison cell? How could I recognize this man if I had loss my memory since meeting him?

I could no longer interrogate him to find out his agenda. Like Stubble, Dr. Tang and everyone else, he probably sought the same information, which might be in my original laptop. The brain that knew and the mouth that could reveal had both expired. Leaving me with questions marks rather than periods. Conspiracy. Nothing less. I must identify the schemers and beat them at their own game.

I pulled out a wallet from the dead minister's pants pocket. About a hundred dollars, and the photo of Dolly and him next to the pulpit. I took the cash and the photo, and returned the wallet to his pants pocket. My intuition had pointed me in the right direction—Dolly and the minister knew each other. A deadly secret, or a lucrative secret, valuable enough to kill for, linked them. Now he had died and I must find Dolly, the key to the secret and maybe to my past.

I turned the photo around, expecting for the best, and got my wish. An address. Dolly's address.

I was about to search the church for my laptop, when a car engine growled. I couldn't see the car through the foyer window, but it, about a mile away, was probably coming from behind the thatched cottages and warehouses. The killer must have driven away and called the police to frame me. The logical step in a conspiracy. The officers should arrive in five minutes, but I didn't care to meet them.

October 15

Dolly's address led me to a villa beside a suburban canal. After stepping off the gondola and paying the fee, I went up to the porch and knocked on the door. The new tenant or owner might know about Dolly. If not, at least I could get the real-estate agent's name and follow that lead. The wind chime jingling in the wind triggered a feeling, a chill perhaps connected to a past incident, but I couldn't recall any images linking to those notes, hard as I tried. The bench next to the door could be hiding a secret about Dolly. No neighbors around. I enjoyed the wind chime's random tune, but the frog's iambic croak annoyed me.

Footsteps shoveled behind the door. I tapped my foot. My fingers drummed the doorframe. I stared at the peephole and composed my questions while the wind chime jingled in the wind.

The knob turned. Perhaps an old lady would emerge with a broom and chase me off the porch. The door opened to a slit but still hid the dweller and I only glimpsed a moccasin. I held my breath to the steady breathing behind the door. The seconds passed while the wind chime jingled.

When the door opened, I stared at the apparition and bit my tongue. Perhaps Francisco was dreaming of me, rather than the other way around.

At the doorway, Ingrid greeted me.

CHAPTER 26 - FRANCISCO

September 19, 2011 (2)

What could I do when Ganesh had just made love to my angel while I listened? Back-stabbing and double-crossing and all that crap. For five seconds, maybe ten, I couldn't move and I couldn't speak, I couldn't think and I couldn't feel. Ganesh was jeering, slapping my face, kicking my butt. I should twist the nerd's neck. I should box his ears. For the first time in years, I wanted to cry. If only Fernando could comfort and encourage me. I stood at her doorway as she had mine but I hesitated to enter for a different reason.

I suppressed the ache in my bosom. I regained my composure. I intended to charm her and reverse the tide. "You mean you expect me to come when the moon and stars are shining in the sky? But you have a beau already." I stepped in and stared at my photo. "I'm very disappointed. How could you forget me? You still need that to recognize me? I usually make very good impressions, unforgettable face and manner. And of course, my choice of words. Where'd I failed?" At that moment, I vowed to rescue her from Ganesh's claws. "You can take a better picture of me. You can take as many pictures as you want."

"Don't take it personally. I have visual agnosia," she said, "so I can't recall faces, not even my own. Every time I look into the mirror I'd wonder at the stranger. To reassure myself, I'd take out my picture to compare. Of course, who else could it be?"

"What? Agnostic? I don't care if you believe in God or not. I'm kind of agnostic, too. I mean, who knows about metaphysical stuff, right? I don't go as far as those positivists who deny everything nonphysical. I'm a humble man, as you probably have noticed." I grasped the vase on the table and itched to squash the roses Ganesh had bought her.

"But when it comes to strangers, whenever possible, I try to have a picture with the name written on it to confirm the person. Of course, after a while, when I recognize the voice, I won't need the picture anymore. So I recognize Ganesh's voice, smell and—"

"Ouch, that hurts." The heartache bolstered my resolve to wrest her from Ganesh's snare. Several certificates, all Ganesh's, hung on the living room wall. In the trophy cabinet his Field's Medal sneered at me. I should fling it into a kiln, but the cabinet door refused to budge.

"Ganesh said you guys still don't have anything yet. The client's getting impatient. She wants results soon. She said, if you don't decipher the code and find the password soon, something bad will happen." She opened the cabinet door and showed me the medal but refused to let me touch it. I'd been waiting to receive that medal for more than ten years but since someone solved Fermat's Last Theorem, I had to find another unsolvable problem. I wasn't interested in differential geometry and had to look into other fields.

"Yeah, I know. They chopped off the Naked Man's hand."

"Naked Man? Does he run around naked? Maybe someone didn't like his exhibitionism." She returned the medal to the cabinet and showed me the trophy Ganesh received in a Math Olympiad more than twenty years ago.

"But naturally the world will come to an end if I don't crack the code. Clients always say that to boost my ego, and I always succeed. Do you know how many times I've saved the world? You'd think I'm a superhero. Of course, in many ways, I am. Well, have your client come and we can chat over dinner. I'm sure she'd praise my progress." I didn't care about the world coming to an end and in fact, after Fernando had died, I'd hoped for it. Now, I only wanted to prevent the toothless thugs from hurting Holly or Suzie.

"You may've overestimated your communication skills. She hired you for your brains, not your mouth." She handed me a can of beer. I asked for whiskey, but she shook her head.

She'd made love to Ganesh, so her face pained me and I couldn't look at her. I vowed not to give up; I'd fight Ganesh to the end of the world, for her. Adrenaline rushed through my bloodstream to energize me and bolster my resolve. A setback couldn't destroy my self-confidence when successes upon successes testified to my charm and eloquence, and intelligence, ingenuity, and creativity. Did I mention self-confidence?

She twirled a lock of hair and glanced through the window, perhaps reminiscing about a dream. I imitated her and twirled my hair. She was thinking of Ganesh, how he'd kissed and caressed and made love to her. I sensed her intoxication and euphoria. I must challenge Ganesh to a duel, with pistol or rapier or even a katana. I must remove that sore, that pang, that itch from my gut and relive the bliss of the mountain peak. I staggered while Faith stared at a snow globe, probably Ganesh's gift.

"You know, he's more of a liability than an asset. He shows off his medals and trophies, but when it comes to solving problems—"

"He's the best. Give him time and he can break any code." She shook the globe and watched the flakes twirl around the house, trees and sleds.

She must've meant me instead of Ganesh. I, not the nerd, could break any code, even the unbreakable. If only Clint could step through the doorway to share how I'd helped the CIA break an Israeli code, an *unbreakable* code based on Aramaic. By the way she smiled at the globe, she was trying to make me jealous. And succeeding in it. Slashing my heart into cutlets, pounding the pieces into gruel. Oh, cruel beauty.

"I'm planning to buy a condo overlooking Central Park." I walked to the fireplace and viewed the photos on the mantel. Their adventures in Banff, Yosemite, the Maldives, and the Swiss Alps. "Care to go house shopping? In some open houses, there're nice buffets. Of course, I can also buy you lobster and Chardonnay for lunch. And afterward, we could take a walk through Central Park."

"Ganesh and I would love to come. I tried to convince him to settle down in the city. He prefers Italian food, though. I know a nice Italian restaurant around Central Park."

Double ouch. I tried to recover from the jabs below the belt, but couldn't find the syllables to defend my honor, or the sounds to express my pain. I, Francisco, wordless, soundless, a canary having lost its voice. My poor, aching heart. I swore to get even with Ganesh. She wanted me to be jealous and I was; I was jealous twice over, and more jealous than a lame cat watching a squirrel bounce from branch to branch.

"Usually, I don't trust anyone. But in your case, I want to make an exception." I had to find an excuse, even by walking on water or healing the lame or raising the dead, to trust her. "So, help me here. Give me anything. Even if you just say, 'Trust me.' But, of course, if we go to dinner and get to know each other, I'm sure that'd work out even better."

"You don't have to trust me. Just keep one eye on the check and the other on the solution. If you can't unravel the code, trusting me won't help."

Her icy fist punched my nose and jaw and my head throbbed with an iamb. On the easy chair facing the vase, I tried but failed to will the roses to wither. I preferred her hatred to her apathy. Before I could go for another round in the ring, a tree trunk or maybe a fire hydrant knocked on her door, denting the center. I followed her to the kitchen and checked the surveillance monitors. Five hooded nobodies tried to open the door with an anvil. That's creativity for you.

Before I could confront them, Faith, having taken the snow globe, opened the backdoor and urged me to follow. She said her brother might've sent his fanatics to locate the holy text. I showed her my nunchuks and my black belt certificate but she insisted on avoiding the henchmen. On the stairwell, I asked her for a date, but no luck. When we reached the ground floor, I volunteered to lure away the hoodlums. We exchanged overcoats and pulled the hoods over our heads before exiting.

Through the doorway we stepped into a nightclub, a few couples dancing in front of the band. Faith left and I stayed to distract the hoodlums. At the bar, I chatted with a lady who turned out to be Ms. Redhead. What a coincidence. I bought her a Long Island Iced-tea and we talked about going to the Caribbean next spring. I hadn't been to Jamaica for three years and missed the chicken jerk. I was delivering my joke's punch line when a shot startled me and a bullet shattered my glass and spilled the whiskey.

On stage, a giant tailless skunk pointed a Smith & Wesson at me. I pulled down Ms. Redhead and dropped onto the floor, and pushed her behind the bar while the bartender shot at the skunk. Since I didn't bring my gun, I crawled to the entrance and rolled through the doorway.

While I turned a street corner under a broken streetlight, a shot behind me saluted the night. The cool breeze caressed my skin and announced the beginning of autumn. I turned into an alley while pedestrians entered shops and restaurants to avoid me. Another shot. The trashcan cover popped into the air and a cat screeched and dodged behind a crumbled refrigerator. Before me, a dead-end. A siren blared in the distance. A homeless man pushing a shopping cart full of plastic bottles and aluminum cans hid behind a trash can. Behind me, the skunk mumbled a prayer and bid me farewell. Should've brought my gun.

CHAPTER 27 - X

October 16

I woke in bed unsure where I was but recalling my dream, I leaped out of bed to look for the diary. I almost tripped over the flower-patterned linen and a photo popped out of my shirt pocket. A woman and a minister. Dolly. I remembered her name. The minister looked familiar but I couldn't recall his name. On the desk next to the window sat my backpack with the laptop and the two ID cards.

After reading the diary, I distinguished Rick's ID from the one Conman gave me. I might not have met them, for the journal entries could be false, but I had the ID cards and could access the government databases.

Outside the window, the water gurgled along the canal. I was in the villa and I had seen Ingrid. Ingrid, the woman whom I longed for in the earlier entries, I must find her. She would be the rock from which I would build my past and future, from which I would rebuild myself. I pocketed the photos and the cards and realized I didn't have the RF ID chip in my arm.

Just as I closed the laptop, the door opened and I turned to greet Ingrid.

Dolly, rather than Ingrid, greeted me and set the tray of oatmeal and orange juice on the desk. Oatmeal and orange juice again, as in the hospital.

Had I returned to the movie set?

I asked for Ingrid even though I had questions for Dolly. She looked confused and I showed her the last entry in the laptop.

Yesterday afternoon, returning from grocery shopping, she found me unconscious in the backyard and carried me into the bedroom. She slept in the sofa.

Should I believe her? At first, I questioned whether she could have carried me into the house, but after checking her physique, I doubted no more.

Sure, I lost my memory time and again. But why was reality shifting? No, the journal entries accounted for the different realities. So I couldn't trust them even though I had to rely on them to jolt my memory.

What was real: I was in the villa with the diary, the photos and the ID cards; I talked to Dolly. Whether I was in the hospital or the prison, whether I had gone to Fermat's Last Stand or not, whether I had met Conman or not, I didn't care. With the facts before me, I would search for my identity and my past.

Except, *Dolly* turned out to be Molly, Dolly's clone. After the factory had closed, Dolly moved away but Molly stayed to tend the house. I bit the spoon with oatmeal in my mouth for a minute before taking it out. She handed me the cup of orange juice but I didn't take it. Was she toying with me? Could she be Dolly? I lacked the strength to leave, so stayed at her place. That night, I slept on the sofa, or rather, pretended to sleep, to avoid talking to her. Molly opened her bedroom door and asked questions that I wanted answered. Around midnight, elevator music filled the house. So, the government installed speakers in every home to broadcast this music during the night and tampering with the electronics would land the felon in jail. "Isn't so bad once you get used to it," she said. According to Dr. Tang's lecture in the diary, we would be listening to subliminal messages. Molly asked another question but I couldn't answer it either. Half an hour later, thinking she had slept, I pulled the blanket over my shoulders, but she asked, "Can you at least tell me your name?"

I said I had lost my memory in an accident and was searching for my identity, including my name. "But you can call me X. That's what they called me in the fake hospital." In the fake diary, I should've added.

"Oh."

I waited but only heard silence. She slept. Probably satisfied she could call me X rather than *you*.

***

Next morning, Molly took me to the cemetery where Dolly would stroll among the headstones and contemplate the epitaphs. And I got another surprise.

Heading there on the gondola, we listened to Leonard Bernstein conduct Copeland's *Appalachian Spring*, which evoked a joy I couldn't describe. Molly prepared mulberry pancake and Java roast, the smell triggering images of a luxury condo in a metropolis. The bay window overlooking the cityscape: the skyscrapers, the bridges, and the smog. Perhaps New York. Perhaps Felast. While eating the pancake and drinking the coffee, I searched for a face from the past, but in the condo was only the LED TV, the velvet sofa, the coffee table. Francisco's place?

As we passed a row of red-roofed Spanish Villas where the government insignia—a bald eagle—decorated the gates, Molly said she had lived in this house for more than ten years. She would cook the meals, wash the clothes, and clean the house. She had asked to go along on missions but Dolly refused to take her.

"Rejected, abandoned." She turned around to look at the villas. "The first time I had that nasty feeling. As if my abdomen would burst."

She had visited neighbors and even crossed the canal to the other side, but had never left this section of Felast. Dolly had set up a bank account with enough money for a lifetime. Molly would shop in the local malls on Saturdays, attend church on Sundays and visit her foster father's house in a nearby community once a month, but otherwise she would stay home.

She pointed at a glass building with scanners and surveillance cameras in front. She would stroll through this shopping center on Saturdays though she could buy everything online. Since only a few neighbors frequented the malls and machines had replaced cashiers and sales clerks, often she wouldn't meet anyone in the aisles.

When I recounted my fake experiences in the fake hospital, she frowned and put an index finger to her lips. I mirrored her posture and could sense her pity, her sympathy, the sentiments I had ignored. Now through empathy I had merged her feelings into mine. Observing, digesting and evaluating them, I also sensed the self somewhere in my frontal lope, as Dr. Tang would say. Of course, Dr. Tang probably never existed.

After breakfast, I steered the gondola along the canal, where marigolds bloomed on both sides. The water reflected my profile against the sky and I hoped to get acquainted with that stranger in the other world. The water murmured beside the gondola while sparrows chirped in the distance. Molly pulled out her recorder and spoke into it, describing my features and manners, my anecdotes and her impressions. I didn't interrupt her to find out her urgency to record the entries. Across the canal, that mother might be pushing a stroller-like surveillance camera, and that elderly lady might be adjusting a camcorder under her wig. Could they be government agents? Then again, surveillance cameras on top of lamp-posts sufficed to monitor me.

"I've taken up writing a diary also." I steered the gondola to one side to avoid a motor boat. "But prefer doing it once a day or a few days. Every ten minutes is too much. Or course, when you meet a strange bird like me, you want to record it right away. I understand." I didn't tell her the journal entries were fictions.

"Oh, I've this sickness." She played with her hair. "I'd forget everything that happened thirty minutes ago. Well, about thirty minutes more or less. And naturally, I couldn't remember anything in the past. So the only way to recall anything is to write it down. And I have to do it often. A strange sickness and a nuisance, I know. "

"You can probably find better reasons to break up with your boy-friends." Faith in my dream also had a similar condition. Not a coincidence. Could I trust her? I shouldn't trust anyone. I stooped as we passed under a stone bridge, under which ducks responded to the quacks overhead. I would like to recall the times in my youth when I lay by the stream and listened to the same symphony.

"So, you and I are very much alike. In my mind, there's nothing beyond half an hour. When I read the diary or listened to the recorder, I'd recall the past, but it would feel like someone else's story." She put aside the recorder and scribbled notes on a writing pad.

An amnesiac should intrigue her, since her memories fade away every thirty minutes. We shared the fear, the confusion, the darkness, the wandering. Of course, her reality wasn't shifting.

On the left shore, a group of tourists waited outside a Cathedral for the first tour. The hundreds of saints chiseled on the granite façade rose about two hundred feet while on either side, towers matched the main building's height. I wanted to tour the church but didn't want to pay the hundred-dollar entrance fee.

As we approached an intersection, I stopped the gondola to let a patrol boat pass and asked Molly about Dolly.

"Are you in love with her?" She dropped the fork and stopped chewing her pancake.

I tried to detect jealousy in her eyes but found nothing. She wasn't *an open book* like Jack Conman. She probably had trained herself to hide her thoughts and feelings, maybe to fend off Dolly, who would know her inside out.

"I don't think so. But after I recover my memory, I might find out I used to love her. Then, I can say whether old feelings are overwhelming my indifference."

The patrol boat approached and the policemen asked for ID cards. After scanning mine, they saluted. The commanding officer put a green flag on the gondola's bow to give me right-of-way over other personal transports. He stopped traffic to let me cross the intersection.

After we had crossed, I said, "Do you hate her?"

"I don't think so." She shrugged and scribbled more notes in her notebook. "I'll help find your identity if you promise to forget her."

"I promise to forget her if you help find her." I showed her the photo of Pastor McCoy and Dolly and inquired about their relationship.

"None. That's me." She crumbled the photo and her face contorted. "I never want to see that hyena face again."

"You won't have to." I expected her to have found out about Pastor McCoy's death. They probably had an affair and the preacher had dumped her. She might've murdered him, shooting him between the legs. I didn't ask.

"He's a bad man. I'm glad he died a month ago." She shredded the photo several times and flung the pieces into the canal, her movements as determined as her demeanor. Anger and hatred rose onto her face, her expression more menacing than Rick's or the hospital guard's. For a second, I seemed to recognize her but might've discerned Dolly's features.

"A month? Not several days?" I located the October 12 entry and confirmed that I had found his body that day. At least, he died in the diary and in reality. The date didn't matter.

"Never mind him," she said.

I tried to sense her pain and grief, but only detected the moisture in the air. She must've killed the minister. If she would tell me, I would comfort her, but she hid her thoughts and feelings. She finished the pancake and lifted her head to let the breeze play with her hair. How much pain and suffering had she endured without comfort or support? I wanted to embrace her but I didn't. I rowed the oar. I steered the gondola from a motorboat reminding citizens to attend the celebration during Government Day. When the officer onboard spotted the green flag, she saluted.

As we arrived at the cemetery, its knolls rising and falling under the gray sky, Molly flipped several pages in her notebook and said, "Oh, Dolly's dead." Raising her head and tapping her lips. "Yes, killed in the line of duty. She joined the Intelligence Agency despite my plea. No one could stop her, not even herself."

I dropped the oar and let the gondola drift. The music scattered my thoughts. A ripple that wouldn't fade. I tumbled into a black-hole that mangled all natural laws, including logic and causality. "But, she was the general manager at that Tristar Clone Factory. I checked the local government record." The single clue to my identity led to a dead-end. Murphy's Law in action. Still, Conman should've known about it. I had to sit down to prevent from falling into the water.

"Oh, only a cover up for a clandestine operation. She'd never learned to manufacture clones, though she knew something about genetics. But certainly nothing about operational efficiency or cost reduction." She scanned through the notebook and said, "The Intelligence Agency wouldn't allow us to have a funeral. They wanted to keep the death quiet for a while. Probably related to her assignment. By the way, it was the Cyber-Clone Factory."

"When can I see a hospital for a hospital, a factory for a factory, a doctor for a doctor and a manager for a manager? Why these disguises and playacting? Can I see an apple for what it is?" The gondola was charging into a pier, so I steered it back to the middle of the canal. Cyber-Clone became Tristar Clone and reverted back again. A name is just a name is just a damn name.

"I'm sorry for your disappointment. But don't worry, I'll help find your past." She seized my sleeve and shook it. "You will find your past. You must. Then, you'll know everything."

A group of boy scouts onshore marched along the dock, chanting an anthem. The clouds still blocked the sun and the mist in front thickened as if the elements were hiding their secrets. The news didn't trigger any memory; the fog in my mind as thick as that on the canal.

"Everything will be fine. You'll remember everything," Molly said.

What did she mean by *everything*? She sounded so ominous that I shuddered. I feared those two statements would contradict each other. As Dr. Tang had said, I might need callousness and resignation to face the past. When *Appalachian Spring* ended, an aroma wafted through the air.

In a piazza, a firing squad aimed semi-automatic rifles at six prisoners along a wall. Behind them, a hundred or so men, women and children on tiers of wooden benches ate and chatted. A vendor walked among the spectators, selling beer and hot dogs. The crowd stopped chatting when the captain lifted his arm. He dropped his arm and the squad fired at the prisoners. After the minister blessed the execution, the spectators gathered around the solders and shook their hands.

"Citizen guards," Molly said, "The community leaders recruited these volunteers to protect the neighborhood. Of course, the government has to approve the selection. And sanctioned the monthly executions. This month, they're executing the local drug addicts. Last month, it was the prostitutes. The goal is to eliminate crime and disease in this neighborhood."

If the spectators knew I had amnesia, they might lock me up for next month's execution. How had Molly avoided the executions? Maybe her foster father financed the community leaders' election campaigns.

"What about Pythagorean Triangle?" The inhabitants there seemed carefree.

She scratched her head, then flipped through her pad and said, "The same. Why?"

"But the beggars and vagrants?"

She fingered the page and said, "None, all executed."

So, in this reality, the government had cleaned Pythagorean Triangle.

When we returned to the house, Molly ran her fingers through the wind chime above the front door. "Even as a child, I like to listen to the scattered notes." She leaned on me, her body warming my arm. The wind brushed against my face and I seemed to drift in the ocean.

"I'll be with you," she said. "We can do this together. You're not alone."

The wind whispered. The water murmured. The vendor barked. They hinted that I was a stranger, trespassing through their world.

She held my arm and showed me the deer she had shot the day before yesterday, its head hanging above the back porch. We would have grill deer tonight. We strolled through the backyard, the marigold's scent attacking my nostrils. She had found me beside the shack. I could stay and live out my years. I could forget about fake doctors and sham diaries, as well as my memories and the past. Yet, as Dr. Tang had said, I wouldn't choose that path. Woe to me.

"I'm sorry for showing the picture. I thought that was Dolly."

At the fence, she pointed to the marsh beyond the field. "Once, Dolly with this grubby guy, unshaven, his hair a mop, well, a loser. Over there by the swamp."

Did she know Francisco Guzman? Had she picked up his diction? "I wish I could be as succinct," I said. "But she should have better taste. Just a wild guess."

"That's what she said." She tightened the lock on the gate. "When I mentioned my thought, she laughed so hard she had to drink a glass of scotch to calm down. That's her favorite drink."

"And yours?"

"The same."

"How could I have told you two apart?"

"You couldn't," she said. "Anyway, she was only working on an assignment with that coworker and she said her boyfriend was more manly. Whatever that means." She took out the notebook and flipped through a few pages.

"You may have the same genes, but not the same experiences. Something would distinguish you from Dolly." A clone couldn't have the same thoughts and feelings and decisions as the original.

"She didn't discuss about the boyfriend. So I couldn't help you." She picked up a boomerang and threw it at a crow perching on a branch. It struck down the bird and returned to her hand.

"Maybe afraid you'd steal him." When I showed her Stubble's picture, she turned her notebook's pages and pulled out a photo: the same grubby man except for the red eyes and nose.

"I couldn't. I could never be equal to her." She leaned closer and compared the two photos. "So you know him, too. Your friend? A good friend?"

Her scent distracted me. A familiar scent. "Not sure. I hope I have as much good taste as Dolly. But, one never knows." I couldn't recall my partnership with Stubble, but according to an earlier entry, I knew him.

"No, of course you have better taste." She touched my hand. As if lightning had struck, I flinched. Before I could grasp her hand, she put Stubble's photo back into the notebook and walked toward the crow while reading her notes. I bagged the bird and threw it into the trashcan.

Several months ago, Dolly mentioned that the grubby man Pratt had fathered seven young women's children but had never paid any child support, his government connections helping him skirt the law. Two ex-wives had to join the rebels to support the children.

So, Pratt exists in this reality. Though he had hinted at the conspiracy, he also blasted X with lies. He mixed facts with lies to confuse X and gain the latter's trust.

"Dolly promised to send the scumbag to jail after the mission."

"Promises are just promises, and usually don't get fulfilled." I turned on the faucet near the barn and cleaned my hands. "I'm right most of the time. Still, I would've liked someone to triumph over statistics."

Dolly had died before she could deal with Pratt. Perfect timing. Perhaps an arranged blade, bullet or cyanide capsule ended her life.

In the dinning room, Molly turned the pages and transferred notes from the writing pad to the notebook. I didn't peep, just wiped the dust from the frame and scrutinized the photos on the mantel above the fireplace. Was Molly or Dolly looking out of the photos? Even my eagle vision didn't help.

"Don't you want to know my thoughts?" She came over, holding the notebook.

"I don't want to intrude."

"If you want something, you have to ask. Otherwise, nothing." She sat on the sofa arm, her lips tightened as if annoyed.

"Even if that something isn't for me to ask?"

"Your amnesia is crippling you."

Dolly's boyfriend had forgotten an episode in his youth. He tried to recall that day but could only draw a blank, as if someone had erased his memory.

A coincidence Dolly's boyfriend lost that memory? Not a chance. After the conspiracies whirling around me since waking up, I couldn't ignore the correlation among random events. I wouldn't play the fool. This boyfriend might've played a pivotal role in Dolly's death. I might have met him. I might even have fought with him over Dolly.

"What about Dr. Tang?"

She dropped the notebook. So, Dr. Tang exists, at least in this reality.

"About six, seven years ago," I continued, studying her facial muscles. "They met in New Jersey."

She tried to pick up the notebook but dropped it again. I picked it up. She took it and scrolled through the diary until she reached the last entry. She scrolled back several entries. She paused and opened one of them. She stared at the page for several seconds before raising her head. "Oh, yes, Dr. Tang. A nice man. She said that. Not much else. She was happy."

"If she was happy, why did she leave him?"

"She didn't tell me. Must be her job. She got depressed once in a while." She dropped the notebook again. When she tried to pick it up, she dropped it several more times.

"Do you love Dr. Tang?" I picked up the notebook.

"Me... No, why... No... What a silly question."

"Does he love you?"

She grabbed the notebook and said, "That's an even sillier question." She rushed through the front door.

I called after her but when I stepped onto the front porch, she had crossed the stone bridge down the canal. I didn't chase after her. Maybe I feared facing her while she relived her love. The wind chime played its scattered notes and the ripples slapped against the canal walls. The scent of marigold mingled with that of durian. What was durian doing in my world?

Molly might love Dr. Tang more than Dolly ever did, since the latter had another boyfriend soon after leaving the doctor. Could the doctor tell them apart? Maybe, he didn't even know about the clone. In the dining room, I examined the photos above the fireplace but couldn't distinguish between Dolly and Molly.

Outside the window, the boy who had fainted in the cafeteria, he walked down a path across the canal. Fake New York must have existed. I rushed toward the front door, but before I could step onto the porch, Molly entered the house. She bought a durian from the fruit vendor, but wasn't going to make durian pie, which would've brought Francisco and his egotism into this world.

Before I opened my mouth to apologize, she said, "I loved him. But it's over." Since Dolly had died, she could pursue her love. But I shut my mouth.

I looked out the doorway but couldn't see the boy. Was I hallucinating? No, he probably entered one of the houses.

She put the durian in the refrigerator, took out Dr. Tang's photo and said, "I only have this." I waited for her to declare she would never give up love, but she threw the photo into the fireplace.

"I'll help recover your memory." She reached over to hold my hand. "Only that matters now." Her warm hand reminded me of the girl in the funhouse but I didn't dare to tighten my fingers, afraid she might be an android.

I brewed chamomile tea while she sat before the fireplace holding her chin in both hands. The fire crackled as the photo turned to ash. After finishing the tea, she rested in her bedroom.

I shouldn't care about her misery. I should fling away the mental image of her twisted face. But I failed. I tried to focus on Dolly, but Molly filled my mind. The same face, the same DNA, but my mind had distinguished between them though my eyes couldn't.

While Molly rested, I read Dietrich Bonhoeffer's *Letters & Papers from Prison* and wondered how his "come-of-age" theology would've affected not only the Christian religion but also western society. Maybe not a bit, maybe a new value system. How would my life have changed if Dolly hadn't died? Maybe I wouldn't have the accident and would still have my memory, but I might not have met Molly, or Ingrid or Dr. Tang. Dolly might not have influenced as many minds as Bonhoeffer, but even if she had only changed my path, she had left her mark in history. Cause and effect in this social network, whether to bless or to harm, whether to advance or to retard, we couldn't escape.

I sipped the tea while listening to the wind chime and the ripples, and before I slept, I checked on Molly, but she was gone.

CHAPTER 28 - FRANCISCO

September 25, 2011 (1)

I was down with flu for several days but am recovering. Damn skunk. What sane person would roam around the streets in a skunk costume? I might've caught the virus from standing naked in Central Park chatting with Ganesh. For the record, I don't usually do that, I mean, stand naked in Central Park.

That night, near the dead-end, just as the skunk raised his pistol, Ms. Redhead swung a trashcan and knocked him down. While she ran down the street and lured away the henchmen, I jumped through a manhole and into the sewage system before the skunk grasped his gun and fired. I'd never visited the tunnels under Yonkers, but with Clint's maps I traveled a few miles and under a manhole called Faith to check with her. I invited her to my office. I'd find her a place to stay and avoid the fanatics. She declined and must've been thinking of Ganesh.

I was strolling down a narrow tunnel and humming "Praise to Fransuccesco" when Clint tumbled out of a nook and beckoned me to follow. Before I could interrogate him, he sprinted ahead and led me through passages descending for a while before ascending again. Every time I asked a question, he'd turn a corner and I'd have to catch up. Annoying gnat. I stepped through a doorway and found myself in the rest area below the West Side. I didn't expect to return to the city in just a few minutes. Clint was probably showing off his knowledge of the underground tunnels, as he'd flaunted his skill in sifting through garbage to locate a grain of poison rice. Well, he didn't impress me. Even if he hadn't come, I would've traveled through the tunnels and escaped from the skunk. I reminded him I knew more about encryption, software, weapons, food, women, etc. He didn't respond and his vacant look reminded me of Fernando. We emerged through a manhole under a horse-drawn wagon along Central Park South. After I crawled on the wet pavement away from the carriage and straightened my clothing, I breathed in the fresh air, saturated with moisture. "About time you show your face. Did you hide in the ditches while I worked my ass off?"

"Don't trust that chick, Faith."

"Jealous she likes me but not you? Come on, ain't I your idol?" Though I wouldn't trust any man or woman or boy or girl until the evidence forced me into a corner, I'd trust Faith without knowing her birthday, her favorite perfume, or the movements of her heart. Yes, all rules must have an exception, even Murphy's Law. Clint must have a motive for shaking my trust. Maybe just jealousy. Maybe trying to impress me and earn a few bonus points. Or, maybe just hatching a conspiracy. I wouldn't blame him for trying, but he'd fail. He'd already lost. Sayonara.

"Yer the smartest and sexiest guy I know," he said.

"For a moment, I thought you're an imposter." I patted him on the shoulder, while a limousine arrived and parked outside a hotel and reporters swamped around it. "But the reward of skipping out for over a month, well, you're fired. In fact, I fired you a month back, as they say, in absentia. And I've given away your junk, so you don't have to remove them. Of course, we can still be friends."

"She's got that manuscript, from yer new sidekick. He stolen it from ya and given it to his lover."

Sure, Ganesh's eyes had fixed on that antique when I opened it. Besides me, only he had the chance to search the office and locate the hiding place. He had the motive: to impress Faith. I believed Clint but said, "Tell me one reason why I shouldn't fire you, after your lack of professionalism and work ethics." When the Governor emerged from the limousine, I hid behind the horse that was munching hay. I couldn't update him on my progress since I hadn't found Holly.

Clint followed and said, "Them thugs chasing me man. Got to run for my life. Was hiding out in Philly for a while before coming back, trying to find out what sup."

"By tailing me? Would I waste money on thugs to scare you, you numskull? I'd rather spend it on drinks in the bar." I munched dark chocolate for some quick energy. The Governor greeted the reporters with his false teeth and declared he'd seek reelection next year. I must have my associates dig up dirt in his personal life and undermine his campaign. Maybe Holly would help me, if I could find her. Four years ago, she'd asked me to sabotage her father's election campaign.

"Nah, ya won't fire me. I won't be punished for nothing I do." Clint clapped his hands and danced in the street.

He must've drunk too much beer while watching Sunday Night Football and I'd lost a loyal sidekick. Tough luck for me. Yet, his blank stare, which reminded me of the zombie cop, alarmed me. Skunkman, zombie cop, Dostoevsky fanatics, now Clint, all ding-a-lings roaming around the city. Even I'd turned into a zombie while eating my sandwich. Could the water or air be messing with people's minds? Was that how Holly's father intended to control the city?

After the Governor had entered the hotel, I stepped away from the horse, which reeked of manure.

"'Cause yer still the smartest man I know."

"Okay, that's a good start." I still enjoyed the comic relief. "But not enough to make me change my mind. Let's mull it over in a bar." I rushed down the block to escape from the hotel and the Governor's henchmen. My phone rang. Ganesh called to request a meeting. He discovered a clue to solve the puzzle but didn't want to talk over the phone. I agreed, since the government must be monitoring our conversations. We'd meet in St. Paul's Nightclub in half an hour.

When I turned around, Clint panted beside me. After drinking some whiskey, he said, "Ya gotta get that manuscript back."

"I'm sure you want to monitor Faith's every movement. No, you don't, you won't pull a fast one over me, you sneaky bastard. I'll watch her myself."

"Someone spilled ketchup on Fernando's gravestone."

"So, while I worked my head off, you went to the cemetery to cut the overgrowth and clean the headstone? Very considerate. No wonder he always praised you." Did Fernando give him the baseball card or did Clint filch it?

"Did he?" Clint sighed. "Seems in his will, he reserved some dough for a task. Quite a pile. Should've let me know and I would've taken care of it for zilch. Could've done something for him."

"Well, so you've been digging around and gotten results, too. Instead of doing your job, like finding out where those diamonds are hiding. As for Fernando's wishes, I'll pry them out of that lawyer's mouth." I ordered him to grab a taxi. Though I'd fired him, I didn't appreciate his spending company time on personal chores, even if the issues concerned Fernando. After listening to the babble, I had to find out more about my brother's will, which I'd never read. When the lawyer read it a few days after the burial, I trusted the expert with his job and didn't attend.

While Clint waved for a taxi, I called my beggar associate and had him wait behind St. Paul's Nightclub. As I stepped into the taxi, the Governor got into his limousine with his new girlfriend, who was about ten years younger than Holly. I had an associate tail him and take pictures. Just the evidence I'd need to undermine the Governor. When we arrived at the nightclub, I had Clint run to a nearby shop to buy a durian pie. In the back of the building, I met my associate. I had him tail Clint and gave him a hundred dollars for expenses. I would track every patch of dirt my ex-sidekick should step on. I would drag out his schemes. After I told my associate that the Governor would run for reelection, he spat and cursed the man. When Holly's father first came into office, he revised the state tax code and taxed income from alms at twenty-five percent while reducing the tax rate on capital gains. So I could understand my associate's anger though my state income tax had gone down. He'd organized SOAR, the Statewide Organization of Alms Receivers, campaigning to unseat the Governor and promote the group's agenda. To encourage him, I mentioned about another associate tailing the Governor and his new girl friend to take pictures.

In the nightclub, I ordered a shot of whiskey at the bar. Downed it in five seconds to quench my thirst and recharge my body, drained after the chase. I ordered another. Then relaxed and enjoyed the respite: the shadows, the whispers, the drinks. I called Clint and checked on his progress. Still waiting in line. I also called Fernando's lawyer, but he didn't answer and I decided to read my brother's will, which had been sitting in my office safe for several years.

On stage, the saxophonist crooned a tune I didn't recognize. Still, I enjoyed it. A prostitute in lingerie approached and solicited business. I declined. I should inform the bartender, but gave her a break. After all, she had to make a living, too.

When two tattooed bikers plopped down at the bar and contaminated the air with their breaths, I picked up the glass and walked to a booth. While passing the dance floor, I noticed a lady dancing alone and was kind enough to invite myself to join her. And surprise, Ms. Redhead greeted me. She must've followed me into the city, after losing the hooded thugs. I thanked her for luring away the thugs. She asked about my escape from the skunk and I improvised a tale of adventure and danger and heroics worthy of Homer.

I shoved the skunk behind my mind and enjoyed the dancing. I jigged, I hopped, I skipped; I dominated the dance floor. The two couples near the back surrendered the stage and even the bikers cheered.

When Clint returned, we shared with Ms. Redhead the durian pie, which tasted flat and failed to stimulate my taste buds. Still, whiskey, durian pie, a pretty lady, what more could I want? I had no idea what was coming. I didn't expect anything else to outdo the giant skunk adventure. Well, one of those nights.

I promised to take Ms. Redhead to The Usual Café to sample the best durian pies in town. I wagered she'd abandon apple pie after one taste. "Of course, I can make killer durian pies myself. So, if you ever have a craving, call me and I'd make a heavenly pie. But, of course, by appointments only. Clint here can start taking appointments, right now. But, if you just want some mean dancing, I'd be glad to contribute an evening. Well, this talking is making me thirsty. Let's have another round of whiskey."

Clint seemed awkward with the ladies at the bar and I could only pity him for refusing to enjoy life. I'd taken him to nightclubs several times, but he could never light a spark with the ladies, even when they flirted with him. And whenever an elegant middle-aged man or a handsome chap entered, the ladies would leave Clint. Since I'd prefer whiskey to his odor, I empathized with them.

I had fun at the nightclub, though what came later that night seemed surreal. At least, I was just holding my underwear and didn't have to clean the blood off the other clothing.

After an hour, when Ganesh didn't show up at the bar, we went under the drizzle to the hotel where the Governor had picked up his girlfriend. I asked for two rooms. Before going to my room, I assigned Clint to return to the nightclub and wait for Ganesh. I also had him check the image processing software's progress and prepare omelet for breakfast by seven o'clock. I insisted on getting the license plate number before breakfast.

***

While I was making love to Ms. Redhead, Ganesh charged into the room with a quantum mechanics textbook in this hand. "I did it. I did it. I found out the meaning of HYMN1. And, of course, on the side, I solved an optimization problem for another client."

I panted. I looked for my pants. Did he ever learn social protocols? Like don't charge into people's bedroom when they're making love. I didn't barge in when he was with Faith. And what's this bullshit about quantum mechanics? As I grabbed my underwear and pondered the long-term effects this trauma would have on my romantic life, Ms. Redhead flung away the blanket, drew a gun from her handbag and shot Ganesh. What a woman. I dropped my underwear as the geek grunted and fell to the ground. Never a dull moment in my life.

CHAPTER 29 - X

October 19

I searched the bedroom. I searched the kitchen. I stepped onto the back porch and the deer head greeted me. I dashed through the back yard and the marigold's aroma again attacked my nostrils. The fog hadn't lifted but the wind chime halted its dance. A folded piece of paper taped to it.

Molly had left, leaving her image in my mind.

You still love Dolly. Your eyes show it. I can't compete with her, even when, or maybe especially when, she's dead. When she had her eyes on a piece of cake, I had no chance of eating it. When she had her eyes on a man, I couldn't come close to him. Her death should've freed me from her shadow. But no, even from the grave, she held onto me. Go to Mr. Smith, my foster father, the deacon. He may know of doctors who can help regain your memory.

I studied the writing. I sniffed the paper. I tried to feel her emotions. But the wind chime's notes again scattered my thoughts.

I knocked on a neighbor's door but no one answered. I searched the canal for the vendors but couldn't find any gondolas. I scanned around the neighborhood and couldn't find a pedestrian or a dog.

Back in her bedroom I scanned the photos on the wall. She took most pictures alone. One with a middle-aged couple, probably Mr. and Mrs. Smith. None with Dolly. I didn't expect them to take pictures together. She took most pictures around this neighborhood, except one. Behind the dead minister's church.

***

I arrived at the church in the evening. The police had left but yellow tapes wrapped around the building, whose lighted cross hung thirty-feet in the air. So the minister had died several days earlier, not a month ago. So what? The crickets chirped and an owl hooted. Behind the church, a lighted shed stood against the woods. I approached, my steps crunching fallen leaves and cracking scattered twigs. The light flickered. Why was I searching for Molly? What would I say to her? I rushed forward to open the door.

I didn't find Molly. Only a boy sat in the corner. The boy who helped me escape from the military compound. Under his father's instruction, he got hired as an extra and waited for the chance to help me escape. Afterward, he returned here, where he had worked for Dolly before her death. So he did help me escape, at least in this reality.

"Who's your father?"

"He's in hiding. He'll look for you when it's safe."

After handing me Molly's message, he strolled into the night. In the message, she begged me to let her go. I should. I should continue my search for my past. I should go to Mr. Smith. Still, I searched the shed for other clues until daybreak.

I looked for Jack Conman in New Jersey but couldn't find him. Perhaps he never existed. Back in Molly's place, grilled deer and durian pie awaited me in the kitchen. While waiting for Molly to reappear at the front entrance, I ate the deer steak but didn't touch the pie. I tried to read but couldn't. I tried to plan my schedule but couldn't. Molly's, or Dolly's, image flickered in my mind.

I had to see Molly again. But what would I say to her? Perhaps I should go back to the movie set. Of course, Ingrid and Dr. Tang had left and I would find nobody there, not even myself.

What would keep me from abandoning this life? Nothing in this world. Maybe fear of the unknown. Maybe plain old laziness. A body in motion remains in motion, and similar nonsense.

***

I hadn't slept for three days.

Today, I visited Mr. Smith, a deacon and a trustee in Pastor McCoy's church. Molly considered Mr. and Mrs. Smith her parents and never asked about Dolly's family. Though I'm not a clone, I understand the parentless mood. Unlike her, I would like to know my parents.

As I approached the secluded community gate, I pulled out the fake ID card, hoping Conman hadn't swindled me, hoping for a miracle. I didn't want to use *Groucho*'s card since the agents were probably tracking it. Just before the gate, someone walked up beside me, grabbed my arm and said, "This way."

Molly. She kissed me.

I stopped.

She urged me forward.

The guard scanned my ID card and saluted me. At that moment, I appreciated the con man's skills. The armed guards on the watchtowers along the barb-wired fence didn't comfort me. If a rebel should drive a ton of TNT through the fence, the guards might kill the driver but not stop the truck. The guards, the first ones to spot the attack, probably would flee before the residents.

Birches and maples along the streets displayed their red-yellow foliages to remind me of the seasons lost. Children playing around the fountain in the middle of the community also hinted at my misplaced youth. Molly picked up a pear from a basket beside the fountain, gave it to me and said, "For residents. Compliment of the community management. Well, the HOA fee covers it."

"But you had other plans." I bit into the pear, the taste igniting warmth. I tried to recall a past instance when eating a similar pear had linked to laughter. I failed.

"That didn't work out. This is plan B."

"What about the shadow?"

"You'll help me overcome it. Just as I'll help you recover your memory."

I sighed when I should dance. I gasped when I should inhale. I shivered when her warmth should energize me. Was I with Molly or Dolly? Had I been Dolly's lover? Would Francisco the egomaniac triumph? And yet, he seemed the only constant.

Molly pulled me along the sidewalk lined with red-bricked houses. The children biked along the road and the parents chatted on porches. The homeless men, women and children near the abandoned factory and the rebels bombing police stations, they dwelled in another universe.

Molly whispered something but I couldn't make out her words.

When we arrived at the house, she put her hand over the scanner to open the front gate. The speaker above the front door broadcast a greeting. A middle-aged man in T-shirt and shorts opened the door. He stared at me for a second before turning to embrace Molly. I looked away from the mole on his nose as I shook his hand.

In the foyer, a dozen Chinese vases lined both sides of the wall. Mr. Smith recounted each one's history and showed me the Van Gogh collection in the living room. None looked familiar. None evoked images.

After scanning me for several seconds, he invited us to sit in the divan. "So, how long have you known Molly?" He poured brandy for us. When I said I was looking for Dolly, he said, "A bad girl. Never much cared for her. Forget about her. Molly here, that's different, a nice and decent girl."

"Were you expecting me?"

"Why, no... of course not... why'd I?" he said, the glass shaking in his hand. "But your face."

"He has a nice face. I like it," Molly said.

"Care to elaborate on what's the problem with my face?" I stared at the mole.

"Have we met somewhere before?"

We might have met in the other realities, but I didn't recall his face or his mole. Before we could continue discussing my face, a woman in her thirties wearing T-shirt and shorts walked down the stairs that curved along the living room wall. Pretty, prettier than Molly, looked like Francisco's neighbor but older. Her gaze pierced into my heart as if she recognized me from the dream. I must've met her before for her to appear in my dream. Yet, her face didn't trigger any images, sounds or smells.

"Mrs. McCoy, the dead minister's wife." Molly leaned toward me and whispered, "Isn't she pretty? She could've been my foster mom. And I would've liked that. But, oh well, life."

Mr. Smith kissed the lady and introduced her as if she were his wife of twenty years. I envied them. When I drank to life with Molly, Ingrid's image burst through my amnesia. I must have met her. I must have been in the hospital, not the prison. I must find her.

"Oh, I'm so happy for you." Mrs. McCoy hugged Molly and said, "I thought she'd never have a boyfriend. It isn't her fault. That Dolly, always dominating over her, always taking away her suitors. But that Dolly never loved anyone. Never knew anything about love. I'm so glad she's gone and Molly's free to live."

"Do you know who killed Dolly?" Who would want Dolly dead? Who would want the minister dead?

"Does it matter? She's dead and that's that. Let's bury the dead and forget them. We have to live our lives, not waste our youth," Mr. Smith said, taking Mrs. McCoy's hand and guiding her onto the sofa next to him. "Are you from the police? Or the Intelligence Agency?"

His eyes sparkled. He was probably referring to the dead minister rather than Dolly. Before I could answer, Molly said, "He thinks Dolly's prettier than me."

"You must replace your eyes. Anyone with a decent pair of eyes could see, even from a distance, that Molly's much prettier." He poured another glass of brandy.

When I expressed my condolences for Pastor McCoy's death, Mrs. McCoy thanked me and said, "If you'd come earlier, we would've invited you for the funeral reception. Soothing music. Palatable food. Professional MC. And, of course, Molly was very pretty in her turquoise dress."

"But I forgot the champagne. My fault." Mr. Smith caressed her hand.

"Maybe next time." I would have enjoyed the funeral reception. More so with the champagne.

"So, you aren't here to investigate McCoy's death? It's a shame, his death. The man made a decent living and had a comfortable life in his mansion. Could've bought several islands to retire in. Could've traveled the world in his yacht. But too bad. Well, that's life." Mr. Smith raised the glass as if to toast to the minister, but just finished his drink and said, "And getting shot in the balls. Damn nasty way to go. I don't recommend it. Of course, I don't recommend dying either."

"Oh, let's not talk about him. Let the dead rest in peace. Let's talk about you two. You should take a trip to the Bahamas and have fun. Get away from this dreary place and the fighting. And if things get worse, don't come back. You're both young so you can always start over."

"Oh, there, there. My poor darling." Mr. Smith embraced Mrs. McCoy and kissed her on the forehead and she snuggled in his bosom. I wanted to comfort her, to tell her that she and Mr. Smith still have many years ahead. In ten years, would I be embracing Molly while talking to a young couple?

"I bet you're too young to remember that at one time, we used clones as surrogate mothers. Even now, even after the government banned natural birth, clones lived as a lower caste. Sent to disable bombs, to mine plutonium, to contain nuclear leaks, to disinfect bio-hazard sites. What about their rights?" Mrs. McCoy wrapped Mr. Smith's arm around herself.

"She went to jail for protesting for our rights." Molly elbowed me and said, "I got to get something from my room. Make me a mango tea, please. Thanks." She jumped up, skipped across the living room and up the stairs, and disappeared behind the chandelier, leaving me alone to deal with the lovebirds.

The government didn't execute Mrs. McCoy or use PC and SP to nudge her beliefs, so the late minister must have golfed with federal and local bosses and might have nudged their decisions. How else could he spy for the Russians?

"Could I watch while people like Dolly bully clones like Molly? But I couldn't stop the executions even with my protests." She kissed Mr. Smith's hand, her tears dropping onto his fingers.

"Did Dolly come often, when she was alive?" I didn't wanted to interrupt them, but had to find out as much as possible about Dolly.

"Wasn't she involved in a covert operation? Just the sound of those two words makes you suspicious." Mr. Smith rubbed the mole with his index finger. "If you ask me, she might've been a double agent, working for both the Agency and the rebels and trying to get the better of both. So, one side wasted her. Probably had enough of her. Well, good riddance." He raised the glass and realized he had emptied it, but he still pretended to drink.

Before I could inquire about the covert operation, Mrs. McCoy jumped off the sofa and stood akimbo. "Hey, so you do like her more than Molly. Listen, forget about the dead. You ain't going to find a better girl than Molly."

Sure, they wanted to forget Dolly and Pastor McCoy, but they couldn't blame me for digging up the information. After all, I would like to have my past. When Mr. Smith realized I was probing into Dolly's life for my missing past, he exhaled and said, "So that's all, is it? Well, that's nothing. Don't worry about it."

He was hiding a secret. Not surprising, since he knew Dolly and the minister. I wouldn't have cared about their hide-and-seek, if it didn't involve me, but I had to unearth my past was buried among their crypts and catacombs.

"I know quite a few folks who'd lost his or her memory and recovered it just fine. And technology is advancing everyday. Who knows? Maybe one day, you can get whatever memory you want and delete what you don't want. No worries. Let me make a few calls to get the best doctors in town and have them fix you up."

Since he didn't want me to inquire about the minister's death, either he or Mrs. McCoy or Molly must've killed the holy man. If so, he would lie, bribe, or kill to protect the killer. I didn't care about their domestic dispute unless it involved the laptop. How would Francisco Guzman attack the problem? With his mouth?

Unable to extract any secrets, I glanced at the carpeted stairs, hoping Molly would rescue me. Mrs. McCoy promoted Molly's virtues, while the mole studied me. I itched to punch it, but controlled my fist. Instead, I praised the Renoir paintings, without understanding my gibberish.

When they made mango tea in the kitchen, I tried to eavesdrop on Mr. Smith's phone call, but the blender masked his voice. I put my nose to the fish tank and scared away the goldfish. The built-in speaker broadcast a citywide manhunt for Pastor McCoy's killer, a fugitive whose features and built resembled mine. The news would confirm Mr. Smith's suspicions. At the bottom of the stairs, I found a piece of paper with the word "Descartes." I had read his book in the fake hospital and debunked his thinking. What linked him to Mr. Smith? No, not him but the minister and therefore the laptop. I must find my laptop. When Molly didn't appear after two minutes, I tried to eavesdrop again, but the grinder still growled. If only I could tap into his mobile phone and listen to the conversation. I checked for police cruisers outside the house, debating whether to leave without Molly. When a patrolman holding a rifle passed the living room window, I waved and greeted him. He nodded and strolled down the sidewalk, brushing away a branch with the gun barrel.

At the front door I grasped the knob and turned but returned to the bottom of the stairs. The fragrance of mango filled the living room. I reread the note and recognized my handwriting, but of course, I couldn't remember having written the word. Perhaps, "Descartes" is a code word, like HYMN1.

Molly came down the stairs holding a laptop. She grabbed my hand, pulled me across the living room and whispered, "Don't just stand there. Come on, let's get out of here."

She must have kept my photo to be able to recognize me after more than half an hour.

"He's making a call—"

"He's contacting specialists to help me regain my memory." I followed her, glancing through the window for the police.

"Not likely the police can help regain your memory, especially the detectives in homicide. Even a profiler couldn't do it." She opened the front door and inspected the street before stepping out.

Outside, the fog had lifted, but the clouds lingered above the houses. I peeped through the kitchen window. Inside, the lovebirds embraced and kissed. When I bid Molly farewell, she said, "I was hoping we don't have to say goodbye. You've lost your memory and must relearn everything. I can help. I can guide you and support you."

I wasn't going to bring her along. Maybe I didn't want to drag her into the mess, a noble excuse. Maybe I preferred to travel alone, an honest excuse. Maybe I didn't trust her, probably the truth. Not that I knew anyone well here. On what ground should I trust her? On what ground should I trust anyone, before the facts could tip the scale?

"I understand you're suspicious of everyone, but give me a chance and I'll show I'm trustworthy. But you'll have to take the first step."

The wind swept up dogwood leaves to remind me of another autumn in a different world. I couldn't recall Dr. Tang's nose or Ingrid's eyes. The dogwood outside Francisco's office had also shed its leaves. Autumn had arrived in both dream and reality, and I appreciated and despised the synergy between them.

A police cruiser arrived at the front gate and the policemen swiped their ID cards over the scanners.

After I agreed to take Molly along, she bought a jacket, a wig, a pair of sunglasses and a tube of face cream in the community shop, while I waited at the back entrance. With the gadgets, I went into the community center men's room. I rubbed the cream on my face. I fitted the wig onto my head and put on the sunglasses. I wore the jacket. I came out as a hillbilly from Whatever. How did I know about Whatever? I might have been there before the accident.

"How long had they been having the affair?"

"They were high school sweethearts. Would've been married if not for—"

"But the minister didn't seem charming. If anything, he's annoying."

"Richly annoying."

"I forgot that some kinds of annoying can be attractive. But she—"

At the front entrance, we passed the police cruiser, which charged toward Mr. Smith's house. I greeted the guard, scanned the ID card and went through the gate.

"She married the pig because she loved my father." Molly scanned her card. "He was very poor, so she married the rich minister. She managed to persuade her husband to give her a hefty monthly allowance, which she'd transfer to my father's bank account. And she'd give him diamond rings, pearl necklaces, Renaissance paintings, Persian coins, and bottles of Yquem. So, my father became rich and started his businesses: biotechnology, consumer electronics, real estates, financial engineering, whatever. He never looked back. All the while, they continued their affair."

We entered the subway station elevator.

"I didn't expect the minister to be so generous."

"As I said, he's a pig."

Her face contorted again. I didn't inquire about her comment and when she held my hand, I grasped Ingrid's. The surveillance camera on the ceiling swiveled and pointed at me, while the elevator descended and I studied the metal doors. The elevator door opened onto the ticketing booth and the heat slammed into my face. No attendants, or other passengers. Only a TV, surveillance cameras and ticketing machines.

Molly used her ID to buy two tickets to New Einstein. We would leave in two weeks on the Intracity Rail System after I took care of business here. The name New Einstein reminded me of cheesecake, its gooey texture. My mouth, like that of Pavlov's dog, watered. "Maybe before I lost my memory, I ate some scrumptious cheesecake there."

"Not only you. Most people connect New Einstein with cheesecake. When we get there, we'll sample some world-famous cheesecake in a shop along Cheesecake Boulevard. But don't confuse it with the Cheesecake Boulevard here in Fermat's Last Stand. The cheesecakes here are imitations. Don't even try them." She inserted her ID card and went through the gate.

A carriage waited for us at the platform and I stepped into it and sat next to her. "That'd be nice. After that, we can continue to run from the law. Do you believe I didn't kill the minister?"

"I wish you did. But no." She entered the destination on the side panel. "Couldn't imagine you killing him for the laptop." She handed me the laptop. "See, I'm trustworthy. Here's your gift for trusting me."

So in this reality, the minister visited me and stole my laptop. I met Dr. Tang and Ingrid in the hospital. Maybe.

"Did he flaunt his thieving skills, proclaiming how he'd stolen my laptop while I turned into a zombie?" The minister must have reviewed my diary entry. Yet, I hadn't recovered my memory when I scribbled those notes and couldn't have divulged any secrets. The man wasted his time. What secret did I have that the Russians want?

Molly opened her notebook and scrolled through her diary and stared at the pages for a while before saying, "Several weeks ago, he sneaked into the church with this laptop. I followed to poison him, but decided to steal this laptop. To find dirt on him. But, I only came across your journal entry. At that instant, I knew I'd found a fellow diarist."

"Just half a dozen bullet holes. No signs of poison." She might've shot him before or after taking the laptop.

The doors closed and the music sounded through the speakers. The carriage moved while the fifty-inch TV broadcast the minister's murder.

"I was going to give him a nasty stomachache and diarrhea, not kill him. But I approve."

Her joy and bitterness, which stirred my entrails, might even revive my memory. I must have loved and hated, laughed and cried; I must have dreamed about flying to the moon.

"Don't you want to know?" she said.

"Only if you want to tell me."

"Like I said—"

"I'm a slow learner."

She looked through the window as if reflecting on a past moment. The twitch under her eye, the tip of an iceberg, beckoned me, but I didn't tread closer.

"I'd never leave you," she said.

I couldn't respond and dared not. I surveyed the tunnel outside the carriage, looking for a light in the dark, a light to shine into my past. But no luck.

After the escape, I vowed to recover my memory even though Dr. Tang, or whoever he was, was no longer treating me. As in the hospital or prison, I refused to allow any anthill or snail to block my path, to stall me from my goalpost. I would find my past. I must.

The subliminal message in the music urged me to attend the celebration on Government Day, reminding me to practice singing the national anthem beforehand. On TV, the broadcaster urged citizens to look for the minister's killer. Mr. Smith would protect Molly and probably not report me to the police.

Back in the water villa, I tried to turn off the TV but couldn't find a switch or a button or a remote controller and we had to listen to the news while eating dinner.

"After I recover my memory, I'd want to help others," I said, "not like the hideous Francisco, but solving problems that'd change people's lives for the better."

"Tell me about this Francisco you hate so much. From my experience, you only hate one person that much. No, not your spouse or your lover, but yourself. Your greatest enemy is always yourself."

"Do you hate yourself?"

"I love Dr. Tang."

"So you hate Dolly, your alter-ego?"

"I had a lover, but he was murdered." She put down the glass. She pushed away the plate. Her eyes twinkled but tears didn't roll down her cheeks. A minute later, she picked up the glass, drank the champagne. "Do you think of yourself as a good person?"

"Maybe the first thing I'd do is to eliminate this war between the government forces and the rebels. But the difficult part is what happens afterward. For one thing, we must get rid of these twenty-four hour announcements."

"Don't even think of crossing out Sunday night football, or you'll have another revolution. Never touch those sacred cows."

"On the other hand, I don't want Francisco's rotten world either. Of course, we must allow people the freedom to be scumbags, parasites, and sewer rats. How else could there be freedom?"

She stared at the darkness outside the living room window. She was still searching for the light, as I was my past. Maybe, we both would fail. She put her face close the windowpane and her reflection fell on the glass. Her eyes gleaming. Her cheeks taut.

She didn't speak. The melody pulsated, the newscaster droned, and the fire crackled. My heart pounded against my chest. But she didn't speak. The fog outside had become so thick that a gray current like a specter drifted across the window. I opened a window to let the fog into the house. I breathed in the night air. Outside, the crickets chirped above the murmur of the canal's currents. I wanted to talk to Molly and to touch her soul but didn't know how. I wanted to care for her but didn't know how. I wanted to flee from the law but didn't want to abandon her.

I shut the window and was about to go for a walk but when I turned around, Molly stood before me and said, "I've got to tell you something."

I studied her voice, heavy and viscous. I expected a revelation, such as she's a rebel, a man or an android, or she had killed someone, maybe the minister cum thief. She trusted me enough to reveal her secret, I was sure. She probably considered me a friend or even more. Whatever filth I could imagine wouldn't bother me. However, I feared those I couldn't imagine.

I checked the windows and doors and after locking them, I returned to the dining room and poured two glasses of champagne. "Should I sit down and take a deep breath?"

"Some pains are so deep that they've become part of me." She leaned against the fireplace and finished the glass of champagne and I poured her more.

"Well, I couldn't even remember my pains. Of course, I'm no masochist. But some pains make you alive." I put the bottle on the mantelpiece and brushed the dust off the photos.

"I could take a break from life. And live in a surreal or even dreamlike world for a while."

"Did Dolly feel your pain? I heard clones could do that."

"Just as we must die alone, we must also bear our pains alone." She removed a photo from the frame and threw it into the fire.

The fire caught the photo's corner, browning the edge and the left arm, and gnawed its way to the opposite corner. The ash fell to the bottom. She drank her champagne.

I had searched my mind for a familiar face, a familiar tune, and a familiar aroma when I woke up not knowing whether I was X or Y or Z and when I read the diary not knowing whether it was fantasy or fiction. I couldn't grasp this world of clones and androids, of cities like Felast, of TVs that wouldn't turn off, of rebels and government forces brutalizing each other as well as civilians. While I related my thoughts and feelings, she held my hand as if trying to remove the pain and I pretended she was Ingrid.

"You'll get used to this place. We all do."

"I hope not." Had Dr. Tang and Ingrid, if they should exist, gotten used to this place? Since they had grown up here, why shouldn't they? I had grown up here also, but without my memory, I entered a nightmare.

The elevator music filled the house, but my thoughts prevented me from tuning to the subliminal message. I hoped my mind could withstand SP.

I had read Erich Fromm's *Escape from Freedom* in the fake hospital and was going to discuss with Dr. Tang whether most people would prefer security to freedom. The rebellion seemed to contradict this premise, but only about two percent of the population had joined the fight. Without my memory, I dreaded the future, its surprises and revelations, so I could understand why someone would give up freedom to live in a safe, stable and prosperous society. But how much?

Twenty-four hour broadcast for up-to-the-minute news and government directives. Subliminal Projection and Pavlovian Conditioning to design thoughts, emotions, attitudes and values. Android policemen that scan ID cards to identify a pedestrian and retrieve criminal records, financial histories, family trees and genetic codes. Surveillance cameras to examine bedroom activities.

She kissed me and I searched for familiar sensations to lead me to my past. The soft lips, the warm breath. Something stirred in my memory. I had kissed her before, but that was Dolly. I must find out my relationship with the latter and how Pratt fitted in.

On the sofa I embraced her while the clock ticked, the fire crackled and the crickets chirped.

"I should but didn't have the courage to kill the minister." She poured another glass of champagne, wrapped a blanket around her legs and snuggled against me, and after emptying the glass, said that while she was a young girl, Pastor McCoy had raped her several times.

CHAPTER 30 - FRANCISCO

September 25, 2011 (2)

About six months ago, after I broke up with a young lady, she tried to commit suicide. I couldn't sleep for two nights and had stopped dating for a month. But the other night, Ms. Redhead shooting Ganesh, trumped my adventures.

"Take it easy," I said. "I'm pissed and embarrassed also and he's certainly a jerk. We can sue him for our emotional traumas, but you don't have to kill him."

She ignored me and again pointed the gun at Ganesh, so I leaped over and grabbed the gun. Two naked bodies wrestling for the gun while the geek groaned in pain. After I yanked the gun from her, Ganesh, his left hand holding the physics textbook with a bullet hole and his right arm dripping blood, staggered out of the room and urged me to follow. I stepped into slippers, grabbed a blanket to cover my body and ran after him with backpack in hand.

Clint didn't answer when I knocked on his door, and the beggar guarding him had disappeared. With the skeleton key, I opened the door to an empty room.

The maid in the hallway ran into the janitor's closet when I grabbed a bathrobe from her cart. I replaced the blanket with the bathrobe and strapped on the backpack while Ganesh took a towel to wrap his wounded arm. We skipped the elevator and went down the backstairs, where we met a British couple who greeted us and told us how much they love America. I bade them a pleasant trip and suggested the durian pie at The Usual Café. When we exited the hotel through the backdoor into the drizzle, someone called, "Hey, look this way." The VE messenger pointed a pistol at us from behind a coupe.

"What's going on? Isn't it illegal to carry guns in the city?" I didn't have a status report, but maybe he came to warn me against trusting myself. "If you want an update—"

"Get out of the way. Scoot. I need a clear view." He aimed the laser at Ganesh's forehead. "By the way, get some clothes on. The sight of your body sickens me."

"Did he steal your girlfriend?" I shouldn't annoy my client, but wasn't going to let the Messenger shoot an unarmed and wounded man. Without my nunchuks, I'd have to use my head. Not literally, of course. I stepped aside and said, "Don't shoot me. I still want to retrieve those diamonds." I walked along the sidewalk toward him.

"Are you going to abandon your friend like a spineless—" Ganesh said.

"When did we become friends? And my spine is fine the way it is." I untied the sash, ready to knock the Messenger's gun from his hand. Before I could release the sash, a set of headlights drilled into my eyes. As I blocked the light with my forearm, a sanitation truck charged down the street toward us. No, toward the Messenger. The engine roared and the smell of burnt rubber reached my nose despite the drizzle.

The Messenger turned his head and dodged to the side. The truck smashed into the coupe, reducing it by a half, and splashed water onto the Messenger.

The driver thrust out his head out and said, "Delivery." The grocer cum cabdriver who looked like the hospital guard in my dream, he threw me a package, must be thanking me for patronizing his bodega and cab. I caught it and asked whether he also picks up garbage, dances in a strip club, mows the lawn and tutors high school students. He praised my outfit and shot twice at the Messenger and turned the truck to chase after him. When the Messenger jumped onto the sidewalk, the truck slammed into a wagon, ran over a puddle and drove over the curb. The driver fired two more shots.

From the pile of scrap I picked up the Messenger's gun in case either madman should return. When I turned to check on Ganesh, he was running across the street into Central Park. The coward. I followed him onto a lighted walkway that guided me toward the interior but the wind and the rain thrust against me. I pushed against the cold shower. Homeless men and women sheltering under trees clapped and whistled to encourage me.

Do I love Faith enough to change my lifestyle? Along the dark path with rain on my skin, I shivered, chill slithering through my spine. For her, I'd plunge into deeper waters and scale higher mountains. Of course, Francisco Guzman could overcome any obstacle. I just couldn't limit my joy, my adventures, my conquests and become that amnesiac, living like a zombie in that wasteland, that prison. Even the thought nauseated me.

Several minutes later, I caught up with Ganesh on a flagstone path and walked alongside him. "How long have you known Faith?" I held the package in my mouth and tightened the sash around my waist.

"Every time I see her," he mumbled, holding the towel over his wound, "her smile would remind me of the first time I met her."

"Never mind. Let's talk about the manuscript, instead." I'd rather eat ice-cream with pickles than listen to how he'd made love to Faith. After learning he'd stolen the manuscript, I should ditch him. Of course, I didn't trust Clint when working with him, but at least my former sidekick scoured the trashcans. With Ganesh, he might swing from tree to tree or jump out of a birthday cake. Sure, I relished surprises. But I couldn't work with a maniac. Still, after working with him, I appreciated his mad genius and I could use his help to juggle these puzzles. Without the psychosis.

We reach the stage where I'd first met him and the drizzle stopped. On stage, actors performed *Romeo and Juliet* to an audience that'd despite the rain filled more than ninety-percent of the seats. Although I'd meet with my beggar-associates in the park at night, I'd never enjoyed any performances. We preferred to meet among the trees, where we could observe passersby, rather than the other way around.

When we stopped, several beggars gathered around us waiting for a strip show, but I shooed them away. To tell the truth, I could tolerate reeking of sewerage if not for standing half-naked in the park.

"It was a moonlit summer night, the warm breeze whispering through the gingko leaves and the crickets humming their iambic tunes." Ganesh turned his eyes toward the stage. "A memorable night, like no other."

"As I said, the manuscript. I knew what you did. Aha, gotcha. Well, cough it up, nerd." I slipped the package under my arm and tried to grab his jacket with the other hand. But he stepped aside and continued to watch the play on stage. I had to stop him, interrupt his rambling, his daydreaming. Maybe, I should shake him loose and depend on number one. He didn't even thank me for scooping his butt out of the sewer. Next time, I'd let the Messenger shoot him.

Two years ago, when an enemy poisoned me with cyanide, I had to choose between dying and begging the dandy, a sadist and a genius, for the antidote. Fortunately, after I'd seduced his girlfriend, she betrayed him and stole the remedy. Close call. I didn't want to kowtow to him, which would scar my soul and dull life's pleasures. I should give the lady, whom I hadn't seen for more than a year, a call and invite her for dinner. If I could find her number or email.

"Every time I see her, I'd smell that fragrance, the fragrance of the gingko leaves mixed with her scent. And I'd be tunneling through a wormhole, back to that night, back to that experience, that warm, soft breeze against my skin. And the joy, the excitement." He loosened the towel and checked his arm. Fortunately, the bullet only grazed his skin after piercing the textbook. He put on antibiotics and wrapped his arm in a handkerchief and I tied a knot.

"Tell me about the manuscript. What's so important about it? Why'd you steal it from me and give it to Faith? Yes, I know. Is that why they ransacked my apartment? Is that why they shot at me? Is that why they tried to grab my laptop? And what about that stinky giant skunk. Come on, I want the truth, nothing but the truth. So spill it out." The wind passed over my wet skin, cooling the surface and raising goose bumps behind my neck. I shivered but grabbed onto the bathrobe.

"Her voice, like a wind chime's melody, mingled with the nocturnal symphony. And every time I hear the whispering wind and the chattering crickets, I'd recall her soft skin again me. And warmth would rise through my body."

"What do you think I am, Freud?" Without the nunchuks I'd custom-ordered from Japan, I couldn't drum his head and shut him up. "Why are you confessing all your complexes? I already know you're psychotic and neurotic and delusional and obsessive compulsive." As the wind whistled through the park, the goose bumps had disappeared and I itched to punch the nerd in the arm and wake him from his trance.

"What do you care about the fake manuscript? If you want to help us locate the genuine one, let me know and we can brainstorm. I'm sure you have the resources and connections to find it. Faith and I would appreciate it. We planned to get a place near Central Park and live together. I would've preferred a place in Long Island with an ocean view, but Manhattan would do."

"You betrayed me and stole it from me." I thrust my nose into his face.

He swung his nose to push my face aside. "I would betray anyone for Faith. Including you. Maybe, especially you. What is a manuscript, even a holy text, compared to love? Please don't take offense. It's not about you. It's never about you. It's about her. It's always about her. I'd do anything for her."

"What's this manuscript to her?" An enemy must've sent me the fake manuscript to frame me. Or to put me in the crossfire and test my dodging skills. Fortunately, Ganesh stole it and diverted the fanatics' attention. Maybe, sometimes two wrongs do make a right. Long live double negations.

"And FYI, she'd do anything for me also. Like helping me start a company, our company, and hiring people like you. Not only with her money but also with her connections. If you want a position, hand in your resume. I'm building a dream team and only want the DaVincis and Einsteins in my field. I can see you as an analyst, maybe a software developer, but you got to be a team player and shed the Prima Dona attitude."

"What'd I care about your pipe dreams and delusions of grandeur? Don't insult me by pretending you qualify to boss me around. Not a delusional chance. You hear me?" The rain-soaked bathrobe chilled my body and I should've looked for a jacket, instead of standing half-naked near the stage. "And why are all these bullets after you? What kind of shady businesses were you into?"

"Shouldn't pick up women who shoots at your boss. Makes managing you so much harder."

"Stop passing the blame. She's probably one of your old flames, who you cheated on with a younger girl or swindled out of millions. She aimed for your heart. Lucky your quantum mechanics textbook took the bullet. Maybe I should also carry one for protection. Though the Messenger would've shot through any textbook, macroeconomics or neurobiology."

"She looked like a professional. Maybe, they're trying to prevent me from revealing the meaning of HYMN1. Like in spy thrillers."

"Well, then, forget about your wound and spill it pronto. And afterward, stay away so they don't accidentally shoot me. I still have to break the rest of the code."

"Here, when there is a thesis, there is always an antithesis. According to Hegel—" he said.

"Didn't you take Communications 101 in college? Cut the crap, will you? Show me the result. I don't care about your Theory of All Nonsense. As a coworker, I'm again advising you to lose the theory and face reality. Or one day, you'd be happily cutting your wrist." I scorned theories devoid of applications, concepts alien to reality, dreamers lost in the clouds, and I would've fired him just as I'd Clint. Yet, Ganesh has skills I could exploit on other projects. As a leader, I'm always seeking talents and leveraging skills.

"Are you convinced yet I'm a bloodhound that won't give up until I corner my prey?" He tooted his horn and exalted himself to the heavens, while I waited for the solution. If I had to write down his monologue, with ninety-nine percent superlatives and florid adjectives, I would've run out of memory in a data warehouse. The amateur, the egotist, the idiot. I removed from this dialogue his self-promotions, which revealed his delusion of grandeur. After all, this diary could become a bestseller and the readers wouldn't care about his self-aggrandizement. I should've brought one of my awards, maybe that statuette, to exorcise him.

Ganesh took out the meadow painting and said, "Voila!" He turned it over to reveal the word "HYMN1" on the back. I should've checked it when Dr. Tang showed the amnesiac the list on the back of that painting. Sure enough, the amnesiac and I must solve the same code, to decode the list of elements. With a breakthrough two days before the second deadline, I leaped up and dropped the package into a puddle.

October 2, 2011 (1)

After resting for several days and eating the mental hospital food, I'd begun to recuperate from the flu. My neighbor's tragedy still grieved and pained me. The roses in her apartment had probably withered without anyone trashing them. I would've gone to her apartment to tidy up the place if I'd been strong enough to leave the mental hospital.

Three days ago, I got out of bed and opened the package the grocer had given me and examined the contents: seven photos of a car accident. Near Hudson Street, a sedan hit my neighbor. The photos worsened my fever and the chill returned to my body. Another delirious day before I could get out of bed. When I again looked at her lying in a pool of blood, my head pounded. Only after drinking the muck from Ganesh could I focus on the images. Four weeks had passed since taking on the project.

Another punishment from the sadist. Someone was kicking my butt and I couldn't flee. Worse, the coward who didn't dare to face me was harming my friends, as she'd promised. My neighbor had moved in two years ago and I'd bought her roses for her house warming party. Sometimes, she'd even come to my apartment to clean up the mess and cook for me. But I didn't want that. I didn't want a maid. I wanted a friend. I only dated her after breaking up with Holly and I would've liked her to be my girlfriend, but a breakup would end our friendship as well. Though my neighbor, unlike Holly, couldn't appreciate my work, I treasured her friendship. Now, because of me... I vowed revenge, but it wouldn't turn back the clock. I'd still blame myself.

I called the hospital and found out she'd survived the accident but was in a coma. She might or might not wake up. I hung up the phone. I locked the door. I drank. I blamed myself for missing another deadline.

I tried but I failed. After Ganesh had revealed the painting's secret, I'd been working everyday to solve the *elements-code*. I must avoid another disaster. That night, after I returned to the mental hospital half-naked, the flu attacked me and weakened my mind. Worse, in my delirium, I hadn't dreamed of the amnesiac, so he couldn't help me. Though Ganesh worked day and night, he couldn't decipher the list.

Though the clue had appeared in the dream, I still rejected intuition or revelation. How did Fernando plant the clue, if indeed he did? Had he hypnotized me so I would dream of the clue? He must've informed the mysterious client about the dream diary. Otherwise, how could she know I'd dream about it? Of course, someone might be shuffling my thoughts.

This morning, I awoke to the day before the third deadline, agitated. The client probably would hurt Suzie or Holly but I vowed to stop the scumbag. I ground the beans to make coffee. I cut the durian to make the pie. I ate and drank to nourish my body.

While Ganesh worked on the elements-code, I asked for direction to the Underground Temple. The Priest's fanatics could see and hear as much as my beggar associates and I needed help to search for Holly. I also had to find out what the Chief-Frenetic knew about the mysterious caller. I must hunt the rascal down and find out his role in this hide-and-seek.

After shrugging his shoulder, Ganesh urged me not to persecute the Priest. "Sure, you aren't very considerate. But, after all, you trespassed on their holy ground so of course they tried to offer you as a sacrifice. Me, I try to grasp their beliefs so I can avoid stepping on tails."

"Like trying to steal their Holy Scripture. That's certainly not stepping on tails. Hey, just because you're petty, don't impose your biases on me. Did I say I was going to harass him or to avenge myself? I only want info from him. I might kick his butt, but only to squeeze data out of his brain."

"Yes, yes, you don't discriminating when kicking butts and boxing ears. Always the pragmatist, always so utilitarian." He asked for caviar and truffle from the supermarket.

"Hey, don't you ever go shopping? That kid always bring you grocery." He'd left the mental hospital only to visit Faith. Whatever he needed, either he bought online or had the lackey get for him. "Anyway, I'm not your errand boy."

"I hate going to the supermarket or the mall or—"

"Or anywhere except Faith's place. You've never been to a concert, I'm sure. You're the laziest guy I've ever known. Very soon, your muscles will wither away."

"I was in the concert hall once, when it was empty. Studying the acoustics of the hall." He enlarged the window on his laptop where he was playing an online chess game and moved his knight for a double check. "And last summer, Faith and I watched the sunrise in Hawaii, and I imagined the fusion of hydrogen into helium creating the brilliant sunlight. And under the sunlight, the plants photosynthesized, converting carbon dioxide into oxygen, nurturing the plant cells. But the next day a cold front confronted the warm front, rain from morning until evening. How I enjoyed that vacation."

Oh, this mad, mad world. How much longer would I have to suffer this maniac? Oh, Faith, why did you send him to torture me? I was willing to share my fee with you. I had to escape the words soiling my mind and I decided to have a drink in the bar, to purify my soul.

"Do me a favor and get them. Will you? Don't worry. I'll pay you back. And if you see nice strawberries and grape tomatoes, please get me four pounds. I also need more antioxidants. You can skip those carbohydrates, unless you come across whole wheat. Thank you a whole bundle."

At that moment, I almost preferred the amnesiac's wasteland. Almost. I would've kicked Ganesh's butt from one cell to another if I weren't rushing to find Holly.

When I left the mental hospital and stepped on chewing gum, a breeze brushed my face, mist and car exhaust greeted me, and a bag slipped over my head. With pain in the back of my head, I passed out.

CHAPTER 31 - X

November 1

This morning, the citizen guards chanting "no more crimes and no more diseases" outside the motel woke me from my dream. After finding a note to go to If So, Inc., I reviewed the diary in the iPad. How did I get to the motel? Still, I remembered I was at the villa. So, the fluctuations must be dying down and reality converging toward equilibrium. I phoned Molly, but no one answered.

At breakfast, the hotel manager reminded me to attend church this Sunday. The guards had expelled two households for not attending the community worships and were gathering burglars, vandals and gamblers for this month's execution. So, Pythagorean Triangle, no longer a sanctuary for vagrants, had copied other communities.

Later, I took the subway downtown. When I exited the station near Cheesecake Boulevard, the glass buildings of If So, Inc., a defense contractor with the Intelligence Agency as its main client, towered before me. The main building's lattice structure extended toward the heavens, its upper levels hidden in the fog. In the plaza between the station and the main entrance, security cameras on two rows of lampposts turned and focused on me while the smell of steel and disinfectant greeted me. A movie star walking down the red carpet. Except my fans sat in front of monitors running image recognition software. At the entrance, four gun barrels above the door pointed at me and probably ready to put a hundred holes through my body in five seconds. I passed through the revolving door where more surveillance cameras followed me to the security checkpoint. I passed through the X-ray scanner and at the other end the speaker overhead greeted me. I inserted the ID card from Jack Conman—reserving Rick's for emergencies—and went through the security gate after the screen displayed my picture, which, along with the fake information, I had downloaded into the Intelligence Agency database two days ago.

Three nights ago, after we had made love, Molly showed me how to hack into the most secure databases, a useful skill in case the identity thief had conned me. She could've acquired the skill through Dolly's generosity or by osmosis. Sometimes, I probably could learn almost anything by osmosis. If I should ever see Dr. Tang again, I would have to ask for an explanation.

Several nights ago, while I searched through my original laptop for missing files, I realized falling into the deep no longer bothered me. Drifting among the waves no longer disturbed me. I might have to swim across the sea alone, but the thought of Molly in my arms would accompany me through the surfs. What Ingrid and Dr. Tang had promised, she had given me.

Again, I imagined living by the hillside, this time with Molly. The same maple, the same warbler, the same canyon. However, the fog outside the bedroom window snapped me out of the dream. I feared another betrayal, another revelation, another earthquake. At some point, I might give up. Still, I would seek happiness just as I would look for my identity. I would risk happiness with Molly.

Pastor McCoy didn't remove the diary entry. He probably wanted to read my confession without having to extract it from me. He had violated my privacy, which this land didn't protect, but since he was dead, I forgave him. Still, that night I raised my glass and toasted to Molly's life and the dozen bullets in the minister, especially those between his legs.

While I waited for the elevator in the lobby, music drifted into my ears and the subliminal message urged me to support the military in defending against domestic and foreign enemies. In the elevator, the TV showed how the rebels had tortured men and raped women and how Jamaican spies had tried to steal military and commercial secrets. I searched for dust on the screens but, even with my bionic eyes, couldn't find a speck.

I exited onto a silver hallway on the one hundred and thirty-seventh floor, where the smell of steel and disinfectant again assailed my nostrils. My bionic ears couldn't hear any sound. I inserted the fake ID card and entered the corporate library where ten rows of computers greeted me. I chose the fifth computer in the fifth row and logged in.

I searched through the online scientific journals, trade magazines and national newspapers for Dr. Fujimoto and found out he had invented cold-fusion alone. Nowhere could I find a co-inventor. I had hoped I could discover my name through this association. But no, I would remain anonymous, and must forgo my achievement. I had to accept this new reality, created to snub me and strip me of my identity and any iota of hope.

When I scanned Dolly's photo and searched through the database, I found both Dolly and Molly. I controlled my fingers and didn't open Molly's file. As expected, Dolly's top-secret file needed a higher-level password. I took out the security device, which would've cost me twenty thousand dollars if not for my benefactor, and stared at the display, the number on which changed every fifteen seconds. Do or die. I inhaled and entered the real-time code from the security device. If Conman had conned me, I might soon be breathing in poison gas or absorbing high-energy neutrons. A smiley face appeared on the screen to indicate the database was checking the password. I tapped my fingers while the seconds seemed to last for hours.

The library door opened and someone shuffled into the room. I ducked behind the monitor, hoping the intruder wouldn't spot me. But footsteps came my way and when they stopped, I pretended not to notice his presence, expecting him to return the courtesy. He greeted me, pulled out the trashcan and replaced the trash bag. I nodded and pretended to enter data. He walked away and continued his work. The icon was still spinning after he had walked down the aisle. My index finger tapped on the tabletop. Even with my superpower, I wouldn't be able to dodge bullets from several dozen rifles hidden in those walls.

After the icon disappeared, a blank screen greeted me. My legs fidgeted. When the janitor left, I stared at the blank screen waiting for poison gas. Then, the homepage appeared.

Before my car accident, Dolly secured some data, codename CP, that a double agent had stolen from Russia. Soon after the transaction, she disappeared and the police found her body three weeks later. One shot in the head, clean and professional. Nothing unusual for an agent. The double agent confirmed the transfer and soon returned to Russia. Did he shoot Dolly and either destroy the data or keep the files for future sales? No, Intelligence Agents pursued a rogue agent, Pratt Calhoun, who probably had killed Dolly and stolen the data.

Pratt Calhoun—Stubble. So he exists.

Pratt had probably visited me only to locate the goods. Did I kill Dolly? Maybe, as Dr. Tang had said, recovering the past would destroy my future. Still, I couldn't fold my hands and let the past slip away. Whatever secret lurked in my past I had to dig it up.

Pratt had no associates. He never mingled with fellow coworkers but had helped the Agency eliminate five double agents. Loner or not, he fathered about a dozen children. After writing down Pratt's old address, I pursued another lead.

I scanned the hospital guard's photo into the system. An intelligence agent named Beta. Though no evidence implicated him, he must also be hunting for the CP data, or wouldn't be monitoring Pratt or me or both. Probably assigned to recover or destroy the files. Nothing interesting about him, just a clone of Alpha, who was murdered as a boy.

The fake guard could also be Gamma, a rogue lieutenant in the rebel force, who joined only six months ago but already bombed several police stations and government offices. He had tried but failed to seize power from the rebel leader. Intelligence Agents confirmed through hair samples that he was another clone of Alpha, but Agent Beta didn't know of him before those bombings.

Even with the newfound information on Dolly, Pratt, Beta and Gamma, I couldn't figure out my part in their schemes, much less my identity. Still a nobody in this wasteland searching for the past. Could I just be trying to avoid reality? Why should the past matter if I couldn't create a future? This instinct, this determination, maybe born of the will to life, the will to survive, continued to compel me forward, the next step, the next piece of the puzzle. Even while the ground in front continued to shift.

In the police record I found the accident report, which didn't name the dead driver. Dolly owned the car, but by then she had died. The surveillance cameras had recorded, moments before the crash, a black sedan pursuing this car. I couldn't find the sedan's license number in the transportation department database. Pratt or Beta was probably chasing me.

I left If So, Inc. and look for Pratt's home in Temporal Loop, a ghetto in Felast. The address led to a red-bricked building with fire-escape stairs along the outer wall. I opened the creaking door and entered a dim hallway where a light bulb flickered above my head. The steps on the stairs creaked as if about to cave in. With every step, I expected a rat to jump out, but only met spider webs. When I reached the eleventh floor, a droopy-eyed man tried to sell me drugs. I declined and walked down the hallway, surprised that the community hadn't executed him. Drawn-out moans emerged from an apartment. Outside Pratt's unit, I met a rat loitering next to the door, maybe waiting for the door to open.

No breathing on the other side of the door, only a clock ticking. I knocked and waited. No footsteps. I twisted the doorknob to open the door, which pushed through a spider web and scared away the host. The rat scurried inside the apartment and entered the kitchen. I waited at the doorway for traps. But no darts, acids, or chlorine. Termites had eaten through the sofa, table and chairs. The rats should've devoured the food long ago but half a cheeseburger lay untouched on the floor.

A rat was nibbling something. Otherwise, just the ticking. A note with my handwriting lay under the dirty underwear:

Send CP data to Mexican client by November 9. Life or death!

I didn't remember writing the note or recall any Mexican client, but he wouldn't be a neighborhood doctor or barber. What was my part in this CP operation? I pocketed the note and, though thoughts twirled in my head, focused on sifting through Pratt's rubbish.

***

I am recording items here (besides the note I am keeping) in case I need the list later.

4 briefs, 4 sweatshirts, 7 socks, 1 bra, half a cheeseburger, quarter cup of whiskey, an appointment book with names and phones numbers, a receipt from a horserace bet, ideas for a Ponzi scheme on a newspaper's margin, a bank's floor plan with arrows and scribbles.

And, under a blanket of dust, a time bomb. Thirty seconds. Don't have enough time to run downstairs.

CHAPTER 32 - FRANCISCO

October 2, 2011 (2)

I woke up leaning over an altar above a roasted chicken, the heat in my face and a blade tickling my throat. The place reeking of goat milk and stale mushrooms. Behind the altar Dostoevsky stared out of his portrait with knitted brows.

The Underground Temple Priest twisted my neck to face him and said, "Where's our holy text?" He turned the blade and scraped my Adam's apple.

"If you've done your due diligence, you would've known that the parchment is fake and someone stole it from my office." I struggled to free myself from the two hooded thugs holding me, but they had tied my arms and legs. Of course, I still could use my head.

"But you know where the real one is."

"If I have it, you would've received an invitation to an auction, you numbskull."

"Let me demonstrate our punishment. It'll refresh your memory." The Priest pushed me from the altar and showed me a man who had desecrated the holy text. He caned the desecrator while his followers chanted. After removing the chicken, he lit the altar and the heat magnified the sanctuary's stench.

My stomach churned and I was going to vomit but when the thugs pushed the man toward the fire and the Priest read a passage from *Notes from the Underground*, I chanted in Russian the first three sentences.

"What?" the Priest dropped the book into the altar and it browned and turned to ashes.

"You just burned your holy book. Isn't the punishment for desecrating the holy scripture forever listening to Descartes' philosophy until Cartesian logic turns your mind into mush?"

"You're trying to trick us. You won't get out of this place alive."

"Come on, Ricky, let him go."

"He'd questioned the Almighty Dostoevsky's work and desecrated the holy text. The punishment is death."

"Damn, you're as grumpy in real life as in my dream. Listen, man, questioning Dostoevsky's work isn't defiling it. So get moving and loosen him."

"As the High Priest, I condemn you—"

"Well, I didn't burn the holy text, you did." I turned to my captors and chanted in Russian several more sentences from *Notes from the Underground*. That was all I recalled from glancing at the parchment.

A fanatic asked in Russian whether I was the Holy Prophet and I nodded and replied in Russian that the High Priest is a sham and a nut. Not that these fanatics weren't crackpots. They released their grips and stepped back but the Priest held his blade under my chin and it tickled me.

"You sham, you've misinterpreted the scriptures," I said. "When I read the original text, I realized how far you've deviated from the truth."

"Deceiver. Rabble rouser."

"You can't read Russian and you don't even recite the Russian alphabet. No wonder you made so many hermeneutics fallacies." I recited the Russian alphabet to show my credentials.

The followers fell on their knees and chanted. I won the gamble but my heart pounded as if about to thrust through my chest and sweat poured down my back. I didn't expect my pony show to work, but then, when you could fall for one nutcase, you could fall for another. Amen.

I had to flee from these lunatics and return to the land of the sane. In Russian, I repeated the first lines of their holy text. They prostrated and chanted more gibberish.

I directed the guard to untie the condemned man, but the Priest raised the blade above his head and said, "He defiled the holy text."

"Hey, you misinterpreted the scripture. I read the text in Russian and I understand its meaning like none of you." I said in Russian that that Dostoevsky would punish him and anyone following him would suffer the same fate.

The fanatic who understood Russian whispered to the others. They swayed their bodies, prostrated before me and chanted, "Oh, Great Prophet."

"Seize the false prophet." The Priest pointed his blade at me and when the followers continued to chant, he approached and put the blade against my cheek. I slipped away and bowed and I thrust my head into his stomach. He groaned and slouched and fell onto the floor.

The followers lifted their heads and as they were about to rise, I said, "The Almighty Dostoevsky has sent me to punish you for your false teachings, for your idolatry."

They prostrated again and chanted, "Dostoevsky gives and Dostoevsky takes. Blessed be His name."

As the Priest got up, I stepped on his dagger. "Then let the Almighty Dostoevsky choose his true disciple." While the Priest stared at the dagger, the followers withdrew from the sanctuary, taking the condemned man with them.

"Well, Ricky, it's just you and me. How should we settle this?" I hoped they'd untie me so the Priest and I could have a fair fight. Still, whether he was a lunatic or a con man, I wasn't afraid of his lunacy, not Fransuccesco.

"You're a false prophet and I'll show it."

"Well, you're a false priest. So where does that leave us?"

"Before I read Dostoevsky's *Notes from the Underground*, I was a lost soul, swimming indifferently in sludge, unaware of its flow toward the edge."

"What are you trying to say? Can you speak like an ordinary man?"

"I would've been caught stealing an apple if an ambulance hadn't plunged into the cop who was chasing me."

"Apple? What kind of apple?" I could imagine this bum crawling around a fruit stall and clawing at a honey crisp apple when Fernando shouted from across the street. Then, the chase, the ambulance, the accident. The bum didn't even glance at Fernando in agony. I clenched my fist and growled to show him my teeth but delusion had clouded the madman's eyes and he paced in front of the altar waving his hands.

"But then my eyes caught the first words of this holy text, the divine revelation, which unknown to me had existed for more than a century. Which was lying on bookstore shelves waiting to save me from this world. It called me. But I hated words, I hated knowledge, I hated books, and I hated the idea a book infecting my hands. Then the e-book came along. No more prints on paper." He lifted his arms and faced the portrait of Dostoevsky.

That night, I identified Fernando in the hospital morgue. I'd often dreamed about punishing the apple thief but realized that cracking the scoundrel's ulna or femur wouldn't compensate for the lost. I picked up the dagger, sat on a bench beside the altar and slid the knot across the blade to cut through the rope. In my mind, the ambulance ran over Fernando, again and again. While the thief fled with the apple.

"Those opening words seized my soul and opened my spiritual eyes. I recited the first sentences over and over again like a drowning man gasping for air. 'I am a sick man. I am a spiteful man. I am an unattractive man.' Divine words of wisdom, of salvation." The lunatic probably had read *Notes from the Underground* once too many. He'd kill me without blinking his mad eyes.

"Before my conversion, I'd always been afraid, of height, of close places, of insects, of strangers, of the unknown, but mostly of the truth. But since my conversion, no more fear. Later I bought a printed copy of the text because the electronic version just didn't feel real enough. As I worshipped the author of this revelation, my soul melted in divine union. I'd found the guiding light, the divine path, the sum of all sums, the end of all ends, the truth of all truths. And guess what, at the same time, he'd found me, from the void of nonexistence, from vacuum emerged I, the Priest. Without this text, I would've been nothing; without meeting those words, I would've been nothing; and if I hadn't responded to those revelatory insights, I still would've been nothing."

Well, he'd become less than nothing. Quite an achievement. The heat from the altar, along with those words crashing against my eardrums and flooding my mind, choked me.

"But, epiphany, catharsis, salvation, transformation, divine bliss, cosmic union. Not afraid of a gun pointing at my forehead, or of a knife flickering next to my throat, or of a fire burning my jacket. I tried to understand it, tried to evoke fear, but nothing. Something changed. Something miraculous. You, who hadn't experienced this holy infusion, couldn't understand it, never could you." He prostrated before a Dostoevsky portrait and kissed the ground.

While the lunatic raved, eyes and hands dancing, I tried to free my hands, but the dagger kept slipping out of my fingers. When he fell onto the floor, I decided not to twist his neck for Fernando's death. His lunacy was punishing him so I shouldn't end it. Still, his suffering, however severe, couldn't numb my pain, couldn't relieve my grief.

I appreciated Ganesh's madness, which compared to the Priest's lunacy seemed like wisdom. I must leave this madhouse—more a mental hospital than Ganesh's office—and take a mud bath to cleanse myself of the maniac's breath. Then again, he might be leveraging this pony show to gain fame and power. He looked like Rick and Nick, but could be another Jack Conman. Still, I mustn't fall for his racket. Once I understood the carrot driving his lunacy, his ravings were as logical as $2 + 2 = 4$. Well, maybe 5.

While I fumbled with the dagger, I promised to interpret Dostoevsky's other texts if he answered my questions. "First off, who's the guy over the phone harassing me with nonsensical questions? I mean, who cares about good and evil when you have to toil for your daily bread? I don't go around pointing at the durian pie declaring it good or evil. I just eat it and enjoyed eating it. It fulfilled its purpose and I fulfilled mine. An equitable exchange."

"Don't know. Never received any phone calls."

"Then find out."

"Sure, you're trying to get me into trouble."

"You're already in trouble. Remember, you burned the holy text." I leaned back to hide the dagger and continued to cut the rope. "Hey, you're the High Priest, not an ordinary fanatic. So, you must have exemption, a blank check, a trump card."

"Doesn't work that way. More responsibilities but no added privileges. Like in any other organization."

"Hey, let me do my job and exegete and you can do your job and serve the grilled lamb or chicken or whatever. Okay?"

"They're direct revelations. No room for interpretations."

"OK, let's talk about how we can exegete blasphemy into piety, sanctification and holiness."

"It's too late for you, but you shouldn't have trusted those VE agents. They shot at you in your battered apartment and at the hotel." He took away my dagger and cut out off a chicken leg. After finishing the chicken leg, he grabbed me and thrust my face next to the altar flame.

The heat slammed into my face and pained my cheeks. "Okay, I accept your offering but lose that cliché and stop telling me not to trust Tom, Dick and Harry. Of course, if you say, 'Don't trust me,' I won't trust you. Anyway, thank you very much." The rope around my hands was loosening and I tugged at it. I must stall the lunatic. "But you'll have to offer something much better for our business venture. Your chance to participate in a win-win negotiation." I must find out why the VE henchmen had shot at me. No, I didn't buy the Messenger's explanation. If he'd wanted the diamonds, he didn't have to shoot me. I hadn't heard of VE before taking on the assignment, so an enemy must be using the front to undermine me. I still hadn't met the boss.

"You stole the original manuscript of *Notes from the Underground*. Give it back or you'll be grilled lamb."

"Never mind salvation according to Dostoevsky, I'll help find that old book, I mean, your holiest scripture, and not charge a finder's fee if you're willing to partner on a business venture. Oh, nothing as risky as an Internet startup. Just this, charge a $100 fee each time a worshipper touches or kisses the holy text to receive blessing. We would gross about $50,000 a month and could split the profit fifty-fifty. Nothing spectacular, but nice supplemental income." At first, I was just stalling him, but while declaring the plan, I found a cash cow.

"You're a wolf in sheepskin, a blasphemer out to deceive us. Get ready to be condemned to eternal hell for such a sin."

"Come on, Ricky. Let's reinterpret the doctrine to have less eternal punishments. You know, to attract more followers." I tugged at the rope but it refused to give way. "And I'm not the one who's a cuckoo. Be realistic, wouldn't you like to preach in a cathedral, instead of fighting with vagrants and sewage rats for drainage acreage? This is no place to glorify the mighty Dostoevsky. With the income, you can rent an abandoned church. Gothic structures, frescoes around the sanctuary, underground burial hall. You'd dreamed about it every night, I'm sure."

"Should've joined me and help me glorify the mighty Dostoevsky. Since you understand the holy texts, you could've enter the holy library."

"Sorry, never considered being a librarian, not that I've anything against the library. I couldn't face books all day long. I need to use my know-how, to open a safe, to break into a database, to save the world. You'd be amazed how many times I'd saved the world. No, sitting in a dusty chamber guarding crumbling pages from fanatics won't do." Even if he paid me a million dollars, I wouldn't waste my precious youth in this underground grave. Just the thought of attending a dying book compelled me to run to a bar and have a glass of whiskey. What fool, what idiot, to waste the months, the years, in this darkness, in this stench, instead of the sun, the roses, the luscious lips.

Before I could loosen the rope, he kicked me in the face and I dropped onto the floor wondering how many teeth I'd lost. He grasped the dagger and approached but before he reached me, a hooded follower entered the sanctuary and came toward us.

"Hey, get lost. I'm not done." The Priest cursed the intruder and promised to punish him for interfering with the rite.

The follower stepped onto the altar, bowed and punched the Priest in the face. The lunatic grunted and fell onto the floor.

"Hey," I said, "if you want to take his place and become the Priest, I won't interfere. But I have a proposition—"

"Shut up. I bet you haven't thought about the question I asked."

The mysterious caller. I tried to get up but fell onto my face as he picked up the blade.

CHAPTER 33 - X

November 2

I didn't die. The bomb exploded, but I didn't die.

I crashed through the window and jumped off the building and, as I dropped past the seventh floor beside the splinters, the bomb exploded and expelled the sofa. I landed on the sidewalk and debris showered on me, but, no harm done, just sore legs and messy hair. Pieces of the sofa missed me by two feet.

Someone probably had expected me to follow the clues, someone who was monitoring the database's access and decided to welcome me with the bomb. I was hunting but became hunted. I brushed away the dust on my jacket and massaged my knees. Who would want to blow me up? The intelligence agents sought the data in my head and wouldn't kill me until they retrieved the data. The agents might've wanted to eliminate Pratt before I could find him.

I checked the iPad to make sure I hadn't damage it while landing on the sidewalk. I was about to leave when an old man, carrying an injured boy, staggered out of the building. Blood staining his temple and dust covering his face. The boy had been looking for me and was knocking on the apartment door when the bomb exploded. I recognized the boy who had delivered Molly's message.

While blood dripped from his mouth, he muttered, "Molly…" I held the boy's hand and brought my ear to his mouth, but he fainted. I imagined finding Molly on the living room floor, a pool of blood collecting around her body. I should call the ambulance but my mind wouldn't rest until I could examine the scene in the villa. I took out the bills and the cash card and gave the old man the money. I had him take the boy to the hospital. After getting the hospital's address, I rushed down the street hoping the boy would survive. I wanted to hear his voice again.

***

In Molly's water villa, a blood trail led from the front door through the living room into the bedroom. Her lipstick, comb, MP3 player, rested among the blood. Soda cans and candy wrappers covered the floor. After drinking a glass of water to steady my nerves, I checked the closet to confirm she wasn't hiding. Opened the windows to let in fresh air. A bird chirped on a branch while the breeze dispersed the scent of blood.

I couldn't suppress my imagination, picturing the struggle and the stabbing. Then, her twisted face scattered my thoughts. I found dust balls and dried roaches beneath the bed, under the floorboard, and inside the ventilation ducts, but not Molly's notebook, which details I had wondered about. She had cheated on her income tax and had an affair with an older man, but she must've had a secret she didn't want to share. Yet, I wouldn't pry into her past even if I found the notebook. She cared about me and helped me escape the police and I didn't have to know more.

While searching under the bathroom sink and behind the toilet, I regretted not having extracted the secret that might've ushered her end. I could've erased the shadow over her smile. Of course, she might still be alive. I found a painting hidden behind the bookcase, an oil painting of Dr. Tang. Had Dolly or Molly painted it? Had Dr. Tang met the latter rather than the former?

While I was rummaging through the kitchen cabinets where the china glistened under the light, Dr. Tang's note dropped onto the floor. How long did I have it? With reality shifting, I didn't bother to look for it. Perhaps I wouldn't find it in the other realities. He asked me to focus on the elements on the back of the painting, specifically their symbols, and requested that I meet him two days later at the playhouse. That would've been the day after I left the fake hospital. Was he going to inform me the hospital was a sham? Or was he going to reveal another secret? About Pastor McCoy? About Pratt? About Beta? Or was he going to feed me more lies and extract information from me? I would like to punch him. I would like to strangle him. But above all, I would like to spit in his face. According to the diary, I had trusted him and considered him a friend, but he had betrayed that trust and that friendship. He and Ingrid. The two people I trusted the most. Of course, the more you trust them, the easier for them to betray you. Another universal truth.

When I was about to leave the villa and search through the neighborhood, I found in the trashcan an ID card the intruder must've dropped. To reveal the name behind this ID, I must again access the Intelligence Agency's database, but I no longer had to enter the defense contractor building, since I had set up remote-access while inside If So, Inc. Must locate the perpetrator and find out what he had done with Molly.

CHAPTER 34 - FRANCISCO

October 4, 2011

I didn't get to see the mysterious caller's face. Was about to wrest the blade from him when I blanked out again. The next minute, I sat behind the altar with a chicken leg in hand, the fanatics chanting and prostrating before me and the Priest bound on the sacrificial table. The mysterious caller had gone, but left a note reminding me to reflect on good and evil.

I held the chicken leg and stared at the Priest for ten minutes while the fanatics worshipped me. Could I be losing my mind? Was the amnesiac infecting me with his mental virus? Perhaps the world was indeed coming to an end. I must convince Faith to be with me before the world ended.

After dropping the chicken leg into the altar, I directed the fanatics to put the Priest in the dungeon and they anointed me the Prophet. I'd locate the manuscript and carry out my enterprise alone. Since the chief lunatic pooh-poohed my creativity, I'd use the manuscript to excommunicate him. I'd replace the holy text with my diary, sentence by sentence, and the almighty Francisco Guzman would soon replace that ancient novelist. My followers and I celebrated with grilled steak from the altar and as I left the sanctuary, a worshipper handed me a message from a homeless man. The message: no one will get hurt for my missing the third deadline but if I miss the fourth I'll find two casualties. Lovely.

***

This morning, the creep called again, this time at my office. "Which means she didn't agree. And in a way, she spat in my face. Can you be-

189

lieve that, spitting in my face? Like I said, I got my dignity. And my face, too."

Had Clint poked his head out of the fog to amuse me? I would've scolded at him for sneaking out of the hotel, without leaving his shirt, pants and shoes. But my former associate didn't squeak like a mouse, unlike the mysterious caller. "So I followed Ganesh down the sewage tunnels past a few nooks where homeless men and women lived. Of course, the rats fought for the same space. Nasty brawls. Glad I don't have to fight with rats for a place to sleep." I slurped the low-fat soymilk and dropped into my chair, putting my feet on the desk.

Long pause. Then, a hypnotic tune. The tune I'd heard in the woods dream.

"What?"

"What yourself." My muscles strengthened and the flu retreated while I annoyed the stranger. If I chatted long enough, I'd recover soon.

"You sound terrible," he said.

"The same to you."

"Did you drink milk at the bar, or something?"

"Just didn't have a chance to kick your butt." The tune from the other side irritated me. "Hey, can you shut your music player?"

"Did you notice that nothing happened after the third deadline? Well, that's a bonus. Now that you feel better, let's get back to business. If I'm satisfied, I may even give you the info you want."

"Where's Holly? Tell me, you faceless mouse."

"Ah, sentimental, aren't you? But sorry, can't tell you that. I'm not allowed to. Part of the rules. But I hope you have enough time to mull over the question of good and evil and come up with the answer. That is, in between casual flings with prostitutes. Of course, someone might've overestimated you. I'm more realistic and don't expect you to have zilch. Just the usual con man. Personally, I'm more interested in that lady—"

"Who allowed you to break into my office and insert old newspaper articles into my book? I didn't recall anyone asking for my permission. Unless you're that drunkard who mumbles nonsense whenever I passed by. Well, get a life, you loser." I pressed a button on the phone to record the conversation and intended to process the speech signal and search through the FBI database for the creep.

"Wow, I expected some bullshit from you about the meaning of life. I mean, the usual crap about love, friendship, spirituality and self-actualization. But this is pretty close to the answer. Quite impressive, though you're off by a conjunction here, a preposition there and two or three articles. As if you could read my mind. But that's my job. Anyway, you passed. Congratulations."

"You'd be more impressed after I kick your butt." When and where (besides in the Underground Temple) had I heard the loser's whine?

Maybe the Governor was nudging me. Or the mysterious client encouraging me to work harder. They should stop distracting me.

The caller was playing chess where each move would preempt several attacks. I must change the game's rules and neutralize his maneuvers.

"Not surprised a loser like you would play such a silly game. But since you started the—"

"But wait, there's more. Don't think because you reached level one that the game's over. Watch out. Your ego will doom you."

The tune gave me a headache. "I demand a meeting, face to ugly face, man to half-man, to show you the real meaning of good and evil. I prefer a dark pier on a moonless night, the best setting to get a job done." I click an icon on the computer screen and sent a file to the fax machine.

"Whatever you do, don't break that code or something bad will happen. I mean something real bad, like the end of the world bad. So relax, have a few drinks at the bar, pick up a few ladies. But remember, skip the code. Okay, ready for the good news yet?"

"If I have to find out who you are, then bad news for you. Since I could get really pissed off and would have to take it out on you. But since I'm a nice guy, I don't want to do that. So, who you are?" I left the office and stepped into the hallway.

"You've no idea who I am. But, call me the Guardian if you want."

"Fine, a mobster." I'd helped a few gangsters transfer money to the Bermudas but none chirped like a canary. I'd stepped on too many tails helping clients pommel their frenemies to remember the sore losers who'd want revenge. "For your information, I charge by the hour. So you'll get a bill for the time I spend talking on the phone. If you shot at me that time, well then, extra charge. So, if you don't have the money, don't shoot at me." Clint might've hired the scoundrel to harass me. Yet, five years ago, Holly had mentioned a Guardian flirting with her and I could be talking to the same loser. I waited for the fax machine to whine so I could put the phone next to it and treat the Guardian to the music.

"Forget the lame guesses. Just know this: you killed your father and buried him. Are you listening? I'm trying to help you remember the past. Remember what you did and how you'd killed him. That's the key to everything. Even your dreams."

The fax machine beeped, but I stared at my hand and tried to recall the day Father had disappeared. If only Fernando could help me recount that day.

CHAPTER 35 - X

November 3

The ID card in the trashcan belonged to Dolly. The Intelligence Agency should've destroyed, or at least deactivated, it after her death. Unless they borrowed it for a subterfuge to fool an enemy. Anyway, the information didn't help locate Molly. Without any other clues, I left the villa and returned to the city to check on the messenger boy.

Well, he died before I arrived in the hospital. Another perished and how many more before I could find my past? The waiting room's fluorescent light oppressed me until the nurse took me to the mortuary, where the silent cold greeted me. The boy's face was serene. He shouldn't have died. He had before him so much life, so much happiness, so much adventure, so much love. Yet, he died while I continued to live. Why couldn't reality have changed this time? Behold, the old man didn't check the boy into the hospital because the latter never went to the building. I wanted to curse but didn't strain my larynx. I wanted to punch through the wall but didn't lift my arm. The stranger with no memory or past, his future as illusive as the morning mist. After an hour outside the mortuary, I inquired about the cremation.

After I arranged and paid for the cremation with the money the old man had left at the reception desk, I walked back to the villa hoping the chill would dampen my fever and clear my head.

I hoped to find Molly there, but no such luck. Reality might shift, but more likely from bad to worse. When I returned a little after midnight, images continued to dance in my head. The music in the house nauseated me. This time, the subliminal message urged me to buy a gold watch.

I couldn't sleep. I had lost my way. Though I still had to recover my memory, even more I had to locate her. Her disappearance must be related to the minister and the laptop. I would return to Mr. Smith's place though he might contact the police. Only then did I realize Molly's place in my heart. I couldn't pinpoint the word, the scent or the feeling that attracted me, but I wouldn't forsake her. Whatever danger awaited me in Mr. Smith's house, I would face it. Without her, I would drift in time from moment to moment. In that instant, the table, the chairs, the drapes, the carpet in the room became ethereal.

While waiting for daybreak, I listened to Seiji Osawa's rendition of Vivaldi's The Four Seasons. Then, epiphany. I realized the secret to the words behind the painting. After the music had calmed my emotions, I solved the elements-code.

***

At dawn, I went to Mr. Smith's place. Jumping over the back fence rather than walking through the front gate where the surveillance cameras would scan my face. Several guards shouldering rifles patrolled the streets but most yawned every hundred paces or so. I waited behind the shrub for one to pass before approaching Mr. Smith's front door. Rang the doorbell and when the surveillance camera pointed at my face, said I wanted to talk about Molly.

Mr. Smith in pajamas opened the door and pointed a gun at me. When I said his daughter had disappeared, he plunged the gun into the wall and said, "It's all your fault. You didn't protect her. She trusted you enough to help you. But you let her down. You useless murderer."

While he pulled the gun out of the drywall and dusted his hand, I walked through the foyer into the living room and said, "No use blaming me now. We've got to find her. Whatever you know, please tell me. I'll do everything I can to find her. And if calling the police will help, do it."

"If the bastard was alive, he would've taken her," he said, tears flowing down his face. "And if Dolly weren't dead, she would've gotten Molly involved in a shady operation. But, they're dead. No one else would harm her." In the kitchen he poured two glasses of pomegranate juice.

"There's you," I said.

"And there's you." He walked into the living room and handed me a glass.

"So, we have a standoff. Now, what?"

"Of course, find Molly. You idiot."

"Do you know someone named Pratt Calhoun?"

"Never heard of him. Sounds like a fake name."

"He knew Dolly."

"I knew it. Damn it, Dolly."

While we sat on the sofa drinking pomegranate juice, the TV announced the rebels had blown up the police headquarter and hung the police chief's armless body under the town square's Triumphal Arch.

"Is there a way to turn off the TV?" I didn't care about the news, unlike the residents who glued their eyes to the screens and absorbed the announcements as if listening to a sermon. This TV, like the rest, didn't have any switches or buttons. "Show me where the switch box is and I'll—"

"Are you trying to get me into trouble? They throw saboteurs into prison. Last summer, my neighbor next door accidentally damaged a wire and the TV went off. And what happened? He disappeared for six months. When he returned, he kept mumbling, 'I'm not a rebel; I'm a good, decent, law-abiding citizen.' Once an hour, everyday. And whenever the TV announced, 'Extra, extra,' he'd sit in front of it and listened like an obedient student. Well, he's just not his old self anymore. They took something from him. So, please, don't mess with the TV."

"Do you know the minister raped Molly?"

"The bastard deserved every bullet." He threw the glass into the fireplace and it cracked and showered splinters onto the firewood.

"I didn't kill him because I didn't know he was a pedophile. So, who killed him? Molly? Mrs. McCoy? You?"

"How dare—"

"I want to find Molly. I don't care—" A sharp pain ripped through my abdomen, and I dropped the glass as cold sweat dripped down my forehead and my back. I smashed the coffee table with my sweating palms.

Mr. Smith jumped off the sofa and after a minute, put down the glass and pulled out his gun. "I'm sorry. I didn't want to do this. You should've minded your own business. But I'll find Molly and bring her back safely. And the son-of-a-bitch who took her—"

With a bang, the front door flew into the living room and half a dozen officers rushed into the house pointing their guns at Mr. Smith. The one with an eye-patch shouted, "Hold 'em up. You're under arrest for the murder of McCoy."

"You got the wrong man. It's him." Mr. Smith pointed the gun at me while I collapsed onto the floor.

"But the security cameras in the church, they said otherwise."

"The damn bastard raped my dear Molly." Mr. Smith dropped his gun and knelt on the floor sobbing.

"Oh, uncle, you should've come to me for help."

Ingrid, I recognized her voice so I must have been in that fake New York. I wanted to embrace and kiss her. I had met her and we had taken the walk outside the hospital. Yes, the acorn was still in my pocket. But could it have been Molly's voice? I fainted before I could raise my head to see her face.

CHAPTER 36 - FRANCISCO

October 10, 2011

I woke up in the middle of the night and drank a glass of whiskey to celebrate finding the password before the fourth deadline. For once, I appreciated the amnesiac. Maybe the Guardian's lie, which I'd dismissed after slamming the phone, triggered my mental agility. I'd strangle him for accusing me of killing my father. Fernando would've confirmed I'd been playing with him that day.

I wrote down the element symbols: Sn, U, Na, Li, I, Ga, Hg, Ti. And the first letters spelled out SUNLIGHT.

I rushed to the laptop and typed SUNLIGHT to unlock the file Faith had given me. I didn't disturb Ganesh so he'd wake up in the morning to admire my achievement. When the screen displayed "Congratulations," I crooned "Praise to Fransuccesco." But how could my dream give me the clue, as the mysterious client had hinted? Something's rotten in New York.

I fist-pumped, I called to invite Faith to Venice, but after several seconds, before the called went through, the screen displayed the message: Ask the Guardian for the next clue. A prompt below blinked and awaited my answer. More rotten eggs. Damn it, the Guardian did play a role in this wild goose chase. I still hadn't found Holly and even the fanatics couldn't locate her, but the fourth deadline would arrive in a week. I itched to punch a hole through the laptop but didn't want to wake up Ganesh, who was snoring in the next suite.

The streetlights outside the window flickered in the fog and cast fleeting shadows on the pavement. Monsters with pointed claws and talons. Once in a while, a hunching pedestrian would scurry along the sidewalk and disappeared into the grayness. I longed for Faith and rebuked myself for the weakness. I didn't even have this feeling when I dated Holly long distance. While I liked the change, this new feeling, I also feared it. I wouldn't want to lose Francisco, even if a new one would emerge.

During the night, the image-processing software had cleaned up the bank video images and I identified the last five characters of the getaway car's license plate. Only one car from the DMV matched the partial plate and the vehicle's color. Registered to Virginia E. Boss. I stared at her picture on the laptop screen and drank whiskey. Would you believe it? Ms. Redhead. Not a coincident, though I didn't expect her to have stolen the diamonds. Of course, I'd find those precious stones, whoever had stolen them.

That wasn't the only surprise. Guess Murphy's Law works both ways.

My contact at the precinct had identified the rat that'd snitched to the police about the stolen manuscript. When I reviewed the surveillance camera video he'd sent me, I could only lament about this wasteland and these scoundrels. How dispirited could an honest man be? Where is loyalty? Where is honesty? Where is decency? I found Clint dialing the phone, his fingers drumming, his hair dancing around his face. Double-crosser; two-time loser; Clint Palmer. Fernando and I had treated him like a friend, like family, but now he'd snitched on me. He should take his depression and middle age crisis to a psychiatrist. Even if the police didn't want to waste their donut and coffee time on such an errand, the fanatics cum psychotics would've skinned me alive and presented me as a burnt offering to old Fyodor.

***

While I was enjoying the durian pie in my office and preparing to contact the Guardian, Faith opened the door and stepped into my office just as she had into my life. She must've missed me. I poured her a glass of soymilk but didn't offer any durian pie, when she pinched her nose and turned from it. I stuffed the pie into the refrigerator and sprayed freshener to drown the odor.

"Very peculiar taste." She still pinched her nose while sitting in front of my desk.

"I'm a connoisseur, and not just of food. Glad you've decided to learn more about me. Go ahead and ask. I can start typing the story of my life. Much more interesting than the usual spy thrillers. And if you want my autobiography, I'll get a ghostwriter to finish it in a month. Not one of those two-dime a dozen writer, the very best." I folded my hands but they shook from the euphoria intoxicating my blood.

When the phone rang, I hesitated for several seconds before picking it up. A representative for battered women pleaded with me to locate Holly before the fundraiser next week. If the shelter couldn't raise any-more money, it'd have to close down. My associates and the fanatics still couldn't locate Holly. If the kidnappers had taken her out of the city or even the country, finding her might take a miracle. I asked the representative to pray, even though I didn't believe in prayer. I hung up. If I had superpower, I'd rescue Holly rather than look for my past.

After drinking the soymilk, Faith said, "Don't trust the Priest."

"Sure, no problem. I promise not to if you agree to have dinner and reveal the client."

"He's my brother."

"The client?"

"The Priest."

"That's a good reason not to trust him. In fact, one of the top ten reasons not to trust someone."

"About the time he first read *Note from the Underground*, he had a car accident and injured his amygdala. The damage eliminated his fear. But my brother, when he got well, attributed it to his conversion. He believed his newfound faith had eliminated his fear and so from that time on, be-came more rooted in worshipping Dostoevsky, his savior."

"You know, just from talking to him, just from watching him rave, without any medical expertise, I guessed his brain was somehow dam-aged, of course not in such technical details, only a commonsense obser-vation. But isn't this very dangerous? Didn't Hitler suffer from a lack of fear? I'm surprised he didn't launch a crusade against the infidels when he was the religious pontiff, leading hundreds of fanatics and would-be martyrs. Close call." Another mental case. And that Guardian seemed deranged also. Even Faith, she had some type of agnosia. Either the air or a mental virus.

When she bit her lips as if mulling over a past event, I wanted to capture her features on video, but she was probably thinking of Ganesh.

"He's delusional enough to believe my Russian copy of *Notes from the Underground* is the original text and that, as the holiest religious relic, it has magical power. He appropriated it from me but a bit over two months ago, someone stole it from the Temple."

"He probably wants to raise the dead, or maybe have eternal youth. I can understand it, and even empathize with him. I wouldn't mind having eternal youth and if I'm going to be delusional, that'd something I want. Better than fearing conspiracies around every corner." I averted my eyes from her face, to avoid thinking about the night she'd made love to Ganesh, but as I stared at the spider on the wall, her image lit up in my mind. "I know this Italian restaurant—"

"So, that skunk was him. He thought you had the Russian manuscript, because I talked to you."

"Nice costume."

"Custom-made."

"Yeah, I smelled something fanatical about the skunk. But the durian must've been a bit strong and covered his scent. So I couldn't be sure. And at the nightclub, there were too many odors. Right, he had a tattoo of Dostoevsky on his forearm. I must've missed it when I talked to him." I offered her another glass of soymilk but she declined. "Naturally, if you worship Dostoevsky, you wouldn't mind wearing a skunk costume. Not for disguise, I'm sure, but a fetish. Of course, the Priest wouldn't have allowed any followers to wear it. He wanted the adventure for himself. Anyway, I'm glad you caused me trouble. In fact, I invite you to cause me more trouble. That'd increase my pleasure in life." I meant every word. Like any John and Jane, I'd avoid gnats and snarls, but I wouldn't mind as long as I suffered for her.

"I've got to get that text back."

"OK, so you want eternal youth. I can understand that, and with a pretty face like yours, it makes more sense than with your brother's scruffy features. But you should stick with those cream things if you don't mind the cosmetics companies fleecing you. Or even better, eat healthy, which I don't care for much. Do you notice healthy foods never taste good?" I took her hand in mine. "But, if you want that old book back, I'll help get it. I like to make people happy, especially if that person is you. But you should've come when the book was in the Underground Temple. Would've been much easier to get it. But, not a problem. Leave it to me."

"I don't have my brother's delusions, just want to prevent the end of the world." She slid her hand out of mine and checked her phone. She was probably waiting for Ganesh's message.

Since the manuscript would help her save the world, of course Ganesh would filch it for her. I would've mimic a thief and steal it from myself. I'd risk my reputation for love, for love of Faith. "Forget about your brother, forget about the world and especially forget about Ganesh, just come. I'll make you so happy you won't care about the world ending tomorrow. What's the end of the world compared to love?" I grabbed her hand again but couldn't find any roses for her. "But I'm curious, how would the world end if you don't get back that parchment? Would Dostoevsky resurrect to haunt us with his madness?"

CHAPTER 37 - X

November 4

I woke up in a cot calling for Ingrid, a name drifting between reality and dream and I chasing after it. Outside the window, rather than the canal and the gondolas, the mountain ridges hid behind fog and clouds, and peeped out once in a while, perhaps trying to reveal a secret dark and grave. I was in a log cabin, the one I had yearned for. Somehow the future had arrived or perhaps I had tunneled through time.

Even without reading the diary in the laptop, I recalled Dr. Tang and his lies. After reading it, again I called for Ingrid. Through slight of hand or plain delusion, Mr. Smith's house had somehow changed into a cabin, but I fretted over losing Ingrid more than tunneling into hyperspace. I could still imagine her features.

So I didn't die. Only had a stomachache. Maybe, I would never die. Maybe, I would suffer for eternity. Of course, Mr. Smith might have bought imitation poison from a hawker and tried to poison me with dirt.

I didn't blame him. Protecting his self-interests and particularly his life is human, even humane. I would've helped him escape if I had known he killed McCoy for raping Molly. Now I only pitied him for wasting time to poison me, rather than planning his escape. If he had known how much I cared for Molly and likewise hated the minister, he would have trusted me. So, I pitied Mrs. McCoy and him. I should try to stop his execution.

***

The fresh air crisp and cool almost swept away Dr. Tang's image. Yet Ingrid, her features fuzzy and fleeting reminded me of his eyes, his nose, his chin. I would have relished the valley, a single ravine snaking through the rocks and the chorus of pines descending the slope, if her distant voice didn't remind me of youth dissipated, time languished, and memory dispersed.

Outside the cabin, no Ingrid. Yet, footfalls beckoned me onto a dirt road along the cliff, my every step grating against the ground and shoving sand and pebbles into the canyon. Pines and boulders, but no Ingrid. In the distance, a bird warbled, the melody echoing between cliffs and drifting into the distant gray. Nearby, the camellias' fragrance drifted into my nostrils, a fragrance as strange as the morning dew. Beside me, my shadow fuzzy as the mist draped over the rock, a phantom that hesitated between the cracks. I followed the footfalls. When the road cut into the forest, I strolled among white birches and reached a stream where the currents gurgled through patches of fern. Crossing the footbridge where several planks had fallen into the water and was diverting the currents.

In the next forest, still no Ingrid. Dr. Tang walked alone through a mountain trail dragging his shadow along the ground. A constant amid the variables. A phantom from my dream, from another reality, which shouldn't have intersected this one. The overcast sky cast light gray and cool on the leafless trees and jagged cliffs. No wind, no sound except for our footsteps. I followed him as the path emerged onto another cliff. His gait slow and steady among the trees and rocks. At the hospital, he had urged me to meet new friends, but he enjoyed solitude as much as I did and he recuperated through these walks.

"I enjoy the company of the pines, the spruces and the cedars. I enjoy surveying from the mountain top, a valley, a lake, or the ridges extending to the horizon." Dr. Tang gazed down at the slope of pines.

"Don't even try to make excuses." I swore not to forgive him and still might have choked him. I trusted him, but he misled me instead of guiding me

"Have you regained your memory?"

"No such luck, for me and for you."

"But you remember me?"

"I'd never forget someone who'd trampled on my trust, never, I swear it." I showed him my diary to confirm his guile.

"Not a hospital and not a prison. The New Einstein High School turned into a hospital." He browsed through the files.

"Not important." Didn't care where he had deceived me, just that he had.

"I don't recall an intruder breaking into the building and threatening people with a cleaver. Didn't play chess with you, or mention the mass-energy equation. I must say, the Queens Boulevard part is quite imaginative."

"You lied to me. You betrayed me."

"I'm sorry for deceiving you."

"But not enough to stop carrying out your mission."

"I still want to help regain your memory."

"In exchange for the data."

"I couldn't allow the Intelligence Agency to get hold of it. Of course, when you recover your memory, you probably won't allow me to destroy it."

"You mean since I stole it to make a profit, once I become a villain again, I'd make sure to reward myself for the trouble? Excuses, excuses. I wish you—"

"I'll help you whether you'll destroy the data or not."

"You're going about it the wrong way. If you want to destroy the data, just destroy me. End of story. And great men don't hesitate. Look at Napoleon. Of course, whether you can is another story. Helping me recover my memory, then destroying the data after I retrieved it, seems risky, inefficient, and almost idiotic." He rambled around his goal, only as a fool would. He could learn a lot from Francisco Guzman; so could I. "And I still wouldn't forgive you."

"You cannot change the person I am." He approached a ledge and sat on a boulder, facing the expanse of sky and mountain. "And I don't care to be Napoleon."

"Since you're so determined to destroy it and the agents are so keen on squeezing everything from my brain, it must be very valuable, though I've no idea what it is. And maybe, I'd keep the data to spite you. That's reason enough. Where's Ingrid?"

He said Mr. Smith is Ingrid's uncle and she would help him get a lighter sentence. I promised to help also and I would, for Mr. Smith and Mrs. McCoy, but also for Ingrid.

I wanted to punch Dr. Tang's face, then shake his hand. I wanted to scold Ingrid for deceiving me, then hug her. I wanted to celebrate the reunion. Yes, Ingrid. But also, Dr. Tang. A wanderer coming upon an oasis. I trudged through foreign soils, meeting familiar faces, of friends who had deceived me, frenemies.

Had he paid Jack Conman twenty thousand dollars to help me access the government databases? He shook his head and said, "Don't know such a shady character and wouldn't use his services if I knew him." So, someone else was helping me find my identity. Probably for the data. Dr. Tang suspected an intrigue but urged me to focus on breaking the Guzman Code and unlocking the secret. My subconscious must've created Francisco as my evil twin, who could breeze through hurdles and pits with his snake tongue, alligator tears and Lucifer mind.

Dr. Tang explained that the government relies on Pavlovian Conditioning (PC) and Subliminal Projection (SP) to purge hatred and violence and breed happiness and obedience.

"Go ahead and deceive me more."

"So, while we're having whisky and chatting with a beautiful woman, or a handsome man, at a bar, we'd hear cigarette ads over the speaker. Or, while we're watching a sex scene in a 3D cinema, we'd hear, actually not hear but receive, a subliminal message 'I'm happy with my life, more than satisfied with this society and this culture, and I endorse our government's plan to route out the rabble-rousers.'" He said these techniques took weeks, or even months, to create lasting effects. The environment might interfere with the programming and a strong mind could resist the intrusion.

Were the ridges emerging from the fog only holograms of rocks and trees and distant mountains? Maybe, hidden cameras and microphones were monitoring us. I mentioned the subliminal messages in the New Jersey lobby and at Molly's home.

Dr. Tang picked up a pebble and wrote "PC" and "SP" on the ground. "PC and SP don't affect about twenty-percent of the population, what the government calls trouble makers. In fact, the procedures make them more violent and rebellious. Well, this twenty-percent, whose minds refused to succumb, they took up arms against the government's social engineering."

"I would've join them if I cared about any of this. But since I don't even know who the hell I am, what'd I care about freedom or oppression." I rubbed away the letters with my sole.

According to Dr. Tang, a new technology, Cerebral Programming (CP), would take only a few hours. I had heard of CP, and might even understand the concept, but hard as I tried, I couldn't yank that bit of memory from oblivion.

"The effect is almost permanent, unless we want to re-program the person. It works on everyone, so we can ignore the Pareto Principle." He wrote "CP" on the ground. Through biogenetics, with a transcranial helmet or similar device, the neurosurgeon would manipulate neurons as a software programmer would bits, and she would alter, eliminate or build neural pathways, and thus memory, perception, and behavior. Already, scientists were testing an artificial hippocampus and a commercial one would be available soon.

I had to flee from this nonsense, but my legs wouldn't move. I had to dismiss Dr. Tang as a lunatic, but the fog lifted and revealed a snow-capped peak. "So, did a Dr. Frankenstein use CP on me? I want my neural pathways back. What kind of a egomaniac would create such a technology for sadistic psychopaths and tyrants to use on innocent people?" I threw a stone into the canyon while I plunged down an abyss.

"Even though in theory we can program any area of the forebrain, the actual procedure is more complicated;" he continued, "we aren't dealing with EPROM."

"You could've fooled me."

"As far as I know, the Russians have developed techniques to change declarative memory and specifically episodic memory, what we usually call memory. Long-term, or structural memory. So, like you, the patient after CP could have amnesia, unable to recall some or all of the past. But also, she could remember past events different from what actually happened. Or, she could recall events that never happened to her. We could re-program the hippocampus. Or neural clusters in the inferotemporal and polar regions of temporal lobe as well as the entorhinal and perirhinal cortices, inducing, altering or eliminating neural pathways." He indicated the regions as he mentioned them.

"Like I said in the diary, skip the technical jargon. You don't have to impress me. So plain English, please." I stamped on the letters he had written. "Treat me like an ordinary John Doe."

"In your case, the accident has slightly damaged your right prefrontal cortex and medial temporal cortex. But I noticed an area... I'm not sure...I'll have to check on it." His shoe scraped the dirt next to the boulder, as if drawing a symbol.

"You know a lot about this CP. Did you work for the Intelligence Agency? Is your name really Dr. Tangenstein, as I'd expected?"

"Like everything in life, the procedure has risks. The patient could lose all memory."

"That doesn't sound too bad. Since you seem to know so much about CP, could you locate those Russian researchers and have them reverse my amnesia? They can do it, I'm sure. But since I don't have any money, they'll have to consider me a guinea pig for research."

"The patient could recall weird memories. Or worse, she could have conflicting memories, like on her tenth birthday celebrating it in Tokyo and at the same time visiting Paris." He walked along the ledge where a few camellias spotted the path.

"Well, with those pleasant memories, I wouldn't mind having multiple personalities. However, I can think of Frankensteinic scenes. Those sick minds who made this possible should have the technology applied on them, to prevent more damages to society."

I had weird memories. I had conflicting memories. Reality shifting before my eyes. Did someone program my mind and reroute my neural pathways?

I followed him along the rocky path, kicking pebbles down the canyon. "Like I said before, I'm willing to take risks to recover my memory. After all, I'd like to know who I am, where I came come, what I'd done, the achievements, the success, the legacy. But I still want to remember you betraying me, in the prison or school or fake hospital. But I can do without *Groucho* and *Skippy*." I also wanted to remember Ingrid.

After mulling over Dr. Tang's explanation and later analyzing his notes, I grasped CP theory and so appreciated its side effects: the damages, the destruction. A wonder my medial temporal cortex wasn't even more damaged. I also understood his excitement about this technology's potentials. I could experience the life of Napoleon or Genghis Khan by programming their exploits into my hippocampus. Read *War and Peace* or learn to fly a plane in a few seconds. Truly Frankensteinic, or maybe Tangensteinic. Of course, Ingrid probably swallowed everything he said. She would.

We continued along the ledge that winded down toward the canyon and the ravine as Dr. Tang revealed his agenda. Through his contact at the Intelligence Agency, he found out the CP data disappeared after a double agent had delivered the files. When the Agency set up the high school to recover my memory, he called in a few favors and became my chief therapist, not to retrieve but to destroy the data.

"Doesn't matter you didn't work for them. You still betrayed me." On the cliff a finch sang and in the ravine a stream gurgled.

"I knew their agenda. But I had my own. And yet, as I got to know you, I couldn't continue to deceive you."

"Just to ease your mind. Nothing you say will make me forgive you. Nothing." I kicked several pebbles into the chasm as the wind sent a patch of fog toward us.

"Yet, I was and am still determined to destroy that data. But with your full knowledge, and not working with those agents."

"Doesn't mean I'll cooperate with you. For so many reasons. Especially since you'd spat at my trust. For that alone, I should refuse." I walked ahead on the path to avoid his face and entered the mist.

"But you despise CP, maybe even more than I do." He caught up and tried to walk beside me.

"Of course, there's Ingrid. But never mind that now. I might want to sell the information to the highest bidder, to collect my retirement fund while I'm still young. I'd like to retire to the Bahamas, or maybe a South Pacific island."

"Let's get your memory back and we can fight that out. My contact in the Agency couldn't find anything on you before the accident. Some big shot there must know who you are, but only a few agents can access the top-secret information."

"Yes, I despise this technology and wouldn't mind getting my hands around those madmen's corrupted minds, minds that had created this evil science." I waited for him to reveal those demon-gods, but Dr. Tang only continued to kick pebbles over the ledge, as if flinging away slime and muck. I tried to study his face, but the fog covered our upper bodies.

"Sometimes," I said, "I feel like my attempt is futile. And I remember your question. Would I be willing to give up the future to discover the past? But, do we have a future in this world? Maybe nothing matters here." I could push Dr. Tang over the ledge, but wouldn't, even if Ingrid should forgive me. I despised him and would take away Ingrid, but I couldn't cross the line separating me from Francisco, not even if I could leave reality and enter dreamland.

"Maybe when nothing matters, we'll find out whether we're truly human. What then will we do?"

"Eat, drink and be merry; for tomorrow we die. No, that's Francisco, not me. Never." Even without my memory, even without Ingrid, even with the grudge against Dr. Tang, I refused to decay into Francisco Guzman.

"Let's talk about courage."

"I don't have courage, only stubbornness. Like holding a grudge to the grave." I tasted bile. Instead of spitting it out, I swallowed it and savored it.

"What we imagine in the future determines our actions now. Do you see the end or the beginning or more of the same?" He stopped. Stood on the path facing the ledges beyond the canyon while the fog lingered on our path.

I saw a future even without the past, even in this fog. I fancied a world different from Francisco's wasteland. "I see the blue sky; I see the green pastures; I see the yellow swallowtails; I see the purple lilacs. I see; I see; I could see myself." With the future before me, I would construct the past, a day at a time until I could reach my birth. Even with my memory, the future must create the past. And whenever my vision of the future changes, so would my past. I still couldn't dissect the dynamics between past and future, but I drifted among alternative realities whenever I imagined the future.

"Then, let's continue, to walk toward this new world." He walked forward and entered the fog, which had flooded the woods and hid the trees.

"Sure, you want to destroy the data and accomplish your mission. Maybe, you're working for the Russians." I followed him into the fog, careful not to step over the ledge. Didn't want to plunge into the canyon. Not yet. "I should sell the data and enjoy life with the fortune." I had to regain my memory by November 9, in five days, or assassins would hunt for my head. I would like to recover my memory to complete the deal, but having superhuman power, I might be able to handle the Mexican client and his henchmen. After that, I could take Ingrid from this fog, from this wasteland, to sun, to sky, to sea, to wind and sails. Perhaps not sails.

Dr. Tang promised to help me regain my memory. "We have to solve the Guzman Code and see what it reveals. After that, I'll use hypnosis again. If everything else fails, I'll have to—"

"I don't want anything to do with your world. Yes, your world. Not mine. And if I find out you're involved in this CP stuff, I'll crunch your neck. I have superhuman power, so no chance you could escape."

"Look for Ingrid in the cabin."

"Don't you ever wonder why Ingrid is always following you? She could be spying on you."

Dr. Tang picked up his pace and walked down the gravel road into the fog without waiting. His footsteps faded and only a distant bird warbled.

I retraced my steps a footprint at a time, to return to the house and find Ingrid. Dr. Tang's voice echoed in my mind and my head fevered despite the cool air. I couldn't admire the camellias' folded petals under the fog, or delight in the chirps amid the wind's whispers. To shift my focus, I tried to recall where I had hidden the CP data but I couldn't picture the location. Only darkness. Maybe I should let him hypnotize me again.

Inside the cabin, I found a slip of paper under a carrot cake. Who still used paper? I picked up the note and read the message:

Don't let the government have the CP data, or Svensson dies. GAMMA.

Ingrid, she was in trouble. Because of me. I dropped the note and let it drift, left the cabin and retraced my steps to look for Dr. Tang. The fog had thickened into a wall of white so I couldn't see five feet away. The moisture chilled me and I shivered though my heart and my head pounded. I had to save Ingrid from the rogue rebel. At one point along the trail, I stumbled and fell beside a cliff and pebbles bounced down the side of the mountain. An andante tune echoed in the valley. When I reached the cliff where Dr. Tang had been contemplating his life and regrets, he was gone. I continued on the path downhill, hoping to locate him or, better yet, Ingrid. I would like to meet up with Gamma and sock the face that looked like Beta's. I wouldn't mind smashing either face. Where the trail turned into the woods, Dr. Tang's footprints lay among the fallen leaves and loose soil. His track led toward the foothill where the fog was dispersing. I fell down twice. My mind twirled with the images of Ingrid, her faraway look, her determined lips, the sense that she never had tasted joy and perhaps would never. Her images overloaded my mind, which had few memories, and every tree, every branch, every blade of grass reminded me of her. Even the sound of wind shoveling leaves. I should focus my thoughts. I should formulate a plan. I should anticipate possible scenarios and lay down the steps for dealing with them. But I couldn't. Images flitted in my mind. Images that combined previous scenes, modifying and synthesizing them into new narratives. Scenes that might never happen in any future, but scenes that played and replayed in my mind so I lived them time and time again. So my memories could be fiction as much as facts.

At the foothill beyond the woods, Ingrid's scarf lay on ruffled dirt, leaves overturned and twigs and branches snapped. On the dirt road, tire tracks led to the main road. I picked up the scarf and ran to the paved road and the gray sky glared through the foliages. The wind twirled around as if frisking me. Its syllables echoed in the woods and spun and spun around my head.

Beside the paved road Dr. Tang etched words in the dirt:

Going after Ingrid.

Despite his limits, he had to play the hero and the fool. A scorpion is a scorpion is a scorpion and though stinging the toad meant suicide, it couldn't help it. At least he was on her trail and he could contact me for help. If he realized Ingrid's life is more important than his pride.

I returned to the cabin, where Gamma's note taunted me. First, I lost Dr. Tang and Ingrid; then, I lost Molly; now, I lost Dr. Tang and Ingrid again. I glanced around the cabin, at the fireplace gray with ash and the cabinet and the framed computer printout of Fermat's Last Stand. Loneliness deep and dark engulfed me.

CHAPTER 38 – FRANCISCO

October 13, 2011

This morning, I visited my neighbor in the hospital with a dozen yellow roses. I might as well be visiting Suzie. Inside the room, the bed was empty. Made but empty.

I dropped the roses and rushed into the hallway, glancing left and right for a nurse. Only a visitor looking for the toilet. I walked down the hallway feeling like the amnesiac in the fake hospital. At a nurse station, I tried to ask for my neighbor, but only gibberish came out. The fanatics must've infected me. After a while, the nurse understood my question, I wonder how, and she pointed me to a room at the other end of the hallway. I ran along the hallway almost knocking down a gurney and when I reached the doorway and looked in, my neighbor was sitting in bed. She stared for a while before greeting me. I walked up to her and held her hand. For half an hour I didn't speak and during that time, I felt closer to her than I ever had. Later, the doctor came to discuss her condition with me. She might not walk again. She'd need physical therapy once she recovered. I returned to the room and held her hand and sitting beside the window that faced the Brooklyn Bridge, I promised to care for her apartment while she stayed in the hospital. I cared more about her than ever. Strange feeling. Maybe, caring for Suzie had changed me. When I questioned how much I loved Faith, I dropped the apple onto the floor. After spending the morning with my neighbor, I walked to Battery Park. On Broadway, I passed men and women in business suits rushing through the Manhattan streets and the fog cooled my head. In my mind,

I reached out to Fernando, Holly, Suzie, my neighbor, and Faith, but they fled from me, disappearing into the fog as Dr. Tang had in my dream.

On the bench facing the Statue of Liberty, I called Faith but she didn't answer her phone.

The other day, she'd left without explaining how the world would end. Anyway, I'd live the same however and whenever it'd end. Still, I had to win her over before the end and enjoy the grand finale together. I couldn't imagine a better way to end everything, especially the universe.

While I was feeding a squirrel under the lamppost and waiting for the Guardian to reply my request for a meeting, my beggar associate texted me the location of Ms. Boss's car. After I threw crumbs at the squirrel, I approached the balustrade and glancing at the waves, decided to crash her hideout tonight. I would've invited Ganesh for an adventure, if he'd run my errands, but the knave had left the mental hospital before I woke up and probably went to Faith's place behind my back, without applying for leave. Clint had never dared to disappear without notice, until now. I could be getting too soft. I must review my management style and adjust it to suit this crumbling society.

***

In the evening, I grabbed my gun, decoder, gas mask, infrared goggles, tool belt and a few canisters of tear gas and headed out for my adventure. I got Beef Chow Fun from Chinatown and ate it while driving through the Holland Tunnel. By the time I entered Jersey City, the clouds had darkened and a streak of purple lined the sky. I passed Hoboken and, within ten minutes, arrived at the abandoned school building, where Ms. Boss's car had changed from silver to red.

I drove around the school through the fine-dusted fog to check for sentries. A couple was kissing in a van across the street, and from a nearby apartment building's third floor window, a pair of eyes surveyed the school campus.

I parked my car two blocks away and called a garage to tow away the van. I finished my dinner and put on my tool belt and I walked under the fog-smeared light to the street corner opposite the school and peeped at the van. A breeze carried the smell of garbage to my nose. A cat loitered around the trashcans. I munched dark chocolate while surveying the campus and tracing my planned path. When the sky had darkened and the tow truck arrived, the couple exited the van and bickered with the driver. While they fought, I sneaked past them, careful to avoid the pair of eyes from the third floor apartment. By the time I reached the gate, the third sentinel had exited the building to help his comrades.

When the surveillance camera had turned away, I slipped through the gate and sauntered across the yard humming a "Praise to Fransuccesco" and enjoying the night air. Only the din behind me disturbed the silence and irritated me. I passed a playground, the swings jiggling in the wind, and reached the red-bricked school building that used to be a church. The front door needed an entry code to enter. Of course, that couldn't stop me. I waited until the surveillance camera had turned to the other side before walking up to the keypad and unscrewing the cover. I detached the keys and wired the device into my decoder, then munched dark chocolate and waited for my helper to crack the code. I could hear the brawl in the distance. Still hadn't tolled away the van. A minute later, presto, the lock clicked. I removed the decoder and replaced the keys and the cover but as I reached for the door handle, the alarm bellowed and a rat scurried away. The door had locked again. I didn't trigger the alarm. A petty thief must've broken into the building, probably trying to steal textbooks from the school. Annoying pest.

Well, plan B. I walked around the building as the three stooges rushed across the yard toward the building. Bars secured the first floor windows. When I reached the circuit breaker at the back of the building, I opened it and flipped the switches, turning off the power. The alarm went off. Only the crickets chirped behind me. I unscrewed the panel cover and with the pliers snipped the wires. After replacing the cover, I walked to the back door, prepared to kick it open. However, I didn't test my tibia with the steel door. I didn't like Ms. Boss's game.

Under the dim streetlight, I munched more dark chocolate and paced around the backdoor. The generator would turn on soon and the guards would arrive to check the circuit breaker. I located a drainage pipe and tested it, gripped it and climbed up to the second floor next to a window without bars. I took out a hammer and swung at the windowpane and my tool bounced off and flew out of my hand, landing on the ground with a thud. Damn plexi-glass.

I was considering my next move, when the power returned and the surveillance camera above the window swiveled toward me. Lovely. I didn't want my handsome face on the control room's monitors, so I took out a wrench and knocked it down. Just as I tried to open the window, the drainage pipe jiggled and my elbow hit the window ledge. Murphy's Law. My body tilted from the building. Beyond the eave a black bird flew above the lampposts. Lovely view. I gripped the drainage pipe and it jiggled again. I didn't have superpower, so unlike the amnesiac, I'd break a few bones if I fell to the ground, even if only from the second floor. I stepped on the window ledge to eased the pipe's load and I grabbed the eave and climbed onto the roof, just as a section of the pipe fell to the ground. Close call, as always.

I tiptoed across the roof as the shingles creaked beneath my feet and I reached an entrance where the door lay two feet away. Inside, darkness. I hesitated for a few seconds before taking out my flashlight and stepping down the stairs that reeked of mildew. My throat itched and I exhaled to avoid coughing. I pressed onto the next step. Then waited. Rats squeaked beneath me. Another step and the plank gave way and I rolled down the stairs, my back and shoulders hitting the steps. I landed on a carpet of dust and I sneezed. I needed a piece of durian pie from The Usual Café to regain my composure but I only had my chocolate. I must repay Ms. Boss for the fun.

I crawled toward my flashlight but after two feet, I touched a hand. Not mine. I bounced away and my head hit something. Stars circled my head. I cussed and held my head. Maybe I found the Naked Man's arm. Ganesh should've taken it to the police station and reported the crime but the nerd might've kept it as a souvenir. In the darkness, footsteps receded. Might be the petty thief. Or he might be lying next to me. I put on the infrared goggle, crawled around the body and grabbed my flashlight. Several rats snooped around the body. I took off the infrared goggles and pointed the flashlight at the body. The man wore a uniform, probably a guard, and blood oozed out of his neck. The petty thief must've killed him. I searched the dead man's pockets but couldn't find his ID cards, so the thief had stolen them.

I pointed the flashlight around the room. A bucket stood in the corner and a mop reclined against the wall. Otherwise, just dusts on the shelves and the floor. When there were no more footsteps, I stepped through the doorway into a dim hallway that reeked of Bourbon. No surveillance cameras. Offices on either side of the hallway led to a staircase. The bulletin boards displayed drawings of Moses, Jacob and Elijah. I followed the scent to the second classroom on the left and opened the door to the smell of money and alcohol. Nice combination. A mechanical hum startled me and I surveyed the surroundings with the flashlight. Next to a bookcase of Bibles, a printer rolled out hundred-dollar bills. I checked the bills. Damn good quality. Like the real ones. I examined the dozen passports on a table nearby. Also good quality. Professionals.

I picked up the bottle of Bourbon next to the passports and drank a mouthful. The dead guard must've been drinking when the thief distracted him and lured him into the janitor's closet.

I was about to put on my infrared goggles when I spotted Fernando's name on a folder next to the passports. Inside, a bank's floor plan and at the bottom of the page the word "diamonds." What did Fernando have to do with the stolen goods?

A hiss, then an odor alerted me. The doorknob wouldn't turn and the door was locked, as expected. The smell thickened and I picked up a chair and threw it against the window, but the chair bounced back and knocked down the table. Damn plexi-glass. Near the door, a card reader. I held my breath. Unscrewed the reader. Wired the device into my decoder. Then waited. Should've gotten the latest model.

The gas nauseated me. My head fevered. After the years escaping from death, no way I'd die in this stinking school. Still hadn't dined with Faith or gone to the North Pole or dived into the East River in the winter. Okay, I wouldn't mind skipping the last item. Still, my bucket list. My face burned from lacking air. Yet, I refused to inhale the gas.

The lock clicked. The door opened. I dropped into the hallway grasping for the stale air. After lying on the floor for several minutes, I beamed the flashlight around to scare away the rats trying to have me for dinner. I unhook the decoder and grabbed the bottle on the floor. Finished the Bourbon. Vowing to kick butts.

I was about to walk down the staircase when a red light flashed above the card reader. I beamed the flashlight at several burnt rats on the steps. The laser beams must've killed those intruders. I hooked my decoder to the reader and waited and when the light turned green, I took off my tool belt and threw it onto the stair. Nothing happened. I retrieved my decoder and tiptoed down the stair, hoping I'd disarmed the lasers. When no beams punctured my heart, I picked up my tool belt and continued down the stair. No guards. Were they snacking in the pantry?

Before I could reach the first floor, a shadow slipped past the bottom of the stairs. Unsure whether the thief had spotted me, I stooped down to hide myself, and after reaching the bottom, looked to the right where the bogeyman had scurried. Nothing. No shadows. A few rats loitered along the hallway, stopping for a few seconds to sniff each other.

I passed a room with a decontamination chamber and reached a gate where the couple from the van lay on the floor. Both throats slit and blood soaking their uniforms. A professional. Before I could open the gate and walk down the stairs, the other sentinel marched down the hallway and blocked my path.

"I didn't kill them."

I showed my ID and informed him about the thief. He examined the card and talked into his phone. I scratched my lower right leg with my left foot to feel the nunchuks. *Make my day. My nunchuks special is better than Salisbury steak.* I hadn't used them for more than three months and wouldn't want my skill to languish.

He returned my ID, and I was about to hurry down the stairs when he blocked my path and asked me to leave. I scratched my head. I rubbed my underarm. I knelt down pretending to tie my shoes, feeling the nunchuks with my forearm. Before I could pull out the weapon, he groaned and fell onto the floor. His eyes stared at me and his throat oozed blood. When I looked up, the gate had opened and the thief charged down the steps.

I went through the gate before it shut and walked down the winding staircase, testing each step before landing my weight. A breeze lifted from the cellar and raised Goosebumps on my skin. I pointed my flashlight at the wall but couldn't decipher the scratch marks on the granite. By the time I reached the bottom of the stairs, the intruder had disappeared. To the right, down the passage, dim light seeped through a doorway. I tiptoed down the concrete path, checking for surveillance cameras overhead and avoiding the rats that accompanied me. My face rammed into a spider web at the doorway, and I had to rub it off my face. On the floor lay a skeleton, a femur beside a coffin in the middle of the room. I cut through the spider webs with the flashlight and shooed away the rats covering the casket. I pointed the flashlight at an opening in the wall and studied the skeleton. Ms. Boss had hidden the diamonds in this catacomb and I intended to find them.

I slipped through an open door at the other end of the burial chamber into a control room where framed computer printouts of 3D graphs decorated the walls. One monitor showed a prominent politician trading briefcases with a mob boss. Another, three thieves breaking into a museum. Still another, Ganesh making love to Faith. My fist came within an inch of the third monitor but I just shut it off.

Ms. Boss was probably going to punish Ganesh for interrupting our lovemaking and do likewise to him. Why else would she monitor his bedroom activities? Something must be rotten. Maybe, Ms. Boss indeed had been Ganesh's former lover. If so, I'd have to tell Faith.

After locking the door and ignoring the rats outside, I sat down in front of a monitor with a clown-face screensaver and hacked into this school's security system. I located the vault, at the center of the catacomb, and after fifteen minutes, unlocked it. I also unlocked the electronic doors in the building. While I scanned the security cameras to locate the thief, footsteps rapped outside the door.

I took off the infrared goggles and put on the gas mask. Hid behind a cabinet beside the front door and waited for the door to open. Silence engulfed the room and I almost choked. When the door didn't open, I rolled a canister of tear gas under the computers, opened the door and slipped out of the room and, taking off the mask, I walked down the passage toward the vault.

This burial chamber had a stack of coffins against the wall. The floor gave way and I fell into a pit. Before I could get up, dusts and dirt covered me, just like walking through the tunnels beneath Manhattan. Maybe I'd find the Underground Temple nearby. With infrared goggles on I searched for warm bodies. Rats crawled above and beside me, but in the distance, a human-sized heat source swayed.

Something hissed. More natural gas. A spark probably would ignite soon so I ran down the passage to look for an opening. I crashed onto a skeleton and fell down and the rats overtook me and rushed down the passage. I got up and followed. A breeze cooled my face and I overtook the rats and reached a door. I pushed and pulled but it wouldn't open and the rats arrived and tried to nip the wood. A card reader hung beside the doorknob and I attached my decoder to open the door. While the rats and I waited, I wondered whether Ms. Boss was the mysterious client harassing me. Fernando should've left a clue for me to figure out the link between the diamonds and the Guzman code.

A boom interrupted my thoughts and I expected to turn into ashes though I preferred burial to cremation. The sound came from above. As I put my ear against the wall, the lock clicked and I took the decoder and rushed through the entrance and locked the door.

A winding staircase led to a storage room. I'd found the vault. The door beside the stairs had flown into the room so the thief must've entered already. Plasma TVs lined the walls and computers filled half the room. When I reached the farther end of the room where muffins awaited me, I ripped off the sign *Designated Personnel Only* and opened the vault door where a passage led to a dozen burial chambers. While on the computer I had accessed the inventory list, retrieved the diamonds' SKU, and located the loculus code. I ambled down the passage humming "Praise to Fransuccesco" and checked the serial numbers on the wall until I found the unit. I took out the bag of diamonds. Left a note to show my appreciation. Too damn easy. Something was rotten. I was about to check the other valuables when I noticed the label above the loculus. *Cli-*

ent: Fernando Guzman. I stared at the name but still couldn't connect it with the diamonds or VE. Fernando had died five years ago but the Messenger had approached me only in August. Were those diamonds Fernando's? Before I could resolve my questions, a red light flashed. Power had returned. The vault door wouldn't open. I had another piece of dark chocolate and took out my decoder but decided to try the vault's back entrance.

At the end of the passage, the wall swiveled to reveal an entrance. Inside the operating room, scalpels lay on an empty gurney and when the door shut, someone panted behind me. I did the dirty work and now the coward would slit my throat with a scalpel and take the diamonds. Lovely.

"What took you so long? I would've left you a donut if you arrived earlier."

"Only you? Where's the army of goons to greet me and congratulate my success?"

"Pretty clever, opening the vault electronically. But, I get the bonus for killing you. Nice price tag on your head."

"Hey, I'm a professional. Of course, I know my head is valuable." I recognized the Messenger's voice. "Hey, you hired me to do a job and I'm doing it. So, what the hell—"

"What? You?" The Messenger stepped in front of me, a Boston cream donut in his hand. "What the hell? It's only you?"

I was about to show him how my nunchuks work when he said, "Hey, your brother's letter—" He grunted and fell to the floor. Two hairy hands grabbed the bag of diamonds.

"I'll take that."

That monotone. The mysterious caller. The Guardian. The creep showed up.

I threw a canister of tear gas at his feet and put on my mask. While he choked, I kicked his butt until he dropped the diamonds.

"What's the next clue, you nincompoop?" I grabbed the back of his collar while he stooped.

He handed me a piece of paper. After I held the note between my lips, I grabbed his belt also and threw him into the bed. "Here's the meaning of life for you."

He crashed into the bed and knocked over the scalpels. I opened the note and confronted the next clue: CHAO. Just great. Another cipher for Francisco the Great. I didn't have time to enjoy this game. Only three days. Though I recovered the diamonds, I'd failed three times already and the momentum was against me. I must protect Suzie and Holly, but how. They depended on me so I must triumph as Fransuccesco would. I must find out the meaning of CHAO from the Guardian.

Something strange happened, again. One minute I was in that operating room walking toward the Guardian, the next minute I woke up and returned to the woods, the red maples whispering in the wind. The scent and the melody seemed to urge me down the wooded path. As I trotted on the earth among lilacs, I dropped the message inviting me to meet at The Usual Place. I would find the blue-dress girl by the brook, to look at her face and the object before her. The lilacs' fragrance along with the tune spellbound me. Then a scream—a painful crescendo followed by a plunge into silence. I stood for a few seconds, as if waiting for the concluding note, before rushing toward the brook. As I approached the brook, footsteps and a curt scream overtook me, while squirrels scrambled up the trees.

At the brook, a girl—not in a blue dress, but in a pink one—knelt beside a body, a young boy, his face half-hidden in the mud. A dagger extended from his abdomen.

I tried to approach them, but someone from behind knocked me out.

CHAPTER 39 - X

November 5 (1)

I struggled through the night, unable to dissect and decipher the double dreams. This morning I woke up in Molly's place, not the cabin. However, I had Gamma's note. After reading the diary, I looked for Molly, but only found blood in the living room. I paced the room for several minutes, before trimming the marigolds that had withered in the villa's backyard. The time for logic and reason had come and I must plot my steps one at a time.

I had to look for Molly and Dr. Tang and I had to rescue Ingrid, but Francisco's dream in the woods interfered with my thoughts, a dream that resembled a forgotten event, and an event that lurked beneath memory. Who were the two girls? Who were the victim and the killer? What was the motive? A secret was drawing me into the abyss. I almost snipped my finger while mulling over the dream, which surfaced and faded like a specter in the fog.

Pulling out the seeds from the withered blossoms, I tried to recall forgotten faces, songs, meadows, forgotten snow, larks, jasmine scents, forgotten bars, lodges, solitary roads, but my imagination, as if tired from a trek, refused to cooperate. Only the withered marigolds' fragrance drifted through my thoughts, a scent that couldn't link the images.

What joy and pain, what love and hatred, what successes and failures, what surge and ebb did I miss? Each one maybe a pixel or an atom, but as a whole composing my autobiographical self, defining me, different from Ingrid or Dr. Tang or that Francisco.

I pushed aside those faces and voices. I knew what I must do.

I left the villa and took the underground transport downtown. In the station, an attendant bade me good morning and x-rayed me for weapons, anti-government leaflets, and other contrabands. As I rushed down Cheesecake Boulevard, a scout handed me a flyer reminding citizens to attend today's execution and the celebration afterward. I was going to dump the flyer into the trashcan when a security camera from a lamppost pointed at me. Pocketing the flyer, I entered New Jersey to look for Conman. To purchase Molly's location.

In the lobby, the TV announcer reminded viewers to attend the execution. While I was crossing the lobby, a hand landed on my shoulder and Jack Conman said, "Looking for me?"

I took out a cash card and requested both Ingrid's and Molly's locations.

"How'd you know I accept cash card but not cash?" He took the cash card and pulled out a scrap of paper. "Don't be greedy. Choose A or B, but not both. Anyway, don't know who's Ingrid and have no info on her. But Molly's another story. Don't know exactly where she is, but this note may help. Someone asked me to forward it."

I took the note while a waitress handed Conman a glass of orange juice. As he complained about not having the privilege to drink alcohol in the city, I read the note: *Check Pratt's hideout for Molly.*

"Don't ask me about Pratt's hideout. No idea. Don't even know who Pratt is." He drank the juice and again complained about civic rules and regulations.

I showed a waitress my ID card and ordered a Screwdriver. Gave Conman the drink and said, "Find Ingrid." Before he could refuse, I entered the café. I had to locate Pratt, who could reveal more about my past and might even show me the CP data. While the music drifted into my ears and the subliminal message urged me to spy on my neighbor and report on terrorists, I took out the photos from Pratt's apartment and studied the background: the building's graffiti, the bent signpost, the smokestacks near the horizon. Sure enough, I recognized the location where he and I had taken them.

When a middle-aged woman with a mushroom hairdo peeped at my photos, I returned them into the envelope, walked over and said, "Don't worry. I'm not a terrorist."

I left New Jersey and took the underground transport to East Thus, a neighborhood by the river, on the outskirts of Felast. After exiting the subway station, I tried to identify the gates along the pavement and the mannequins behind cracked windows but could only recognize the scent of charcoal. Though I located the graffiti and signposts in the photos, the fog had covered the smokestacks in the distance.

Around a trashcan, a group of homeless children stoked a fire. A leg inside. They were burning a boy who had died of rabies. Among them, the boy who had died from the bomb. Except now he had pimples on his nose.

"You're alive." I grasped his shoulders, glad that he had resurrected from the dead to soothe my conscience. "I still haven't met your dad." I couldn't find any scars on his face.

"Do I know you, sir?" He scratched his head and warmed his hands with the fire.

Of course he wouldn't know me. He never met me so he didn't die. I could accept that. For once, I rejoiced in reality shifting. Of course, he might have reincarnated. I could accept that, too.

When I showed Pratt's photo, he said the man had gone to his Maker. A month ago the government agents had shot him in the head. Another dead-end. The wind swept charcoal into my face, and I drifted in the ocean, the sky meeting the water in every direction. I crumpled the photo and threw it into the fire. The agents had silenced him, but I swore to dig out the secret Pratt had taken with him.

The pimple-nosed boy offered to take me to Pratt's place for a price. After we agreed on the amount, he led me down a deserted street to a gray stone-front building, a mural of a riot on the wall. He opened a squeaking door and we entered a hallway where spider webs decorated every corner and edge. An incandescent bulb overhead lit the passage. We descended the creaking stairs at the end of the hallway until we reached a steel door. The boy unlocked the door. The stench of decaying flesh assailed my nostrils and I stumbled backward. I covered my nose and entered a room with a mat, a table, a chair and two corpses, on which maggots squirmed. Intelligence agents in uniforms. The boy shut and locked the door as if the corpses didn't exist. I covered the bodies with a mat, preferring not to watch the maggots feast on them. Roaches beneath the mat scattered, and the boy stepped on a few as he strode to the opposite door. He said he would open the other doors while I examined this room. Before I could ask how he had the keys, he disappeared behind the door and shut it. When I touched the table, it crumbled and collapsed onto the floor while termites scattered. How could Pratt have lived here a month ago? How could anyone? No, not even those homeless boys. Sleeping with the roaches and eating dinner while the termites ate the table.

A hiss startled me. Gas seeped into the room. Car exhaust. Those agents must have suffocated from carbon monoxide. I tried to open the door the boy had gone through but it was locked. I stood back. Kicked open the door. Stepped through the doorway into a storage room with empty boxes, spider webs and three corpses, or rather, skeletons. The boy's footprint on the dusty floor led to another door. A concrete door. Locked.

He had led me into a trap. Maybe an agent or a rebel had promised him dinner, or just lunch. My life for a meal. He had to survive. I sympathized with the boy and blamed myself for trusting him. I hadn't learned an iota through my experiences.

Back in the two-corpse room, as I raised my leg to kick down the steel door, a red-nosed beggar opened it and beckoned me to follow. Holding my breath I rushed through the doorway.

Outside the building, as I was about to thank him, the beggar again beckoned me to follow. He led me through an alley of prostitutes to a redbrick building, where his fellow comrades sat along the wall, playing poker and backgammon. I studied the graffiti on the wall but the scribbles didn't trigger any memory. The beggar lowered the fire-escape ladder and led me to the fifth floor, where we entered through a broken window into the hallway. We scaled two flights of stairs and reached a door with crisscrossing scratches. He said Pratt lived here rather than the basement.

I inquired about Pratt but he ignored me. He inserted two pieces of wires into the keyhole and fiddled for a few seconds, opening the apartment door. The moldy air assailed my nostrils and I choked and coughed. Inside the apartment that reeked of stale garlic, the beggar stepped on the soggy carpet and navigated through the landmines of stains and soiled underwear and socks. Just like Francisco's apartment.

No decaying flesh, nor muffled sounds.

"Where's Molly?" I pulled out his wig. He stepped backward and slipped on a sock and crashed onto the coffee table, the red rubber nose rolling into the kitchen.

"Don't kill me. Don't kill me. I beg ya. It's me, yer old buddy, remember? Visited ya in the hospital. Warned ya against 'em."

So, this time the hospital, not the school building.

Pratt, pizza against cheek, held his hands together and cowered toward the sofa. His pupils dilated. Like a cornered dog, he would lunge to save his life. The will to live. He had disguised himself as a beggar to hide from enemies, and would lie his way to a longer life.

I relished the fear behind his dilated pupils, pale cheeks and trembling nostrils, the pleasure so delicious as to remind me of the night with Molly. Demons surfaced from the chambers of my heart. My past self might be taking over this present one. Dr. Tang's words, like specters, surfaced upon my mind and flashed a red light but I refused to succumb to my DNA. I would rather embrace the probabilistic world, where accidents disrupt design and destiny. I waited for reality to shift and rewrite my past.

"Trap's for them agents. Not you," he said. "Been hiding from them bogeymen."

So, he must have laid other traps around the neighborhood and employed the homeless boys to secure the area. Collecting skeletons, how many I didn't know.

"No games, please." I enjoyed Pratt cowering before me. Was I a sadist? How many people had I brutalized, injured and killed in my past? Would I, as Dr. Tang had said, lose my freedom, my future by regaining my past? I stood at the crossroad, one path leading toward an inferno, another into an abyss, both enticing and welcoming. How much courage and strength would I need? How much callousness and resignation did I have? My past self didn't enlighten me.

"No, no, no games. Please. She ain't here, man."

I searched the bedroom, the bathroom, the closets, the cabinets, the refrigerator, but couldn't find Molly. I examined the note. Had Conman conned me? Perhaps, a schemer, expecting Pratt to subdue me, had given Conman the note to invite me into this trap. Big mistake.

In the living room, I swept away the T-shirts and socks with a bat and sat on the couch rubbing my forehead and tapping the bat on the carpet. I had expected to see Molly's face, to hold her hands, to hear her voice, but hope dispersed as I stabbed the T-shirt with the bat. The stench seemed to sneer at me. Maybe I should've looked for Ingrid instead. I struggled against the sea of amnesia, its waves surging to drown me.

I pressed Pratt on my relationship with Dolly. Indeed, she had been my lover for three months but she later tried to kill us—Pratt and me. So, I was the amnesiac lover.

To my surprise, I had lost some memory even before the car accident. Those lost images and sounds and smells had stood out in the abyss, but afterward, they merged with those I lost through the accident.

Now, only a single level of oblivion. Then again, maybe I could still separate the first set from the second.

When I smell a rose, when I touch a silk dress, when I listen to Beethoven's Moonlight Sonata, which memories will respond?

"She seduced ya justa steal the CP data. At first, we dunno, but when she tryna kill us, we knew everything. She's a double agent." Pratt wiped the cheese and tomato sauce off his face, licked his fingers, and lapped water from the kitchen sink.

According to the Intelligence Agency files, both Dolly and Pratt were looking for the data. Maybe Pratt killed Dolly to prevent her from replacing him as my new partner. Of course, they could've been working together but more likely each was vying for the same pie in the sky.

After working as an agent for years, Dolly must've become disillusioned with the crimes she carried out to receive a paycheck. I could understand her anger, not with the agency, but with herself, for believing she had been toiling for a better world. That fury must've pushed her to seek revenge against herself, to destroy the vision she once had. Maybe I had confronted the same abyss, but didn't have the courage to walk down a different path, fearing a wasteland stood behind my fantasy. Dolly might've tried to kill me but I would keep the image Dr. Tang had conveyed of her and therefore picked and chose Pratt's jabber. Fortunately, he didn't inspire trust.

Pratt could be a mercenary selling the juiciest secrets to the highest bidder and maximizing his gain given the boundary conditions—staying alive and out of jail. And to success he would toast, after winning another zero-sum game. His achievements probably compelled him to take on greater risks for larger rewards and now he was playing me for an amnesic fool and trying to profit from the CP data. Which fiction should I believe in? Perhaps a different one in each reality.

"Ya trusted me, remember? That why ya asked me to help ya." Pratt scratched his face with his right hand. "I been loyal, following all yer instructions. Even tryna rescue ya from the hospital."

In this world, a hospital might turn into a prison or a school, and I could never take someone's word at face value. I would have to decipher each syllable as if it were part of the Guzman Code. I had recalled Pratt's and Dolly's wedding at sea but now questioned that invention. I doubted I had cooperated with Dr. Fujimoto. I searched for the past but might only be creating it. Perhaps, to search is to create.

I scratched my face, but with my left hand. Pratt had shot Dolly in the forehead. Like target practice. Like any competent agent. Endorphins rushed through his body as he hunted down the prey, as he wiped out the target. When I felt his thrill, I inhaled and bit my tongue, and pain flushed away the endorphins.

"Know ya'd understand," he said. "The data's worth a whole bundle. Enough for us to retire to Tahiti, those babes in bikinis." He wiped his mouth and panted like a sweating dog, then swatted the roach walking across his neck.

He looked and sounded human, but he wasn't. Every word and every action seemed programmed, a reflex responding to a stimulus. Mechanical, unfeeling, inhuman. Based on an algorithm. He might as well be an android. "How did you kill Dolly?" I turned away as if to avoid her mutilated body. Several roaches marched single-file from the wall toward the coffee table.

"Hey, man. Like I sez, didn't kill her. She gotten killed. Someone done her in. Maybe her partner sold her out. Maybe that why we almost gotten killed with them agents chasing us for them data." He flicked away the roach and wiped his hand with a sock. "A shame. Nice chick. But hey, that's life. Right? I knew ya liked her. But think about the dough, the beach, the piña-colada, the babes."

"Thank you for escaping and leaving me to die in the burning car. If those agents weren't after the data, they would've let me burn. You probably had the data so no use sharing the profit. Might as well reduce the number of claimants." I opened the drapes and scanned the street below the balcony. Two beggars near a fire hydrant played poker as the smell of ash wafted through the air. The homeless boys had removed the trashcan after the cremation. Where were the citizen-guards?

"I scared man. Scared them bogeymen come get me. Them cutthroats killed her, woulda killed me, too." He wiped his mouth with the sock.

"Never mind the cutthroats. Show me the CP data." I ground the tip of the bat several times on his chest until it tore a hole in his T-shirt, then swung and drove a roach from his hair. At least a double, maybe a home-run. "Facts are to laughter as lies are to screams."

"Hey, of course I won't tryna con ya. Yer my partner. We always share and share alike. Remember the time we went to that whorehouse—"

"I'm beginning to recall things and sooner or later I'll remember everything. Try to trick me, if you're a gambler. But remember the stakes." I dropped the bat, picked up half a tabletop and shredded it, just to motivate him. After retrieving the data, I would use the trump card against the agents, the rebels and everyone else, including Francisco.

"Oh, no, no, no, of course not. Know where them data is. Even made a note just in case, um, need to prove it to someone." He bounced up and tried to back away, but tripped on a T-shirt and fell onto a puddle.

"The data please, I want the data."

"Well, ya have it." He whispered, grasping the couch to get up.

"Like I said, bad answers equal screams and sleepless nights."

"I ain't pulling yer legs."

"OK, I have it. Where? Last chance for redemption, before purgatory."

"It's in yer head, in yer head."

"I guess I wasn't sincere enough. I'm sorry. I promise to do better this time."

"Don't, don't. I'm telling the truth, I tell ya. I dunno how ya do it. You put them data into yer brain and destroyed the disk. See here." He shoved his notebook at me.

I didn't look at his chicken scratch. His raisin face and gelatin lips convinced me he didn't lie. Still, how had I inserted data into my brain? In this surreal world, with Dr. Tang rambling about CP, I certainly could have used such a science-fiction-like technology to store the information. More likely, I had memorized the data, and in the abandoned school those agents probed my brain to search for the treasure.

According to Dr. Tang, I had injured my medial temporal cortex. If the link to the neural cluster storing the CP data had severed, I would have to regain my memory before retrieving the files. So I was thinking like Dr. Tang. I could be adapting to this wasteland and might even succeed as another mad scientist, and help create super-soldiers to defend the rights and privileges of dictators and drug lords.

The nonsense mixing with the stench motivated me to find my identity. In this world, the impossible had become possible through insanity and I might succeed through this madness. Of course, I might have to face the reality that could destroy not only my future, but also this earth. Still, even if this world should disintegrate, I wouldn't return to Francisco's sewer and devolved into that loud mouth.

Pratt scattered the flies buzzing around a quarter glass of beer, where one had drowned. Picking up the glass and finishing the liquid. He burped and wiped his mouth with a sock before reclining on the sofa handle.

My skin itched at not finding Molly or the data. I shoved the note from his previous apartment in front of his nose and said, "What's the deal here? Who's this Mexican client?"

Pratt choked and coughed into the air for half a minute before saying, "A bad man. Very bad man. Had a deal to give him the data. Ya got half the payment already."

"He'd probably throw a tantrum if I couldn't remember the deal or deliver the goods." I opened the sliding door and stepped onto the balcony. In the distance black smoke rose into the sky and down the street sirens blared. I could imagine the client's toothless thugs vying with bounty hunters for my head and the million-dollar reward. November 9. Only four days. How could I regain my memory and retrieve the data in four days? More likely, I would have to face his henchmen.

After returning to the living room, I requested the client's name, but Pratt, wiping his mouth with a T-shirt, said I had contacted the man and I didn't trust him with the details. I believed him. I wouldn't trust him. Not even with a soiled T-shirt.

"Ya called him El Diablo and told me how he lops off people's fingers and limbs before killing 'em." He gulped and pulled on my sleeve. "C'mon, man, please get yer memory back. Or we're goners. Wanna die a peaceful death in old age."

"Okay, since we're partners, I don't mind splitting the money."

Pratt, a man responding to stimuli rather than prodding toward any goal, licked his lips. The intelligence agents probably had toyed with his mind and if I could find the relevant tunes, I could probably control him.

"Help me make it happen, or else, nada, amigo."

"Anything, anything ya say, boss."

I needed him to bait Agent Rick so I could extract information from the agent's brain.

"Sure, will do, boss. Anything to help ya."

"When we finish this, you'll be able to retire to the Bahamas and drink rum from morning until midnight." Sure enough, beach and rum and ladies in bikinis motivated him. The reason my past self had chosen him as a partner. I wouldn't mind partnering with him again and providing for his needs. Like an insect, he would devote himself to the expected rewards. He would yield to his genetic programs.

"Yeah, love the Bahamas and love rum." Pratt licked his lips while saliva dripped down his chin.

***

On the balcony I rehearsed the tactics to trap Agent Rick. While beggars and homeless men and women gathered in the street below, the fumes in the distance gushed into the heavens, the charred smell refreshing me. The searched for my self energized me but I feared finding this stranger, perhaps a psychopath as inhumane as this wasteland's other dwellers.

Pratt strolled out of the building and walked up to the tattered men and women. After greeting them he punched a muscular beggar. The man stumbled backward, but two beggars charged at Pratt. The group divided into two fractions, one for and one against Pratt, and brawled. Sticks, pipes, broken bottles swung through the air. Shouts and screams echoed through the neighborhood.

Pratt no doubt belonged to this world. He enjoyed this fog and smog. Even the moldy pizza and stale beer. He would perish if this world changed.

In the distance, rumbles shook a building, and the charred smell thickened. The fighting was approaching this neighborhood and I hoped to capture Rick before fire and smoke engulfed the streets.

Half an hour later, a siren sliced through shouts and screams, a tune as commanding as the police cruiser. Red and blue flashed along the street and sped toward the crowd, while onlookers raised beer cans and cheered on the brawlers. Before the police cruiser reached them, the beggars had dispersed. Pratt rushing back into the building. The policemen chased after the vagrants through the alleys but no limousine arrived to deliver Rick.

In two minutes, Pratt stood beside me on the balcony, watching the policemen question bystanders. He wiped away the blood rolling down his cheek and licked his fingers.

"He'd want your head, I'm sure," I said, "at least to the extend your head can lead to mine."

After locking Pratt in the bedroom that reeked of sour milk and rotten mushroom and warning him to be quiet, I shut the sliding door and pulled the drapes together. Then unlocked the front door, pushed away the T-shirts and socks and sat on the couch, reading Henri Bergson's *Matter and Memory*. Rick must have spotted Pratt and would come after him and I must squeeze from the agent every byte of data on Dolly and me, and maybe even on Molly. No more hide-and-seek with the truth. I feared confronting the psychopath within me. Unlike Francisco, I must have a conscience.

While I was meditating on Bergson's concept of continuous time, an old lady in a gray dress entered holding a wrapped box. I had expected a man in black suit wielding a shotgun, not an old lady with a gift. Spotting me, she retreated, almost dropping the box.

I recognized her eyes, glistening like pearls. I recognized her lips, trembling like petals. Despite the wig and dough or mud or whatever hid her features, I recognized her. Mrs. McCoy. Her slender fingers grasping the box.

"A gift?" I said.

"I came to look for Pratt Calhoun," she said.

"Sorry, he doesn't have the data." I navigated through the socks and T-shirts and stared at the box. "So you wasted your money on the gift."

"I came to kill him, to avenge my mother." She handed me the box. "Someone in a black suit asked me to deliver this to him. I agreed to help the man only because this gives me a pretext to knock on the door."

I accepted the box but didn't ask the gripe between Pratt and her. On the side of the box were the words "Compliment of Agent Rick." Should've guessed that *Groucho* didn't dare to appear in person. Since he had sent a gift rather than come and shoot the rogue agent, the box should have explosives or anthrax. Mrs. McCoy tried to grab the box but I pulled away. Never take back a gift.

I considered tossing it over the balcony, but didn't want to murder the policemen and beggars below. Maybe leave the box in the apartment and escape with Mrs. McCoy, letting the bomb or the poison gas take care of Pratt. I entered the kitchen and opened the refrigerator, which reeked of the East River, put the box on a shelf with the inscription facing outward and closed the door. I leaned on the refrigerator, watching a spider weave its web above the cabinet. I hoped Mrs. McCoy had fled.

The refrigerator groaned and shook while its door pushed against me. I pushed back as my body shook. The rumble died as quickly as it had started. I didn't open the refrigerator to check the leftover shrimp pizza Pratt might've saved for dinner.

No scream or wail from Pratt. Maybe he was napping. With a hiss, gas seeped into the kitchen. In the living room, a canister spewed gas and Mrs. McCoy lay unconscious near the doorway.

I held my breath. Grabbed the canister. Took it to the balcony. And left it there. Back in the living room, I shut the sliding door and opened the kitchen window, and the draft dispersed the sleeping gas.

After checking Mrs. McCoy's pulse I carried her to the divan near the bedroom. Before I could wake her, footsteps approached in the hallway.

I grabbed the broken bat and a table leg and tiptoed to the doorway. Stood behind the door. Waiting for *Groucho* to enter the apartment. He was probably going to search the compartments behind the drywalls after blowing up the rogue agent. The bomb didn't destroy the refrigerator, so Rick intended to preserve the apartment in case Pratt hid the data disk here. He should've had a surveillance camera in the apartment to make sure he had killed Pratt.

From the balcony, a gust wafted into the room, carrying an aroma. The beggars weren't barbecuing in the street. After the bombing, the fire was burning the bodies.

The footfalls stopped behind the front door, and I held my breath, tightened my thigh muscles and flexed my fingers. Time to show my superpower. The burnt flesh and the chilidog, their aromas wafted through the balcony...

Then, it happened.

I dropped the bat. I dropped the table leg. Someone on the street shouted, "Chilidogs. Three dollars."

My arms went limp and I couldn't lift them, not even feel them. As if my nerves had severed. What had the intruder done?

In the hallway, someone crashed into the wall, groaned, and thumped onto the floor. Several screams. A groan. Then silence.

I prepared to kick the table leg toward the intruder...

My legs wouldn't lift. My knees wouldn't bend. I stood like a statue...

Again, footfalls stopped behind the front door. I struggled, but still couldn't move. Unable to free myself from the body. Well, not my body anymore.

At that moment, enlightenment struck me. A light flashed before my eyes. The feeling that I couldn't enunciate ever since waking up from the accident, the ephemeral sense that haunted me, now clotted in my mind. Like an ALS patient. The self confined in an alien world, trapped in a foreign body. This world oppressed me and this body confined me. Perhaps, as Dr. Tang had said, this world is an abstraction and this body is an abstraction. Enlightenment freed my mind but I couldn't escape from this super body.

Is that how a superhero feels, the sense that his body isn't his? Am I a superhero in this story?

More likely, I was Francisco's dream figment, a sap lost in some Hilbert space.

The knob turned. The door creaked. On the floor, the shadow of the gun crawled along the carpet. I imagined the heat from the bullet piercing my flesh and the chill from the blood leaving my body but smelled the aroma of chilidog, the beans and the ground beef.

"Make my day," I said. "Test my superpower." Maybe the intruder would pull the trigger without greeting me. Maybe I would find out whether I could overcome the elements, whether I could save humanity time and time again. Or, whether I would wake up and return to Francisco's world.

I shut my eyes.

CHAPTER 40 - FRANCISCO

October 14, 2011

Woke up sweating and sat in bed. Held my head and tried to recall the sounds and smells of the dream in the woods. Couldn't recognize the boy lying beside the brook with a dagger in his abdomen or the girl with the pink dress. No chrysanthemums were near the water, so I didn't dream of the brook in the Catskill Mountains where Fernando and I used to sit and chat. Did I recall a memory or create a story? Maybe, recalling is creating.

When I opened my eyes, I couldn't find the window beside my bed or the night sky beyond the pane. Only darkness. Not in my apartment. Not in the mental hospital. Fear from the pit of my stomach gushed into my chest and I shivered as if on a winter night. I slid off the bed. My heart pounding. I feared reality had shifted and I, like the amnesiac, had plunged into Hilbert space. When I turned on the light, Dostoevsky stared from paintings on the four walls. The fanatics wouldn't let me remove them for fear of holy punishment. They should instead fear me, the new prophet. One day, I'd excommunicate anyone who refuses to follow my reform. I'd even excommunicate old Fyodor. Amen.

The bag of diamonds sat on the nightstand. Sure enough, I was kicking the Guardian's butt in the catacomb's operating room when I entered the maple woods dream. Same as when I was walking with Ganesh across the Queensboro Bridge. A disruption of consciousness. Some damn neurological disorder.

I picked up the note from the Guardian and phoned Ganesh to give him the next clue and he said CHAO should refer to something called the Chaocipher code. Very annoying. Why does he always have the answer off the tip of his tongue, even when he's clueless, as if his only purpose in life is to impress the universe and annoy me? Anyway, I'd come across this code before, but would have to reread it to refresh my memory, which unlike the amnesiac's, could recall Pi to more than a hundred decimal places, maybe two hundred.

I put on the slippers and left the room, looking for whiskey. The Priest must've stored a few bottles. What'd communion be without it? Unless he used vodka to honor old Fyodor. In the sanctuary, every footstep echoed for several seconds. Annoying. At the altar, I stooped down, not to kowtow, but to open the compartment the Priest had shown me. Inside were whiskey, Champagne, cigarettes, and a few pornographic magazines. Good man, preferring whisky to vodka. I took the bottle of whiskey, put on the robe and took the elevator up to the manhole. I pushed away the cover and sat on the pavement. The fresh air and the whiskey cleared my mind while the clouded sky turned a dull gray and the fog dispersed. At the corner where the road meets Broadway, six teenagers sang and danced and drank. Nearby, a familiar tune resonated through the air. Guess what, the same tune I'd heard while talking to the Guardian.

The girl in the woods, I knew her. I'd seen her somewhere before, not from a dream, but from a memory, yet a dream-like memory. My father had bound her hands and feet. She was crying, struggling to get free, begging for help. My father ripped off her blouse and I smashed his head with a stone. I killed my father. In the Catskill Mountains, on the trail where I'd planted the chrysanthemums.

While the breeze played with my hair, I downed half a bottle of whiskey to clear my mind, but remorse surged through my bosom. Yes, remorse. But why remorse? I confronted my father; I stood up against evil; I saved her. Yes, I was David taking on Goliath. Anyone else would've stood by and watched him rape her. Not I, no, not Francisco Guzman.

Still, killing your old man isn't another day in the office. Not something to shrug off. No, not even for Francisco Guzman. The blood on the stone, the blood on the ground, the blood on my hands. Or did I imagine it? I'd never deny my actions. But had I done it?

Throughout the years I'd learned to forget that episode, but now, I could recall the details as if it'd happened yesterday. Only as fanciful as a dream. If only I could ask Fernando about that day. Of course, he'd praise me for confronting evil.

Still, the law wouldn't give a damn about that. The law would only seek retribution. If John harmed Joe, the law would punish John, to equalize pain and joy on the cosmic scale. No, probably just the terrestrial scale.

The Guardian, the loser, by scooping up the past, by dispensing guilt and remorse, was playing that ultimate equalizer, God. To enjoy the power of dispensing suffering, of rewriting my destiny. To relish his victim's wails. No, I wouldn't bow down, or kiss his feet, or beg for death. I'd fight him and slash him and vanquish him to savor my revenge. He'd soon endure the wrath of Mighty Francisco.

When a sports car raced down the deserted street, I ducked into the manhole before it ran me down. After it had passed, I waited fifteen seconds for the air to clear before emerging from the hole. I gulped down more whiskey and gaze at the sky looking for stars beyond the clouds.

The homeless men and women emerged and barter empty bottles, leftover pizzas, used jackets, and I returned to the Underground Temple. I dressed and looked for a fight in a bar, but ended up picking up a lady. She hated her dead-end job as the assistant to the governor's daughter. Her parent didn't understand her. She just broke up with her latest boyfriend. I should've fled from her but ended up giving her free counseling. After dancing for about half an hour, we came back to the Underground Temple. She liked the place, except for Dostoevsky staring at us in bed.

After she'd left, I drank more whiskey, alone with Dostoevsky in the Holy Room, and I kept recalling the incident. The stone smashing the head. Dad shrieking. The girl crying. And I just dreaming. I recognized the girl's eyes and her nose. I must've known her and projected her image into my dream. Like it or not, I'd stepped into alien territory. I couldn't remember how I'd planted the white chrysanthemums or how I'd buried Dad. Of course, I must've buried him, or the park rangers would've found him. So, I wasn't in school playing basketball with Clint and several other boys. I might've created that memory. I waited for Fernando to enter the room, not to comfort me—I didn't care for consolations—but to stand by me. He didn't.

To turn my mind from random thoughts, I accessed the National Cryptologic Museum's website to download a paper on John F. Byrne's Chaocipher encryption. While the grandfather clock ticked away its seconds. After reading the paper under the Temple Library's dim light, I tried to decipher the code, but images of Fernando, Dad, and the girl

drifted through my mind. I tried to, but couldn't, hurl away those specters. I couldn't concentrate on the code and ended up finishing the bottle
of whiskey.

Only three days to the fourth deadline.

I couldn't sleep or solve the Chaocipher code, so I read Fernando's
will in the Prophet Office, where more Dostoevsky portraits decorated
the walls. I laid the will on the marble desktop. He'd given almost everything to me, but his favorite baseball card and ten thousand dollars had
gone to Clint and a hundred thousand dollars to VE. That imbecile Clint
must've dropped the baseball card while visiting the grave without my
permission. And why'd my brother transferred more than a quarter of his
fortune to VE?

I called my beggar associate, who should've reported once a day but
hadn't for two days, to check on Clint, but the bloodhound didn't answer
his phone. Clint should be prepping a gotcha and I needed my associate
to dig it up before the lunatic could serve his masterpiece. Since my former lackey believed he could avoid punishment for any crimes, he was
probably searching for gadgets to torture me. I should've called the police to lock him in a mental institution but now would have to parry his
blows.

At 5:00 a.m., I phoned the Messenger and advised him to meet me
tomorrow and bring a million-dollar ransom for the diamonds. Before he
had time to complain or cuss, I hung up and turned on the radio to enjoy
my favorite New Age tunes. I intended to collect my fee in tomorrow's
meeting. That rascal the Guardian would also come for the diamonds
and I'd squeeze out his identity and *reward* him for resurrecting my memory. Most of all, I had to discuss Fernando's hundred thousand dollars
and find out his involvement in this conspiracy.

I was planning my moves to outwit the Messenger and the Guardian,
when Ganesh intruded into holy ground and reported Faith had recovered the lost manuscript. I'd hoped to locate it and impress her. Rotten
luck. I asked for her new address, but the nerd refused to betray her. As
my new sidekick, he should've obeyed my "sit" and "fetch."

"Instead of wasting time, let's talk about something we can cooperate
on."

I didn't care how loyal he was to her. I only cared how much I loved
her. Though he was her lover, I wouldn't allow him to interfere with my
love for her. I'd call her and find out her whereabouts. Easy enough. Still,
I hate sidekicks who burden me instead of easing my workload.

"Let's try to decipher this Chaocipher code."

"You're trying to evade the subject—my love for Faith."

"I haven't evade it. I've dismissed it. Now, please focus on the code. After all, we'll solve it sooner if we work on this code together before one kills the other."

I had to agree, though I preferred to resolve the love triangle ASAP. I still admired his robotic reasoning, rare in this day and age, so I didn't swat his triangular face. I still had to leverage his brain and crack the code before dumping him into the sewer.

I put the parchment back onto the self and sat in the Prophet Chair. I folded my hands and related my conversations with the Guardian. "Obviously, the guy's trying to cripple me through this tragedy."

"Come on, why'd you believe him? Use your brain for a second, will you. He's probably trying to deceive you. Anyone who claims to a Guardian or any authoritative figure, well, you've got to be skeptical and suspicious." He sat down across the Prophet Desk and wagged his index finger. "I never trusted teachers, coaches, ministers, and community leaders."

"Of course, I won't fall into his trap. Who do you think I am? A numskull? Haven't you been around me long enough to know that I'm smarter than the average genius? But I'd like to reveal his identity and hidden agenda." I'd like advice from Ganesh's electronic circuits, lacking empathy, sympathy, consideration and kindness, assets in dealing with the Guardian. When my servant in a hooded habit entered and folded his hands and bowed, I ordered a scallop omelet, lobster scramble eggs, French toast and Chai for breakfast. I also ordered Ganesh a glass of skim milk.

"Ahem, I'm much humbled by your generosity." Ganesh took out his phone and called Faith but she didn't answer. "Listen, don't be a willow in the wind, trust yourself and check everything he says. Sure, he's got an agenda. But, he may just want to hurt you, a sadistic craving."

"Of course I only trust myself. Who else would I trust? You?"

"Don't worry about him now, focus on breaking this code."

"Come on. I can crack the code and his bones at the same time. The trouble with you—"

"No, the trouble with you is you think you're a superhero. Listen, if he claims to be your Guardian, fire him. That's easy enough. I'd fire anyone who claims to be my guardian."

"Naturally, I'd like to box his ears and kick his butt, but not before I flush out his slimy intrigue." I put the napkin around my neck while the servant set my breakfast on the desk.

"Oh, your priorities, please. A before B and B before C."

"Hey, you're my assistant, not my father. Don't lecture me on priorities." I sampled the scallop omelet and approved of the cooking. "Naturally, I wouldn't believe anything he said. But, the newspaper articles, my brother's obsession and his will with the strange provisions. Giving Clint the baseball card." I slid the will into the drawer, before Ganesh could pry into its details.

"Listen, it was the Guardian, or whoever he is, who convinced your weak-minded friend Clint that he wouldn't be punished for his actions. Hypnosis, or some cheap trick like that. Isn't he nice, manipulating behind the scene to bring you down?"

"All right, all right, so you know everything. But don't look so happy yet. I'll find a way to get him into Sing Sing." The last time I talked to Clint, I'd sensed the Guardian toying with his mind. My former sidekick used to look forward to Saturdays when he could cook for Fernando, but after my brother died, he befriended alcohol, which weakened his mind so much that he turned to fortune-tellers and motivation speakers.

"Maybe he's trying to stop you from breaking this code. So, don't be a fool and fall for his trap." Ganesh finished his skim milk and said, "By the way, no need to hide the will. What I need to know, I know."

What an annoying gnat. Still, I needed him to help me crack the Guzman code and deal with Clint and the Guardian. I asked him to join me at the bar to brainstorm but as always he refused with the same excuse: he hated bars. How could a cat hate fish? Next time, I'd force him to go to Atlantic City's casinos. One try and he'd return again and again. Trust me.

***

In the evening, while I reviewed the Chaocipher code and reread the journal entry where Holly gave me a code, my bloodhound beggar reported that Clint had thrashed him in an underground tunnel. My former assistant had been tailing Faith since this morning, from her apartment to Greenwich Village to the subway station, but he disappeared among the tunnels. Faith went missing. My associate had checked Ganesh's mental hospital, but couldn't find her.

I had my associate check into a hospital, expenses on me. Called Faith several times, but she didn't answer her phone. I slammed my desk. I threw the penholder into the trash bin.

What if the mysterious client was referring to Faith rather than Holly? I'd hoped Faith was only hiding from Clint, but soon I found her bloodied body. Damn it.

CHAPTER 41 - X

November 5 (2)

When the door opened, I expected Rick's angry face, but Dr. Tang entered and said, "The trouble with you, is you think you're the Lone Ranger."

"No, not at all. The Lone Ranger had a partner."

Dr. Tang must enjoy popping up and helping me out of trouble, though I could rescue him more than he could me. His DNA probably had destined him to try to save the day and he couldn't standby and enjoy the show. Just like Francisco the narcissistic alcoholic who couldn't keep his mouth shut. Dr. Tang should rescue Ingrid rather than play the masked adventurer. "Where's Ingrid? You're supposed to rescue her, not me. Has a virus impaired your neo-cortex?"

"You shouldn't question my brain. If there's anything I'm proud of, it's my brain."

"Who cares about your brain. Where's Ingrid?" He babbled like Francisco. Perhaps the virus that infected my dream self had also infected the good doctor.

"Safe." Dr. Tang picked up the broken bat. "Whatever tricks you were up to, you won't need them now."

If only I was playing tricks. Still couldn't move or feel my arms and legs. Maybe someone had hexed me with a voodoo doll. Mrs. McCoy still slept on the divan and I worried the gas might've harmed her.

"I can't move my arms or legs."

"Someone drugged you and paralyzed you?"

241

"Paralyzed, yes. Drugged, not sure. I was standing here—"

While a rumble in the distance loosened the curtain, a dog whistle provoked a bark. How could I hear a dog whistle? Superpower, of course. The bark didn't come from the hallway, but from Pratt's bedroom.

The bedroom door flung open. Pratt barked and growled and saliva dripped from his mouth. Fear soaked my body. I didn't want to die. I wanted to recover my memory and my past. My skin and flesh tingled with pulses as if shocked by static. How had he *turned into a dog*?

"Someone used PC or SP on him," Dr. Tang said, "Or worse, CP."

"I hope you know what to do."

Dr. Tang slid his index finger in front of Pratt and snapped his fingers, but Pratt barked and lunged, his teeth aiming for my neck.

I willed my arms and legs to move, but no luck. Dr. Tang crashed into me and we fell beside the sofa while Pratt flew overhead and crashed into the TV. After he dropped onto the floor, the TV collapsed on him.

Someone blew the dog whistle a second time and Pratt shook off the splinters on his head and charged again. As a gas canister flew into the room through the front door.

"Beta," Dr. Tang said, "It's him."

I must live. I had to see Ingrid again. I had to find Molly. Strength surged through my breast. I felt my arms and legs. I could move them.

I pushed away Dr. Tang and with Pratt's teeth six inches from my neck, I leaped up, grabbed his jacket, and threw him out the door. He landed across the hallway, crashing into the wall. When I stepped into the hallway, he ran after a balding man, probably Agent Beta. The agent must've hypnotized Pratt and convinced the feeble mind that he is a dog. Would Dr. Tang start biting me? No, he could overcome mind control.

I didn't want to live in this world, where advertisers manipulate the mind for profits and programmers customize memory to create the perfect citizens, where a man could turn into a dog and try to bite me.

While I dashed along the hallway, Pratt tumbled down the stair. I was going to chase after the agent and the dog, but recalled the gas in the apartment and returned to check on Dr. Tang and Mrs. McCoy.

Inside the apartment, the canister was gone and the gas was dispersing. Mrs. McCoy had disappeared, probably having woken up and left. Dr. Tang was on the balcony gazing at the distant smoke, which gushed into the sky.

On the balcony, I sniffed the charred air as another plume of smoke rose into the sky. In the street the canister spewed gas. Farther away, students demonstrated in a plaza as another black plume shot into the air.

That day, after I left him and returned to the cabin, Dr. Tang continued on the trail down the mountain where he expected to find Ingrid. Near the foothill, shouts alarmed him. Concerned for Ingrid, he hurried along the path and reached the edge of the woods as Gamma and several rebels forced Ingrid into the transport. He had never met Gamma but dealt with Beta several times, so recognized the slanted nose. He ran toward them and was about to shout when a hand from the back covered his mouth and silenced him. He flew backwards and landed in the bushes, the hand still over his mouth. After Gamma and his gang had left with Ingrid, the woman who held him down released him. She was the rebel leader. Since Gamma had defected with a group of militant rebels, those who cared nothing for the civilians, she intended to quash the radicals before they turned public opinions against all rebels. She let them kidnap Ingrid so as to draw out the mastermind guiding Gamma's hands and legs. She would followed them to their hideout and destroy them. Dr. Tang objected but he could do nothing. The rebel leader invited him along as they tracked Gamma to the hideout but he could only observe. If he should try to sabotage the operation, she would lock him up. They followed Gamma to an abandoned industrial complex in Pythagorean Triangle, a hideout that only Gamma's five personal guards could access. The rebel leader's spies couldn't wheedle the info from those confidants.

Dr. Tang and the rebels hid in a warehouse across the complex and waited for the mastermind to come. That night, Doc tried to leave the warehouse and enter the complex to rescue Ingrid but the leader caught him and tied him to a post.

The next morning, Gamma's puppeteer stepped off her transport and entered the complex.

"I couldn't believe my eyes." Dr. Tang kicked the broken bat out of the apartment. "I almost fainted. I requested the leader take me along."

From the sweat pouring down his forehead, I guessed who she was but I refuted the fact. I must be wrong. I had to be wrong. Otherwise...

"Dolly didn't return from the dead," Dr. Tang said. "It was Molly."

"No, it can't be. You're lying." I went for Dr. Tang's neck, but before reaching it, I stopped myself. If I hadn't, I would have broken his neck. I refused to believe him and I still don't. He had mistaken someone else for Molly.

The rebel leader ignored Dr. Tang and stormed the complex. Shots hammered out their tunes and bombs drummed out their notes. Shouts and cries. Smoke emerged from the buildings and soon obscured Dr. Tang's view. He worried about Ingrid's safety. He struggled but couldn't untie the double fisherman's knot. The smoke was filling the warehouse and Dr. Tang kept scraping the rope against the post and soon tired himself. Amid the din and chaos, the warehouse door opened. Dr. Tang thought the rebel leader had returned for him and he shouted to untie him, but when a breeze thinned out the smoke, Ingrid emerged and embraced him. Then untied him and pulled him out of the warehouse without explaining what had happened. He found out from Ingrid that Gamma and Molly had escaped from the rebel leader.

"I didn't care that they had escape, I only held onto Ingrid, a second chance at life."

Would I have another chance at life?

"Well, I'm glad you came," I said.

"My friend from the Intelligence Agency, actually he's no longer there but still gets access to the information, he told me about Pratt Calhoun's scuffle. So I came to look for you."

"Who's your friend anyway?"

"You know better than to ask." Dr. Tang leaned on the balustrade, surveyed the street and said, "The rebels probably blew up another police station, or a military depot. Or the police raided a rebel hideout."

"I was going to hand you Pratt so you could take revenge. But too bad, he's become a dog." In the empty bedroom, the linen tied into a rope dangled out of the window. "Guess he isn't a gambler."

"I've learned from Ingrid that we can turn pain into whatever we want. We can become angry, bitter and vengeful, or we can become wise, strong and compassionate. She still believes we can make a difference, while I've given up." Dr. Tang punched a hole through the drywall and white powder covered his fist.

I agreed with his every word about Ingrid's spirit and character but still would *kick his butt*, as Francisco would sum up. She must have revealed her past, her pain and struggle, and her indomitable spirit. What had she shared with me that she hadn't with him? What uniqueness could I claim before him, except the loss of memory?

"After her brother had died," he said, "she tutored other students and saved money. She invested the money in treasury bonds and eventually paid her way to college. While living in the foster home, she learned martial arts and fought off the bullies."

I should punch Dr. Tang for knowing Ingrid's childhood when I didn't. No, he created these stories to taunt me. I ignored his tale and looked through the window at the burning buildings.

Several pops echoed from the street below. The students weren't opening Champagne bottles to celebrate a cease-fire. After more pops, they dispersed and fell along the street. So the fighting had reached this area.

"What kind of people should we be?" Dr. Tang glanced at the students for several seconds before turning around and walking into the bathroom.

"First of all, living. That trumps everything else. I hope you aren't thinking of something silly like shooting the police."

"Let's do something." He rummaged through the cabinet and after taking the first aid kit overtook me.

"Like putting on Band-Aids?" I should protest, reason with him, convince him the futility of helping zealots who would continue to protest and take in bullets when they could walk again. Instead, I stowed away my backpack in the kitchen cabinet and followed him into the street, where the charred smell mixed with a fishy scent.

While leaving the building, Dr. Tang said the plain-text for the Chaocipher code would be the sequence A-Z and the cipher-text the sequence Holly had given Francisco on August 13, 2006.

"Glad you recorded Francisco's diary entry." Dr. Tang stepped into the street where smoke and dust obscured cars and buildings.

"Glad Francisco recorded it." I pinched my nose to avoid the stench.

The smoke shifted and the pops reached the street corner. Dr. Tang grabbed his toolkit from the car. We searched for blood. We sterilized infections. We anesthetized twitching flesh. We took out bullets. We bandaged wounds. We closed blank eyes. All the while, the pops retreated but the fog descended to replace the smoke. A cool, refreshing fine dust.

Unlike Dr. Tang, I couldn't find a lamppost, a fire hydrant, or a mural on a wall to detain me. Sans the doctor's passion I helped these students who had fallen without taking arms. Maybe I knew that for each person we saved, another ten would fall. Maybe I couldn't relate to the earth, the air and the people and I didn't want to. At least, I cared about Molly, Ingrid and Dr. Tang.

An explosion on the next block spewed debris and smoke into the street. I ran toward the smoke where a young man, right arm two-thirds missing, staggered for three steps before falling onto the ground. I approached him and called Dr. Tang. The body convulsed while I held it down.

Someone approached and knelt beside me. A syringe jabbed into the man's right shoulder. I thought Dr. Tang came to help, but Ingrid, her blonde hair tied into a ponytail, treated the man.

"You should stop tailing Doc, so he could pick up a lady or two at the bar." I backed off when the man's convulsions subsided.

"It won't work. So, stop wasting your time." She put away the syringe.

Dr. Tang approached and covered the man's nose and mouth with the anesthesia mask. I held it down while he applied nitrous oxide. He opened his kit and laid scalpels on a towel while she cut away the man's shirt and applied isopropyl alcohol to the wounds. As I watched, Dr. Tang cut open the flesh around the right shoulder to remove fragments of bones, glass and splinters and Ingrid stitched up the openings, both of them so natural at their tasks. I envied their camaraderie.

As I applied pressure to slow the bleeding and watched them finish the operation, I decided to help Dr. Tang eliminate the CP data. I wouldn't sell the data to the highest bidder and retire to the Bahamas. I didn't like the Bahamas anyway. After my decision, I inhaled the air that continued to reek of blood and charcoal. Had I been wasting my time searching for my past? I should seize the future instead of digging up my annals though without the past I would be half a man.

"The rebels are counterattacking and sweeping through this area. So, we better leave soon." Ingrid finished stitching and bound cuts along the body's right side.

When they had finished, I carried the man into a nearby building's empty apartment. I was about to look for Dr. Tang when the pimple-nosed boy who led me into the trap charged out of the building and said, "Help! Help!" He approached me and grabbed my sleeve. "Help my dad." Before he could take another step, Pratt, clutching his torn shirt and bloodied abdomen, staggered out of the building and fell onto the sidewalk.

So, the boy's father was Pratt. No wonder he went to that fake New York. Molly must've known him through Dolly. Did he go to the building to look for me or for Pratt? He might have been returning home. He helped me escape from the military compound (or prison, or school) and died delivering a message to me, and yet I couldn't even save his life. I had to wait for him to resurrect in a difference reality. Why should I look for my memory and my past when I couldn't even save a boy who had helped me? Of course, I might have revived him by jumping from one reality to another.

Pratt twitched, raised his hand and he begged me to kill him. His eyes clouded over and he gazed into empty space. I knelt down to ask for the perpetrator. The boy said, "My mom."

So, an ex-wife had punished Pratt for not paying child custody. Or for some other grievances. I had to leave this world, to avoid this air and these people.

Dr. Tang approached and examined Pratt, who after convulsing and moaning for a while grabbed my sleeve and again begged for death. Dr. Tang shook his head and opened the toolkit, then took out a syringe and filled it with solution. "This is why I didn't want to be a medical doctor."

He was going to do it. He had to do it. Before he could inject the solution, I took the syringe from him and said, "Let me do it. Go help the others."

He hesitated, but I said, "I'm more callous than you are." He lowered his head for a moment before joining Ingrid to help another student.

I stared at the needle and at Pratt's pulsing cheek. The boy held Pratt's arm and looked at me. After glancing at his abdominal wound, I jabbed the syringe into Pratt's chest and injected the solution.

Pratt opened his eyes and stared at me. He tried to push away. "Ya... ya... killed... killed my boy..." His open mouth, dilated pupils, stretched cheek froze, the expression preserved in his final moment.

His mouth could no longer explain his words and reveal the secret. He seemed surprised, as if he had just recognized me. He probably had recalled his son's death and mistaken me for the killer. I couldn't have killed his son. I couldn't have killed anyone. Still, I had enjoyed his fear.

When I raised my head and surveyed the street, the boy, with Pratt's knife in hand, ran along the sidewalk toward the intersection. I called after him, but he didn't slow down or turn his head.

He was probably going after his mother. I called after him, to stop him from crossing the line and jumping into the abyss, to rescue him the inferno. I couldn't stop him, but he would never have the chance to kill his mother either.

As he passed a liquor store, a bomb inside exploded and the debris rushed out and swept him into the air. He shot into a car parked across the street, cracking the windshield.

I shouted no, no, no, while life and hope and salvation vanished before my eyes. Darkness descended as another explosion muffled my voice. A typewriter seemed to tap out continuous notes. A familiar melody. Perhaps an elegy. I didn't care. I had tunneled into another world. The boy resurrecting from the dead had given me hope that with enough changes in reality, I would regain my memory. His death sealed my fate and wiped out my hope. As another series of taps sounded nearby, I prepared to take the shower of bullets and leave this wasteland.

Someone shoved me. In midair, I turned. Dr. Tang was pushing me away while bullets rushed at his head, neck and back. Something stirred in my stomach. From darkness and the abyss, I returned to this world. Strength filled my arms and legs. I swung my arm and swept away the bullet. I hated these guns and bullets.

We fell to the ground and I said, "Doc, like I said before, you don't have to impress me or Ingrid."

"Bad habit. Next time, remind me not to save you." Dr. Tang brushed away the powder on his face and ran down the street to help Ingrid with a wounded woman.

When a rebel, who looked like Virginia E. Boss in my dream, staggered out of the building that Pratt had emerged from and held her right arm in her left hand, I approached and treated her wound. I told her a wounded student in the building needed surgery. The rebel, who turned out to be the leader Dr, Tang had met, called her unit and had them rush a van over to pick up the student. After showing the student's location, I returned to Dr. Tang and Ingrid, who were binding another wounded student two blocks away. I carried a youngster to the sidewalk and waited for Molly to appear around the corner.

Ingrid wrapped the scalpels in another towel and returned the bundle into the kit. She urged us to leave before the squadron of rebels arrived.

I returned to Pratt's apartment to pick up my backpack, but couldn't find the laptop in the kitchen cabinet. Either it had walked out of the bag or itchy fingers had taken it. I searched the cabinet. I pushed away the debris. I lifted the smashed TV. No laptop anywhere in the apartment. Beta might have returned to snatch it. Fortunately, I had put a GPS receiver with transmitter in the laptop to send its location every fifteen minutes to my phone.

When Ingrid and Dr. Tang stepped into the apartment, an explosion shook the ground and the building a block away spewed out flames. The pops advanced again, probably three or four blocks away.

When I mentioned the missing laptop, Dr. Tang gave me the thumb drive into which he had copied my diary. I abandoned the search, but before we could exit the building, the rebels had flooded the neighborhood. We returned to the apartment and waited for their retreat.

In the street, thirty to forty policemen fled toward a warehouse, but the rebels cut down half of them before they could go one block. The last one fell in front of the warehouse. The rebels burned a post office on the next block and chanted a slogan in the street. Their band played a paean. Then more pops, but they were only shooting into the air, to celebrate victory. As intermittent gunshots saluted the air, vagrants emerged from manholes to rummage through the carcasses, but after a bomb blew up a store on the next block, they scattered.

When the rebels entered the building and came up the stairs, Ingrid cleaned her hands of blood and said, "Let me take care of this."

"You don't have to prove yourself to impress me." I glanced at Dr. Tang and said, "Or him. We think you're fascinating, fantastic, fabulous."

She opened the door and walked down the hallway, where footsteps thundered. Before I could step out of the apartment, Dr. Tang shut the door.

CHAPTER 42 – FRANCISCO

October 17, 2011 (1)

I didn't sleep the night my beggar associate lost Faith. According to her building's concierge, she hadn't returned since leaving in the morning. I called again but she didn't pick up the phone. Back in the Prophet Office, I asked my police associate to post Clint's stubble-face at bars, brothels, fight clubs, and gambling dens. The fanatics also distributed wanted posters in the underground tunnels.

This morning, my beggar associate left the hospital, and I had him post his homeless scouts from Bedford-Stuyvesant to the Lower East Side to the South Bronx. I ran the image recognition software on police surveillance videos across the city, but searching through thousands of videotapes might take more than a month. Ganesh had tracked down the transmitter I'd put in Clint's shoe but my former sidekick had donated his footwear to a vagrant in the Bowery.

While my associates scoured the city looking for Faith, I drove to the Catskill Mountains, not to picnic, but to revisit a memory and to complete a transaction. Under light fog, trees along New York State Thruway shed their leaves and the breeze tossed them across the road. In late Octobers and early Novembers, Fernando and I had hiked in these mountains. Our car would plunge through the shower of leaves, just as mine was doing. Except, he no longer sat beside me.

The white chrysanthemums I'd planted seventeen years ago blossomed beside the gurgling brook, probably, even after these years, still drawing nutrients from my father's decayed body. He bound the girl's hands and feet and ripped off her blouse. I grabbed a rock and smashed his head. The girl sobbed. My hands dug through the soil. The anger and the fear seventeen years ago, the trembling and the panting, the sense of betrayal and lost, they had fled from my bosom and dispersed among time's moments. The chatter between wind and brook calmed my agitation with not having broken the damn code. I no longer hated my father because I no longer cared. I no longer cared about his betraying my trust and his shattering my illusion of him, because my heart had long ago shredded his image. Time had cleansed my heart and I could enjoy the morning air without regard for the stench below the ground. The young Francisco who had killed his father and saved the girl, who had buried the body and planted the seeds, a stranger from another eon, another planet, traveled through the years and months and days and held out his hand. As I stooped to smell the chrysanthemums, to examine the white pedals and yellow pistils, I only cared about the autumn fragrance. I waved my hand and bid him adieu as the foliages hummed a crisp tune, but prayed for him to visit again and revive the courage and chivalry I'd need to face tomorrow.

I didn't want to delay cracking the code—I didn't want my head to part way with my torso—but I couldn't put off finding Faith either. As I checked the results from the image recognition software with my laptop, a thick fog descended on the brook and the surrounding woods. I couldn't see ten feet away. I couldn't see the path, the fork, or the rocks waiting to trip me. Yet, even on a murky path, my past triumphs convinced me I'd reach Faith.

I was about to leave the white chrysanthemums, when the Messenger, his nose bandaged, walked toward me, whistling a Dixie tune. "Nice place for a retreat. I can see why you come to clear your brain."

"Nice place for burials. You're standing on one now. So, if you want to reserve a spot, move ten steps to the right." I put the laptop in the backpack.

"Don't tell me you've decided to abandon problem solving and become a serial killer. At least finish our job first, before switching your profession. Professional ethics, or just plain courtesy." The Messenger kicked a rock into the brook and the water rippled for several seconds.

"I wouldn't miss out on my fee. In this day and age, even a serial killer needs money for daily expenses and monthly bills. So, show me the million dollars and I'd show you the diamonds."

"Change of plan."

"Not a problem. You're still trying to impress me with your tongue-licking-frozen-lamppost routine. FYI, that broken nose's pretty impressive." I stooped and smelled the chrysanthemum. "All right, plan B, then. So, I'll sell the diamonds. Not as difficult as you'd think. I know a Russian millionaire who'd pay a handsome price." At that moment, thinking I had the upper hand, I was willing to play his game. I enjoyed my moment for about thirty seconds.

"No, you won't." The Messenger shoved his hands into his pants pockets, probably to grasp a gun or a knife.

"Since when have you become a prophet or a fortuneteller? Did you predict the Guardian would break your nose? If you want to succeed and keep a good reputation, read someone else's fortune." My eyes tracked his hands while my foot eyed his groin.

"Here's the amount we promised you." He pulled out a check. "Get it into your head. You ain't getting anymore than this."

"Do you really want your diamonds back?"

"No, we don't."

"Sounds good so far." I grabbed the check and pocketed it.

"You're to deliver the diamonds to the Guardian. You know, that dolt who tried to steal them from you while you're stealing it from us."

"You mean the dolt who broke your nose?" I thrust my head forward to examine the bandage. "There's something irrational, illogical, contradictory in what you're proposing. Something so wrong that I might've stepped into an anti-universe, where up is down, right is wrong, good is bad."

"Cut the crap."

"Wow, you've impressed me. First off, why give the diamonds to that loser of a Guardian? And then, did I hear you right? I stole the diamonds from you? So, you had the diamonds all along and spent the money to play a game? Are you testing my capability? For playing games with the client, I charge a twenty-percent overhead. And then, the most ridiculous idea, why would I give up the diamonds for this pittance, when I could sell it in the black market for millions? What am I missing?"

"Certainly, you're missing your friend, Holly. And she's waiting for you to rescue her. Now, do you want to cower, to slither, to scrimp? Or do you want to save the damsel in distress?"

After wiping my sole on the grass, I threw a piece of dark chocolate into my mouth, adjust my jacket and whistled "Praise to Fransuccesco." I lunged at him but that snake slipped away and shook his index finger.

Holly must still be alive or he wouldn't threaten me. He had better not tortured her.

"People who threaten me, they usually get their noses cracked," I said. "For your information, she'll kick your butt, to put it lightly. After she's done suing you, you'd want to be a Bowery bum, not that I have anything against them."

Ms. Redhead was probably the mysterious client. She'd cut off the Naked Man's hand and run down my neighbor with her sedan. She'd kidnapped Holly and probably planned to harm Faith, to force me to crack the code. Instead of pulling out my nunchuks to show the Messenger my Bruce Lee moves, I decided to play a different game. Cat and mouse. I had to rescue Holly and protect Faith before the final deadline tomorrow and I intended to beat the Boss at her game.

"Hey, cut the crap and choose. You can't talk your way out of this. If you hadn't try to blackmail us, we wouldn't have to resort to such drastic measures. But we're here to get a job done and we'd do it." He folded his arms across his chest, as if he had the upper hand. However, I had a wild card in my pocket.

While the fog covered the brook and obscured his features, I picked up a two-foot branch and swung a wide arc to disperse the mist. "Getting your nose broken isn't fun. On the other hand, I naturally want to be a hero. Sure, I've enough credential to prove I'm a hero. What more do I want? Then again, I have a soft heart and don't want my friend to get hurt by losers like you."

"What's this blabbering? You know, once you open your mouth, you can't shut it."

"All right, I'm feeling generous. So, I agree to deliver the diamonds to that loser of a Guardian. I still don't understand why you bother with that creep." Of course, I wouldn't deliver the diamonds to the Guardian. I'd only follow this dolt to his hideout and rescue Holly. Simple as that. After that, I'd sell the diamonds on the black market and retire to the Bahamas with Faith. Yes, Faith, I must find her. After getting my retirement fund, I would *reward* Ms. Boss for messing with me. Always repay kindness.

"Oh, you won't understand even if I try to explain. Just keep in mind, we want that creep who calls himself the Guardian, not the diamonds. He's the hero of the story."

"But I'm the hero of the story."

CHAPTER 43 - X

November 6

Even before I returned to the water villa, the transmitter had sent my laptop's position to my phone. After confirming the location, I led Ingrid into Next Market. Even as I searched the crowd for the thief, I found out more about her and so had to choose between betraying her or Dr. Tang.

Among shoppers in cardigans, blouses, saris, and sarongs, I basked in the aroma of foods and spices, yesterday's battlefield still vivid in my mind, the bullets, smoke and blood mingling with the sirens, shouts and groans. The children now chased each other as if the other world didn't exist. Only the patrols among the stalls reminded shoppers of potential rebel attacks.

I should tell Ingrid I love her, but I didn't. I began to doubt my resolve in finding my past, in facing reality, in building myself through previous experiences. The past buried beneath crimes; reality clouded behind intrigues; and previous experiences tainted with blood. As I inserted my ID at a checkpoint, I vowed to leave this land for an island or a mountain, perhaps a desert. First, I had to catch a computer thief.

"Do you know how Rainier would put his chin on his right palm and stare at a stapler or paper clip on the desk?" she said.

Yesterday, after shutting the door, Dr. Tang said, "Trust her. When she said she'd do something, she'll do it." I patted him on the shoulder for playing the coward and elevating me in Ingrid's eyes. Still, I couldn't stand his confidence in her, as if he knew her inside out. I believed in her ability but worried about her safety, while he seemed to neglect her well-being.

I prepared to rush into the hallway if the discussion should turn hostile, but after the voices of Ingrid and the rebels rose and fell, laughter and singing drifted into the unit, as if they were celebrating. A few minutes later, the footsteps retreated. A knock. I opened the door and Ingrid urged us to leave before the government forces could return to avenge their comrades. She led us out of the building without revealing how she had persuaded the rebels.

She hadn't mentioned a word about her conversation with the rebels. Even now, squeezing through the crowd and tying her hair into a ponytail, she said, "I imitated him. But don't tell him about it. Or he might be angry with me."

"For a while, I thought you're their leader." I would never be angry with her but before I could reveal my thought, the scent of cumin wafted through the air and I sneezed. Taking out a tissue I blew my nose, but nothing came out of the nostrils. I could feel the saliva in my mouth but it seemed the fluid couldn't reach my nasal passages. I threw the tissue into a trashcan and expected never to have to blow my nose again.

On the day Gamma kidnapped her, she could've escaped, but she stayed to talk him out of his crusade.

"I had to try."

"Who is he to you?"

"I failed. I knew I'd fail, but I had to try."

"You left that fake hospital in a hurry," I said. "Didn't even say goodbye."

"Thought I'd never see Rainier again. But—" Ingrid took out a chestnut and walked to the turmeric stall.

"But, you would've search for him to the ends of the earth, until the end of time, until all matter and antimatter annihilate each other. I know, I know." I tasted bile and almost vomited. "You don't give up, do you?"

"One of the bad habits I'd picked up, growing up in a rough world."

In the hospital or high school, I would have fought Dr. Tang for Ingrid's heart, until the sun collapses into a black-hole, but she had defeated me on his behalf by refusing to be our trophy. A glorious victory for her. For Dr. Tang, who had abandoned civilization for the desert, an unexpected oasis. I still held onto hope and searched for a flagstone path out of this night.

"He wasn't working for the Intelligence Agency."

"I know."

"Only wanted to destroy the CP data, not help them retrieve it."

"I know."

"His friend at the Agency got him into the hospital. But of course the Agency wanted him—" Ingrid dropped the chestnut and tried to pick it up but her fingers trembled and she dropped it again.

"I know; I know; I know everything. I don't care about him. You, who did you work for? The Agency? Dr. Tang?"

"He didn't want to work with the Agency to deceive you. Only to destroy the data and prevent Armageddon. But he couldn't go through with it, deceiving you. He realized how cold, how inhumane he'd been." She grasped the chestnut in her palm and veins appeared on the back of her hand.

"But do you think he's cold, hard and jaded?" If only she would despise him for his callousness. If only she would crush the chestnut.

"Often, he took solitary walks through the path of chestnut trees. I sensed his troubles and was determined to join him in that path, to search for, to construct meaning."

I had forgiven her and would've accepted any excuse, but she didn't make a single one. She made excuses for Dr. Tang and the more I listened, the more I struggled for breath. I had to sit down beside the chutney stall and bend over the bench. I should grab the chestnut and crush it.

"He struggled against the slavery of necessity, the need to save humanity by deceiving you. In the end, he freed himself and decided to inform you about the set up at the risk of your hoarding the data. But you no doubt found out about the hoax and escaped. He's still determined to destroy the data." She put the chestnut into her coat pocket. Paced to the bench but returned to the stall and surveyed the sauces.

"Can he subdue me?" I knocked down the bench with my left leg and waited for her excuses. But none came.

"I'd never allow you to touch him" She turned from the scenery and focused her eyes on me, like a lioness about to leap at an antelope. She turned and walked away rather than lunge at me.

I called after her. I chased after her.

I extended my hand and tried to understand her hopes and regrets, but the mist like a wall seeped between us and I averted my fingers before touching hers. "Sometimes you have that hard expression, as if you're determined to ram through a door. And I realized I don't know anything about you." While a police captain announced the community patrol would be executing gamblers in an hour, the scent of lavender reached my nose and yesterday's scenes of smoke and bullets and bodies flashed through my mind.

"Please tell me why you couldn't forgive me," I said. According to the coordinates in my phone, the laptop, or at least the transmitter, was less than a hundred feet ahead. I search among the faces for the thief. How would a thief look like? Probably, like me.

"I could sense his struggle, his pain, the gray sky and foggy swamp. I understand why he needs those solitary walks. And sometimes, I had to restrain myself from walking beside him."

A man in T-shirt and jean, who looked liked the Naked Man in my dream, blocked the path and peddled cowboy hats and boots. I pinched myself to confirm I wasn't dreaming. I must have met him before losing my memory and I dreamed of him. I grabbed his bag and pulled out assault rifles and automatic shotguns and ammunitions, but no laptop. Before I could return his belonging, he ran into the crowd and several policemen chased after him.

When I checked my phone, I had lost the signal. Pushing away the bodies. Squeezing through the crowd. I searched the faces for the thief, unsure how a scoundrel or a criminal would look like.

"I was once a rebel," Ingrid said.

"If only I was once something, just anything would suffice." These men and women in the crowd, what had they once been? A dreamer? A painter? Only a boy or a girl? In the distance, Molly's face flitted between a sombrero and a fedora. Just an instant. Just a mirage. While I gazed at that spot, she disappeared. I surveyed the crowd but couldn't find her face. I had to confirm that she didn't work with Gamma. She wouldn't tolerate Gamma's violence even as a rebel. Did she steal my laptop, after helping me recover it?

"Joined when I was young. Not sabotaging government buildings and military depots, but counseling fellow fighters, from war trauma and all that. Killing's not easy for most people. It exacts a psychological toll and some never could recover. But for most rebels, the therapy helped them cope with the atrocity and the looming sense of death. I even worked with the leader on her psychological trauma." Ingrid pointed at the policemen handcuffing the Naked Man. "We do what we have to, to keep ourselves sane."

No wonder she knew Gamma. No wonder she wanted to dissuade him from violence. No wonder she could talk the rebel leader into letting Dr. Tang and me alone. Of course, the leader didn't harm Dr. Tang when he tried to interfere with her plan to capture Gamma and the mastermind, so she didn't care for random violence. She was cold, like Virginia E. Boss, but not evil.

"I wish to be disillusioned about something. Some failure, some unfulfilled aspiration, something to illustrate my past years, my joy, my grief, my anger, my jealousy. Yes, I'd like to know I envied someone." At that moment, Mrs. McCoy's bonnet darted between a turban and a fedora, but before I locked on the face, a ten-gallon hat blocked my view. Afterward, the bonnet disappeared. A truck stopped at the market entrance and the patrolmen unloaded men and women in chains and striped uniforms.

At a shooting gallery, children blasted life-sized targets of beggars, prostitutes and drug addicts, while the parents chatted about having a picnic after the execution. Had I seen Molly and Mrs. McCoy? Were they meeting to plan Mr. Smith's prison escape? Should I wake up from this dream? No, I didn't want to return to Francisco's world.

Amid the shots, Ingrid glanced beyond the children and their parents, as if searching for someone among the red, yellow and blue apparels. She was probably looking for Dr. Tang. I didn't ask. The faces round and slender in the crowd, could they appreciate having a name and a past? I wouldn't, if I had never lost my memory.

"I apologize for whatever I've done. But I need to know and I want to—"

She left the shooting gallery and rushed along the walkway, as if running from her past. Or, she might be running from me.

"Tell me about my evil past." I ran after her. I yearned to hold her hand. A boy pushed me aside and ran to the ice-cream stall. In the distance, the prisoners filed past the tent and ascended the stage.

"Like so many other youngsters, I was idealistic, passionate for a cause. I wanted to make a difference, to fight for justice, to help build a better world. Now, it sounds so cliché, so naïve, so foolish." She stopped and pointed at the gallows. "The first corpse woke me from my romantic visions, or perhaps illusions. Death as a concept, as an ideal differs from death in flesh and blood, the latter so much messier and uglier."

"Can you forgive me?" I took her hand. I caressed her hand. I led her from the gallows to a Malaysian food stall where the proprietor was serving laksa to a customer. I offered to buy her dinner in a nearby mall but she declined the offer. Sure, she would meet Dr. Tang. I didn't want to find the laptop anymore. Or maybe even to recover my memory. I would just like to see Molly again.

"It takes years of training, like martial arts, to get used to the blood and bullets," she said. "When I joined the rebels, my anger had intermingled with excitement and hope, hope for a better tomorrow."

How had I wounded her? I must recall. She must tell me.

"When I left, I still felt that anger, but anger had mixed with disgust, disgust with human savageness. After meeting my former comrades again, I've rekindled anger and disgust. But, unlike the Ingrid who'd left the rebels disillusioned and unable to direct those emotions, I've blended them into an apathetic stew. So if I see them slaughtering again, I'd walk down another road. Rainier could empathize, because of his own disillusionment." She closed her eyes and a lock of hair dropped over her forehead.

I reached over to kiss Ingrid and share in her grief, but those lips waited for Dr. Tang's, not mine. "I have something to tell you." I was about to snitch on Dr. Tang when a boy snatched an old lady's purse and disappeared into the crowd while she shouted after him. Several patrolmen ran after the pickpocket and the crowd opened a way for them. I hurried after Ingrid without knowing the boy's fate.

"I mourn the loss of the other Ingrids and sometimes waited for them to visit me, to remind me of the fresh air, the warbler's song, the lavender's scent. But time like a dungeon master has locked them in the cages of past moments, unwilling to release them to the present. So, like Rainier, I've also released my past so I could trot on a new path. Yes, we still believe in a better future. He hasn't abandoned his past selves however childish and silly, and so I wouldn't either. Together, we'll help each other search for the beacons in the past to shine a path into the future." She took out a chestnut and rotated it.

I grasped the acorn in my pocket, letting pedestrians dressed in red, brown, yellow and purple pass me. Two girls ran around me and chased each other, their giggles as distant as my past. The image of Molly among the crowd surfaced onto my mind. I glanced around but couldn't spot her. "How could I mourn my past selves if I don't know them? How could anyone mourn for a stranger except in the most general way? Yes, we have our common humanity, but we need connections to hurt deep within the heart, to taste pain that could tear our flesh apart." My phone beeped to signal it had received data from the laptop, but I ignored the sound and focused on my pain.

"I love you." I held her hand.

"I hate you." She didn't pull away.

"I don't mind. At least you have feelings for me. At least you aren't indifferent." I tried to lift her hand but it slipped from mine.

"I wish you're someone else. I wish you're anyone but you."

"As I said before, I'd be whomever you want me to be. Just name it." I tried to take her hand again, but my hand froze beside my leg. The fog seemed to be seeping into my bones and slithering through my spine.

"It wasn't by accident I was Rainier's colleague in that charade."

She was probably spying on me. If she also wanted the CP data, I would give her everything, to show my love. Only a fool would choose the CP data over love. Even Dr. Tang, a fool for years, could appraise those options.

"I came to spy on Rainier." She said, as a wave of men and women separated us and the moisture thickened in the air.

Why Dr. Tang? Why not me? What secrets was she trying to dig up from the doctor's past? Was she seeking revenge?

The crowd pushed her away and rushed toward the gallows where the patrolmen put nooses around the prisoners' necks. I cut through the mass and was about to reach her when I spotted Molly behind an antique stall.

CHAPTER 44 - FRANCISCO

October 17, 2011 (2)

After the Messenger had left, I shadowed him from the Catskill Mountains back into the city. Soon I would see Holly. By the time we crossed the George Washington Bridge, the fog still covered the skyscrapers' upper sections. Along Hudson Parkway I negotiated through the moderate traffic and managed the distance between our cars. By the time we reached Bleecker Street, the rush hour traffic had congested the roads. Tailing him through the crowded streets, I phoned my beggar associates for help. The Messenger walked to Washington Square to have coffee and cheesecake. I ate a piece of durian pie while waiting for him. When the Messenger went into a massage parlor, I sent an associate to enter through the back door and check on the loser.

While waiting in a teahouse across the street and thanking the Messenger for wasting my time, I solved the Chaocipher code. Voila, another unsolvable code solved. Anyway, CHAO, besides referring to the Chaocipher code, was also the coded word. After that revelation, I only had to decode this word.

I turned to the August 13, 2006 entry to retrieve the cipher-text. As I reread the diary entry, I couldn't recall Holly having given me that sequence. After we'd finished the champagne, we made love and her law firm partner called. I still remembered the details. Yet, the cipher-text in the diary entry stared at me. Ever since the Guardian had helped me recall *that event*, I couldn't trust my memory anymore. It Then again, someone might've tampered with my diary.

I finished the green tea and used the cipher-text to decipher the code word CHAO and I got NFTU. I entered the word to unlock the file from Faith, but the screen showed the question: *What does NFTU stand for?* Just great, another code within a code. Testing Francisco's limits. I should walk across the street and enter the massage parlor. I should find the Messenger and squeeze out his boss's holding cell, which wasn't in the school. But I waited.

After an hour, the Messenger left the massage parlor and skipped down the sidewalk. The sky had darkened and I had to follow closer. He stopped at a liquor store to buy vodka and my beggar associate slipped a tracking device into his coat pocket while he whistled at a lady. I had my associates wait at the piers and the bridge and tunnel entrances just in case I should lose him.

I tracked him to Varick Street, but lost him at the Holland Tunnel entrance where I had to shoo away several squeegee men. When my car exited the tunnel, I picked up the signal and tailed him through Newark, where every pedestrian had his hands inside his pockets and every pair of eyes peeped at my BMW. When a young man blocked the way at the crosswalk, I was kind enough to drive around him rather than over him. I sped down the street as a slug bounced off my bulletproof rear window. Close call. Soon, drizzle blocked the signal and I had to call my police friend to locate his car. I drove around the warehouses near Newark International Airport, hoping to spot his car. In the twilight, I took out Faith's picture. I could be dining with her rather than tracking the Messenger. Of course, I had to find Holly and rescue her.

My friend at the police station had located the car and gave me the address. I drove to a bowling alley in Union. Inside, the Messenger bowled while his friends booed. I should throw him down the lane for a strike but I stepped out of the building and waited in the parking lot, waiting for his friends would throw him out. I munched dark chocolate under a tree while an owl hooted above me. When water dripped from the branches, I got into my car and listened to Bizet's *Carmen*.

Close to midnight, I called my Underground Temple assistant to come to the bowling alley and have a few games while keeping an eye on the Messenger. When he arrived, I drove to Hoboken to have a midnight drink. At the bar, I ordered a Manhattan and checked my watch. The Messenger might be waiting for midnight to harm Holly. The Priest had assured me this assistant could track a rat in the ditches and I hoped he wouldn't lose the Messenger.

While I was drinking my Manhattan and talking to the bartender about the meaning of life and other nonsense, the Guardian called to request a meeting. I'd expected him to call. He wanted the diamonds. If I could ferret out his connection with VE and his reason for harassing me, the puzzle would fall into place. Of course, I also had to check out his ugly face since I didn't while kicking his butt.

"If you're nice, I got some juicy info for you," he said.

"I'm never nice."

"Good, good. I like that."

"Spill it."

"What's in it for me?"

"When I kick your butt, I'll consider your service."

"Hey, you're a sick man. Just like that underground man."

"Are you done?"

"Aren't you looking for Holly?"

I almost dropped the glass but steady my hand and drank a draft. When the alcohol steadied my mind, I said, "Did you kidnap her? You know—" I sent a message to my friend at the police station to track the call. I'd locate the Guardian and squeeze out the information.

"Ha, I got your attention. Didn't I?"

"If you hurt her—"

"Chill out, man. I'm not the one. Do you or don't you want to know where she is?"

"You want the diamonds, don't you?" I finished my drink and left the bar, heading for my car.

"What's one thing got to do with the other?"

"One—"

"What?"

"Two—"

"Okay, okay." He gave me an address in Long Island City and hung up.

When I started the car, midnight had passed. My assistant reported that the Messenger had just lost another game. Was the Guardian toying with me? Still, I had to check the leads. I ran several red lights and got on the highway. How could he know Holly's location? Of course, he might be working with Ms. Boss to harm me. Who hired them? I went through the Lincoln Tunnel and the Midtown Tunnel and under the drizzle drove toward Long Island City. I parked the car near Northern Boulevard and walked under the rain toward the junkyard several blocks away. I brought the nunchuks to practice on the henchmen.

Near a warehouse, a clunker passed and honked. In the next block, a figure darted around the corner and in the distance, a dog barked. I sniffed the moist night air as I arrived at the junkyard beside a waste disposal site. I went into an abandoned lot under the rain, past used cars and electronics and appliances on the ground, and approached a warehouse, where three pit bulls greeted me with wet canines. To return the greeting, I threw beef jerky over the fence. Those puppies ate, almost fighting over the delicacy, and in five minutes fell asleep. I bound their jaws and legs with ropes and walked toward the warehouse, a lone spotlight gazing at the ground. I turned the knob but the door wouldn't open and I had to connect the decoder to the keypad to unlock it. The door squeaked open. I turned around to check whether I had alarmed the vagrants and beggars nearby, then stepped into the warehouse, which reeked of stale fat and blood.

My eyes adjusted to the dim light and I sidestepped several slabs of fat near the doorway and tiptoed across the slippery floor, pushing aside the slaughtered cows hanging from the ceiling. I kicked an empty beer can and it rolled across the storage room, the notes echoing between the two walls. I huddled down and listened for footsteps. Besides the rain knocking on the windows, only the rats chatting with one another. Several minutes later, I tiptoed across the room and went down the stairs.

Darkness greeted me. I put on my infrared goggles and stepped down the stairs to the odor of goat cheese. At the bottom, rats chased each other around beer cans and chicken bones. I scattered them. In the dark, taps echoed among the rats' squeals.

A passage led deeper into darkness. Beyond a dozen crates of Cuban cigars the tunnel ended. I opened the door and a skeleton fell on me but I just grabbed its femur and stepped through the doorway.

Several dozen crates of sub-machine guns lined against the left wall. Good quality. Russian made. Beside the opposite wall sat a crate of fake passports. Good quality also. Made in the U.S.A. The table in the middle of the room displayed food. I pushed aside the milk, bread, cheese, and roast beef and grabbed a can of beer. Without turning on the light or taking off my infrared goggles, I opened the can of beer and drank. Am I an alcoholic? No way. The folder next to the milk had pictures of Ganesh and Faith, in Battery Park, Carnegie Hall and Madison Square Garden. The report only detailed the nerd's activities during the past two months and didn't reveal his background. Could someone have hired VE to eliminate Ganesh?

Behind a door at the farther end of the room someone tapped on the wall. I leaned against the door and finished the beer. Then lifted the latch and watched the person prepare to swing.

When the door opened, I sidestepped to the left to avoid the bottle aiming for my cranium and said, "Well, I was hoping for a more friendly greeting. Like a hug, or a kiss. But then again, anything less would make me suspicious. That someone else is posing as you."

"Hey, back off." She threw the bottle with a shout and her right heel aimed for my jaw, which I'd extended for her benefit.

Well, I'd found Holly but after the deadline. I ducked and blocked but her foot had already switched target: my butt. We used to spare before making love. "All right, all right, you win." I turned and grabbed her foot. "We can play this game another time."

"What'd you want, creep?" She circled me, raising her fists and ready to kick my butt.

"This creep is here to rescue you. Now, do you have any problem with that? If you do, I'll leave and lock the door so you can continue to enjoy your solitude."

I flipped a switch to turn on the light. Then took off the infrared goggles and bowed. "It's me. Good old Francisco. Don't pretend you don't recognize me. That'd be cold, even for you." I tilted my head to show my profile so she could recognize the contours of my nose and jaw.

"Francisco?"

"You usually call me Fransuccesco."

She dropped onto a futon in the middle of the cell. I sat next to her and picked up the lipstick. I examined the two red strokes on the wall she probably used to count the days. Smart girl.

"My head hurts where the jerk hit me with something, maybe a karate chop."

Was Holly, like Molly in my dream, also a clone, a clone of someone whom I'd known but no longer existed? How could I be sure she was Holly? I couldn't.

She lifted her hand and caressed my left cheek, and I also extended my hand and caressed her left cheek. The longing, the hope swelled in my bosom, so delicious, so aching, so distant. Yet, not my longing, not my hope, only hers. Must be hers. She'd missed me; she'd longed for me; she'd hoped I'd save her. She touched my lips and I touch hers. Happiness flooded her bosom and intoxicated her mind. Only not hers, but mine. The first time we'd met, the first time I'd kissed her... The past revived to haunt me, to taunt me. Only six weeks ago, Holly had reproved me for being heartless, insensitive, and most of all, egotistical. Now, she held onto me, as onto her very life. Outside, the wind continued to whistle and tapped on the windowpane, warning me not to be sentimental. My dream self, I pitied the sap. He should confront the doctor and vie for Ingrid, the lady whom I'd known from a forgotten incident. Likewise, I should crush Ganesh to win over Faith just as I'd toppled what's-his-name to have Holly. Or had Holly demolished my previous girlfriend? No, only a glitch in my memory, or maybe an episode cut and pasted from someone else's.

I returned the lipstick to her and helped her out of the room. She looked as refreshed as if she'd been taking a vacation.

"Hey, there's food. Let's have something to eat first." I left the holding cell and headed for the table. "Well, you know, Maslow's Hierarchy of Needs. I wouldn't want to upset any natural laws." I opened the pack of roast beef and a loaf of bread.

"It says I have to tell you something important." She approached the table, grabbed a can of beer and gulped it down in less than a minute.

"I'm listening." I made two roast beef sandwiches and gave her one.

Holly bit into the sandwich, chewed for ten seconds and downed it with beer. So glad she hadn't lost her habits. While eating the sandwich, she glanced through her diary. Then she approached and grabbed my shoulders and said, "Don't trust Clint."

"Hey, come on, it's me. Did I ever trust him, or anybody, for that matter?" I didn't like each Jane telling me not to trust the next John, as if I'd ever committed such a crime. I could understand the Messenger, the Priest and Faith, mistaking me for gullible Thomas, but Holly, even if she'd lost her memory, should've known better than to insult me. "You must've been in this place for too long. Or maybe they put something in your food."

"For some reason, he's after one of your lady friends called Faith. He's pretty upset with her. Maybe, with you. But anyway, you'd better find him soon. Or there'll be blood." She munched on a wedge of Swiss cheese.

"Damn it. I never found out where he dug his hole. Wouldn't have been difficult to find it. But, I don't have time now." I worried more about Faith now that I'd saved Holly. She flipped through her notepad and stopped at a page. "Do you know The Usual Place? Oh, I'm to give you the address."

The Usual Place? The maples woods in my dream? Or the place in the Catskills where I'd killed Father and later planted the chrysanthemums? No, an apartment in the Bronx.

I copied the address and led her out of the room though she was interested in the fake passports. We left with the food and as we walked through the tunnel, she beamed the flashlight and scanned her notes. "Clint used your social security number and birthday to get a credit card."

I kicked away the rats blocking my path. "An old trick. But what he'd want with the credit card? To fill his apartment with beer? Maybe, he decided not to watch football at home anymore and bought season tickets." Since I didn't trust Holly either, I didn't ask how she'd sniffed out the information. Since Clint bragged that he'd exorcised punishments, he must be releasing his repressed desires by shopping nonstop and ruining my credit score.

"He carried a book outside The Printer Shop. Dostoevsky's *Notes from the Underground*. Could be the Underground Temple's sacred text." She kicked a beer can and the din echoed through the tunnel.

"If that's true, he's in big trouble. My fanatics would slaughter him." I kicked aside the empty cans and chicken bones and showed her the stairs. Since he was kind enough to inform the police I'd stolen the fake manuscript, he might've also been generous enough to buy it with my credit card and send me it. Of course, I'd have to confirm it before incriminating him. Anyway, only Faith's safety mattered now. I followed Holly up the stairs into the slaughterhouse.

"Oh, he'd disguised himself as a fat policeman to steal your laptop. Must be very angry to go through the trouble to hurt you."

"Well, the reward would more than compensate his effort. You know, risk and benefit. Not that anyone has ever succeeded. But everyone is after the Holy Grail and would pay with his/her dear, or not so dear, life. So, I'm not surprised." So Clint, after serving me for years, learned my tricks. Growing a hundred pounds is a standard gimmick and I should've recognized him as the fat cop, at least his beady eyes. Must've used colored contact lenses. I downed the beer and threw the can across the room. Before I could run across the room, I almost fell on the slippery floor.

"I've no idea why they kidnapped me or who they're or how long I've been here." Holly stepped out of the warehouse and inhaled the night air. The rain had returned to drizzle.

"Nobody important, just the typical losers. Strange thing, I've been bumping into them quite often during the past two months or so." I led her past the dogs and into the junkyard where several vagrants were rummaging through garbage. Wiped the rain from my face and wondered whether Clint had kidnapped Faith. "Has it become fashionable to be a creep? Or, is my scent attracting them? Scary. But anyway, nice hideout. I like to have a hideout like this. To avoid giant skunks, trigger-happy ladies, and mysterious guardians. Maybe, I'll start looking around for a place like this. But you'll have to support me, financially, that is."

As we walked to my car, Holly recounted her ordeal.

She was minding her own business, which after years of experience I don't recommend, filing court papers for a client at the district court, another word, clerking. When she left the court, she bought a chilidog, the genuine article not the imitation, and was about to chomp on it when a grocery bag covered her head and a stick knocked her out. A kidnapper had probably wolfed the chilidog down his esophagus.

After she'd passed out, she dreamed, but wouldn't share the contents. That's fine, since I wouldn't want to divulge my dreams either.

She woke up in that coop, no idea where she was. A client's ex-husband, a sore loser might've resented the settlement and tried to reduce his alimony. Not as strange as it sounds. Well, the creeps warned her not to make troubles and promised to release her after the transaction. She didn't know what they meant, but I sure did. They fed her well, angel hair in garlic sauce, Salisbury steak, tandoori chicken, Mediterranean salad and even Vietnamese beef noodle soup. Nice hostage meals. Better than some of my dinners. Anyway, they bolted the door and she couldn't leave the cell to stretch her legs.

"Yeah, I was minding my business also." I said, after opening the car door for her. "And guess what, all of a sudden, a Guardian harassed me, a giant skunk chased me, and a lunatic priest tried to roast me." I got into the car and started it and my hands shook. "These days, minding one's own business isn't good enough. You have to take the initiative, rout out the nuisances from life. Like these creeps who kidnapped you. But, they're my clients, so we'll have to wait until they pay me." I reminded her about the fundraiser for battered women and rape victims and said, "Don't worry about those creeps, just raise money for the good cause. I do it all the time without knowing the cause."

"I'll have to trust you on that."

"Then trust me."

I phoned Faith again but she still didn't answer, and I almost dropped my phone. What if Ms. Boss had intended to target Faith all along? After all, she'd sent Faith to me.

***

After taking Holly to the hospital for examinations, I rushed to The Usual Place, speeding through red lights and stop signs that tried to slow me down. Since I'd passed the deadline by about two hours, I hoped to rescue Faith before the thugs could carry out the torture. I called Ganesh and urged him to meet me there, not sure whether I'd given the correct directions. I also called the Governor to inform him Holly was in the hospital. While I drove along the Long Island Expressway, the Printing Shop's owner sent a message to confirm Clint, using my name and credit card number, requested the Underground Temple's holiest text duplicated. So, Holly hit the bullseye. The confirmation gave me license to kick my former sidekick's butt, but I worried about what he might do to Faith, whose smiles had been strumming my heartstrings. I yearned to hug her and kiss her, but still feared committing myself, and I loathed my usual solution, or for that matter, the unusual ones also.

As I left the Triboro Bridge and drove along a main street, the streetlight cast a lone shadow onto the sidewalk. I'd faced similar shadows time and time again while tailing politicians, ministers, businesswomen or housewives, but not the void in my stomach. I gazed at Faith's picture on my phone. I'd scanned her picture on the fireplace mantel while she was busy praising Ganesh to the abyss. Come to think of it, I only heard her first sentence, enough to sicken me.

My phone rang and I picked up the call from the hospital. Suzie had died. The nurse mentioned some complications but I didn't listen. The car wobbled and I grasped onto the steering wheel. A breeze chilled my back when I ended the call. Though she hadn't said a word to me, I cared about her as much as I cared about Fernando. I should rush to my brother's grave to relay the news. That Virginia E. Boss, the sadist, even killed a girl in coma. My hands slipped from the steering wheel and the car smashed into the guardrail. The airbag exploded. Steam rose through the dented hood. I wanted to sleep. I wanted to give up the project. But I remembered Faith. Faith, waiting for me to save her. Already two hours after the deadline.

I got out of the car and my right leg throbbed with pain. I waved for a taxi and gave the driver the address. In the car, I held my head. I'd talked to Suzie. Telling her how Fernando had died and wouldn't visit her anymore. Promising to visit her once a week as long as I lived. And I'd kept my promise.

When I arrived at The Usual Place and stepped out of the cab, four tattooed fists were looking to break my ribs, but my nunchuks drummed their knuckles until the hands opened and the legs took them away. Under the streetlight, my shadow was as murky as my mind. I ran up the stoop and opened the front door, its whine echoing along the hallway. A wedge of light from the streetlight shone on the hallway floor and right wall. I charged into the hallway that reeked of mildew and spoiled shrimp, ready to save my damsel in distress. My face smashed into a spider web and scattered the occupant.

Unit C. I kicked down the graffiti-decorated door. A single light bulb flickered in the windowless room reeking of blood. The image in the apartment still haunts me now as I record the scene. Intermittent light shone on her face. She lay on the floor, her face and body bloodied and bruised. I hesitated for a moment, not daring to check her breath and heartbeat. I was afraid, yes, Francisco was afraid, to find her dead. I slipped on a burnt book cover and almost fell onto the floor but managed to grab a chair to balance myself. I rushed to her side and confirmed she had heartbeats. I didn't dare to wake her up as I looked at the blood on my palm.

CHAPTER 45 - X

November 7

Last evening, I couldn't find Molly even after inspecting all one hundred stalls. The antique vendor didn't remember her when I showed her photo. Still, I had seen her, her cheeks' contours etched in my mind. I continued to search after Ingrid returned to the villa, and when night had fallen and the last vendor had left, leaving only the wind and the fog, I wandered around the campground amid the chilly air, my mind replaying the gondola trip. I reviewed the diary to confirm we had gone on that ride. So, we didn't listen to Beethoven's *Moonlight Sonata*, but it didn't matter.

An hour later, I left the campground and tracked my laptop to Gauss, a suburb of Felast, and trudged through the bustling streets, the neon signs overhead escorting me from theater to boutique to pastry shop. Lost among strangers and novelty shops, I studied the faces among the crowd, hoping Molly was also looking for me, but their looks only reminded me of phantoms as ethereal as the mist. I expected to meet the Governor in a bar complaining about his job or Francisco's beggar sidekick in a limousine kissing a woman.

The subliminal messages in the night music invited me into video arcades to empty my wallet and max-out my cash cards, but I went to a coffee shop, where two old men reminisced about their first dates and argued over who had more lovers. According to Ingrid, Conman might hang out in this café at night, but the proprietor said Jack had several business transactions and wouldn't come that evening. I would have to wait until the next day to ask about Molly.

This penal colony, I would leave after regaining my memory and forget the people and the experiences. Probably to a mountain or a desert, or a Pacific island with enough moisture and vegetation to block satellite signals, maybe an undersea city, like Atlantis, where I could live as an amnesiac, free from agents and rebels, and mad scientists sporting with citizens' minds and directing their destinies.

Maybe I should leave now. Forget about my memory and the past. Forget about Ingrid and Molly, and Dr. Tang. Even if I recovered my memory, the government or a syndicate or a secret society could take it away anytime, the contents only goods for seizing and bartering. Yet, my instinct wouldn't let me.

The transmitter signals led me to the Möbius Strip by the sea. The fog had so engulfed the entire coast that I couldn't see the water beyond the cobblestone walkway. Only the crashing waves alerted me to the boundary between land and sea, and only the beacon, its yellow beam struggling to penetrate the mist, hinted at the lighthouse location.

Under the fog, I entered the dark alleys that wound through the neighborhood. An occasional gas lamp lit the cobblestone path, but shadows seemed to lurk behind every wall. The chill, the water vapor grainy like dust, seeped into my bones. Footfalls ahead as I approached my laptop. When a breeze drifted through the street and the fog cleared for a moment, a pair of eyes down the alley glared at me. Not the thief. The cat meowed and scurried into the dark.

I hummed a tune—an unfamiliar tune—as I dreamed of living in a stone-front house by the sea. As I imagined walking along the beach with Ingrid, a figure darted into a side street. I jogged on the cobblestone. Cut through the mist. Turned the corner. Confronted darkness thick as molasses. Amid the booms of waves crashing onto the shore, the footfalls light and agile tapped the cobblestones like a drummer beating out the chord.

I followed. Almost crashing into a lamppost. Almost stepping on vomit.

I didn't care about the laptop, but the thief might help me recover my memory. In front of a brick building, a figure rushed down the stair and entered a cellar. After the door had closed, I tiptoed toward the entrance, went down the stair and listened for sounds. None.

I turned the knob. Listened for footsteps. Pulled open the door. Stepped into darkness. The silence choked me and the air chilled my face, my hands and my body. The thief must have noticed me and was lurking in the dark, waiting to ambush me with a baseball bat, a hockey stick or a golf club.

Though I didn't care about dying, my heart drummed out fear, the iambic rhythm sending waves of chill down my spine and through my limbs. Fear of what?

A metal container descended and engulfed me, the walls the scene of a beach sunset, which I had experienced before. Somewhere. I couldn't remember when and where and with whom. The rays golden and shading the evening clouds soothed my mind and drew me toward a dream, reverie as fleeting as reality, even as my heart beat harder and harder and blood pulsated at my fingertips. Would the sun come out again so I could recapture that dream?

What would the thief do, now that he had trapped me?

The container moved toward my end, but I just enjoyed the scene, imagining the rays warm against my skin, which hadn't touched sunlight for months. Pretending Ingrid was leaning against me. This scene would burn into my memory and, one day, I would reflect on this experience, real as the street battle or the confrontation with Pratt and Beta.

I was about to kiss Ingrid when the container door opened to an office that smelled of coffee and bread. The door closed after I stepped out, and a bookcase slid along the wall and blocked the exit. I couldn't remove the fake books, wood blocks attached to the shelf.

A poster of Descartes hung over the desk at the far end of the room, the corners of his mouth curled as if in a smirk. Liberty Lair.

When had I entered Francisco's world? Was he dreaming of me? Or had I come to this office before and dreamed of it as Holly's hideout? I couldn't distinguish between dream and reality, just as I couldn't between Molly and Dolly.

"I only want to get back my memory." I tried to open a glass sliding door that led to an ocean-view balcony but it was locked.

"I only want to retire to the Bahamas with him." Mrs. McCoy's voice trembled through the ceiling loud speaker.

"You're as mistaken as your husband. The data isn't in my laptop." Mrs. McCoy couldn't help recover my memory anymore than I would give her the CP data. Sure, if I had my memory, I would retire to an island, too. Get hold of several million dollars before the government collapsed. I searched for the rainbow after the rainstorm and if I had the money, I would hire the rebels to free Mr. Smith from prison.

"But you have the data in your head."

"Your late husband's mansion, paintings and vases should fetch a few millions."

"How much is your head worth?"

"No idea. Maybe tens of millions."

A viscous silence, as the beacon outside the sliding door flashed through the fog. If only the fog would lift to reveal the waves, the clouds, and the lighthouse. A seagull landed on the balustrade, its head twitching back and forth. I would like to turn into a bird and fly from my mental fog.

"Any information to help find Molly, please let me know. Believe me, I want to find her."

A section of the back wall swiveled open and Mrs. McCoy, her hair in a chignon, emerged. "I have bad news." She pushed aside a plate of chocolate-chip cookies and put a tote bag on the desk. She opened the tote bag and handed me the laptop. "I'm still down two-million dollars. These mercenaries are expensive."

"Okay, I'm ready for the bad news," I said.

"I'm not a bad person." She poured a cup of coffee from the thermal bottle.

Mrs. McCoy had grown up in a farm with only carrots, tomatoes, potatoes, chickens, pigs and a few dairy cows. When her father drowned in the river, she bought a bottle of wine to celebrate his death. He wouldn't get drunk every night and beat her mother anymore.

I didn't interrupt her but wondered why she was revealing her life story.

"My mom soon died…"

Her mother passed away after a mugger called Pratt Calhoun had stabbed her and taken her cash card, about twenty dollars.

"I'm sorry for taking your time. You're probably not interested in my story."

"After I sell the data, I'll give you two million dollars to get Mr. Smith out of jail. But maybe by that time…" I envied them. Whatever storm they faced, they could anchor on their pasts, renew their strength and march forward, into their destinies. I had no such anchor. When I sulked over Ingrid's love for Dr. Tang, when I lamented about never seeing Molly again, when I doubted ever recovering my memories, I mustered the strength that waxed or ebbed according to the wind's bearing, to prevent from falling off the chair.

Mrs. McCoy handed me photos from the tote bag. Molly's? Or Dolly's? She was on a swing. She was with Mrs. McCoy in a carnival. She was with Mr. and Mrs. Smith in the amusement park.

I wanted to see Molly, not her photos, but flesh and blood, to hold her hands and kiss her lips, her warmth against this cold and damp world.

"We found out Dolly had been dating Mr. Smith's nephew only after the boy was murdered. By another boy." Mrs. McCoy arranged the photos in two rows as I put them onto the table.

Mr. Smith was going to adopt Dolly after meeting her at his nephew's funeral, but she had retreated into herself after her boyfriend's death, only glaring others from afar. Her parents took her to counseling but she soon left town after killing a cat and a dog and hanging their bodies on a tree branch. Mr. Smith thought she would become a prostitute or drug dealer and end up in prison, but years later she returned as general manager of Pythagorean Triangle's new clone factory. Enforcing the production schedules and disciplining those who under-perform and firing those who missed a deadline.

"You could feel her anger and hatred," Mrs. McCoy said. "By that time, her bitterness had seeped into her marrow. But she converted that bitterness into strength, cold and cruel strength, treating the world as her enemy, and fighting it with all her mind, all her heart and all her soul."

Well, Dolly had killed cats and dogs, blacklisted troublemakers, and threatened to sue her neighbor for building a stall in the front yard to sell produces. So what attracted me to her? I could picture her cold eyes behind the snowflakes and her taut cheeks in the gust. I could picture the leafless branches, the white landscape, the cloudless sky.

"When Dolly and Molly first arrived, I thought they were twins."

Soon after they had arrived and bought the house by the canal, Mrs. McCoy found out Dolly had cloned Molly sixteen years ago, to shop and cook, and to clean and repair the house. Somehow, they looked the same age. While Dolly disappeared for days or even weeks, Mrs. McCoy befriended Molly and took her to church every Sunday to soak in the minister's wisdom. Trying to persuade her new friend to leave the tyrant and start a new life. Even volunteering to help support her livelihood for the first several months. Yet, the servant refused to betray the master.

"Dolly had trained her servant well. Molly was prim and slavish in those days. Now, after Dolly couldn't oppress her anymore, she's a little more free-spirited." Mrs. McCoy crushed the cookie in her hand.

Mr. Smith, church deacon then, soon adopted her, and he protected her.

"I would've adopted her. Yes, I envied Mrs. Smith." Mrs. McCoy picked up a photo of Molly on a rowboat, the sunlight glistening on the lake surface and lighting up her face.

One summer afternoon, Mrs. McCoy found Molly lying in the front yard, having fallen from the roof while repairing the eave. She called the ambulance to take the clone to the emergence room. After staying for six weeks in the hospital with three broken ribs, Molly returned to paint the back of the house and fix the barn in the backyard. All that time Dolly hadn't returned. When Molly complained of back pain, Mrs. McCoy gave her some ointment and again urged her to flee.

"Dolly treated her more like a slave." Mrs. McCoy wiped the crumbs off her hands and sipped the coffee. Dolly was probably shooting an enemy spy in the head while making love to him, then cleaning the gun and showering while the carcass bled on the bed. Another day at work.

During that time, Dolly fought to nullify the adoption, claiming the clone had no rights and she—Dolly—had ownership. Molly was going to give in, but Mr. Smith insisted on fighting. In the end, the court allowed Molly to choose and granted the adoption. From then on, Molly took turns living with Dolly and the Smiths, and Mr. Smith could protect his adopted daughter. Still, Dolly continued to usurp Molly's suitors.

Once, Mrs. McCoy chatted with *Molly* on the porch about a pie recipe until the latter snickered and revealed she was Dolly. The minister's wife, alarmed and distraught, realized she couldn't distinguish between master and servant, though the former was more than ten years older. Molly later apologized for her master's farce, but Mrs. McCoy worried that Dolly would again impersonate her and might even implicate the clone. When Molly had to get a crown for her molar, Mrs. McCoy paid for it and requested the dentist mark its side with an "M."

Munching on a cookie, I dreamed of looking at the marking on Molly's crown. I had to know more about Dolly, my previous lover. I could imagine the aura that had attracted me to her. Cold, calculating, seductive.

"I caught Dolly repeating the trick several times. Of course, she found out about the crown." Mrs. McCoy picked up a picture of Molly and her in Next Market. "But not the marking."

The minister-spy never had a chance against Mrs. McCoy and I didn't want her against me. Though anxious about the bad news, I didn't interrupt her.

"I was the one who found out the pig raped her." She put down the cup and gnawed the cookie, a wrinkle sliding down her cheek. I wanted to embrace and comfort Molly, who had suffered enough from Dolly, without the minister.

A few weeks after Molly had begun going to Sunday worship, Pastor McCoy asked to talk to her alone on a weekday morning. Molly, not suspecting his scheme, went to the church at 10:00 a.m. The minister took her to his office and persuaded her to have monthly counseling sessions. He doped her. He raped her. She was only sixteen.

That was the first time.

She wouldn't remember it. If Molly hadn't recorded the incident, she could live as if it had never happened. Should I erase the entry from her notebook? No, that would be too cruel. Just as if someone erased an event from my memory without consulting me. My fist tightened and I crushed the empty bottle.

Mrs. McCoy found out about it.

She began to suspect the minister when he disappeared at night for several hours at a time to visit hospitals overnight. Usually, she would pretend to sleep and wait for him to go to bed, before getting up to look through his wallet for the safe's new combination, which he would change every time valuables disappeared. She collected a few million dollars before having to steal his bank code for withdrawals. After he had disappeared during the night several times, she followed him. In bars, casinos, and brothels, he would meet men in trench coats and wigs. Yes, she'd seen through their disguises. At first, she thought he employed private investigators to catch the thief stealing his valuables. Soon, with Mr. Smith's help, she found out her husband was spying for Russia part-time.

She hired several private investigators and they pretended to join his congregation. They bugged his shoes, briefcase, office desk and in his office set up a hidden camera. They watched him flirt with female parishioners and sell top secret documents. Soon, they discover a hidden safe and its combination.

"Guess what I found in the safe." Mrs. McCoy got up and walked to the bookshelf. She pressed a book and a compartment opened to reveal about a dozen tapes. "There were more tapes, and more victims also. But I gave those to the police."

"I wish Mr. Smith hadn't killed him." Imagined scenes swirled in my mind and I rose, took a step and cracked my knuckles. I had to drink a bottle of the water, but my head still fevered.

"So do I."

I envied Mr. Smith for having taken the action and relieved his pain and anger. For Mrs. McCoy and me, no such relief. What could we do when both Dolly and McCoy were dead? Except to take care of Molly. I must locate her before... I held my head and waited for the *bad news*. "You didn't have to tell her."

Mrs. McCoy handed me a photo. "If you love her—"

"If the rebels topple the government, perhaps they will grant a general amnesty. Or you can bribe the warden and the guards, which should cost less than the mercenaries." The photo showed Beta's ugly face, maybe Gamma's. "But, time for the bad news." I should introduce her to Dr. Tang. If he released Ingrid from his talons, I would step in to comfort her and show her my love.

"If you love her—"

"What does she have to do with this rascal?"

"She was with this guy. Seemed friendly with him. Might be trying to pry out something. But he might be holding her, to extort the data from you. A bad man."

Sure, she wasn't colluding with Gamma; she was trying to squeeze out some info. I would ally with Gamma to infiltrate the Intelligence Agency and show that *Beta* was leading the rebels.

"Since the pig failed to destroy the data, his Russian colleagues would come to finish the job. So, watch out for them."

"But he was a mercenary doing side jobs to buy a yacht. Hard to believe he'd only served one master."

"A free-lance agent. But, he'd been renewing his contract with the Russians for a few years. He said a prayer after your car flattened into the side of the building. For Molly's sake, I'm glad you're alive."

Another constant, the car accident. But the perpetrators and my enemies might change from one reality to another.

I again dreamed of life with Molly by the hillside, the sun smiling at us from the eastern sky, the breeze sweeping through the canyon and whistling a soft summer tune, the scent of jasmine wafting through the hillside, and her smile lighting up my soul.

How much would I give up for her? Would I forgo recovering my memory? I didn't know and still don't. Sure, I would give up the future to find my past and if the future included Molly, then I should also give her up. Yet, like everyone else, I wanted this, that and the other things.

If Gamma asked to swap the CP data for Molly, how would I choose? By hesitating?

Molly would never scheme with Beta or Gamma to extract the data from me. She might have known the agent or rebel through Dolly and was just sweet-talking him into loosening her chains. From the beginning, even when I didn't know he coveted the CP data, I didn't trust those eyes, neither in this nor in the other realities. Since he hadn't come to blackmail me, he must be cooking up a scheme.

"Do you know who gutted Pratt Calhoun?" Mrs. McCoy took out her phone.

Pratt sprawled on the sidewalk while begging for death. Sure, she would avenge her mother, but she wouldn't marry Pratt. Anyway, her husband was Pastor McCoy.

"I took that woman's picture." She flipped through her phone album until she located the picture. "Here, just an ordinary woman. You probably don't even know her."

The rebel leader whom I had helped after saving Dr. Tang, she had tied Pratt to the bed and was thrusting a knife into his abdomen. I couldn't imagine the ruffian and her as a couple, but of course I knew nothing about the affairs of the heart. She probably didn't see the bomb kill her son or she would've rushed toward the burning car. I didn't care she killed Pratt. I wouldn't avenge Pratt or thank her.

***

In the alleys of Möbius Strip, the mist obscured my view, and footsteps trailed me along the cobblestone paths. Distant waves continued to boom against the shore and nearby shadows flitted amid the fog. I turned several corners but couldn't throw off the footfalls and considered stopping and facing the stalker but continued toward the coast where the beacon shone against the darkness.

Come on, make my day. Not fear, but anger surged through my veins, my blood warming me in this misty night.

Beyond an intersection where trash hindered my way, the footsteps neared and a voice said, "I know what NFTU stands for." Dr. Tang, a phantom in gray raincoat, stepped out of the fog, both hands in his pockets. Only after several seconds did I understand his words.

The pieces were fitting together into a picture, my dream linking to this wasteland and Francisco linking to me. So far, the Guzman code had remained constant through the alternate realities. After the hubbub about the Underground Temple and the holy text, I should've guessed the code word, but Ingrid and Dr. Tang, Molly and Dolly, they distracted me, as the waves likewise did at that moment.

Dr. Tang gave me a watch with his name on it and asked me to switch it with Beta's. Then I should find the doctor's watch, with location tracking, in Gamma's pocket. I didn't ask. I hadn't met either Beta or

Gamma, and knew nothing about their watches. I thanked him for the watch, in case I didn't meet either Beta or Gamma. I could use it.

Along the shore toward the lighthouse, the mists sprayed onto my face as thoughts crashed in my mind, the water droplets unable to calm the mental storm. I would like to give up Ingrid and Molly if I could, but their voices threatened to drown my reasoning, which was fading into the mist.

"Hey, doc, be careful of the eyes around you."

"You have something to say?"

I should tell Dr. Tang that Ingrid was monitoring him and reporting him to the Intelligence Agency, but how could I betray her? Instead, I asked for ways to tune my dreams and get rid of Francisco the scumbag. Of course, I would like to have Ingrid in my dream, but didn't mention it.

"He may be the key to recovering your memory. Your dark side trying to reveal the truth."

"Ganesh will help me solve the puzzle. I don't need Francisco."

"Rivalries among your divergent selves is common. I can't stand my dark side either. But we have to bear it, part of the growing process."

"I heard of sibling rivalries, but self rivalries?" I believed him and would leverage Francisco to find my memory. Still, I had to trounce my dream self, to show who is in control. Oh, how I detest this Francisco, the slimy crawler who had contaminated every cubic inch of space with his bodily fluids.

"Some memories you might never recover."

"I'll recover as much as I can. And if I try hard enough, I should be able to bridge the missing ones."

"But when they're intentionally deleted, then—"

"Wow, you tell jokes."

"I don't."

No smirk on the doctor's face, only the wrinkles between his eyes. Was he a champion poker player?

We reached the fog-covered lighthouse and entered the café, empty except for the waitress leaning against the jukebox and watching TV. We picked the table beside the window and when the waitress walked over, I ordered soymilk and Dr. Tang chai.

While a seagull wove into and out of the fog, I asked for the scoundrel who had erased my memories. "With my superhuman power, I can reconfigure his skeletal structure."

"As they say, knowledge brings sorrow. I wish I didn't find out, but sometimes the desire for truth destroys us."

"Hey, Doc, forget about these philosophical musings. We can discuss the nature of wisdom and sorrow another time. You have an obligation to reveal the scoundrel. As a friend." Not sure whether he considered me a friend and I struggled to consider him one. No matter, I valued his expertise and appreciated his help.

The waitress put down our drinks as the seagulls yelped through the fog. Unable to discern the waves behind the sea of gray, I raised my hand to grasp the fine dusts of fog blowing through the window.

"Can you not consider me a friend?"

"I'll consider it after you tell me. Who?" If Beta had erased my memory, I would shake him until the details fall out of his mouth. As I grasped the doctor's sleeve, I prayed neither Ingrid nor Molly had toyed with my brain. When the fog cooled my head, I released his sleeve and smoothed its wrinkles.

"You."

You. I tried to understand what that word implied, but for several seconds couldn't grasp the sound. The word, stripped of escorting syllables, revealed a void as gray as the fog outside and as blank as my mind. Then, after drinking the soymilk and gazing out the window, I understood his accusation. "For a second, I thought you're the culprit, trying to shift the blame by implicating me. And if I didn't trust you, I would've believe you're the mad scientist."

"My colleague who used to be in the Intelligence Agency told me you'd volunteered as a test subject in the Moscow CP project. One of ten subjects the researchers had tested on."

"You mean, a guinea-pig."

"They removed some of your memory."

"No."

"Yes."

"Impossible."

"December, last year."

While the seagulls continued to yelp outside the window, I leaned against the table and held my head in both hands. Rubbing my cranium. Staring at the drops of soymilk beside the spoon. Trying to recall the crowd in Red Square and the scent of formaldehyde in the lab, the feeling of waiting to lose my memory, to plunge into the unknown.

"Might be a traumatic memory that'd haunted you for years."

"You mean, I might've been molested as a child and had that memory erased." After trying to recover my past... I should kick myself in the back. I should smash my head through the wall. I should punish this culprit. In the end, I banged the cup against the table and the waitress scurried into the kitchen.

"Maybe you couldn't endure a painful memory."

"Maybe I was curious about what this technology can do. Maybe I needed the cash." I drank my soymilk but wanted whiskey. "I volunteered before the accident, and would've lost that chunk of the memory anyway. So, I wasted my effort." I could've been insane, my reasoning compromised by a mental virus.

"Maybe solving the Guzman code will give us the password to reconstruct the neural pathways," Dr. Tang said. "CP has that capability. Like a code word to release the subject from hypnosis."

I left my seat, prepared to look for Molly and forget about my lunacy, but recalled the code and asked about NFTU. Before Dr. Tang could open his mouth, his cup shattered after a pop.

In the doorway, Jack Conman tipped his fedora with a handgun. "Tang, you've got a guardian angel."

"I'd like one who doesn't stop me from drinking chai."

"Correction, cyanide." Conman said, "By the way, want to know who killed Dolly?"

"You? Okay, I won't hurt you. But Doc here, he'd probably pulverize you."

"I don't understand what she sees in you." Conman glanced at the doctor as the latter approached him wiping his hand with a handkerchief.

"Maybe you don't understand women." Dr. Tang knocked the gun out of Conman's hand and grasped it in midair. "What happened to Dolly?"

Conman pointed at me. "Hey, man. He killed her, to steal the data. Now, do you understand? He stole the data. That's why everyone's after him. He's a rogue agent."

"I don't like people who lie to me, especially con men." Dr. Tang poked Conman in the ribs with the gun barrel.

"She was my lover." I spat at the lie, especially one from a con man.

"What does one thing got to do with the other? You're a pro." Conman backed away until his back hit the jukebox.

"I wouldn't have hurt her even if I knew she'd seduced me to get the data."

"You got the seduction part right. Hey, she never loved you. It's always been you, Tang. Just couldn't understand her."

Dr. Tang turned to face me. His face, calm and blank, frightened me. Even if we had been rivaling for the CP data, I wouldn't execute Dolly. Never. A point-blank shot. When I recalled how Dr. Tang had loved her, I averted my eyes from his face. The air stifled me more and more with Conman's every breath.

I didn't move. Just waited for Dr. Tang to act. Would he shoot me? Would I dodge?

Dr. Tang banged the gun against the table and dented the tabletop. I waited while he rubbed his hand.

"Hey, breaking the table won't help you any. The murderer's in front of you. But before you kill him, consider the data. My client would pay plenty for it."

Dr. Tang collapsed onto the chair, propping his elbows on his laps and his head onto his palms, almost doubling over, as if about to vomit.

Jack Conman was rubbing his hands and looking at me like a piece of steak when the waitress stepped out of the kitchen. After spotting the spilled chai, she sprinted back inside. Conman pulled out another gun, tipped his fedora and ran after her.

"Now that we both know I killed Dolly, what should we do?" I didn't believe Conman just as I didn't believe Pratt. The con artist would spread fake news for a fee, and a nominal one, too. Either Beta or Rick could've hired him to drive a wedge between Dr. Tang and me.

Dr. Tang held his head for several minutes, got up and paced around the café.

"The simplest thing would be to kill me, but I don't want to die. At least, not yet. Not before I recover my memory. I still want a life with Molly. I still want to have a hillside house." When I thought of Molly, Dolly's face distracted me from Dr. Tang's anger and grief.

"I should avenge Dolly."

"You should."

"An eye for an eye."

"A tooth for a tooth."

"What kind of world do we live in?"

"You tell me."

"She knew what she was getting into. She killed enough people to die a thousand deaths."

No, his look betrayed him. Dr. Tang couldn't convince himself that Dolly deserved to die. His heart vied with his mind for control over the man, the moderator who must decide yes or no given limited and perhaps corrupted data.

"Do you still love her?"

"That's not it. In this desolate land, under this gray sky, I'm scared of not feeling, of not caring, of unwilling to extend my hand or lend my voice. Yesterday, I considered shooting you in the head to destroy the data, but I feared dropping into the abyss." He kicked the trashcan across the café.

"Funny *you* should fear the abyss when the gun barrel was pointing at my temple. What should I feel then? Excited or delighted? Next time you want to get frightened, go for a Frankenstein thriller or walk between the rebels and government forces. Don't think about shooting me. Please."

"How much bitterness can I harbor?"

"I should hope as much as I can."

"No, I refuse to become a monster."

"Not even for justice? I didn't forgive you for betraying me. So why should you forgive me?"

"No, not justice; just revenge."

"The same difference as between decapitation and hanging, or cesspool and quagmire, or Napoleon and Genghis Khan."

"Or fire and ice, ocean and desert, or birth and death."

"So, you focus on the differences between an apple and an orange, rather than the similarities. A discriminator rather than an integrator. But note this, unlike you, I don't forgive."

He wouldn't kill me. He wouldn't avenge Dolly's death, not because he didn't care about her, not because he accepted her death, but because he didn't have enough hatred and anger and bitterness. I knew. I could kill.

After staring at the spilled chai for a minute, Dr. Tang revealed that NFTU is the acronym for *Notes from the Underground*. Then left the café. I had read the book in the fake hospital. The text had also appeared again and again in my dreams. Should have seized this key to the puzzle days earlier.

After gazing at the spill for several minutes without finding wisdom, I left the café to sulk over giving up my memory. Beyond the lighthouse the waves tossed a plank and swooshed against the shore. The fine dusts of mist unable to soothe my skin. Why did I volunteer to remove my memory? Did I find a dead body? Did my parents dump me into a trashcan? Did I torture a cat? Did I betray my best friend for a slice of pizza? I shivered not from the morning chill, but from the shadows in my past, which threatened to resurface and devour me.

Two pops startled me but I continued to stroll along the shore, the waves tossing me in the ocean of amnesia. My life drifting from crest to crest, all about no shore in sight. Would memory ever shine into this darkness and enlighten my life, giving me sparkles of my past and my monster?

Beyond a fishing boat, the waitress lay outside the roadside café in a pool of blood. Conman was nowhere in sight.

I must leave this hell, to drift in the ocean, no man, no voice, not even the stench of human flesh, to be an island among islands.

Amid the mists, the TV over the café entrance broadcast today's headlines. The rebels had stormed the Intelligence Agency's local head-quarter and taken over the offices and were executing an agent once every five minutes. I should punch a hole through this omnipresent elec-tronic intruder.

Dr. Tang must have heard the news, also.

I returned to the lighthouse café, but he had left.

He had probably strutted toward trouble like a warrior out to slay a dragon, like a fool out to face Napoleon. Since I had planned to look for Beta in the Intelligence Agency headquarter even before the news, I might as well head over to check on Dr. Tang.

According to Doc, after her daily jog this morning, Ingrid had gone to the city's orphanage center to distribute apple, bread, and soymilk. So I walked up the ramp onto the expressway and sprinted into Felast, the car horns blaring out a cacophony and the dark clouds tracking me. I would inform her of Dr. Tang's suicide mission, and hoped she wouldn't care, but of course she would convince the rebels to delay the disaster until the fool pretending to be hero had left. I arrived in the evening and walked up the garage adjacent to the complex, the glass building reflecting the nearby cityscape—the skyscrapers, the traffic and the black smoke downtown. A covered walkway over the street led to the orphanage en-trance. The breeze soothed me and relaxed my mind though I worried about Dr. Tang's safety. In the building lobby, where children's pictures decorated the walls and six surveillance cameras eyed me, Ingrid was talking to the superintendent. This place appeared more like the Intelli-gence Agency Building (IAB) than an orphanage. I might find androids instead of orphans.

"I love him." Before I could open my mouth, she projected her voice across the lobby, and everyone hushed and turned their heads toward her.

I held her hand and said Dr. Tang might have gone into the IAB, while trying to determine her thoughts and emotions.

"Yes, he must do what he must." Ingrid put on her overcoat and tightened the strap. "And so must I."

I knew what she would to do. I knew what she had to prove. Would she do the same for me?

I knew what I must do.

She handed me a Styrofoam box and said, "Spaghetti the orphanage gave me. Have it all. It's quite good." She strolled to the door and bid the superintendent farewell. Phoned a former comrade while walking out of the building. From the way she walked and talked, she seemed like going to the supermarket to buy milk and bread, rather than into a war zone. I forgot to chase after her until she had left.

Would she rat on Dr. Tang? Then again, she might resolve her dilemma by dying with Dr. Tang, a fool's solution.

What do I care? I care.

I ate the spaghetti and left the orphanage. By the time I rushed along Cheesecake Boulevard toward the smoke, where my friends were converging, the city was under curfew. Sirens blared from the loud speakers and red lights flashed on lampposts. The police ordered civilians to stay off the streets.

I stepped into a side street to avoid the police and the security forces patrolling the main streets. A group of homeless men and women gathered around a trash bin. They probably come out of hiding from various quarters to take advantage of the chaos and loot the stores. Several blocks later, I had an acute stomachache and passed out outside a bar. If I hadn't fainted, I might've reached the building as it collapsed. Somehow, I couldn't control my destiny.

CHAPTER 46 - FRANCISCO

October 20, 2011

I stooped next to Faith and held her hand. I stretched my arm but dared not touch her face. Several seconds later, I rushed to the futon to grab a tattered blanket. A driver's license with my name and Clint's picture fell onto the floor, but I ignored it and wrapped Faith with the blanket. Her legs kept sticking out of the blanket and when I wrapped the blanket around them, her left arm poked out.

As I lifted her, my arms shook and I almost slipped on the book cover again. Blood had smeared my arms and clothes but I held her tight against my bosom. If she hadn't been tortured, I might still be singing in the fog. If the tragedy had happened but I never knew about it, tonight I'd still relish my lobster and Chardonnay. Or if I'd damaged my brain and couldn't sympathize, I might continue to solve the code without the distractions. Even if I'd felt different about her, I might just pity her and nab the fiend for justice. No, I, Francisco Guzman, sympathized with and, what's more, cared about her, and that made the difference. I sensed myself as I never had, as if I'd woken up the little guy in my head, examining Faith's bruises, listening to her moans, smelling the blood, aware of bad breath and hissing syllables, but ready to take action. Maybe I'd been drunk and the Priest sober. Maybe I should reread *Note from the Underground* and imitate the underground man.

I tried to go through the doorway, but Faith's legs knocked against the doorframe and she fell onto the floor, and I only grasped the blanket. I knelt down and apologize to her but she hadn't woken up. I wiped the dirt from her face. I embraced her, then wrapped the blanket around her again, my palms sweating and my knees aching. I lifted her and took ten seconds to steady myself. I lowered my head to gather strength. *I am Fransuccesco and won't fail her.* I stepped through the doorway.

As I walked down the flight of stairs, as I trudged on the sidewalk under the streetlight, I swore to take care of Faith. Yet I feared committing to her and losing the freedom more precious and dear than the SOAPS awards. How I'd suffer, how miserable, how suffocating, how unbearable. Yet, I held onto Faith. How could I prefer freedom to Faith? What would I want with a gilded coffin when I could have life?

Across the street, several pairs of eyes shone in dark corners. The scumbags should approach and make my day. I was going to kick butts, to box ears, to pull hairs, but in the end, those mice scurried away.

At the hospital, I forced myself to gather my thoughts, to direct my pain and anger, to plan my revenge, revenge grander than a wedding banquet. Only Clint's groans could relief my pain. Only his suffering could quench my anger. He'd beg for death but I wouldn't grant it. He'd curse himself until the pain forces him to curse his life. When he couldn't lift his fingers, I'd hand him a knife. Perhaps I was a sadist like Ms. Boss. So be it.

Only when Ganesh called did I remember not having waited at The Usual Place. I related the crime and requested that he confirm the mysterious client's identity. Ms. Boss probably colluded with Clint. Ganesh ended the call without revealing his thoughts or emotions. The annoying robot.

Later, I took a taxi to another hospital to visit Suzie. She looked like that girl in the funhouse. I tried to recall Suzie's face without looking at her, but I couldn't. Anyway, I kissed her cheek, which had begun to stiffen. I brushed aside the lock of hair over her forehead. I straightened her gown. I bid her farewell. She'd lived for such a short time. While I... What had I done with my time? At least I'd been visiting Suzie every week, for the past four years. I left the mortuary to arrange the funeral.

Outside the hospital, the breeze against my skin chilled me to the bones. The shadows under the streetlights evoked and dispersed my mental images of Faith and Suzy. Part of me had died and I shivered in the night.

Francisco would never be the same again.

Back in the Underground Temple, I swigged half a bottle of whiskey (okay, I'm an alcoholic), but my stomach continued to squeeze like a tightened fist and I finished the other half. I swore to get my hands on those scoundrels, but I blamed myself for not protecting Faith and Suzy. I should've known. I should've stayed with Suzy. With all the stochastic algorithms and estimation software, I should've predicted the event. With Ms. Redhead's threat, I should've prepared for the possibilities. Damn the Black Swans. A draft seeped into the room but my head burned like an oven. I had a fever. I embraced Faith and kissed her, but I was only holding my pillow. The room spun and I dropped into an abyss, the plunge seemed endless and my legs lost sensation.

I woke up in the maple woods, the breeze against my face. The oriole's melody rose above the foliage's hissing. I trotted through the lilacs, waiting for the shriek. Near the brook I searched for the girls, but only found the squirrels playing with the acorns. Then the scream. The oriole fled from the branches and the leaves fluttered in the breeze. The squirrels scurried away without their toys.

I ran to the brook. The fallen body lay on the bank.

When the pink-dress girl arrived and threw herself on the body, I chased after the sadist and overtook him at the brook's elbow where several willows draped into the water and swept ripples to the other shore.

"You've gone far enough. You won't be walking along this bank anymore. Time for you to exit my dream." I grabbed his arm, ready to kick his butt into the brook. "But first, who are you? Sadists always want the limelight."

"So, you're here, after I've killed him so many times. For someone who claims to be the best, you suck big time. You're right. I won't be coming here anymore. But you've no idea where I'd be." He plunged the dagger into my abdomen and I fell onto the ground, the cold spreading through my body.

I hate dying in dreams.

October 24, 2011

I buried Suzy next to Fernando. He'd appreciate it. That their decayed molecules lay next to each other comforted me. For the past several days, I'd gone to the hospital, but never walked up to Faith's room. I dreaded her swollen eyes and her bruised arms but even more the sticky silence. What should I say? I had to recuperate before facing her.

This morning, I woke up with a headache. I vomited in the bathroom for about two minutes as my stomach convulsed. After rinsing my mouth, I cleansed my face with cold water, but my head still ached. Back in the bedroom, I tried to remove the portraits of Dostoevsky so he wouldn't stare at me, but the cement held the frames to the walls.

I called the hospital to check on Holly but she'd checked out three days ago. I called her but she didn't pick up her phone. According to the Governor, Holly had raised two million dollars at the fundraiser, but she'd left town for business. I couldn't believe she was still working. Maybe she'd recovered and didn't want to laze around. That sure sounded like her.

After croissant and eggs for breakfast, I lay on the divan with a glass of whiskey and stared at old Fyodor's face for two hours. I couldn't identify the killer or the victim in the maple woods dream. At the thought of my younger self as the sadist, I couldn't drink the whiskey or eat the durian pie. The victim could be the amnesiac. Of course, the real amnesiac should've died and I dreamed of him. Yet, I wouldn't harm that sap, much less kill an innocent boy. Not my style.

I'd prefer not to be a sadist or a psychopath but whether I'd killed that boy or not, I'd destroy Clint and Ms. Boss. I still grieved for Suzie and Faith and the grief had strengthened me and would drive me to avenge them. Unlike Dr. Tang or the amnesiac, I favored an eye for an eye.

With Faith in the hospital, solving the puzzle didn't thrill me as it once had. I drank the whiskey to numb the new sensation. Would Fransuccesco disappear? No, I mustn't decay into that amnesiac.

"So, Fyodor, since you're the Almighty Dostoevsky, what wisdom could you impart upon this mortal soul?" In front of the largest framed picture, I stared into those eyes. The wisdom in *Notes from the Underground* couldn't help me anymore, though I'd studied the underground man's thoughts and actions.

No, I needed concrete methods.

I took a book from the shelf and scanned through the ancient punishments from Rome to Persia to China. I was selecting a special torture for Clint and the Guardian when the phone whined. Did Ganesh call to update me? Did the Guardian long for another dressing-down? I would've obliged if I weren't conversing with the Almighty Dostoevsky. I finished my whiskey, pushed away the glass of whiskey and picked up the phone.

Clint.

"Ya got wha ya deserve."

I squinted at the speaker as if staring at Clint, who tortured Faith to punish me. I'd caused her the pain and suffering. Light flickered around the corners of my eyes. The floor tossed. I dropped the phone and, knocking over the chair, almost fell onto the floor. I leaned on the table and steadied myself, while Dostoevsky stared.

I picked up the phone. I cursed the madman, but the expletives lost their blows the second they left my mouth, the venom having remained between my teeth and under my tongue. Faith's limp body in my arms and her faint breath against my face. Until that hour, I'd never tasted such bile, not even when Fernando abandoned me. I vowed to nurse it and strengthen it. I straightened up the chair. I nodded at Dostoevsky. Wiped the sweat off my forehead, feeling like a new man after baptism through hatred and pain. Perhaps I'd evolved into the underground man. No, that wimp, loser, and social outcast just whined about his misfortunate and blamed everyone else. No, I'm Francisco Guzman. I invited Clint to meet me. I'd reward him for his tutelage in pain and relieve him of his misery and suffering.

"Ya shlub." His voice grated into my heart.

Could this be a dream, the amnesiac's dream? How else could Mr. OCD become a sadist? How else could a man claim to be the Guardian of Memory? No, his world of clones and zombies, of government surveillance and random violence, of subliminal projection and cerebral programming, that had to be a nightmare.

"Treated me like a dog and I tolerated yer abuses and been loyal."

"Your problem is your obsessive-compulsive disorder. Always doing the same thing and expecting different results. Haven't you learned the law of causality?" What could be his Achilles' heel? I must turn his madness against him.

"Couldn't forgive ya. It's yer fault Fernando died. Never took responsibility. Never apologized at his grave. Losing him was bad enough. But yer arrogance, yer insensitivity, yer cowardice. Man can only take so much from a scumbag." Clint's voice cracked through the phone speaker and my ears rang.

I recalled his tears over Fernando's tombstone and tried to figure out the missing piece of the puzzle. The soft spot I could jab my dagger. The baseball card. Why did Fernando give it to him? "Cut the excuses. You never cared about him. Just a leech hanging onto him."

"Ya, ya drove him to madness, to depression. He thought he killed his father. But it's ya, ya killed his father." Clint cursed me with an expletive that surprised me. "That drove him to run in front of the ambulance. Probably couldn't take it no more." He sounded like he was choking or sobbing.

I didn't believe his nonsense, but the tide had turned. Time to attack this madman's left flank. "More than once, he said that you're less than half a man, that you're a pitiable loser, that you're a leech sucking the life out of him. I've always wondered whether he threw himself in front of the ambulance to escape from you." I took out a pad and scribbled notes, hoping to stumble upon that Achilles' heel.

"No, no, no. Ya lied." His voice shook with a rage that soothed my heart. "Listened to him when he was troubled by his father disappearing and when he was troubled by yer selfishness. Had fun joking about yer sexual life, hiking in the Catskill—"

"Wake up from your delusions. You're a loser. How could my brother—"

"He was my lover. I'll love him forever."

CHAPTER 47 - X

November 8 (1)

I walked down the same lilac path in the familiar maple woods. From Francisco's description, I recognized the oriole's melody, the foliage's murmur, the squirrels' acrobatics. Near the brook, I hid behind the bushes, afraid to see the boy's body in a pool of blood, but he stood at the bank, humming the familiar tune Francisco had followed in his dreams. Where had I seen those eyes, those lips and that jaw?

He raised his head and turned to my right, staring beyond the lilacs. Another boy came along a hidden path. I knew this boy. I knew his gaze, slicing through the air. I knew his stride, trampling on the lilacs. I knew his swing, cracking the branches. I knew his countenance so well I couldn't identify him. From another dream, from another nightmare, from another fantasy, which had surfaced from my unconsciousness for one night only to retreat and vanish into the fog of amnesia. I knew him as I knew my red blood cells.

"I hate HYMN1, but you still asked me to come." The handsome boy raised his fist as if to strike the cement-face. "Only for Dolly's sake. But it's the last time."

"You're right." The cement-face showed his stained teeth. "It's the last time, at least, your last time."

"What'd you want?"

An elongated scream rose above the stream's murmur and echoed from trunks to branches to leaves to blossoms, and the petals and foliages shivered and hissed. A squirrel fell onto the ground and scurried into the woods while a breeze brushed against my back, chilling my skin and flesh.

Cement-face grasped the dagger that he plunged into the handsome boy's abdomen. He leaned forward and studied his victim's eyes like a doctor examining his patient. After shaking off leaves from the nearby trees with his scream, the handsome boy fell onto the ground while the sadist wiped his hands with a handkerchief and strolled along the bank, whistling that familiar tune.

Like Francisco, I ignored the pink-dress girl who rushed to the handsome boy and chased after the killer, tracking the footsteps along the muddy and snaking bank, but in the woods, I lost his scent. As the foliage became denser and the path darker, I sensed another presence behind a mossy boulder with orange-spotted mushrooms.

The blue-dress girl stepped out of the boulder and approached me. I searched my memory for the familiar eyes. She plunged a knife into my abdomen, the chill, the pain, the refreshing sensation tingling through my gut. As I clutched the clothed handle, as I fell to the ground damp and musty, as I gazed at the girl pristine and calm, I smiled at her, the girl I loved.

Ingrid.

I might have known her as a child, her features etched deep in my hippocampus. Since she had never mentioned it, even while sharing her childhood, she either didn't recognize me or was hiding her past. Why would she stab me in this dream?

Like Francisco, I hate dying in dreams.

I woke up in the afternoon on the same side street outside the bar, the ugly face of Agent Beta—the grocer cum taxi driver in my dream—hovering over me. I vomited. After filling the gutter with spaghetti in gastric juices, the pain and nausea lessened and I spat out the remaining food.

I pushed the Styrofoam box toward him and gestured for him to sample.

"No, thank you, cyanide doesn't do well in my stomach. Not like yours." He tossed me a paper napkin.

"Why did you poison me?" Poisoned sashimi pizza in the *hospital* and now cyanided spaghetti. I wiped my mouth and put the napkin over the food.

"With people like you, we would do well against those government thugs. Everyday, agents pretending to be hawkers, caterers, cooks and waiters poison dozens of our comrades with Anthrax."

"You aren't Beta?"

"Gamma," he said. "You're eyes must be damaged. I look nothing like him. If you scrutinize, you'd discern that I'm not Beta, that sadist lapdog with an ugly olfactory organ. But soon, you won't have to suffer his face. One less thug to contaminate this society."

He should find a better excuse than pretending to have multiple personalities. Then again, I might have to retune my eyes. I could distinguish Gamma's scarred bald head from Beta's.

"I'll believe you when I see him. And you, at the same time." I wouldn't have believed him if I hadn't met Molly. But now, but now. Why must I choose between this mad air and Francisco's rotten streets? "I'll tell the rebels you're really an intelligence agent posing as a rebel."

"Are you prejudice against clones? Do you think all clones look alike?" He took out a handkerchief to polish his shoes. "Don't trust that Dr. Tang. He wants the data to further the experiments. Of course, he's probably dead by now." He threw a folder marked *The Tang Profile* onto my lap.

"Even in that fake hospital, I didn't trust you."

I couldn't trust him anymore than I could Pratt. Gamma had turned this penal colony into Francisco's wasteland, each John telling you not to trust the next Jane. To break the cycle, I would trust Dr. Tang even if the evidence indicated otherwise. The only reasonable approach in this nightmare. I had wasted enough time with Gamma. Down the street, toward downtown, smoke had thickened. I had to chase after Ingrid to prevent her from entering the building.

"You can't let the government have that data. You can't allow them to develop the technology."

"When you tell me what I can or cannot do, you probably expect me to rebel and do the opposite. But I'll do whatever I want without your interference, right or wrong, good or bad, pretty or ugly."

"Do you know the power of this technology? With the data, the agents will brainwash us. They'll enslave us. They'll turn us into androids."

"You want to topple the government so *you* get to brainwash and enslave others. A taste of divine power."

"Do you value your freedom? Do you value your individuality? Have you taken your head out of the sand? Look around." He pointed an accusing finger. "The TVs broadcast the government's agenda and ideology. They dictate what you can or cannot do. Any decent man or woman will fight against such evil and oppression. For freedom, for dignity, for humanity."

"I don't care about the government. I don't care about the rebellion. And I don't care about your fanfare. Chant your slogans to someone else. Your buzzing is hurting my ear. We're here to bargain, to exchange one action for another. Which has nothing to do with what you or I believe." As I disdained the minister for wasting my time with apple-pie recipes, so I also despised Gamma for diverting my attention toward ideological propaganda. "If your freedom was encroached upon, then fight for your cause. I'm for freedom and nothing wrong with having ideals. But don't drag me into your fight with your slogans. We each have to walk our own paths."

"Ignorant mass." He patted my shoulder.

"No such luck. Life's not fair. I want to be an ordinary Joe. But I ended up being X, as in an unknown."

"Well, I won't let the government have that data." Gamma sat on a trashcan and crossed his legs. "Let me make it clear. I want the data in your head."

"After the smoke and fog about justice and equality. I don't trust you just as I don't trust the other you. You want the information in my head, no different from the government. So, let's negotiate instead of blowing smoke."

"Stop insulting me." He grinned.

I cringed before those icy eyes that aimed at my jugulars as if trying to pierce into them. He didn't shout. He didn't rant. But his slow breaths seemed to empower him as his face tightened and his lips stiffened. The silence stifled me but I inhaled and said, "I state a fact. And if that fact insults you, you better move into another universe with a different reality. If I want two plus two to be five and you want it to be four, we can agree to disagree, shake hands, and find our own universes. The problem with you gunslingers is that you always have to be right. In the end, you have to destroy the world because it doesn't conform to your *truth*." I wouldn't mind two plus two equals five as long as it doesn't switch between four and five every ten seconds.

He clinched his fists and his knuckles cracked. He moved his jaw but silence came out of his mouth. Like a wolf preparing to attack. He didn't shout or throw the trashcan. In the end, he relaxed his fists, exhaled, and said, "I offer something very valuable." His voice calm and subdued frightened me.

"Perhaps, my memory in a memory stick. An exchange of data for data." I could walk away and he wouldn't be able to stop me, but I didn't. He had confined me with his silence and his inaction.

"Between you and me, your past's worthless. Don't bother with it. Forget it and move on." He jumped off the trashcan and rubbed his soles against a paper bag to remove the dirt. "Let's exchange your CP data for Molly's life. Agreed?"

Molly's name rang in my ears and froze me. Gamma's soft level voice spiced up the dread. A butterfly fluttered in my stomach.

He's buffing. He's trying to con me.

My inner voice couldn't dispel the butterfly. I calculated the chance he had kidnapped her and I didn't like the odds. I raised my shaking hand. Reaching for his neck. Blood throbbing in my neck, surging through my arm, hot and lively. My hand waiting to grab, to squeeze, to release the energy building in the muscles. His neck wouldn't withstand my grip. His life wouldn't withstand my anger. But half way to his neck, he nodded as if encouraging me and I lowered my arm. I wouldn't turn into a monster, a sadist, a murderer. Never, never to be like him.

"Maybe you don't care about Molly," he said. "In that case, collateral damage."

As long as I had something he wanted, I could bargain with him. As long as I wasn't dealing with a fanatic who cared about nothing except his deluded principles, I could beat him. I swore to save Molly, even if I had to sacrifice an arm. Yet, according to Mrs. McCoy's photo, Molly might have been helping Beta (or maybe Gamma) con me. Doubt lingered like a parasite but I shook it away.

"You don't trust me. Reasonable. Let's confirm the merchandise is still in decent shape." He dialed his phone.

His confidence and poise disturbed me. I considered subduing him and exchanging him for Molly, but the TV next to the bar's entrance distracted me and I itched to punch a hole through the screen.

The call having gone through, Gamma asked his comrade to get Molly and handed me the phone. I kept my poise and took the phone, but my hand trembled. When I pressed the phone to my ear, Molly's voice resonated like a temple bell. "X, is that you? Don't listen to them. Don't make any bargains. It's a trap." A slap, then a groan.

"The article is genuine. No counterfeit. A deal? Or, maybe get rid of her and try someone else?"

"You're a sadist who enjoys killing people."

"Sorry for not explicating. If I kill someone you care about, it's only to show I can do the same to someone you care about even more. Like the girl Ingrid. So, I only torture. Physical or mental or emotional torture. And only to get results. Savages and thugs only kill, but an artist tortures. I'm artistic. Of course, I may have to show my art to convince you."

I seized his jacket. Pulled him close. Lifted him. I slipped my hand into his pocket and exchanged his watch for Dr. Tang's. His eyes showed nothing, as if he didn't have a soul, so I dropped him onto the ground.

Even with Molly and Ingrid and Dr. Tang in it, this world is as bad as Francisco's wasteland.

He got up, straightened his sports jacket, and brushed the dust from his trouser legs, then pulled out a pistol, cocked it and pointed it at my heart. "Molly or the data?"

Even without my memory and my past, I still valued my life. To soak in the smog, to suffer the broadcasts, to breathe in the violence, to live without a past. I preferred not to die before finding my past or, at least, my name. I estimated the bullet's trajectory and my hand's reaction, so I could catch the slug.

"Don't even try to make me shoot your brain, it won't work. Anyway, if you die, Molly suffers."

I pushed back the barrel with my chest. Unsure whether he would fire or whether my skin could repel the bullet. I didn't like gun barrels pushing me around, and would've charged at him if I didn't have to worry about Molly. "Sure, you have the gun and you have Molly, so you can monopolize the truth." I shut my eyes to feel the barrel. Trying to evoke fear. Losing my name and my past seemed to have numbed my sensations. What's the correlation between fear and the sense of self?

"Beta. You hate Beta."

"He's my first target," he said. "That is, if you cooperate."

Gamma stared and I could sense the hatred and bitterness running through his blood. More than anyone else, he would want to eliminate his clone, for taking a different path. As he blinked, his heartache slithered through my abdomen.

"At least," I said, "you have memory to feel painful about."

"You pray for pain from memory? Be careful, my friend. When that memory slashes your heart, you can tell me how it feels. Right now, you have no idea. Living in fantasyland, detached from the pains of this world. While the storms of anger and hatred rage around us." The gun barrel shook, for the first time.

I had weighed the pain of knowing my past and begun the journey. Now, turning from the wretch's smirk to the fog that snaked through the alleys, again I evaluated the possible cost, the possible pain, the possible suffering, and reaffirmed my intent. Sure, he delighted in taking apart a human body and prying out screams and moans. I would like to flee from these sadists but I wouldn't be able to escape from myself.

"I only need your brain to get the data. We'll perfect CP and defeat the government's police state and create a new society, a utopia. Freedom, human dignity."

"Have you considered working for an advertising agency?" Even without my memory and my past, his words and his utopia sounded as flimsy as the wind. After executing the top government officials, he would upgrade the monitors in every home with the latest equipment, high-resolution scanners and the latest discrete-cosine-transforms for more accurate image recognition. Change the music over the broadcast, but keep the same subliminal messages. Wear a different uniform, a jazzier jacket, but issue the same commands.

"People like you make slavery possible. Fear, indifference, saving your own ass, sitting on the border, waiting to kowtow to the winning side." Gamma put his finger on my forehead and pushed away my head. "Anyway, your brain's coming. Decide if your body will come along."

"So, your new freedom of choice. I'm quite impressed." I folded my arms around my chest. How sad that Francisco's world might be as close as possible to utopia.

"You'll be more so when we extract the data from your brain." He patted my cheek.

"But I had a deal with this Mexican client already. And I wouldn't want to disappoint him. Neither should you. So put your gun away. Then go home and enjoy a glass of scotch."

"About that Mexican client. One of these days, I'll tell you about him. But for now, ignore him. He won't bother us."

I stared into the gun barrel. Stared into darkness. Trying to be afraid. Trying hard. Still nothing. I sighed and imagined the pines, the ledges and the ridges. Relishing my dream. I smiled at the barrel. Ready to charge at Gamma and catch the bullet.

"Careful." He pulled away the gun. "Don't put you brain in danger."

"Sorry for jeopardizing your chance to retrieve the data and get your promotion."

"To entice you to make the deal, I'm throwing in a piece of news, for free." He straightened his jacket. "The IAB has blown up. The whole slab collapsed onto nearby buildings. Wasn't us. The Air Force bombed the building and killed everyone inside. To tarnish our image. To turn public opinions against us. They sacrificed those loyal servants just—"

The TV broadcast confirmed the news.

In my mind, a voice shouted. Loud and incoherent. I couldn't understand it until silence returned and the images of the building's debris fixed onto my mental screen. In slow motion, the dust and smoke drifted into the sky while red and blue lights cast shadows on the gray.

I would never see Ingrid again, her body buried in the debris, her hair burned into ash, her past, her memory, her she-ness dispersing with the smoke. Or Dr. Tang. A breeze brought the aroma of roasted meat and I pinched my nose and, steadying myself against the wall, tried to collect my thoughts, to review my plan, to mull over the next step but my mind couldn't focus, random thoughts and images and sounds darting into and out of consciousness, emotions churning my stomach and paralyzing my limbs. I had lost my friends. I had lost the anchors, the foundations of my existence in this world, and now I drifted in the sea of amnesia among agents and rebels, among strangers trying to seize my brain.

Yesterday, I went into Dr. Tang's room when he was out, and found, beside his Jung anthologies, a painting of Dolly with his initials. He had never shown me that painting, but it had ignited a sparkle of hope, that he couldn't release her even after she had died. Now, that didn't matter anymore. Funny thing. What appeared so vital then had become trivial, as time passed and events unfolded and sentiments changed, and we headed toward our graves.

"Now, back to business. Now that Tang is gone, you don't have to worry about him anymore. But Molly's fate is in your hands. Two minutes to decide if she lives or dies. Not often you get to play God. Enjoy the moment. As they say, it won't last."

CHAPTER 48 - FRANCISCO

October 25, 2011 (1)

I loaded my Smith and Wesson and prepared to meet the Guardian.

After sausages and eggs and a cup of coffee, I left the Underground Temple and headed for the rendezvous with my automatic pistol, a pair of handcuffs, my statuette, and the box of diamonds.

As I drove across the George Washington Bridge through the night fog, I studied Fernando's baseball card. No way Clint was his lover. He had more taste. After all, he was my brother. Besides, he would've confided about his lover. Clint might've had a crush on Fernando and hallucinated about being the lover. Then again, he might be trying to ruffle me, but I wouldn't fall into his trap. I must pay him extra for trying to taint Fernando's name.

The eastern sky hadn't lit up and I drove on the New Jersey Turnpike under fluorescent light. As I passed a solitary truck, I longed to have Faith by my side, to see her eyes and feel her hands, to show my achievements. Damn it, I'd never considered her wishes. Would I fail to love her? I'd never flopped and didn't intend to, but then, even if I should succeed...

I exited the turnpike and headed down the local road, the occasional houses passing on either side, their shadows spectral, their lights sallow. I drove into the junkyard and parked my BMW next to the skeleton of a luxury sedan. I shut my engine but continued to think about Faith for several minutes before getting out, the smell of spoiled fish and egg wafting through the air. A path between an abandoned car pile and a trash pit led to my office. In the pit, a few stray dogs were sniffing and chewing through the trash but stopped and eyed me. I greeted them and after I'd passed, they toiled again. A crow perching on a rusted crane cawed and I took out my pistol and aimed at it and it shrieked and flew into the night.

After reaching the shack, my makeshift office for *special* clients, not used since last winter, I kicked the door and entered the room that reeked of mildew, and stooped and picked up the femur I'd found when rescuing Holly. My beggar associate had delivered it before my arrival. I cleared the spider webs with the femur and dusted the desktop and the armchair.

After putting the diamonds on the desk, I called the hospital to check on Faith but Ganesh had taken her home last night. The nerd had raced ahead again, but I wouldn't give up. I'd win her over. I took her to the hospital, while he was loitering in the night streets, or worse, getting drunk in a bar, and she could rely on me more than on the loafer.

Since the geek would cower in front of a shadow and hide behind Faith, I had my beggar associates tail them and fend off any thugs or assassins. Ms. Redhead, a professional, would carry out the threat if I didn't solve the Guzman code by tomorrow, THE DEADLINE.

Just as I hung up the phone, Ganesh texted me: Faith had sketched the mysterious client's profile. I should forward Ms. Boss's picture to impress the nerd, but against my better judgment, my St. Francis alter-ego held me back. For Faith, just for Faith. In fifteen seconds, I received the digital file.

When I looked at the sketch, I dropped my phone. My office seemed to toss about the raging sea while I struggled to balance myself on the chair. The storm (my mental and emotional storm) wouldn't subside. Several minutes later, I picked up my phone but my eyes averted the screen for several more minutes while I held my head with the right hand. I took out a bottle of whiskey and a tumbler from the locked cabinet and drank a quarter glass before looking at the sketch again. I didn't want to believe my eyes. I exit the office and screamed and scared away the stray dogs. Then returned for another drink.

Holly. She is the mysterious client.

I checked the contract on my phone. Sure enough, Holly signed it. If not for the signature, I would've kicked Ganesh's butt into the East River.

Why didn't she hand me Fernando's file? Why did she have to threaten me with a deadline? Did she know VE would kidnap her? Did she chop off Naked Man's hand, run her car over my neighbor, kill Suzie, and have Clint torture Faith? Why did she have to inflict pain on those I cared about? OK, not the Naked Man, though I had nothing against him.

Someone knocked.

After having the visitor sit in the waiting room, I polished my trophy and checked the emails on my phone. I finished the whiskey and called my beggar associates and had them gather around the junkyard, ready for hand-to-hand combat.

What were Holly's intentions? The office became stuffy and the fever impeded my thoughts, so I drank more whiskey. (Damn it, even if I wasn't an alcoholic, after these traumas I'd become one.) Outside, the dogs returned, toiled over the trash and chased away the rats. I let down the black cloth to cover the window and returned to my chair to study the sketch of Holly. A nice sketch. Faith should change profession.

An hour later, I commanded the visitor to enter. No response. The Guardian could've left, but when I shook the box of diamonds, the rattles the melody of wealth, a thud broke the silence. The Guardian probably fell off the bench, his nose knocking on the hardwood floor.

"Hey, did you read the sign? No sleeping in the waiting area." I commanded him to enter. "Either I see your ugly face in five seconds or I'd sell the diamonds in the black market."

After the rumbles, footsteps approached my office and a shadow draped over the stained glass. I drew the pistol.

The door opened.

Beta the grocer cum cabdriver came into the office. He'd disguised his voice so I couldn't recognize him on the phone and in the school, but I should've known from the beady eyes, the crooked nose and the twisted lips that this loser is the Guardian. Had I known him for ten, maybe twelve years? I didn't like having shopped in his bodega and rode in his cab, and subsidized his plot against me. So, though a picture of the scheme was emerging, the twines had tightened around me. "Now, I know you're a loser. Tailing me like that. I shouldn't have given you any tips."

"Didn't even recognize me when I was right under your nose. Too busy talking about those SOAPS certificates. What ego. What hubris. I told you that'd be your downfall." The Guardian stepped into the office and dusted his sleeves. "Before we start, I remind you that you killed your old man seventeen years ago along that trail in the Catskill Mountains. Just a friendly reminder. You know how memories are, fading with time and all that. I don't mean to be long-winded, but only doing my job.

And a dirty job, too. By the way, can still find the rock you used. Buried near those white mums."

"One chance to redeem yourself. What's the code word inside *Notes from the Underground?* Be careful, your only chance." After Faith had been tortured, after Suzy had died, after Holly had turned out to be the mysterious client, I should toss in the white flag and leave for the Bahamas. Yet, when the Guardian stepped into the office, I vowed to defeat his trickery. I vowed to fight to the end. I wouldn't succumb to remorse or turn into X. I wouldn't waste Dr. Tang's insight about NFTU referring to *Notes from the Underground.* As Francisco Guzman, yesterday, today and forever, I'd kick the Guardian's butt and his foreseen suffering spurred me onward.

"Don't try to evade the subject. Your old man, you killed him."

"You're beginning to annoy me and when I'm annoyed, the grizzly inside me comes out." I rubbed the pistol's handle, mulling over where to shoot him. I didn't want to kill him but couldn't let him off without his reward.

"Like I said, if you break that code, you'd seal your doom. So stay put and let things run their course."

"Would Caesar or Napoleon or Genghis Khan ever let things run their courses? Look at me. I'm Francisco Guzman." I checked the text message on my phone: my associates begged me to kick the meatloaf out of the office for kneading and pounding.

"Damn it, you're sidetracking. You hear me? You did kill your dad. You killed him. Your past always affects you." The Guardian pounded his fist on my desk. "Your memory, the past perceptions and sensations stored in your brain define you. You're Francisco Guzman because you and only you have those memories, those adventures, those successes, those pleasures. They're you."

"You forgot I'm Francuccesco. Whatever I recall won't stop me from shredding you to pieces. You see, I don't allow my past to shackle me though some experiences might annoy me." I waved the gun at the lunatic and shook the box of diamonds. "But convincing Clint he wouldn't get punished for whatever he did. Nasty. Your hypnotism will really do him in. He may try to jump down a skyscraper and chase after jets." I'd punish him for digging up past maggots and peeling my scabs.

"But what do you care? You never cared nothing about him before." He stared at the diamonds, his jaw hanging and his tongue licking his lips. He approached and extended his arm.

"Hey, listen carefully, I'm holding you responsible for what happened to Faith. Without you screwing Clint's brain, he wouldn't have dared to hurt her. Or believed he was my brother's lover." I put the empty whiskey bottle in his hand. "We're doing business now so I'm polite. But after this, well, all's fair in love and war. And there's no love between us."

"I toiled and toiled to guard those memories that are fading over the years. Do you remember what you had for dinner on May 6, 1995? I remember the moments when you received these certificates. I remember the meals you had and the ladies you picked up." He studied the bottle for a while before staring at the box again.

"If you're supposed to guard my memories, then you've failed at your job. Look, you lost my memories. And you failed to grab the goodies, too. So, if I were your employer, I'd fire you."

"But, I do work for you." He grasped the bottle by the neck and smashed it onto the edge of the desk, cracking it in half. "Of course, you ever paid me anything, you cheapskate. Should've let more of your inane memories go by the wayside."

"Usually, I don't talk to lunatics, but since I need info—"

"Hey, come on, I'm your Guardian of Memory. Don't you remember me? That time you're having so much fun kicking Clint's butt on July 4, 2004." He waved the cracked bottle in front of my face as if trying to scribble on my cheeks.

"I only know you tried to steal these diamonds." Clint probably disclosed the Independence Day incident. Clint and Holly and the Guardian must be colluding to pull me into their snare. Just as I'd prepared the handcuffs for this meeting, I'd design a trap worthy of their crimes for the showdown.

"And that time you dreamed of being a knight, thrashing your enemies and saving the princess."

"Never mind those cheap. Let's get back to business." I'd never told anyone about that dream, or written it down, so the knave must've hypnotized me and extracted the info. I suspected someone playing with my mind when I dreamed about the amnesiac. I should've guarded against the hypnotist and lamented that my mind yielded to the quack. I put the box of diamonds in my left pocket and the gun in my right. I walked over, knocked the bottle out of his hand, grasped his collars and lifted him off his feet. "So, redemption or condemnation? Tell me the code word."

"So I'm just reading your mind? Fine, fine." He struggled for several seconds but couldn't loosen my grip. "Be warn, if I get mad, I'd lose your memories by the bundle. By the time this ends, you'd remember less than the poor devil in your dream. Now, that's a loser and I know you agree."

"You've no right to enslave me with my past." Had X dreamed up the Guardian and this world, and I just a figment of the amnesiac mind? Of course, I'd prefer to be Dr. Tang's figment. "I'd forgotten the killing for so many years. Without a bad conscience. I was enjoying life. You were jealous. You didn't have your own experiences and could only relish my joy. Note this, you'll fail. I'll shred my conscience and regain my freedom." I sensed his pleasure, the pleasure in tormenting me, the pleasure that energized him from morning until evening. I had felt such pleasures, sad to say. "Like you said, I create the future and at any moment, I choose from the paths before me as if I am a new man. Who is Francisco Guzman? Not the guy who killed his dad." I shook him until his face flushed and his eyes lost focus.

"But listen, what you experience, both the details and the old feelings create new sensations, new reactions, new responses, new memories. So, even when you delete the memory of the event, those sensations will trickle through your life and help to recreate that experience."

"Last chance for diamonds."

"The key lies in your dreams."

"Who's the guy with amnesia?"

"I mean the other dream, the dream in the woods, with the kid killing the other kid."

"But that's not my memory, it never happened."

"I don't know. I'm not sure. It may or it may not be."

"How can you not know? Will you protect that dream?"

"You're confusing me."

"That's a lame excuse."

"The girl in the dream is important."

"There were two girls. And I identified one already."

"The one closer to the action."

"She looked familiar."

"You must believe I'm—"

"Well, Guardian of Memory, help me create my future. I'd like to own the Rockefeller Center and a vacation island in Abu Dhabi. I'd like to access the CIA and Interpol databases for my work. Just for starters." I shook him until his toupee fell off.

He nodded as if agreeing but said, "Sorry, I only protect your past. I don't create your future. Not my department. You ask a knight to act as a rook; you ask a square peg to fit into a round hole; you ask Napoleon to knit a sweater—"

"Right, I shouldn't ask a moron to add one and one together." I dropped him and picked up the femur. He stooped down and picked up the toupee and I yanked it out of his hand. Just great, just like him, trying to disguise himself, trying to deceive me. How could I trust someone who hides his baldness?

He tried to grab the toupee but missed by an inch. I opened the window and tossed it out. Two dogs charge at it, each biting one side and they growled and tried to tear it from the other.

"Here's the deal, you'll locate Clint and bring him to me, alive but in handcuffs. Be glad I'm not vending my anger on you. Of course, I can if you prefer." I shut the window and tapped the femur on his cheek. Outside, the dogs tore apart the toupee.

"But, that's not my job. I ain't no good at that. I could get killed."

I pushed him against the wall and took out the handcuffs. "After what happened to Faith and Suzie, I've got nothing to lose." I shook the box. "Diamonds, or no diamonds?"

When the two dogs barked outside, I checked on the toupee, but kept my eyes on the Guardian, who disclosed Clint's new hideout. He tried to grab the diamonds, but I pull away the box and cuffed his hand to the box of diamonds. I ordered the madman to bring back Clint, though he'd flee to the Bahamas with the diamonds. No, I let him go, so he'd take me to his accomplice and reveal more secrets.

Dawn had arrived but the fog hadn't left, and the dogs, having shredded the toupee but unable to eat it, continued to scour the trash for breakfast.

I ate breakfast in Washington Square while my associates sniffed the Guardian's scent from Newark to Hoboken, across the Holland Tunnel to Chinatown. I was munching lobster pancakes when Ganesh phoned and said, "Don't trust Holly."

"Here we go again." I rinsed my mouth with coffee. "I seemed to be stuck in a time-loop, where everything repeats itself. Except in my case, each person says not to trust the next person, until the loop closes on itself. Well, someone said not to trust you."

"Well, don't trust him either," Ganesh said. "Anyway, you received Faith's sketch—"

"FYI, I don't have amnesia." I waved to the girl at the next table, while the businessman with her boasted of his bonus. When I recalled

Faith's bruised face, I lowered my head and stuffed pancake into my mouth.

"Remember the note you found in her place, the one that urges you to crack this code so she wouldn't die?"

"How you know this? Have you been tailing me?"

"Well, Holly wrote it."

"All right, I believe Faith and her sketch. So Holly's the client. But why should I believe any word you said? You didn't even exist before August. And don't say I should believe you because you're my friend."

"While you were in her apartment, she thrashed your stuff to find the laptop you'd hidden inside your spring box."

"Why were you snooping around my apartment?"

"She either changed or deleted your previous diary entries. So, don't believe any entry before this August."

"And, most of all, I shouldn't believe you. If you're such a know-it-all, who stole my *pate de foie gras*?" Holly had lied. She'd been captured for only two days and she betrayed herself by marking the days on the wall. For the record, I could remember such details. During that time, she'd contacted Faith, so she also lied about the phone running out of power. She didn't even strained her brain to fabricate more convincing tales.

"Do you remember that homeless man in the back alley who scours through the trash for leftovers? Well, he was quite hungry and finished the paste in three days. By the time I reached him to have a share, he'd finished everything, and won't touch leftovers anymore."

"And you led him to it, I'm sure, just to spite me and ruin his appetite. Who are you really? Which of my enemies sent you?"

"Not yet. Soon though. Have patience. But you'll have to trust me."

"Now, that's a new one." I didn't trust him anymore than I trusted Clint or Holly or the Messenger. At that time, I had to focus on the Guardian, who'd lead me to a revelation. While I talked on the phone, the lady from the next table walked over, dropped a card on my table and headed for the lady's room.

"I know where Clint is and I'm going after him," Ganesh said. "I hate violence and detest those agents and rebels in your dreams, but for Faith, I'll shred my decency and integrity. Sure, I'd become a monster, but I'd analyzed the cost and benefit and decided to mutilate the scoundrel."

"Always competing with me. Sure, trying to trump me and win her heart. Trying to prove you're a better man." I picked up the card and turned it over. The girl had kissed it and left her phone number. "Well, you aren't there yet, not by a stretch across the Sahara. If I can help it, I'll stop you from shredding Clint and avenging Faith. I want him. You hear me? I want him."

"Well, each person seeks his or her own hell. I've chosen mine and must strive to get there. If you choose to follow me, then let the best scoundrel shed his decency. But I'm more than a step ahead."

"Hey, I don't lose. Never have and don't intend to."

Damn it. Ganesh would reach Clint's neck before I could get half way there. I must use the trump card in my pocket. "Also, when it comes to kicking butts, you aren't even in my league. Go play in the Minors, with those petty thieves and con artists." I paid the check and left the restaurant.

"Since you've wasted your time with that con artist," Ganesh said, "just have some durian pie in The Usual Café and wait for my good news. My treat. Maybe, blue sky tomorrow."

After Ganesh had hung up, I called my Underground Temple assistant to free the Priest. I reinstalled the chief lunatic to his former post and informed him Clint had thrashed Faith. I gave him the scoundrel's location and urged him to *shake-a-leg* before a fool could snatch the prize. I hoped the Guardian had given me the correct address. Otherwise, the nerd would suffer through the rest of his life. Of course, he'd win Faith's heart. No, no, I must prevent it. Then again, he couldn't torture or kill even if I pointed a gun at him. His genes would halt his hands; he lacked the resolve, the courage, the flexibility, and the ingenuity.

I checked with my associates on the Guardian's location and took a taxi through Manhattan. As the cab sped down Broadway, running red lights and honking at pedestrians, chants, cheers and shouts reached my ears and disrupted my thought on how to punish the Guardian. Soon, a procession blocked the way, and the cab had to stop and let me out. On the street, shouts echoed among the buildings and down the street several booms shook the ground. Smoke rose into the air. For a moment, I thought I was in Fermat's Last Stand and the rebels were bombing government buildings.

As I approached a building on Broadway, the Guardian stepped out of a toy store with a model car and skipped down the sidewalk whistling the familiar tune. I followed him across the street toward Greenwich Village while pedestrians rushed down the street, saying terrorists were attacking Manhattan. The traffic was at a standstill and the *horn concerto* blasted through the early winter morning.

When I saw the Guardian's accomplice, I slit my forearm with a pocketknife to dispel any illusions. I could only lament today's smog contaminating tomorrow's sunshine. Dreams lost; love dispersed; Francisco beaten.

CHAPTER 49 - X

November 8 (2)

Atop a trashcan I read *The Tang Profile*: Dr. Tang had formulated the concepts for cerebral programming and advised the Russians on the CP experiments. So, after all, he was Dr. Tangenstein, and had continued to hide his past. Why couldn't he trust me? With no chance to interrogate him, I dropped the report onto the ground.

On the TV screen, which I should smash, the rescue teams pulled corpses out of the collapsed IAB. So far, no survivors. Had Dr. Tang dragged Ingrid with him into that graveyard? If so, I wouldn't forgive him, though he had perished. I would miss him but I didn't want to mourn for her also. The debris was collapsing onto the rescuers when Gamma's face blocked the screen.

If I could forsake Molly, I would grab Gamma's throat and try to turn the hunter into prey. I didn't intend to give him the CP data even if I could retrieve them, but I couldn't risk her life. I would stall him and with the added time try to rescue her. So, I agreed to the exchange. I sensed an intrigue but at that moment I couldn't pinpoint the problem and couldn't consult Dr. Tang to analyze my misgivings and isolate the misplaced piece of the puzzle.

"You've got one week. So recover your memory by then and save the damsel in distress. Like the hero you pretend to be." Gamma took *The Tang Profile* and left.

He was probably going to check on Molly. Rather than give the rebels the CP data, I would crash their party and rescue her. Though I would desert this wasteland, I wouldn't help create a society of automatons.

I tracked Gamma to the main street, where a jeep waited for him. After he had climbed in, the vehicle sped away and headed toward a plume of black smoke among the skyscrapers, where the IAB's debris must still be burning. I followed along the sidewalk. Of course, I could track him even without the jeep, since I had dropped Dr. Tang's watch into his pocket and the transmitter was sending me data.

Near the smoke, ambulances and fire engines clogged the main street but a few pedestrians rushed down the sidewalks. The symphony of sirens blasted in the air while helicopters hovered above the buildings. Spectators poked their heads out the upper floor windows and chatted while sipping grape juice and skim milk.

No officers or soldiers patrolled the streets, so I treaded near the buildings and under the awnings to avoid the surveillance cameras. Near the jeep, which was crawling in the traffic, music wafted through the air and a subliminal message urged citizens to inform the police of rebels hiding in the buildings. The jeep stopped and Gamma got off and jogged toward the smoke.

I was about to follow him when someone behind shouted, "Stop." Halting under the awning, waiting for the footsteps to approach, planning my moves, I cursed the man for holding me up and forcing me to subdue him. Several policemen ran past me and headed toward the jeep. After a pop, an officer collapsed. The rest darted behind surveillance stations and security checkpoints and bullets flew back and forth.

I sidled next to the buildings and passed the jeep, dodging two stray bullets and reaching the street corner. Gamma had disappeared. Not among the pedestrians hiding behind cars to avoid the bullets. Nor among the patrons in the cheesecake shops.

When the jeep exploded, I slipped into a side street. I would track Gamma's movements with my laptop in a café or restaurant while planning Molly's rescue. I had to focus on locating Molly, and couldn't work on the code. Francisco, with Ganesh's help, would have to break the remaining code, whether or not I would fall asleep and dream.

I was walking across a piazza and shooing away the pigeons when a figure darted into a side street. Gamma? No, a lady who looked like Ingrid. The hope that had fizzled out again flickered, a spark in the darkness of despair. Perhaps she hadn't caught up with Dr. Tang when the building collapsed. I called after her and passed the fountain toward the other end of the piazza. As the wind lifted my hair and my jacket, I persuaded myself that she hadn't entered the IAB, that she still lived, that the lock of hair still curved behind her ear.

In a side street between two rows of jack-o-lanterns, the melody of "Amazing Grace" wafting through the air, I reached an intersection where the head-trauma patient from the *hospital*, dressed as a minister, handcuffed Dr. Tang. On the cobblestone path, a dozen parishioners pointed their automatic shotguns at the mad scientist, the phantom that should've left this world for a better one but returned to haunt me.

Joy? Anger? Indifference? Feelings stewed. How to describe the sensation that moved in my chest? A simmering cream of tomato?

No, I didn't wish him dead. Still, his face reminded me of his lies and deceptions, which after many winters had not faded from my mind. On the other hand, meeting the head-trauma patient reassured me that reality was settling down. Maybe. I might have seen him in the hospital or the school, but I didn't fret over trifles.

I should turn around and look for Molly, rescue her from Gamma and take her to a world where we could toil in the sun and reap the fruits of our labor, where we could stroll along the beach under the evening rosy clouds. The booms in the distance and the gunpowder in the air, the sounds and smells in this wasteland, these intruders would stay in my mind and torment me.

I grabbed a parishioner's shotgun and threw him into his comrades. They fell one after another while I approached the minister and tapped his shoulder. When he turned toward me, I took his hand and squeezed. He opened his mouth as if to greet me, but his face contorted before he could say a word. He knelt down and begged for mercy while tears rolled down his cheeks. I shielded Dr. Tang with the minister's body and ordered the parishioners to drop their weapons and go to the pub. When the minister whined and repeated my order, they left. After getting the handcuffs keys, I released the minister's hand and he collapsed onto the ground, his shoulder crushing a jack-o-lantern. I unlocked the handcuffs while the minister's footsteps receded into the distance.

The mad scientist rubbed his wrists. Instead of disclosing Ingrid's mission and destroying their love, I asked for her whereabouts. At that moment, I had forgotten about Gamma, but even if I hadn't, I would have waited for her.

Well, I would see her soon and she would plunge a dagger into my abdomen, to end my amnesiac misery.

He led me along a cobblestone path under brown awnings to look for Ingrid, who was nearby talking to the rebel leader and avoiding the intelligence agents. Two blocks away, the minister ordered his men to spray bullets into our bodies, his voice echoing between the buildings. They should have gone to the pub.

Turning a corner and sprinting down an alley, Dr. Tang said, "I would've gone into the building if Ingrid hadn't caught up and insisted on coming along to persuade her former colleagues from massacring the rest of the agents."

I blamed him for my plight. Without CP, I wouldn't have volunteered to erase my memory and I wouldn't have joined Dolly in stealing the data. I wouldn't have had the accident and lost my memories. Most of all, I couldn't forgive him for lying. He deceived me in the hospital/school/jail, in the hillside house, and in the lighthouse café, not once, not twice, but time and time again across several realities.

He had never considered me his friend, in neither this nor an alternate universe, but just as I couldn't force Ingrid to love me, I couldn't force him to trust me. These empty streets and closed shops only a microcosm of this world: shadows lurking in nooks, smoke obscuring the view, and booms echoing in the distance. After recovering my memory, after finding my past and my self, I would probably discover I didn't have any friends or family. The other lives disconnected from mine. To discover the self is to walk into the desert.

"I can't waste my time or Ingrid's," he said, "especially when the world seems to be ending, or at least going mad."

"Congratulations, you helped make it a mad world." I jogged up the slope between two concrete walls with government insignias. My hope to win over Ingrid had evaporated and I could focus on finding Molly, but as he couldn't forget Dolly, I wouldn't Ingrid either. I would recall her in solitary nights and days, in solitary springs and summers. "If I ever regain my memory and locate the CP data, you may destroy them. That is, if I find them." The government agents or the rebels would apply CP to manipulate the citizens' minds and recruit supporters and soldiers like the Underground Temple fanatics. I wanted to talk to, to associate with, to share my ideas with intelligent beings, not zombies. I wanted to say no, even if others would stone me. I didn't want to be an android, not until one could transcend its algorithms and rebel against its master.

In front of a pet shop, Dr. Tang held out his hand but I didn't shake it. Why should I? He left his hand hanging as if begging for alms. Were I Francisco—thank God I wasn't—I would spit on his hand.

A boy stepped out of the shop holding a puppy and a man and a woman holding hands followed him. They talked and laughed as they walked down the slope but they might as well be androids. Why did they shop during a curfew, when police and rebels were shooting each other down the street?

I was about to call after them when the minister appeared at the bottom of the slope and ordered his parishioners to seal off the area. I scanned my ID and we entered the pet shop where goldfish swam in the tanks and parrots babbled in cages. Their eyes could be surveillance cameras.

"Not only our education and backgrounds, not only our temperaments and preferences, but also our visions of the future, no matter how false, how surreal, how distorted, set our decisions and directions, and create today." Beside a cobra in a glass tank Dr. Tang peeped through the display window into the street where the wind tossed propaganda leaflets into the air.

"So, you believe in self-fulfilling prophecies." The cobra's eyes didn't look like lenses, but I couldn't trust my eyes.

"I believe in no prophecies, whether self-filling or self-evident or self-contradictory."

"A true believer." I pulled him farther into the shop as the first agent's gloved hand appeared at the window edge.

We turned around and I pretended to admire the gecko in the back of the shop. When a parrot greeted me, I pretended I didn't understand its tongue, but it continued to echo the phrase and tempted me to tie its beaks together. Perhaps its ears were receivers to capture customers' conversations.

The door opened and the bell jingled. Footsteps approached me. Dr. Tang looked at an oriole and I prepared to shove him onto the floor to avoid the bullets. As long as I didn't have to worry about him, I could handle the agents.

Rubbing my hands, I prepared to turn around when a little girl pushed her face against the tank and stared at a snake's hissing tongue. No parishioners waited for us outside the display window.

We continued up the slope and Dr. Tang said, "Sure, my excitement when I was formulating my theory. Yes, I looked forward to using CP to ease needless sufferings and ushering in a new era of healthier mind and body without the side effects of PC."

"I wouldn't have ratted if you'd told me." I should strangle the mad scientist for creating CP. Instead, I pitied him for having to bear the guilt of creating the weapon that would destroy this world, a just punishment for his crime. So, I shouldn't blame him for my memory loss or for my part in stealing the data. He didn't need my words to taste his guilt.

"But after I worked on the Moscow CP Project. How they tested the subjects. How they'd use it to eradicate dissension. Well, I helped usher forth Armageddon."

"Congratulations, Dr. Tangenstein. Now, what part of your participation couldn't you disclose?"

We reached the top and a side street led to a church.

"With PC, government officials have to spend months or even years changing someone's behavior. Also, the effect will fade over time. So, the procedure can't create a society of human androids. But CP, that's different. It reroutes neural pathways in hours. So, with the new technology the government can forge that apocalyptic utopia within a few years."

"I see. You guaranteed your name in history books. The Father of A Perfect Mind and A Perfect Society. And you wanted to surprise me." If he had extended his hand, I would have spat on it. For once, I would mimic Francisco.

"And so," he said as we passed the church, "the drive that had propelled me onward, that had fooled me into living like a savior, that had given meaning to my life, all turned negative. Disaster as from a tornado or a tsunami or a forest fire. Not only that, I've been the chief designer, initiating this Armageddon, this holocaust. So, what part of this did you want to know? And why?"

"The part about trust and friendship, which you obviously don't understand. Even though you have your memory. Of course, playing God isn't easy."

"Yes, indeed, I've become a god who's going to destroy the world. The exhilaration and bliss from the past and the guilt and sadness from the future integrated with that moment to brew a storm that churns my stomach and jostles my mind, the past, the present, the future, bliss and grief, triumph and defeat, a melting pot." He turned around and said, "Why'd you want to know any of this?"

"Obviously, you're clueless."

We were turning left onto an alley when footfalls thundered behind us. I turned around. The minister led the agents out of the church and pointed his gun and fired. I seized Dr. Tang's arm and pulled him into the alley as the first bullet whizzed behind my head.

We ran. Down the alley. Over the cobblestone path. Amid the smoke and ash. Through several intersections. The minister and his men shouting and firing their guns, the bullets passing us. Could I protect Dr.

Tang? Could I dodge the bullets? I still had to see Ingrid and Molly. And maybe, even to shake Dr. Tang's hand.

A bullet grazed my neck. I turned to check on Dr. Tang and he turned left onto a lane with lanterns hanging from the eaves.

I followed. Turning left, then right. Through backyards and patios, through passages inside buildings and tunnels below homes.

We lost the minister and his men and entered a maze of alleys and byways, no surveillance cameras anywhere. When we stopped at an intersection, I had lost my direction but still smelled the smoke.

Dr. Tang looked down the alley and turned to glance around. Before I could open my mouth to demand that he show me Ingrid, he dashed down the alley, glancing through the windows on both sides. I ran after him until he stopped at an intersection with another alley and glanced left and right. No one down either end of the alley. Only more jack-o-lanterns sitting on lampposts. Only the traffic and din in the distance. I must see Ingrid. He retraced his steps and stopped at a doorway, staring at the flag flapping in the breeze. She should be here talking to her rebel friend, but she wasn't. No blood or splinters on the ground or cracked windows and collapsed doors. While Dr. Tang searched through the alleys, I looked in the empty buildings, but couldn't focus. I couldn't lose Ingrid now. I had to say farewell before she and the doctor could leave for paradise.

In the abandoned buildings, dust and cobweb draped the offices, and rat droppings paved the hallway floors. But no signs of life. Back in the alley, Dr. Tang grabbed my sleeve and pulled me along the flagstone path. He and Ingrid had agreed to meet in a nearby café after she had reminisced with her friend.

"Maybe they had to avoid the agents." Dr. Tang continued to glance through the windows into the buildings on both sides. He was trying to comfort himself and me.

Had the agents spotted her with the rebels?

Footfalls echoed through the alleys and we ran again.

After steering through the maze for ten minutes, Dr. Tang said, "And so I again sensed myself more real than ever, only not as a god, not as a savior, but a deluded man, a defeated man, who must face his mistaken pride and assured failure." He stopped at a corner to let the militiamen pass before crossing the intersection. "Alive again, alive to pain and suffering, alive to the vacuum in my stomach, alive to the futility of life. That continuous time, that integrated self, the past and present and future selves meeting at this point in time, this eternal now, reconciling one with the other, trying to synthesize a new world."

"Hey, Doc, you keep philosophizing and conceptualizing instead of living. Forget about the technical mumble jumbles. Forget about continuous time. Forget about eternal now. Forget the integrated self. Just live your life."

At an intersection, rebels bashed a TV monitor with pipes, the screen cracked and the circuit board halved. So we hid behind a trashcan. The rebels would riot downtown to avenge their comrades in the IAB, so we had to locate Ingrid soon and leave the war zone.

"In the end, I left Moscow before the project ended for fear of losing my humanity and becoming a monster. So, I didn't meet you and didn't know you had volunteered as a test subject."

"Smart move. Otherwise, I would've blamed you for that also."

"I searched for wisdom and found folly. For several years, I'd escaped from people to search for myself, no, to search for a path to re-create a new self. But that integrated self, a present pregnant with the past and the future continued to haunt me. Even now."

He took out a chestnut, probably the one Ingrid had taken from the hospital yard. "Don't worry. She'll be here."

"Do you guarantee it with your life? Even if you do, should I trust you?" I gazed at the chestnut as if looking at Ingrid and my heart ached.

"I must do what my better self would do, to create a future I. Despite my errors and my crimes. Even though the fog covers the streets now, tomorrow the sun will shine on the pedestrians. After all the follies, that bit of wisdom I've learned." He twirled the chestnut with his fingers.

I took out the acorn from the hospital yard, the one I had keep across several realities, and I recalled the days and hours that had passed since then, the crimes and treacheries revealed. The versions of reality. I knew more of myself and this world but understood less about either. Would I want to understand even less?

"I was very tempted to wipe my hands clean of CP and let the government do whatever with the technology. But, in the end, I couldn't. So I tried to get access to the abandoned school and destroy the data. Guess I still have a conscience. When I told Ingrid about my mad creation, she volunteered to help me destroy the data without blaming me for bringing forth a monster. And she helps me overcome my struggles, encouraging me whenever I lack the energy or the will to move forward."

"Doc, I tried time and again to trust you." I tried to spin the acorn. "But you have so many secrets that even with my superhuman speed, I couldn't get near you. So what should I believe? I'll believe in sunshine when I see it. I'm just afraid you may turn out to be an android, or worse, a hologram."

Dr. Tang fumbled the chestnut and it fell onto the ground. Was he indeed an android? I didn't dare to ask. Only prayed he wasn't one. I also prayed Ingrid wasn't one. I was in for a surprise.

I picked up the chestnut Ingrid didn't give me.

"I'll bear the burden, the responsibility for creating that technology." He extended his hand for the chestnut.

"Forget about burden and responsibility. I have a favor to ask." I should keep the chestnut or crush it but I returned it.

We waited until the rebels had flattened the TV and left, before crossing the intersection. We turned right and walked downhill until we reached another intersection and continued on a cobblestone path. Several helicopters hovered above the buildings scanning the streets with laser beams, perhaps trying to execute loiterers.

"You want to sock me in the face? I wouldn't blame you. But that can wait." He rushed toward an intersection where another smashed TV lay on the ground and walked up to a coffee shop on the street corner. "We have more important things to do. Once we have the code word, we'll locate the data in your brain and destroy them."

"The code word may or may not recover my memory. Anyway, tomorrow's the deadline. So, if Francisco still couldn't solve the code, then I must have Plan B. Would you use CP to help me regain my memory?"

"When I left Russia, I swore never to touch that stuff again. As you shouldn't tempt an alcoholic with whiskey, you shouldn't tempt me with this." He grabbed the handle but didn't open the door. He clutched the chestnut as if about to crush it. I waited for bits to slip through his fingers. The veins on the back of his hand wriggled as if about to jump out. When his shook, I rolled the acorn with my fingers and imagined sweat dripping down his forehead and along the wrinkles on his cheeks. A breeze thrust smoke into our faces and hid his features.

"But, of course, you'll do it anyway. You owe me it."

"When I become addicted again, I'll hold you responsible." He released the chestnut and dropped it into his pocket. Then picked up a bottle at the doorway and smashed it against the wall. A laser beam burned the TV scraps as if to seal his doom.

"Thanks, Doc. And don't worry about the side effects. I wouldn't mind losing my memory, since I only have less than three months' supply. And with the shifting reality, I couldn't isolate the genuine from the fake ones anyway. So I'll just start over again, like in that hospital room or classroom, that's all." I wiped the splinters from his jacket and kicked aside the fragments in front of the doorway.

A boom shook the ground. Inside the shop, the ceiling lamp dropped and the splinters splashed across the floor. Several screams echoed in the distance and a woman passed the burnt TV scraps.

Dr. Tang entered the cafe. I followed before the door closed, then sidestepped the splinters. Ingrid wasn't drinking tea at a corner table. No one was in the coffee shop. I demanded to see her but he sprinted toward the back and called for her.

A framed photo hung on the wall. The meadow, the sun, the lilacs, the stream, and the bird. The same picture... I was in the seat below the frame tasting a piece of durian pie—the café owner's new recipe—when Dolly walked through the doorway and sat facing me at the next table. I turned to look at the table where she had sat. How had her fingers moved across her cheek as she smiled?

Taking out the meadow painting from my backpack, I compared it with the photo on the wall. Had Dr. Tang painted the picture from the photo? I didn't ask. It didn't matter anymore.

Outside the café, two boys holding bats marched down the cobblestone path. I was about to step out when the doctor walked up to the counter and announced he couldn't find Ingrid. He didn't say he worried about her. I raised my hand to grab him, but he exited and peeped into the side street. Another TV crashed onto the ground two feet from him. He surveyed the grayness while a cloud of dust mingled with smoke and fog to obscure the view. Several more pedestrians hurried past the entrance and a man walked up to the TV and bashed it with a bat. Dr. Tang would search for Ingrid while I waited for her in the café. He held out his hand but I refused to shake it. Before he left, he took the photo from the wall.

After he left, I wished I had shaken his hand. He didn't emerge through the fog and extend his hand. Inside the café I stepped behind the counter to pour a cup of soymilk and take a whole-grain muffin. Sipped the soymilk that tasted like starch-water and watched a man flatten the TV. After the laser beam scared him away, I took down from the wall a plaque with the inscriptions JACK CONMAN, FERMAT'S LAST STAND BEST PROPRIETOR OF THE YEAR and threw it into the trashcan. At a table in the middle of the café, I bit into the muffin and facing the door devised a plan to deceive Gamma with fake data. As soon as I could ensure Molly's safety, my only concern, I would fight it out with him. Outside, a platoon of soldiers passed the doorway, probably chasing after the saboteur. Behind them, a cat scurried into the alley.

After I had completed my plan and tracked down Gamma's location, Dr. Tang still hadn't returned. Nor had Ingrid shown up. I logged into the Intelligence Agency's database and checked for Dolly's autopsy, accessing the top-secret report. Sure enough, the forensics department reported a crown on a molar. The crown had an "M" on the side.

Duped, again.

I dropped the cup onto the floor and the splinters scattered like sunrays while the soymilk thrust toward the counter. Leaning closer to reread the report I still spot the "M."

Molly was shot. Molly had died. So, I was with Dolly, the spy, the deceiver, the schemer. I recalled the shock when her hand first touched mine. I recalled her smile, her lips against mine, and pushed away the laptop as if it were Dolly.

My dream of a house by the hillside dispersed again. Like another part of memory fading. Only not the past, but the future had scattered in the wind. I stood alone in the mist, unable to see left or right. In this reality, I lost everything, plus some.

Was Beta scheming with Dolly to extract the data from my head? He might have kidnapped Dolly, believing she was Molly, but he wouldn't care as long as I gave up the CP data. Then again, maybe Mrs. McCoy had seen Gamma rather than Beta. Could she tell them apart? If Dolly had killed Molly to play dead and deceive everyone, I must deal justice. I would do it for Molly, though I had never met her, and I wouldn't hesitate. Not this time.

The door opened.

There she was.

Ingrid.

She walked around the fallen lamp, stepped over the shards and approached me. Before she could open her mouth, I revealed Dr. Tang as the Chief Mad Scientist on the CP Project.

"I am sure your boss in the Intelligence Agency would want to know he was helping the Russians," I said. "And would pay you a hefty bonus for that tidbit. I ask for nothing but your gratitude. If you need anything else, just ask." I promised to help implicate him.

She didn't thank me. She didn't assign me a mission. She didn't initiate me into a conspiracy. She only said the agents had lured him to the abandoned school so she could check whether he had indeed participated in Moscow's CP Project.

I held the acorn and recalled the day we had first taken a walk together, in either a hospital courtyard or a schoolyard. I longed to take her hand and exit the café into the smoke and fog, to stroll down the street with her while the agents and rebels gunned down each other as well as pedestrians, to walk into eternity. I almost crushed the acorn as I imagined standing in the fog searching for a path through the quick sand.

"You know what? He trusted me. He opened his heart and considered me a friend. He divulged everything, everything to convict him, everything I could take to the Agency to collect my compensation." At the counter she poured a cup of chai and said, "He even told me he likes chai."

"But you followed him to the IAB rather than collected the compensation. So, he told you in vain. Should've kept his heart closed." I closed my hand on the acorn, pretending to strangle Dr. Tang.

"Sometimes, a foolish act is the only rational act."

"I see. The Doc has infected you with his pseudo-wisdom virus. Stay away from me."

"I'll report to the Agency."

"But, I thought..." I thought I understood her. I thought she loved Dr. Tang. I thought she would sacrifice everything for him. Of course, I might have overrated my intelligence or my intuition. At that instant, I struggled to awake from this dream, though preferring not to return to Francisco's dunghill. Maybe, I would awake to a new dawn, in a new land, with a new mind and body. I opened my palm to free the acorn opened my mouth to ask a question, but only silence emerged.

"I need a favor," she said.

"Anything." I closed my palm and gripped the acorn, swung my arm in an arc and knocked the plate off the table. It cracked next to the spilled soymilk and its fragments mingled with those of the cup, just as the events in my life blended with those of Ingrid and Dr. Tang.

She picked up the lamp and put it on the counter, pulled a chair next to me and sat facing me. When she requested that I close my eyes, I obeyed and waited for her gift. She inhaled and grasped my forearm as if to calm me and when I nodded, her other arm moved, slowly, deliberately, determinedly. Then, I sensed it. Chill and pain bored into my abdomen, a force pushing me against the back of my seat. Then, peace and calmness. Opening my eyes I studied the knife in my abdomen. A kitchen knife with a brown handle. Nothing special. Closing my eyes again to suck in the sensation, the coolness fading, the pain spreading.

When I reopened my eyes, she released the knife and my arm and wiped her hands with a paper napkin.

She stabbed me as she had in the dream.

Could I be the boy in the woods, after being stabbed by the young Ingrid, lying on the path, dying and dreaming of this wasteland? Whether an amnesiac or a boy, I would die in her hands. Amen.

"I'm sorry for doing it before you regain your memory. I would've waited, but must hurry to finish one last task." She poured me a cup of chai and handed me a paper napkin before walking toward the doorway, ready to escape the crime scene. "I'm also sorry I couldn't forgive you."

"Don't you love him?" I crushed the acorn, its fragments leaking through my fingers.

"To stand against the tide, to create the Ingrid I want to be. To love, to live, to die."

I didn't hate her, just didn't understand. Anyway, if I had to go, I would prefer to die in her hands. Why would she want to kill me when I could have helped her rat on Dr. Tang?

"I love you. And I forgive you." I didn't stand up and chase after her, lest my intestines spilled onto the floor. I sipped the chai, but I didn't like it. I would like to enjoy it but I didn't. When a girl entered and asked for alms, I gave her the cash card, which I wouldn't need anymore, and shooed her away before she could see my intestines. As another rumble shook the ground, I sipped the chai again but still didn't like it. Damn it.

CHAPTER 50 - FRANCISCO

October 25, 2011 (2)

I tailed the Guardian through Greenwich Village, but a din on Eighth Street distracted me and I almost lost the villain. Onlookers' panamas and kerchiefs blocked my view while chants and shouts and cheers engulfed me. I cut through the crowd and tracked the diamonds' rattles to the Guardian, who stepped out of a café, cappuccino in hand. I phoned my associates to have them tail him.

At the next block, shouts drowned the onlookers' chatters. After scattered screams, smoke rose to the sky. A torch zipped through the air and landed on a stall, burning the fruits and vegetables. The crowd dispersed—men and women, boys and girls, dogs and cats crashing into each other. While store signs collapsed onto the sidewalk, fire hydrants spouted torrents, and looters carried tablet PCs and plasma TVs out of electronic stores. I would've joined the festivities if I didn't have to chase after the damn Guardian.

I tracked the diamond lover through fire and smoke until the hooded rioters, one hand carrying a book and the other a torch or bat or lighter, marched down the street and forced me to step into an alley to avoid them. They chanted the beginning verses of *Notes from the Underground*: "I am a sick man. I am a spiteful man. I am an unattractive man."

I showed a rioter the holy sign and he fell on his face, chanting gibberish. I asked about the festivity the Priest initiated without me, the Prophet, but it turned out, the fanatics, without my guidance or the chief lunatic's consent, rioted to protest the burning of the holiest text. Sacrilege and blasphemy and all that crap. He asked me to rally with a speech, but I excused myself and continued to tail the Guardian. The police siren whined through the smoke and New York looked more and more like Fermat's Last Stand. The amnesiac's wasteland was invading my world and I must end the incursion and once again save it from destruction.

I kept close to the buildings, looking out for flying rocks, bricks, bottles, and Molotov cocktails. When a torch descended on me, I dropped to the ground and wrapped my hands around my head. It shattered the display window and burned the mannequins and wedding gowns inside the bridal shop. Fortunately, my leather overcoat parried the shards and splinters. I'd punish those lunatics once the fire and smoke had settled. After I sidestepped a flying toilet, an associate phoned to report he'd found the Guardian two blocks ahead of me.

I sprinted down the sidewalk toward the villain. A block later, a young man lay on the street, dead, blood oozing from his temple. Bullets whistled through the air, flattening tires and shattering car windows, one almost hitting me, and I dodged into a side street to leave the battlefield. I almost expected the amnesiac and Dr. Tang. My associate phoned to update me on the Guardian's location. By the time I reached Fifth Avenue, the villain had crossed the street. After giving my beggar friend ten dollars for lunch, I chased after my target, avoiding the rioters, who destroyed parked cars and display windows. I followed him to a roadside café, where Holly greeted him with a smile.

At a table nearby but behind two landscaped screens, I peeped through a slit. I ordered a piece of durian pie and a glass of whiskey but neither could cure my grief. The evil duo discussed their scheme, which was as twisted as a snake slithering through reeds. Damn it, the Priest and his fanatics were saner than these two sadists, and Dostoevsky's underground man, a sage.

"Wow, those nuts rioting just because an old book was burned. And taking on the police, too." The Guardian ordered a Bloody Mary. "I'd like to have followers like them. I'd be able to get loads of diamonds." He shook the box of diamonds cuffed to his hand.

"A wonder you're still in such a good mood. " Holly sipped the gin and texted a message. "If I were you, I'd prepare to dough out that thousand dollars. That's the punishment for disagreeing with me. I'm always right, especially when it comes to Francisco. I can read him like an open book."

"The game's not over yet. He still hasn't cracked the code. He still has a chance to break down. You never know. Maybe, he'll commit suicide tomorrow. That's life. I'm still betting he'll collapse. He isn't as tough as you make him out to be." He took out a key and tried to unlock the handcuffs.

"Are we talking about the same Francisco Guzman? Even if you've confused someone else with him, I'll still take the money. A thousand dollars is a thousand dollars." She waved to the waiter and asked for another gin and a piece of cheesecake.

"My dear, I'm sure the mental virus will crush him. Unless, he's a sociopath or a psychopath." He rubbed his shoes against the table leg to remove dung.

"Care to raise the bet? Two thousand dollars. You've no idea who you're dealing with. He's no ordinary Joe. His unconsciousness can resist any virus." She took out a bottle of perfume and sprayed around the Guardian.

As smoke and fog cleared, the buildings on either side of the street flaunted their scars—beads, streaks, blotches like paints on a canvas. I lamented that I couldn't continue to fantasize in the fog. I also envied the amnesiac's loss of memory, which shielded him from shock and grief.

"You have too much faith in people like him. Steel outside but gelatin inside. I could feel his bones wriggling just now, even though he barked like a mad dog. What do you see in him anyway?" The Guardian drank the Bloody Mary and a red patch colored the corner of his mouth to match his swollen eyes.

"Like I said, you don't know him like I do. And if he knows what you're doing to him, he'll turn you into gelatin." She raised the glass and toasted to me. I should step over with a glass of champagne to celebrate Fransuccesco, to turn the Guardian into a damn Bloody Mary, and to find out why she'd stabbed me in the back. I had to ferret out the details of their intrigue, their manipulation, and their atrocity, against me, Francisco Guzman. I swore I'd avenge myself. I swore to be Fransuccesco. Now that the picture emerged, for the first time, I grasped how the amnesiac was tossing about the sea, unable to spot land or even the North Star. Of course, he shouldn't be fumbling around.

"You must've forgotten who I am. I'm his Guardian of Memory. Do you know what that means? I know everything about him. You know, omniscience." The Guardian tapped his head as he leaned against his chair.

"I'm not a five year old. I don't believe in fairytales. Yeah, Guardian of Memory. Sure, and I'm the Tooth Fairy. Back when we first met, Francisco thought you were hitting on me. So did I. But you didn't make any moves. So, who're you anyway? A Freudian quack? A motivation speaker? A snake charmer? Or an out-of-luck politician?"

"Have more respect for the Guardian of Memory. Or else you may lose your memory, or worse, get unwanted memories." The Guardian asked the waiter for a bottle of gunk.

"Well, you couldn't charm that Priest. Only his own insanity can seduce him, the loony. And he'll get you for burning the manuscript. A stupid idea. Now, his loonies will come after you, each fighting to pierce your heart and sacrifice his or her life. Look at them rioting, killing any policeman who'd dare to stop them. They don't give a damn about their lives, as long as they can exorcise you. If you're really the Guardian of Memory, you'd have wisdom—"

"I'm not scared of that nut job. I burned that manuscript to prevent the end of the world. We're talking about the end time, Armageddon. If it weren't for me—"

"Aha, another madman. So, you'll start your Anti-Dostoevsky League soon."

The scorched book cover in Clint's hideout that I kept stepping on, it turned out to be the remains of the holy text. The Priest, after finding out his holy text's final resting-place, hunted for the desecrator. Not Clint, but the Guardian, who came afterward to burn the book. As the Prophet, naturally I'd hand the Guardian to the Priest, a burnt offering to appease the Almighty Dostoevsky.

I vowed to mete out the appropriate punishments to Clint and everyone else involved. An eye for an eye; a tooth for a tooth—the Guzman code of justice. Of course, I'd still ache for Faith and mourn for Suzie. Good old Francisco forever lost, and durian couldn't entice my taste buds anymore.

The Guardian must've hypnotized me with that jingle in the maple woods, so I'd dream of the amnesiac. Yet, no shrink had touched my mind. When had he violated me and planted the mental virus?

I had to confront them but at that moment, someone walked up to the table. I waved my hand; I didn't want anymore whiskey. As I was about to stand up a hand pressed on my shoulder.

"I bring good tidings."

I looked from the hand to the ivory arm to the bare shoulder to the smiling face, and leaned back and raised a hand as if to fend off a blow.

Ms. Redhead. Virginia E. Boss. She pinched her nose and stared at the durian pie.

"Hey, Ganesh was way out of line when he barged into our... our business, but he didn't mean it. Just was so excited about... anyway about something. No need—"

"Oh, that was a mistake." Ms. Boss sat opposite me and crossed her legs. "Got the wrong person. Can't believe it happened to us. What an embarrassment. But, it happens when we couldn't filter the noise from the data." She shrugged her shoulder and twisted the corner of her mouth as if lamenting a deal gone sour.

"Well, next time you make a mistake, stay away. I want nothing to do with your mistaken bullets. But at least this—"

"We've got unfinished business." She leaned toward me, the look in her eyes suggesting intrigue.

"Um, maybe some other time." I pushed away my chair and even if I weren't spying on the evil duo, I'd prefer to stay away from women who keep guns to eliminate underachieving lovers. Still, I didn't want to vex a client and ruin my reputation.

"Well, let me join in to snoop on those two schemers. Seems like an interesting conversation. You have to share juicy secrets. Otherwise, what's the fun?" When the waiter came over, she ordered tequila and put her handbag on the table.

"Um, I've nothing against you. But I prefer to spy on others alone, rather than with a stranger. You know, I couldn't see it as a social event, not that I object to others doing it together." Though I tried to shoo her away, she stayed for the party and the fun. I certainly didn't expect the surprise and the fun she had for everyone. Scary woman.

"We mistook your indiscreet friend for the Guardian. For some reason we got the wrong info. Still evaluating how we blundered. Lucky for him, I missed his heart. By the way, how's his arm?" She took out cigarette and lighter and smoked.

"Him, the Guardian? He couldn't even guard his own butt. You should've shot this bastard, instead." I pointed at the Guardian, who was describing one of my dreams.

"Maybe if you wish it hard enough, it'd come true. Dreams don't have to remain dreams." She puffed out a smoke ring while glancing at Holly and the Guardian through the slit. "Dreamers don't just dream but take actions."

"I don't want to see your gun."

"I don't have to use my gun."

"I didn't bring a gun."

"I don't want to see your gun."

"So, who draws first?"

"Let's wait for the drink. In the meanwhile, we can chat. By the way, I'm Virginia E. Boss. They call me the Boss, but you can call me B." She puffed out another ring and as it drifted beyond the screen above the Guardian's head, the waiter put down a glass of tequila. In the distance, the chorus of sirens continued to blast through the air.

"Yes, I know. I've got my sources also. Lovely name. So, you're associated with the mob and VE is a front for money laundering? I have quite a few clients who are or, for some, who were mobsters. I haven't stepped on your turf, so I hope we're cool with each other."

"Do I look like a mob boss? Maybe you should have your eyes examined. Look at these lips. Look at these legs. No, no, as owner and CEO and Chairwoman, I make sure VE is legit. Or kosher, if you prefer." She toasted to success and sipped the tequila.

"Oh, I see, I see. I see very clearly now."

"Do you?"

"Should've given me the million dollars. But anyway, you probably came because the loser over there's got the diamonds." Now that the Guardian had the diamonds, she had a reason to shoot him in the heart. Though I could practice my nunchuks on him, I'd let the Boss finish her job. Courtesy, you know.

"You're very confident of yourself, aren't you? I like that." She held the glass and leaned forward. "I could use a brain like you. And I treat my people generously. You could even take a share in every project. At VE, we run a legit business with shady nuances, just your cup of tea."

"Thank you for the offer. But some people don't work well with others. I can only work for myself. A bad habit I'd picked up through the years." I'd rather be a poor vagrant than a rich slave. I'd turned down more than one six-figure job just to be able to hack into corporate databases under moon and stars, and in my underwear, not for job security and not for yearend bonuses or golden parachutes. Why'd I want to clock in at eight in the morning and out at five in the evening when I could work twenty-four hours a day, and, as a bonus, on Thanksgiving and Christmas, too? Why'd I want to wear three-piece suits when I could work in my underwear? Only for Faith did I ever consider suffocating under slavery. Yet, even with her, I struggled to breathe the free air.

"Nasty habit. It might doom you someday."

"But, if you need to subcontract out a task, I'd be glad to consider it. But no assassinations, please. I prefer digging dirt out of people's past."

"Well, business calls. So now, I give the signal." She tapped her cigarette on the ashtray and raised the glass and she sipped the tequila and smiled, a twinkle in her eyes.

The aroma of roasted chestnut wafted through the neighborhood, amidst the pedestrians, the vehicles and the buildings. The Guardian giggled like a kid. Someone should snuff out the bozo's laughter. He was picking up a peach tart when his face twitched and he stared straight ahead, open-mouthed. I followed his gaze to where a cat was licking spilled Screwdriver. Down the street, an Underground Temple fanatic threw a rock through a store window. When my eyes returned to the Guardian, he was convulsing and a hole on his forehead oozed blood. About two seconds later, his face smashed onto the tart, cracking the plate into pieces. Holly fell off the chair. She crawled from table to table until she reached the café next door, where she got on her feet and ran down the street, losing both her pumps.

I stared at the crushed tart for a minute before turning to the Boss. She wiped her lips with a napkin and said, "And you mocked Agent Z. Must admit he has an accurate shot. Probably better than mine. If he were a vengeful man, he'd shoot you now. For insulting him."

"Certainly didn't look like he had it in him to shoot like that." I surveyed the rooftops but couldn't identify the Messenger's location. Yes, if he released his anger, the second bullet would pierce my forehead. They'd murdered the Guardian to retrieve the diamonds, and his blood soaked the tablecloth and dripped down onto the ground where a piece of tart had landed. No, I couldn't have tortured him, let alone killed him. I didn't have the stomach to snuff out another life.

What's more, I didn't understand. I simply couldn't understand how I could've killed my old man. Sure, I might've done it in rage or fear, but I wouldn't forget it. I couldn't. The nightmares should've haunted me. Until it possessed me. How could I have managed to forget it? I could only admire my will to survive.

"Don't worry. He's a professional. Like everyone in VE. I only pick the best. But, of course, the Guardian breaking his nose does motivate him a bit. So, thank him the next time you meet. Buy him a gift, or at least a card." She drank the tequila, put down the glass and raised her thumb, probably to signal to the Messenger. A job well done.

I gave her a key and she walked up to the Guardian, bent over and unlocked the handcuffs. She lifted the box of diamonds and a letter from his pocket and returned. She put the letter on the table.

"A gift."

"Guess you want these diamonds after the trouble stealing them from the bank and hiring me to steal them from you." I forked a piece of durian pie but its aroma, though as alluring as ever, didn't whet my appetite.

A pedestrian screamed. The waiter dropped his tray and two glasses. After the clangs and splashes, more screams. Soon, onlookers gathered around the café and gesticulated, some pointing at the Guardian, others pointing at windows and rooftops. While several children chased each other around a van.

"Be careful, your self-confidence might undo you. Sometimes, you need humility. I know, I know. That's not your forte." She puffed on the cigarette and shot the smoke into the air. "Listen, these are fake diamonds. Got it? Fake. As fake as your love for that girl Faith." She opened the bag and poured the stones onto the table.

"Were you helping the bank test their security system? So, they failed."

"I stole these *diamonds* from my own security box. Just a show for the Guardian. And he took the bait. Doesn't that sound fun? Really, come work for me and have more fun. Instead of picking up questionable women in shady bars."

"I might've finished that loser myself." I picked up a *diamond* and examined it.

"But your brother didn't want it."

"Okay, since you're inferring Fernando's alive. You better show him to me. Otherwise, leave him out of it." Why the excuse? She killed the Guardian to retrieve her loot. Carpe Diem. She shouldn't have dragged Fernando into her scheme.

"Tsk, tsk, the cuckoo virus must've infected your brain." She took a document out of her handbag. "He was generous. Hundred thousand dollars. Guess you didn't read every part of his will. Too focused on your inheritance, huh?"

I remembered my brother's words while celebrating his promotion. I also recalled the money sent to VE. Still, I couldn't help trumpeting out, "Here's the flaw in your logic. Fernando wouldn't waste that much money on such a loser. You might want to reread the contract again. Because I'm holding you accountable for what he ordered. If you don't finish the job, you won't get a penny."

"No mistake. My lawyer scrutinized every word. Your brother wanted your Guardian of Memory dead. End of story." She opened the document and pointed to a paragraph.

"Of course, that contract won't be binding in a court of law. Contract killing is illegal in New York. Should've killed him somewhere else. But that aside, Fernando cared too much about me to hire you to kill my Guardian of Memory. Well, that is, if there's really such a nutcase."

"Well, there's your nutcase." She pointed the cigarette at the Guardian.

"Come on, give me a break. Don't tell me you believe in that stuff." I threw the contract onto the table, knocking half of the *diamonds* onto the ground. Maybe Fernando wanted to play a joke on me, for old time sake. Did he design the Guzman code or did Holly and the Guardian cook it up?

"I don't have to believe in the tooth fairy to do my job. I've executed the contract to its letters. This lunatic claimed to be your Guardian and now he's dead. Another project completed." She took the contract and swept the rest of the *diamonds* onto the ground. An old man tiptoed toward the Guardian, licking his lips and scratching his butt. The children charged into the café and ran around the tables.

"Besides, even if there was such a loser in this dead-end job, Fernando wouldn't want him dead. He'd want me to remember our good times together." I kicked several *diamonds* out of the café onto the sidewalk.

"Not so. He had the Guardian killed, to free you of your memory and your past. So you can live a new life, without the past as burden." She finished the tequila and snuffed out the cigarette in the glass. "So you can recreate your past."

The stone crashed on Father's head. He whined and groaned and whimpered. Blood...

I believed her: Fernando got rid of the Guardian dead to set me free.

Down the street, two policemen arrested a rioter and I wished Fernando were sitting beside me. Just like seven years ago on a summer evening, when I was going to introduce him to a waitress. We had two bottles of Chianti. We roamed through Washington Square from gallery to bakery to café to arcade. In the end, after the fun we had, I took the girl home.

Fernando and I had dined at the restaurant across the street and we joked about my flings and discussed his career path. Now, at the entrance, two policemen stepped out and also walked toward the café. I searched among the pedestrians converging on the café, but couldn't find my brother.

"Well, now that I've delivered the gift, time to go." She bagged the contract and handed me her business card. "Like I said, we've unfinished business. Call me anytime. And I'm sorry for shooting your friend. Just a mistake. I'm sure he'll understand." She patted a brunette girl on her head and disappeared down the street before the policemen could reach the café.

The old man poked the Guardian with his cane. The waiters and waitresses surrounded the bloodied table and more passersby gathered in clusters to chat and point their fingers at windows and rooftops. The children picked up several *diamonds* from the sidewalk. I finished the whiskey and picked up the letter: Fernando's letter to me. The Guardian had stolen it from that security box. I should've recognized the creep's handwriting. I couldn't recall my brother's face, or remember his voice, his gaits, or his eye color, as if I'd only met him in a café one sunny afternoon and I might only find his face among my photo collections.

Could I have begun to lose my memory minutes after the Guardian's death? No, that scumbag couldn't guard my memory anymore than the amnesiac could exist.

As my mind was whirling through hyperspace, the brunette girl approached and handed me a note from Ganesh. The nerd sent a courier rather than called me probably to prevent me from tracking the phone signal and locating Faith, but the evasion wouldn't stop me.

He rebuked me for interfering with his chivalry and vowed to find Clint wherever he was hiding. Well, Ganesh should've known that I don't lose. Tough luck. The Priest probably had kidnapped Mr. OCD and would prepare the sacrifice to old Fyodor. Lovely. I cheered Clint's deserved end, but mustn't miss the celebration in the Underground Temple.

Ganesh had cracked the code and found the code word on the sacred text's charred front cover, which though over eighty-percent burnt and scarred by my footprints, still showed a handwritten word: *Descartes*. The Guardian had burnt the holy text, but hadn't destroyed the cover.

He failed.

I scolded myself for allowing Ganesh to discover the secret when I could've picked up the cover while attending to Faith, but at that time, my thoughts were swirling and my arms and legs were trembling. I couldn't blame anyone else except myself for missing the chance to crack the code.

Faith had written the philosopher's name inside the front cover before the Priest stole the text, and Holly, after stealing the manuscript from the Underground Temple, adopted the name for her mind game.

Did Holly steal the holy text for this game? For it, she could've asked the Priest for a few million dollars but she didn't need the money to retire to the Bahamas. Whatever her motives, more than ever, I have to discover the file's content, Holly's masterpiece—Fernando didn't create the code. I also have to face her but she's disconnected her phone and I don't have time to find her. She might've moved, but I'll locate her.

As I read the note, I realized tomorrow would be the deadline. Perfect timing. Of course, since Holly and the Guardian had cooked up the scheme, the deadline meant nothing now.

I'll soon find out the surprise they prepared. With Holly, I expect nothing less than havoc. What greater pain and suffering will she lavish on me? The file may activate a military satellite or trigger a nuclear reaction. Or unleash nuclear warheads to target cities around the world. New York, London, Tokyo, Beijing, Moscow. In New York, I won't survive. Thank goodness. I don't want to mutate into Franciscozilla. More likely, Holly only targeted me. The file may play a tune to destroy my mind, or signal an assassin with my face to kill the Governor, or broadcast on TV how I killed Father. Make my day.

October 26, 2011

In Liberty Lair, I took down the poster of Descartes, turned it over, and signed my name under the word *Congratulations*. Holly should've returned after the Guardian's death to witness the end, but could be avoiding me. Beside her photo, I polished the SOAPS statuette with a handkerchief from her desk drawer and now it shines golden on her shelf.

On the desk sits George, the robocat I bought for her birthday, last year or the one before. We traveled to Japan for two weeks and bought the mechanical feline in a Tokyo toy store. We didn't know whether we'd lovers in a year or two, but she couldn't imagine life without me. Amid the Tokyo crowd, her loneliness touched mine. We promised to always be friends. Even then, I knew we'd empower or destroy each other, or perhaps both. Now, George meows and walks around the desk to remind me of our loneliness together. Why doesn't she come to face the end? If she destroys me, she won't last a week. I pat George and it brushes its face against my palm. Why did she leave George here?

Before coming, I visited Fernando's and Suzie's graves under a haze. The grass swayed in the breeze as I walked among rows of headstones toward my destination. A yellow rose lay in front of my brother's headstone. Clint had cleaned the grave and taped a picture of Fernando and him next to the rose. My brother would've liked the picture there, so I didn't yank it away.

Sorry, brother, Suzie's dead. But I buried her next to you. That's the least I can do. I know you'd like it. And it saves me the extra trip.

Before leaving the cemetery, I called Faith but she didn't pick up. I longed for her to come with me and encourage me. I would've given her the statuette to show my love. I would've persuaded her to leave Ganesh.

I struggled to work with Ganesh and yet, I'm glad he helped me during this crisis. He and Faith will be getting married and last night he invited me to be the best man. Of course, the geek was taunting me and I didn't fall for his bluff and on meeting Faith would expose his lie. No, he must not marry her.

The air damp against my skin irritates me, as it never did. I want to fling away the moisture just as I want to fling away the sadness. I want to embrace the sun just as I want to embrace Faith. But I only embrace Lady Liberty, that cold steel statuette.

After this project, I'll locate Faith and stop her from ruining her life. I must list the hundred and one reasons why she shouldn't step into the alligator pit. Of course, before approaching her, I must dig up enough dirt on Ganesh. He must've bullied a girl in kindergarten, or stolen candies from a grocery store as a boy. He might also have smoked pot as a teenager, or cheated on his IRS returns.

He didn't chitchat or dine with anyone besides Faith. Sure, he talked to a few associates, including the errand boy, but only about business. Maybe he's an android. How could Faith love someone like that? What a waste. I must rescue her, if not for myself, then for humanity.

I won't have any woman except Faith, and for her I'll fight Ganesh until time ends. On the Staten Island Ferry, as I proclaimed my allegiance, my heart skipped a beat and chill traveled through my spine. I still fear losing my freedom, my companion since Mom entered the mental hospital. Am I willing to depart from this longtime friend, who's walked beside me through storm and flood and chaos? To exchange one companion for another. To walk a different path, to face a different sun. What melodies, what fragrance, beyond?

On the phone, Ganesh questioned whether I could give up my certificates for Faith, and he urged me to take care of the statuette instead of her. I didn't and won't apologize for my certificates and statuette, or for my wine collection and *pate de foie gras*. I'm Francisco Guzman and that's that.

After hanging up the phone, I threw the statuette into the trashcan. I decided to give up the certificates for Faith, and fight Ganesh to the end. Maybe, one day I'll regret it, but today I fight.

The Guardian said not to trust anyone. Sure, I won't trust him, or Ganesh, but I've trusted myself since a small boy and I can't help doing so. Who else can I trust except myself? Ganesh said that my biases would lead me astray. How then should I decide? Can I bootstrap from nothing? I open the blinds. Drizzles obscure the Manhattan skyline, but don't hide the ferry docking at the pier.

I was parking my car near Battery Park this morning when traffic on both directions stopped while a cab driver strutted toward a biker with a crowbar while his foe swung a chain. Drivers got out of their cars and watched from a distance. I looked up into the dark clouds, singing "Praise to Fransuccesco." I'll miss those fights if the world ends.

Before the laptop I study the prompt that awaits my input. Even while searching for the password, I sensed the destruction this word will unleash, even as my revived memory tormented me. After learning that Holly had initiated this scheme, I imagined catastrophes cascading from air to land to sea until every molecule in my body detaches from the rest. I should like to confront her one last time, to sort through our love and hate, but by this time, the Priest may've eliminated her along with Clint. Having reviewed last three months' reveries, I've prepared to check out of this world, this hell.

I enjoyed my life. I helped clients break unbreakable codes. I charmed more ladies than I could count. I pulled enough beards, boxed enough ears, kicked enough butts. Alas, I ate enough durian pies. So, onto my next journey, to scale the next mountain and cross the next rainbow.

My love for Faith helped through this storm. I wish I met her earlier. I wish I sacrificed for her and revealed my love. Thrashing my statuette and certificates. Leaving my clients and paychecks. Giving up durian pies. I didn't love the way I do now, but time has run out and I must face the last act. I must enter the password before Ganesh gets here, and find out the secret and face the holocaust.

Faith, oh, Faith, my beloved. Be happy with Ganesh. He's a scoundrel but he cares about you.

October 27, 2011

I was in the woods. I heard the tune. I passed the lilac. I knew where I was going and what I was looking for. I took another path.

I met Ingrid and inquired about the two boys, but she smiled and walked deeper into the woods.

I didn't chase after her. I continued down the path. Before reaching the stream, I blocked the sadist, the killer, while the sunset lit his face.

I grasped his shirtfront and lifted him up as a breeze rustled the foliage. "I know who you are. And you aren't me." Yet, even as those words left my mouth, I questioned whether this murderer could be my younger self, the self I'd abandoned along the road to maturity. Maybe I'd begun my journey toward patricide here among the lilacs and maples. "Why'd you choose HYMN1 to kill that boy?"

"What'd I care what you know? Why bother me with such trivial stuff? You want me to kick your butt? You're a figment of my imagination. When I wake up, you'll vanish. Put this into your head: you don't exist." He imitated my tone and manner, his lips arching and his words slashing into my thoughts. The bloodstained dagger flashed before my face and the sunlight reflected from the blade and flickered in my eyes.

I despised the impersonator, but I steadied my voice and turned his face toward the sun. "Your older self will regain his memory and he'll find out that you, or rather he as a child, had murder the innocent boy. For no other reason than to enjoy the thrill. Yes, pleasure and satisfaction from plunging that dagger into his gut. Catharsis. Even rebirth. You're sick; you're demented; you're a psychopath without any remorse; you're worse than the underground man."

"That amnesiac feels remorse and even loves someone else. Can you? No, not you. Besides, your hands aren't clean. Remember, you killed your old man. Patricide." He tried to avoid the light but I turned his face toward the sun.

I'd saved Ingrid from my father. I'd visited and comforted Suzie during her coma. I loved Faith such that I blessed her marriage with Ganesh. These thoughts crushed the devils inside me and steadied my legs. Ingrid and Suzie and Faith, they were the angels protecting me, guiding me from darkness into light. What I'd given them, they returned ten-thousand fold.

"When he regains his memory, he'll become a psychopath again." I dropped him onto the ground and took the dagger. "I'd never become a sadist." I'd killed Father to save Ingrid while this sadist killed the boy for fun. We belonged to different species, the amnesiac and I. The sunlight warmed my back as another breeze cooled my face. If I could snuff out the dream, or rather the nightmare, I'd eliminate the sadist, that amnesiac. I'd prevent him from hurting Ingrid, just as I'd saved her from Father. I should plunge the dagger into the boy's abdomen to eliminate the amnesiac, but I couldn't. I couldn't even kill the murderer. What happened to Fransuccesco?

"No, he won't become a psychopath again," a baritone beyond the setting sun said. "He wasn't one after he lost his memory." Ganesh, his eyes sharper and his cheeks tauter, like an angel or a demon but probably both, emerged through the sunrays. In the wind, his hair fluttered and his striped shirt ruffled. His sandals kicked up a dust trail that darkened the sunlight. I almost didn't recognize him.

"Then you also believe the amnesiac is the psychopath. But how could I be sure? I didn't remember the incident, but neither did the sap." I rushed toward him, almost thrusting the dagger into his abdomen.

"Do you care what I believe? Anyway, I've no such belief." He took the dagger from me and flung it over his shoulder. The foliage fell as a gust swept up his hair. For a second, he looked like someone in my dream.

"That's right. What'd I care what you believe? I can change my destiny." I turned around and said, "Now, you little sadist, I want to know—" The boy had vanished.

"He's your dream self, not you. So don't worry about being a psychopath." Ganesh sat on a boulder and crossed his legs and he whistled Beethoven's Moonlight Sonata.

"Hey, I know you're smart, but stop pretending to know everything."

"Not everything, only what you want to ask."

"Oh, wise guy, huh. Well, tell me, then. Who'd he kill? That boy looked familiar. But, I couldn't match the face. Not you, not Clint, not the Priest, not the Messenger. Maybe he had a sex change, but still, I'd recognize that face." I kicked up the leaves and they swished in the wind and fell on Ganesh. Amid the melodies of foliage and wind, I almost identified the fallen boy, but my mind didn't match his image with any name or object or place, as if someone had severed the neural cluster.

"You've seen him before."

"But where?"

"From your dream, of course."

"Very funny. Of course I've seen him here getting killed. You should do standup comedy."

"I don't mean this dream in the woods. I mean the other dream."

"Oh, damn. Him. I mean, them." The boy's eyes and his nose and mouth, sure, they resembled those of Beta and Gamma. "Holy Dostoevsky, it's the Guardian. So, the boy didn't die? And he grew up to become the Guardian? That's why the sadist killed him. I might, too."

"Not quite. And he isn't related to the Guardian, just Beta and Gamma."

"No, not another clone?"

"His name was Alpha."

"Of course, A, B and C. And X killed A, leaving B and C."

Did Beta and Gamma know the amnesiac had killed Alpha? Beta should and was probably playing cat and mouse with him. "Damn it, clones, cerebral programming, omnipresent TV broadcast. How did my mind create such a Freudian dream? Why not reveal universal truth with a fable? Of course, I prefer action and adventure." Still, I admired my mind for creating the surreal world and plotting the story's twists and turns. "Naturally, Beta and Gamma are trying to avenge their clone, but their political ambitions must've taken precedence. So, before killing the amnesiac and then each other, they have to extract the CP data. Definitely sounds like the kind of plot I'd create for my dream. But where's the action hero? Certainly not the amnesiac. I have to put a nasty twist to the ending and kick everyone's butts, except Ingrid's." I sat next to Ganesh, rubbing my hand and mulling over how to torment the amnesiac. I didn't ask my sidekick for help, so I could save the fun for my brain.

"I came to prevent that fake Guardian from turning your world upside down, but failed." He brushed aside the leaves in his hair and on his shoulders.

"Don't worry about it. He's dead anyway. I must look to the future." The horizontal sunlight cast a tree's shadow along the riverbank until it faded at the elbow. I must take that turn at the elbow and walk down a new path. A new world awaited me, one without the Guardian and his madness.

"But first, let me return your real memory." He clapped his hands.

"Hey, what the hell are you doing?" The familiar tune. The tune in this maple woods. The tune over the phone while I talked to the Guardian. The tune Nick hummed in my dream. The tune from the computer after I'd entered the password. I fought the hypnosis, trying to fix my thoughts on Fernando, Holly, Clint, and Faith.

Ganesh reached over and touched my head. "This is the reason I came. Of course, I also came to help Faith retrieve the manuscript."

Heat from his hand warmed my scalp. I tried to dodge, but my muscles forsook me, those damn traitors. I recalled laughing and drinking with Fernando. I recalled flirting with my many lovers, including Holly. I recalled meeting Faith on that August morning. "This is only a dream. You can't erase my memory."

I dozed off. I fell onto the ground, ruffling the fallen leaves, which swished around my body. The sweet maple scent mesmerized my nostrils. I called to Fernando. I called to Faith. I called to Suzie. I called out Fransuccesco's name, the amulet that'd protected me.

When my mind cleared up and I could move my arms and legs, I sat up and leaned against a tree. "Are you Dr. Tang?"

"I'm the Guardian of Memory, your memory. That diamond hoarder was as fake as the diamonds. Now, you have your memory back." Ganesh waved his hand and walked down the rocky path toward the sunset. "Have a well-lived life. I'm done here, so we won't meet again."

"Sure, Faith should choose whoever she wants. But that won't stop me from winning her over." Whether she'd choose me, I still loved her and would fight for a life with her.

He raised his right thumb above his head without turning or stopping. The sunlight cast a shadow that stretched from his feet to a spruce behind me while the wind caressed my face. I tried to examine his back to detect Dr. Tang's features, but the sun blinded my eyes and I had to turn around to face the darkness.

I didn't believe in the nonsense about Guardian of Memory, but mulling over Ganesh's jumbled syllables, I recalled an event that shook me to the core and that would trample and crush me. I realized what Fernando's letter would reveal. I must stay in this dream to avoid reality, or have Ganesh remove my memory. I chased after him, but he'd forsaken me. Fransuccesco would have to rest in peace.

It's not fair. It's not fair. I killed Father. I killed him.

CHAPTER 51 - X

November 9 (1)

Well, I didn't die. Not even when a knife, however plain and cheap, had plunged into my abdomen. Woe to me, the immortal wretch. I woke up early in the morning from the dream's dream, from the brutal crime, that young boy's murder, and realized my name is Descartes: Francisco's password to the Guzman Code, the key to unlock my memory, to restore my past, to reveal my crime. Except, I didn't find any CP data in my mind. Ingrid's knife still in my abdomen, so reality hadn't shifted, but I didn't care. I could live forever but I didn't care either. Dragging guilt for eternity. No, never such a life.

I lifted my face from the table to the darkness inside the café. Outside, the streetlights shone on the debris strewn across the sidewalk. I faced the boy in my dream's dream, who had snuffed out a budding life, who had rejoiced after the murder, who like a needle had pierced into my consciousness to burst my amnesia, who was my younger self, the self I had forgotten or pretended to have forgotten, and I found a stranger, cruel and sadistic, more so than Pratt or Beta or Gamma. How could I respond to such a monster, a fiend, an incubus? Time might have dampened the shock, but the buried memory, resurrected through this nightmare, still traveled through time's tunnel and bypassing the years and decades, delivered the stench of the past evil. I couldn't understand the thoughts running through that mind, the shadows and silhouettes, the hisses and sneers, the taste of slime and blood, the phantom resurrecting before my mind's eyes. Never would I live with it through the days and months and years. Never would I live in hell. I would rather live without a past, without the demon lurking in my memory to remind me of the snake pit within. I must destroy it, erase it from my mind. I had volunteered for the CP Project and erased it, to free myself from the demon, only to revive it through my dream's dream, through my search among lost memories. My pride; my pig-headedness. I tried to integrate my selves by piecing together memory bits into a portrait, but instead found a fragmented self, scattered across time, the moderator leveling out praises and rebukes, laughter and tears, yesterdays and tomorrows through arithmetic and geometric means.

I couldn't get rid of the murderer, the sadist, the psychopath. I couldn't get rid of myself.

Could this sadist have learned remorse? Could a psychopath change? I still relished Pratt's screams and groans and I still tasted my younger self's delight in killing the boy. The sensation etched in my cortexes, the neutral pathways constructed to retain not only the memory of the event but also the delight and excitement, they composed me, and time added new connections to augment the old self, never deleting the old ones. I had tried to erase those connections, but failed, as deleting a file only removed the link, while the data remained in the hard disk, ready to be accessed. Could I ever become a different person, even if I changed my thoughts and habits and attitudes and character?

Sure, I had integrated past and future moments in camaraderie, into a present pregnant with memories and possibilities, a present marching through the dream we called reality and life. Sensing myself as my self, the self who would carry this moment's fullness and labor through life. Just as Dr. Tang had described.

My existence like the moon reflected on a serene lake. Though my limbs and torso and organs were decaying, I continued to reflect on myself, my brain more alive than in the previous life.

So who could this self be, standing akimbo and watching the arms raising, the legs walking, the eyes scanning, the heart pumping, the lungs expanding and contracting? In what sub-brain would this I reside? What neural cluster, what cerebral subsystem could be housing this awareness, this observer, this evaluator? The same questions I had asked when first awoken in that *hospital*. But still no answers.

Am I as real as Dr. Tang? I am stronger, faster and more alert and might even live longer. And yet...

Outside the café, smoke wafted through the dawning street as several soldiers sprinted past the door. I shifted in my seat and scanned my wound. Instead of blood, a yellow liquid seeped out. I felt its texture. I smelled it. Oil. Motor oil. Could I have mistaken about blood running through a human body? But a lady outside the café was bleeding. Red streaks down her cheeks. Red blotches on her arms.

So I am an alien.

Leaning back on the chair, I grasped the knife handle. My hand shaking. I closed my eyes. Wheezing, sweating, grinding my teeth. Exhaling and sighing, I opened my eyes and tighten the grip. Before I could pull out the knife, Dr. Tang stepped into the coffee shop and I covered the wound with my jacket.

"Something came up. Delayed me." Dr. Tang switched on the lights and leaned on the counter to pant. "So you haven't left. But you wouldn't. You want to see her."

"Doc, your prophecy has come true. I've discovered the seed of destruction in my past and eliminated my future." I related the dream in the maple woods and its revelation. That I was a monster, a murderer, a psychopath, a devil.

"At any moment, an infinite number of worlds open before us, waiting for us to choose, to step forward, to enter. And even though the past has directed our paths and limited our choices, we still have enough of them in the future to create a new man, a new woman." He put a hand on my shoulder.

"Possible futures mean nothing. I have to face my past." I flung my arm in the air, almost lifting the jacket and revealing the knife.

"I won't allow my research to define my destiny and you shouldn't allow your childhood incident to define yours."

"Maybe you're stronger than I am."

"Sure, your future will differ from your vision and you'll need courage." He pulled out the chair, but didn't sit down.

"There's no CP data in my mind, only my hideous memories." I couldn't remember the moments after killing Alpha. Nor my growing up as a teenager and a young adult. Most of the memories lost through the accident remained hidden. I could piece together Dolly's scheme through my research, but couldn't identity the Mexican client. I would meet him or his thugs soon enough.

"The data you had stolen—"

"Only my missing memory, the memory I'd volunteered to erase. That's why I volunteered for the CP research." I held my head in both hands. "But, in the end I recovered it, through this elaborate game."

Dolly had probably used the CP data to lure me into the trap. So I would regain my memory and remember I'm a psychopath. So I would regret killing Alpha and suffer the nightmares. She seduced me to destroy me.

When Dr. Tang took out his phone, I grabbed his arm, careful not to reveal the knife. "You better skip town now before those agents come." Outside, a siren blared and debris and dust fell onto the sidewalk.

"One more thing to take care of, just one more thing, and I'm out of here." He grasped the phone as if about to crush it.

"Forget about Ingrid."

"I believe you're jealous."

"Of course, I'm. I've never hidden that." I said Ingrid had been working for the Intelligence Agency to spy on him and was probably snitching on him at this very moment. I urged him to accept the ticket bought under Mrs. McCoy's name and take the flight to New Einstein. "If you value freedom, seize it without delay. May be your last chance."

"She confessed everything and I forgave her." He thrust the phone in my face and showed Ingrid's message, which said she would *take care of everything*. He pressed his left hand on the table to support his body. "When I found out her secret mission, I grieved, I lamented, but what does that matter in the span of a lifetime. There are enough moments to grieve and to lament. No, I refuse to hold any grudges against her." He straightened himself, flinging his arm and knocking down the chair. "By forgiving her, I also forgive myself, which before seemed so impossible and required so much courage. I've searched for knowledge all my life and now find wisdom. Isn't that refreshing?"

"Looks like a decoy to confuse you, so the agents would have time to catch you."

Yes, she would sacrifice for him. She was looking for something to sacrifice herself, to make her life worthwhile, and found it: for Dr. Tang, for love, for hope, for the possible tomorrow. She had found that rainbow even while dragging her hatred through the rain-soaked dirt road. For her sake, I hoped she could forgive me and release her burden, and fly into tomorrow's rising sun.

"I asked her not to go." He paced from table to counter to table. "I promised to escape with her to a small island without surveillance monitors. She tried to avoid the crowd, to touch nature. To lose our pasts, to lose our names, to lose our identities. What is the past if it blocks my future? What is a name if it confines my growth? What is identity if it snubs my character? From the wasteland, a single lotus emerges through the mire and flings away the sludge. Life. I hadn't lost it forever. Ingrid gave it back to me. When I opened my heart and confessed everything, when she opened her mind and listened to everything, redemption and freedom. And life enough."

"I was going to fight you for Ingrid until the world ends, which might not be too long." I shifted on the seat to a more comfortable position, but couldn't feel the pain anymore. A bad sign.

"Then let's fight. Before, I might not have." He kicked aside the shards. "But now, I'll fight because I've found out she'd fight alongside me. For her." He hung the photo of the meadow back onto the wall. "Despite the destruction, despite the terror, despite the suffering, despite the evil, this life and this world continue to blossom. And tomorrow, the sun will still rise in the east." He raised his hand and dropped the phone.

"I still have to trust you on this sun stuff. But I'm losing my faith, not just in you, but in everything." I would help them, though unable to dodge the coming storm.

He picked up the phone. "Her resilience, her wisdom, her strength, her courage. Her belief in building character despite situations. From the quagmire, a blossom. After the rain, rainbow. At first, I was afraid I might lean on her as crutch. Not anymore."

Though the news might comfort him, I didn't reveal Ingrid had pretended to spy on him while waiting to kill me. I would like to believe she had gone to the fake hospital and followed him just for me.

"They'll erase her memory whatever she says and she'd lose herself. She pretended to spy on me but was trying to accomplish her own mission, which she'd pursued since her youth. Searching, training, suffering. A goal as alluring as the Siren. An obsession that has destroyed her years, her days, her laughter. Maybe, to erase the painful memory of her brother's death. She seemed unable to dispel its shadow and sway. Her expertise could help others but not herself."

"Sure, when you've known the tricks, when you've seem through the hocus-pocus, they won't work anymore." He would risk his life to rescue her, but I would stop him.

"She might've wanted to use CP to avenge her brother, but had agreed to help destroy the data. Still, whatever her goal, she continued to struggle with it."

"No, she didn't really care about CP." She had opened her soul to him also. So I didn't reveal her lifelong mission—to kill me.

"I wish she'd reveal her obsession, so I might help her."

"You might; you might. But you'd fail as she did."

He would've enjoyed plunging a knife into my abdomen, before finding out he couldn't harm me.

"Do you still believe freedom to be possible?" I reread our exchange in the hospital and with the past months' experiences, doubted freedom in this world.

"I believe that each of us is unique, that we can have our own views and styles, that the only way this world can continue is through this diversity within the unity that is humanity."

"All right. All right." I waved my hand. I waved aside his wisdom. We had stepped beyond wisdom. Even beyond the Underground Man's insights. Only folly would do now. But not Francisco's whiskey and durian pies. I pulled away my jacket to reveal the knife and my wound. "What the hell is this? Why am I bleeding motor oil?"

"I have bad news." Dr. Tang glanced at the knife, putting his hand on my shoulder. A boom shook the counter and a coffeepot fell onto the floor.

"That I'm alive? I already know that. Anyway, I'm in the mood for bad news."

"No, you're not."

"Okay, I'm not. But I enjoyed killing an innocent boy, even as a kid. What can trump that?" I had plunged the knife into that boy's abdomen, and the resulting joy and peace and catharsis had nourished me. If I had a month to live and the recovered memory wouldn't haunt me for decades and decades, I would welcome the bad news and buy him a cup of chai latte with extra cinnamon.

"A single act, a single decision doesn't reap destiny. I refuse to believe it. I refused to believe it for myself and I refuse to believe it for you."

"Doc, I forgive you."

"I'm sorry."

"Don't be."

"You died in that car accident three months ago while escaping the intelligence agents. They couldn't save you." Dr. Tang bent down and gripped the knife handle. Nodded and pulled it out. "The Intelligence Agency had your body cremated and the urn with your ashes is sitting in one the government storage warehouses."

So I had died and still lived. Was I in Purgatory, or hell? Would I have to live in this wasteland and dream of Francisco forever? Talk about eternal punishment. I would rather plunge into a black-hole and enter oblivion.

CHAPTER 52 - FRANCISCO

October 28, 2011

Dostoevsky stared through his portraits. How had I returned to the Underground Temple? After I'd entered the password, twirling patterns flashed on the screen and the computer played the tune from the woods. I blacked out and dreamed the double dream.

Maybe Ganesh had hauled me here from Liberty Lair, while I slept. I phoned him but received the busy signal. The encoded file had disappeared from my laptop, probably self-deleted after the password unlocked the content. I'd cracked the code and received the messages: Fernando, rather than I, had killed Father; and the boy psychopath was the amnesiac. The world should've ended, so Dostoevsky portraits wouldn't haunt the Temple anymore. Perhaps, nuclear warheads or biological weapons had destroyed the world aboveground, and survivors mutated and moved underground. Just like in the movies.

I checked the Internet news. Another foggy day. A chance of light snow. I could buy turkey at forty-percent discount online, and get tickets for tomorrow's Thanksgiving Rock Concert in Lincoln Center. The police had suppressed the riot and jailed the fanatics and the looters and would fine each prisoner a hundred dollars. The Underground Temple would have to pay a hundred-thousand-dollar fine.

I'd looked forward to the chaos and destruction and the world ending. Now, I must bring Fernando's letter to his grave.

In the letter Fernando said he'd killed Father to save the little girl. When the old man abducted the girl in the school parking lot, he slipped into the trunk, not sure what the fiend would do. The tires screeched and the car sped off. The girl cried through the entire journey, but he focused on what he'd do to stop the crime. After Father had dragged the girl from the car, Fernando opened the trunk and slipped onto the ground. He picked up a rock and approached as the girl struggled to free herself. Father read a passage from Leviticus, ripped off her blouse, and raised the dagger to cut out her heart for the burnt offering. Fernando struck the old man's head. Father groaned. The girl screamed. He struck again, and again, and again and the girl screamed with each blow. Only after Father hadn't moved for a minute did he stopped and took off the jacket to cover the girl. After asking her to stay in the car, he took the shovel from the trunk and dug a pit next to the stream and he threw the body and the bloodstained rock and soil into the pit. He filled the grave and smoothed the ground and he threw the shovel into the stream. When he drove the girl back into the city, he worried a police cruiser might stop him because of his age. But none did. Maybe, he looked like a teenager despite his age. Next day, he and I cycled to the spot to plant the chrysanthemums. We'd returned each week for three months to water the flowers and they bloomed. I began to believe I took him there to plant the flowers.

When no one found the body, he convinced himself Father was missing. He enforced that *truth* through his obsession with finding cats and dogs along with Father, but by the time he'd become a police office, he decided to face his past and confess. He would've divulged the secret on the day we celebrated his achievement, but he couldn't tell me face-to-face. He wanted me to read the letter before proclaiming he didn't regret killing Father.

I should've killed Father. I should be the hero. I could still pretend to have gotten rid of the monster and saved Ingrid, but I'd give Fernando credit for his courage. Wherever Ingrid could be, she'd prefer the truth. I should spit in the Guardian's face and kick his butt from New York into the Atlantic Ocean for messing with my memory. The loser.

After replacing the letter in the envelope, I put on my cloak and left the Prophet Office. Along the hallway, chants from the sanctuary echoed Dostoevsky's quotes on the walls. Probably fanatics, those who avoided the riot and the jail, were worshipping old Fyodor. I stopped to straighten my framed photo and removed the Priest's. His photo shouldn't contaminate the walls any longer. I'd modernize the Temple with security cameras, eye scanners, multimedia equipment, and a control center. I'd replace Dostoevsky with Descartes as the new idol and update the doctrines to suit the postmodern times.

Near the worship hall, the aroma of barbecued meat tickled my nostrils and triggered my appetite. I hadn't eaten last night and longed for grilled T-bone steak. The Priest had probably sneaked in the barbecue worship after finding out I was sleeping. The double-crosser.

When I slipped into the sanctuary from the side door, the Priest was stuffing the last chunk of meat onto the altar while about a hundred worshippers in ten rows folded their hands and chanted. The flame swung out of the altar and almost licked the Priest's face. I must buy a gas grill with glass cover and ventilation to replace this tub. Or else, one day the lunatic would burn down the entire temple. I didn't intend to sacrifice myself to the Almighty Dostoevsky.

I waved to my followers and strutted toward the Priest. He was poking the meat when I confronted him about partying without me. His excuse: he couldn't locate me when the service began. Yeah, right. The aroma intoxicated me and I forgave him so we could begin the meal. He whined that we couldn't eat the burnt offering, but as the Prophet, I revealed the Almighty Dostoevsky wanted us to share in the offering.

"Communion, you know," I said.

"I wouldn't eat that." He flung off the apron and left the altar.

He probably feared the holy punishment so I assured him the Almighty Dostoevsky wouldn't punish us. I'd eat the first piece to show I'm a man and he's a mouse. I rubbed my hands and sniffed the aroma, my saliva pushing against my lips and my stomach growling like a lion.

He pointed at the meat and said, "Do you know what I offered?"

"A deer? So you don't eat deer? No? A skunk? Yeah, I might reconsider. Did you sacrifice a cat, you savage?"

"I love cats."

"Well, as long as you didn't harm any pets." I poke the meat with the skewer. "A snake? They should taste like chicken though I've never tried them before."

"No."

"Well, it isn't rabbit. And doesn't smell like lamb."

"It's Clint."

I dropped the skewer. I stared at the femur. The aroma of burnt fat nauseated me and the heat stifled me. I leaned against the wall and puked while the fanatics continued to chant as if they were hypnotized. I had enough of this hell and these nutcases. Then again, I was the CEO of this franchise and I could rewrite their beliefs and values and likes and dislikes, but I couldn't give them free will.

"I suppose if you really want a piece. Since you're the prophet—" The Priest picked up the skewer and approached me.

"Forget I mentioned it. Dostoevsky probably would want everything for himself." I waved my hands. I couldn't rejoice in the savage receiving his *reward*. I didn't want to kill the fiend. I couldn't. This priest, on the other hand, would do anything for Dostoevsky. Torture, kill, even self-immolate. I had to agree with the amnesiac that I'd rather deal with crooks and thieves and Wall Street bankers than saints and lunatics.

"Isn't it a crime to murder, even under the city?" I wiped the sweat off my forehead.

"Damn it, I have religious rights."

I decided to leave this hell. Forget Fyodor; forget a multimedia temple; forget postmodern doctrines; and above all forget these lunatics. Soon, the police would arrest the Priest and raid the Temple. Before I left, he patted my shoulder and asked me to take care of Faith, something I would've done without his reminder. He should skip town and avoid the police. After the public had lost interest in this killing, he could return to lead the fanatics in worship.

He refused. He'd sacrifice himself for the Almighty Dostoevsky.

He proclaimed a celebration after the offering. The fanatics chanted. I sipped whiskey while the altar's flaming tongues flickered from side to side like serpents searching for preys. The fire danced—my heart matching its beat—until it'd consumed the fuel and returned to its calm, blue flame. A draft stirred the flame and reminded me time wouldn't reverse, wouldn't return Faith to a former morning.

I finished the whiskey, a drop of tear falling to the ground.

After the Priest had prayed to the Almighty Dostoevsky, I told him the Guardian burned the holy text, but the desecrator had taken a bullet in the head and couldn't serve as a burnt offering. The chief fanatic cursed the Guardian and vowed to retrieve the body and offer it on the altar. He asked me to join his quest, but I declined, citing my aversion to cadavers and stenches, not to mention the mortuary.

He prostrated and kowtowed thrice. "To show my faith, I'll bring another offering. Please accept it with pleasure." He extended two open palms toward the ceiling.

"Thank you. I'll accept the original manuscript of *Crime and Punishment*. But if you brought a slaughtered lamb, I'll pass. I prefer beef to lamb. Nothing against them. Just a personal preference. I'm sure you have your own quirks." I laid my hand on his head and blessed the lunatic even though he should be blessing me.

"Holly informed Clint that Faith was your new lover. She also helped him locate her." He kissed my hand. "If you want her arms, I'd be glad to bring the offering."

I hadn't decided on how to deal with Holly for conspiring with the Guardian and toying with my memory. I would've condoned her for the pain she'd caused me, for altering my memory, a reason or even an excuse would suffice, but I couldn't forgive her for fostering Faith's torture. While eating durian pie or hacking into a database, I'd probably recall Faith's leg sticking out of the blanket or her body in my arms. The image had glued into my hippocampus and pain drilled into my heart and the trauma would leave a void for the rest of my life. Where should I turn when whiskey couldn't heal my emotional, mental and spiritual wounds? Certainly not Dostoevsky, and not even the underground man.

As I rode the elevator to the surface, Faith's swollen lips haunted me and would do so until my last breath. I punched the elevator panel and my knuckles turned red. I ignored the pain and when the door opened, I stepped out of the elevator and stood under the manhole to inhale the morning air. Above the manhole, car horns played a cacophony to announce another Big Apple day. The inhabitants would inhale more smog and eat more trans-fats and pesticides and slave through another day for their paychecks as if the fundamental constants of the universe had remained the same and Francisco hadn't saved humanity once again. Oh, blessed fools.

I climbed up the ladder and pushed away the manhole cover, and stared into a car's under-belly, the muffler and exhaust pipes. The car inched forward in the rush-hour traffic. Half a minute later, the clouds, dark and churning, gazed at me. Before I could poke my head through the manhole, another car belly had blocked the sky.

I crawled out of the manhole, careful not to bump my head against the muffler, and lay flat on my stomach. Two columns of tires stretched down the road and exhaust filled the air. I rolled on my side to get away from the tires. Then jumped up to greet the cabdriver talking on the phone. He dropped the phone and darted toward the passenger side, but the seatbelt prevented him from leaving his seat. I turned around and steered through the sea of cars, ignoring the horns and shouts.

On the sidewalk, patrons had lined-up outside a cheesecake shop, the line wrapping around the end of the block. I didn't recognize the stores or the buildings, or the loud speakers atop lampposts warning pedestrians not to jade-walk and vehicles not to speed. Down the block, the hotel New Jersey rose like a mainframe server into the fog. I was on Cheese-cake Boulevard instead of Fifth Avenue. In the distance, the Intelligence Agency Building had replaced the Empire State Building.

Holy Fyodor, I was in Fermat's Last Stand.

CHAPTER 53 - DESCARTES

November 9 (2)

After Dr. Tang joked without even a smirk, I patted him on the shoulder and said, "Nice try. But you need to work on your timing. The punch line's about three months late. Would've found it funny when I first woke up in the fake hospital. Like 'Oh, poor chap, sorry, but you just died from a car accident and now you're stuck here, in limbo, between heaven and hell.'"

"Just found out now from my source, the former Intelligence Agent. About the accident, not the official version of course, but the top-secret one." Dr. Tang pulled up a chair and sat next to me.

"But you raised me from the dead. Right? So, your real name is Dr. Tangenstein." With the back of my hand, I checked his forehead's temperature, for fever.

"My source could only access the top-secret file two days ago."

"Maybe, you've been at your job for too long. Studying those lunatics takes a toll. Should take a vacation."

"But haven't you been feeling strange, like something's off?"

"Not from losing my memory, but from being dead? Anyway, do dead men dream of Guzman Codes and Guardians of Memory?"

"To be more precise, your body's dead. But you're still more real than Francisco."

"Touch my hand to check whether I'm real. You're a scientist; you must believe in the empirical method. Right?" My body felt real enough when I made love to Dolly. Yet, Ingrid's knife had plunged into my abdomen but couldn't injure me. Maybe, I didn't invent Francisco's Sodom and Gomorrah. Maybe, Francisco dreamed of this Armageddon, and through his delusion, he fancied this sadist who had murdered another boy just to enjoy the thrill. So, he created me.

"Unfortunately, the evidences—" He put the knife on the table.

"Now I understand everything. Francisco is dreaming of us, you and me. And he decided whether I live or die. How else do you explain that I'm still alive." I pointed at the knife and at the gash oozing motor oil. "That she couldn't kill me." But then, how did Francisco arrive just now? He might even enter the café and greet us.

"That could've been an explanation."

"You don't seem convinced." I picked up the cup and crushed it. "But this mad world, clones and omnipresent TVs, agents and rebels, PC and CP. What, besides a nightmare, could this be? And what twisted mind, besides Francisco's could've dreamed of it?"

"It could've been a nightmare."

"Maybe, only one of your abstractions. So it couldn't hurt me. But then maybe I'm an abstraction."

"There's another explanation."

"That I'm a super hero?" I grasped the blade in both hands and bent it.

"You're an android." He opened the gash to reveal the wires and IC chips and circuit boards inside me. "The knife didn't cut through the inner wall, so it didn't damage the vital circuitry. Only the lubricants spilled out."

I threw the knife over the counter. I didn't believe the illusion or accept the deception. I am human, not an android. I am flesh and blood, rather than electronics and mechanical pumps. I touched a capacitor and a plastic tube. The nano-devices within my transparent *intestines* helping to process the food I had eaten several hours ago. I had tasted the food. Caressed the wind. Smelled the smoke.

I should curse the world but only laughed. I should punch Dr. Tang in the face but only broke off the table's corner. I willed the nightmare to end, but the café, the counter, and Dr. Tang didn't vanish. What could one do when life turned into a sham or an illusion, except to play along or quit the game?

"Unlike other androids, your body can process food, so you would believe you're human. But you're special in a more important way."

I smashed the table with my fist and it collapsed onto the floor. I didn't ask to be an android; I didn't want a mechanical pump for a heart, nor a CPU to control the circulation of motor of oil. I had to tunnel to an alternate universe, but reality wouldn't shift anymore. This nightmare embraced me, no, choked me.

Dr. Tang caught my laptop before it crashed onto the fallen table. "You're not quite dead. Your brain is in that metallic cranium and so you're like no other android."

"Doc, every time you try to comfort me, you make me feel worse."

"So you searched for those lost memories buried inside your brain. The agents saved your brain after the accident. To retrieve the data. So don't ask for a new body. You should keep the android body, which would last about several hundred years. You've experienced the strength, the dexterity, the stamina. So, you got a good deal. Even a millionaire won't get one of these state-of-the-art units when her body breaks down." He handed me the laptop.

"I should've died in peace. But they wouldn't even allow me that much. Have to let me live as a sub-human. You, you helped create CP and now everyone is after me." I grabbed his lapels and shook him and I could take his life. He didn't resist. Steel limbs, engine fluids, optical sensors, a mechanical pump, they gave me life, life brisker than with flesh and blood. In the end, I let him go.

I wouldn't let him stitch up my *skin*. I would rather demolish this alien body than allow the agents or the rebels or Dr. Tang to retrieve the data.

My body is an abstraction to me, Descartes.

Just as I took the laptop, the minister a.k.a. the head-trauma patient stepped through the doorway.

"So, do you remember killing my brother while escaping from us?" He took off his jacket to reveal the bomb strapped on his torso, grasped the power switch and blocked the exit. "I rammed your car to kill you. I did kill you, but they have to preserve your brain."

"Show us decency through your treatment of friends and enemies," Dr. Tang said, "in your fairness toward the innocent, in your respect for life. Show us your humanity."

"Um, Doc, we're in a war. Like they say, all's fair in love and war. We should stick with the truth that survival equals goodness, justice, and honor. So, the first thing's to survive anyway you can. Like we must do now," I whispered to Dr. Tang while the man shook the bomb. Should have warned the doctor never to provoke a bomber. Should have reminded him the man held the truth along with the bomb.

"Just because you're once Dolly's lover," the bomber said, "you think you're special? You're a mad scientist, an ignorant fool, who never looks out the window to see what the hell's happening in the street. I should kill you and save the world from your idiocy. Damn it. Let's get this bullshit over with, since you want it so much." He grasped the handle near his ribs.

"Let the doctor go. He has nothing to do with this." What happened before the car crash? Damn it, only images of plunging a blade into the boy came to mind. I didn't doubt him. Probably had killed several agents while escaping from them. I couldn't waste anymore time. Ingrid was waiting for us and we had to stop the agents from programming her mind. I must disarm this man without detonating the bomb. No, I didn't want to kill him, enough dead bodies already.

"The bomb in that building was for you, not Pratt."

Pratt's son died delivering me a message. His lifeless body in the hospital still haunted me, and would do so till my last breath, which I hope would come soon. Did the boy resurrect and die again in this reality?

"It's your fault."

Without a pit or a nut in my mouth, I retreated toward a table, sidestepping the debris on the floor. Dr. Tang pressed his lips together and glanced around the café probably looking for a way to disarm the man. The bomber's fingers tightened, the veins squirming on the back of his hand. He was going to press the switch. He was going to end our lives. At that moment, I screamed in my mind for life, for another second, another minute, another day to enjoy this amnesia and suffer Francisco and his super-narcissism. So I could rescue Ingrid? So I could punish Dolly? No, so I could delay dying and live like a beast, my survival instinct had trumped my desire for peace and rest and my fear of pain and suffering.

Let me suffer longer, even just for a day. Let me grieve and sigh for several more hours.

I lunged toward the minister as a bang rang in my ears.

I faltered. Fear and anger and peace and joy, those emotions seized me to the extent that, despite the graphite limbs and mechanical pumps and IC chips, I proclaimed *Cogito Ergo Sum*.

I should charge, but only wrap my body around the bomb, to save Dr. Tang, the man who pretended to help me but had a different agenda.

In that nanosecond, Dr. Tang looked with a plea and perhaps a sense of regret. He signaled for me to dash out of the café, to save myself and rescue Ingrid. I hadn't shaken his hand and he hadn't seen Ingrid. I couldn't depart, not this way, not with regrets, not without having hunted a lion, raced a bullet train barefooted, or turn New Jersey into IAB before an audience. No, I wanted to live, and live like no other human.

The gunpowder irritated my nose.

I grasped Dr. Tang as the bomber fell onto the ground. His hand releasing the switch, tears gushing out of his eyes. He lay on the floor, a pool of blood spreading around his head. I should laugh; I should pump my fist; I should leap into the air and clap my heels; but I just studied the contour of red, jagged and expanding, my will to live gone. I would live and savor my crime.

Jack Conman stepped through the doorway with a gun, his hair and coat covered in dust. Shaking his head he greeted us, and after kicking the bomber in the ribs, walked around the counter and picked up the cash. "You owe me ten thousand dollars for saving your lives. It's a bargain."

"How does it feel to escape death?" I studied Dr. Tang, searching for fear, relief, or gratitude, but he only gave Conman four cash cards, shook my hand and said, "Goodbye, my friend. Take care. And leave this place. Forget about the CP data and mad scientists. Forget about agents and rebels. Live your life." He left the café before I could reply. Again avoiding his feeling and falling back on his savior complex. For sure, he would contact the Ex-Intelligence Agent to locate Ingrid. He had to be a hero.

How could I forget my crimes? How could I abandon my nature and transform from a psychopath to a saint? No more than he could abandon Ingrid. Not even if I leaped into an alternate universe.

"Hey, man. Get out of here. The rebels are coming."

"How much did the agents pay you to protect my brain?"

"Not enough. And Dolly still owes me ten-thousand."

I lifted Conman over the counter and asked for the rebel leader's phone number. At first, he asked for two thousands dollars, but I convinced him to revalue his life. After he had given me the number, I thanked him and tossed him behind the counter. Leaving the café and sprinting down the side street toward a boulevard.

At the intersection I turned left and spotted Dr. Tang five blocks away where gunshots echoed among the buildings. While I navigated against pedestrians fleeing from a burning cheesecake shop, I phoned the rebel leader to report Ingrid meeting with the agents and requested that they track my location with GPS.

Near New Jersey, where a carol's melody filled the air, several rebels retreated from a fire, so I asked them to gather their colleagues and prepare a car. They asked for the CP data but I only promised to help rescue Ingrid. When a police cruiser pulled up and four policemen emerged to chase after the rebels, I slipped into a street where a police siren greeted me. While the policemen and rebels shot at each other, I ran with the traffic, passing ambulances, fire engines and police cruisers. Outside an electronic store, Dr. Tang pulled out his car key. Somehow, the police ignored him. Before I could reach him, he stepped into his car and drove off. I ran after the car, confident he had located Ingrid through his source. A policeman stepped out of his cruiser and called after me but I ignored her and chased after Doc.

Gunshots rang behind me as I sprinted past several surveillance cameras and a group of rebels. Several bullets whizzed by but I ignored them, hoping the police wasn't aiming for my head. A bullet lodged into my forearm, but no harm done.

Dr. Tang detoured two blocks before the collapsed IAB and took the expressway out of the city. At first, cars fleeing the city jammed the four-lane highway, but after a junction with another expressway the traffic thinned out. Two exits later, the skyscrapers disappeared. I was running in the right lane, the wind against my face, when a rebel van caught up and honked. I slowed down and after the passenger side door opened, I hopped into the van to join the rebels inside and exhaled several times to slow down my mechanical pump. Twenty more rebels in two trucks followed the van. The driver, who turned out to be Pratt's ex-wife and the rebel leader, stepped on the gas and caught up with Dr. Tang's car. Did she know a bomb had killed her son? I didn't poison her with knowledge after it had tainted me.

After I recounted Ingrid's suicide mission, the other rebels cursed Dr. Tang and suggested dumping him into their torture chamber but Rebel Leader decided not to torment Ingrid. By the time we arrived, the agents would probably have erased her memory and she wouldn't want to kill me anymore, but I preferred her hatred to a void. I imagined torturing those agents but shook my head to disperse the images and the sadist's sense of oneness with the universe, as when he (not I) had plunged the dagger into Alpha's guts.

The colonial houses along the highway gave way to ranches, which in turn yielded to farmhouses. Though the clouds continued to hide the sky, the trees replaced the houses around noon. The woods gave way to hills, which in turn yielded to the plains. The fog thinned out but the sun still hid behind the clouds. Reeds on the left swayed to the wind's rhythm.

The expressway gave way to a local road, and the cement yielded to dirt. Soon, besides sky and earth, only Dr. Tang's car.

I came here before. I recognized a lone tree in the plains, its branches clawed at the sky for prey. Dolly and I had made love beneath the tree, and I might still find a heart etched on the trunk.

After passing the sign *HYMN1*, we entered the maple woods, where the foliages had abandoned the branches. I still recognized the rocks, the trunks, and the stream. After about five hundred yards into the woods, Dr. Tang's empty car blocked the path. Before the van could stop, I jumped off and scanned the path for footprints. Sure enough, my friend didn't bother to hide his trail.

I was a fish returned to water. The trees, the rocks and the smell of rotting leaves enlivened me, as they had when the sadist killed the boy.

"Well, well, well," the rebel leader said, "so we missed this facility. But don't worry. We brought enough explosives to blow up a ten-story building." She strapped a rocket launcher on her back. Each rebel fastened about half a dozen grenades on his belt and grabbed an AK-45. Besides a dozen rockets, they also brought along two trunks of TNT. They should have more hi-tech weapons, but they probably were short on money.

Though they objected, I led the way, tracking the footprints along the stream, where a section had dried up. Fallen leaves still swished on the path, but I tried to ignore the din and tracked Dr. Tang's footfall. A slanting headstone stood on the spot where I had killed Alpha, but I didn't stop to examine the epitaph. After turning at the stream's elbow, the path cut into the woods where more leaves gathered on the path.

Voices wafted through the air. I rushed forward ignoring the rebel leader's pleads to slow down, crunching the leaves for about a hundred yards before spotting a shack, in front of which Dr. Tang talked to a ranger. I jumped from rock to rock to approach them. The leaves swishing in the wind hid my footfalls.

"Go ahead," the ranger said. "The entrance's in the bathroom, under the toilet."

Dr. Tang approached the shack, his gait steady against the wind that rose and fell according to my mood. Two campfires in the front yard sent smoke into the sky. The twin beacons probably signaled the guards inside to receive visitors.

When the ranger took a water bucket toward the campfire, I knocked him out before he could drop his load and lift his rifle. With the rebels, those slowpokes, nowhere in sight, I phoned to hasten them, but the call didn't go through. Without waiting, I rushed into the shack, determined to prevent Dr. Tang from flinging himself against a legion of agents even if I had to tie him up.

The living room reeking of maple returned me to my childhood. I had played cops and robbers with Alpha in a log cabin, probably this one, and one day I was chasing him through the kitchen when his mother brought us apple cider. Her voice echoed in my ears while the taste of the cider stirred my taste buds. I slapped my face to purge those sensations, preferring to forget my childhood. If possible, I would remove the memories I had regained, with CP. If possible... But I had to save Ingrid.

Tiptoeing around the divan and passing the fireplace where maple branches burned, I savored the aroma for a second, only a second, and took out a stained dagger from a cabinet. The dagger I had used to kill Alpha. Rust had mixed with bloodstain but the handle nestled in my hand, its curves reminding me of the fatal thrust. I sliced the air several times before putting it away and closing the cabinet. If only I could fling away the afterimages of the incident by closing that door.

I grabbed the poker on the coffee table and searched for the bathroom. No footfalls. Dr. Tang must have entered the secret passage under the toilet. Rick's framed photo—I recognized Rick's frown—hung above the fireplace and his stare pierced into me. In the dinning room reeking of beer, half a pepperoni pizza and six almost-empty steins sat on the dining table. The agents must have left their meals to set the trap.

I picked a cowhide whip on the dinning room wall and entered the kitchen and the stench of durian triggered a headache. I probably wouldn't need any air so I held my breath, but the odor had already woken up more childhood memories. Such as, I used to enjoy durian pies, like Francisco, but not anymore. I despised durian just as I abhorred my childhood, and would fling both into the incinerator.

A rasp startled me. I wouldn't have heard it if the wind outside hadn't hushed for a second. With whip around my waist, I tiptoed across the kitchen, the poker demolishing spider webs and my soles picking up dust. I turned the knob and opened the door beside the dishwasher.

I thrust the poker at the flutter behind the door and pierced a piece of paper swaying in the draft. Then stepped into a lounge. The sports section lay next to the rest of the newspaper on the countertop. The coffee maker cackled and gurgled. Francisco's office. How could it appear in reality? Had I reentered the playhouse? Maybe I had returned to my dream. If so, I must unload a burden.

Inside Francisco's office at the end of the hallway, I put down the poker, opened the trophy cabinet's door and took out the statuette. I bent it. I twisted it. I pulled it into two pieces. Then threw it into the trashcan. I removed the frames from the wall. Removed the certificates and piled them together. Ripped them into four piles and threw them into the trashcan. I shut my eyes and enjoyed the moment. Catharsis. If Francisco walked through the door I would spit in his face. But no such luck.

I was searching for other awards when laughter below alerted me. Dr. Tang should have entered their offices through the bathroom, so the agents must have captured him. In my dream, the bathroom was near the lounge.

I left the room with the poker to go to the bathroom. In the lounge, Rick—Nick didn't have those V-shaped eyebrows—in a black three-piece suit sat on the sofa, as he had in the funhouse. Except Conman didn't stand behind him.

"Get your memory back already." He pulled out a semiautomatic handgun. "Don't you remember your damn office?"

I unleashed the whip and knocked the gun from his hand. Whether trapped in a playhouse or in my dream, I intended to save Ingrid from the agents.

"You should thank me. I authorized the lab to create your body."

I wrapped the whip around my waist. He should have let my brain expire, but of course, he couldn't. He needed the data. I didn't remember using this office. I didn't remember the events before the car crash. Only the childhood incident still haunted me.

He snapped his fingers and the bathroom door opened. Six agents shoved Dr. Tang into the lounge. I walked up and shook his hand. He didn't seem frustrated or restless and might have a plan B. Anyway, I could protect him and take out these agents, just had to make sure Ingrid was safe before I could *kick their butts.*

"Where's Ingrid?" Dr. Tang said.

"We want you, not her. So help us perfect CP."

"Don't be greedy. You have PC and SP already," I said.

"I'm sick and tire of using Subliminal Projection. I need something efficient. How could I program a whole army of super-soldiers with that crap? I don't have time to bullshit around."

"Only if you didn't erase her memory," Dr. Tang said.

"If we didn't erase her memory, how the hell could we test your CP." Rick pushed the doctor aside. "Your CP better be able to recover her memory. I have no time for crap."

I had expected Agent Rick and his henchmen to erase Ingrid's memory, but when he proclaimed the verdict, I still squeezed the poker and warped the handle. Dr. Tang punched him in the jaw and he fell onto the floor. When the agents rushed toward the doctor, I blocked the path.

"Let them take care of it man to man," I said. "Get a cup of coffee and watch the show."

Maybe Rick couldn't erase Ingrid's memory with PC or SP in only eighteen hours. Of course, the Agency might have improved these technologies.

"Not a problem," a chubby agent said. "But don't kill him. We still have to arrest the double-agent and interrogate him."

Before I could ask about Agent Rick's double life, the front door collapsed onto the floor. I pulled Dr. Tang onto the floor, as the agents dropped their rifles and dodged to either side, one agent knocking down the coffee maker.

After a crash, footfalls, shouts and shots intermingled into a concerto. Bullets whistled above me, one lodging into my arm. But no harm done.

As I fainted, Agent Rick darted into Francisco's office.

***

The next moment I held a poker in the living room, while an explosion shook the cabin. When the dust settled, Ingrid stood in the doorway to the dinning room, her hair covered in dirt. Her eyes had the same look that mine had in the hospital mirror. I could understand her fear, confusion and anxiety. Her search for a self that had dispersed like ashes, a past that had evaporated like morning mist. When Dr. Tang asked for her name, she asked for ours.

"We've failed. You've failed. How can you fail her?" I didn't care how many other men or women, boys or girls the agents had tested the technology on. I cared about Ingrid. Instead of embracing her, I swung the poker at the cabinet and broke its glass door. I grabbed the dagger to stab the agents for removing Ingrid's memory, but it dropped onto the floor. She, whom I love, who loves Dr. Tang instead of me, who had tried to kill me, they had removed her soul.

Through the kitchen backdoor, we stepped into the backyard where the fallen leaves had gathered near the house. Dr. Tang held Ingrid's hand and led her through the yard. The wind played with the leaves and two squirrels chased each other from branch to branch, as we walked toward the barn fifty yards away. The rustles and occasional caws escorted us but I walked alone on my path. The withered leaves and barren branches reflected my soul. Ingrid must remember me and hate me. She must try to stab me again. I would give her my dagger so she could avenge her brother's death.

A branch cracked in the distance, maybe a thousand yards away. I turned to check for movements but the trunks blocked my view. Before I could inform the rebel leader, she walked off to confer with her band, so I followed Dr. Tang and Ingrid into the barn where hay stacked against the wall on both sides and a straw hat sat in the corner. I checked the stalls to make sure no one hid inside. Nothing, not even dung. I took the rusted pitchfork and shoved away the hay. A trapdoor lay under the piles. I opened the trapdoor and a cold draft swept through my face.

Dr. Tang was dusting Ingrid's hair and shoulders when the rebel leader approached and said, "Cover your ears."

After twelve rebels rushed into the barn, she gave the command to detonate the explosives. A boom shook the ground. The cabin's windows and doors flew out. The structure swayed for several seconds before collapsing. The debris burned and the smoke rose into the sky.

"All a day's work." The rebel leader took off her beret and dusted it.

When I pointed at the trapdoor, she said, "We won't need that escape tunnel. But in case there're agents down there…" She ordered a rebel to throw a canister of teargas into the tunnel and shut the trapdoor. Then tried to talk to Ingrid, but only an inquiring look returned her greetings.

"Damn these agents. I'm glad they're buried under that cabin." The rebel leader kicked up a bundle of hay.

"Except for their leader Agent Rick," I said.

After giving Dr. Tang and me pistols, the leader took twenty rebels to scour the ground and get the van. The remaining two guarded the doorway. I opened the trapdoor to let out the teargas. I listened for footfalls, but after several minutes, the gas cleared away without anyone coming out.

Near the stall, Dr. Tang wiped Ingrid's face with a hand towel.

"You're supposed to protect her. You're supposed to solve problems." I stroked Ingrid's hair. Her look frightened me. "I trusted you and I want to continue to trust you. Do something: medicine, surgery, hypnosis, anything. Even if you have to lay hands on her. I don't care how you do it, as long as you can return her to normal."

Dr. Tang took out his music player and played Beethoven's Moonlight Sonata. While she scrutinized his forehead, nose, cheeks and jaw. He extended his right hand, his thumb touching the bridge of her nose and the rest of his fingers her forehead. His thumb slid down her nose while the other fingers caressed her forehead and reached her left temple. I was only rambling when I suggested laying hands, and would have objected to the witchcraft, but at that moment, I waited for a miracle. I would have prayed if he had asked. At the same time, I doubted such gestures, however sentimental or desperate, could reconnect Ingrid's neural pathways or repair her temporal lobe.

Then by a miracle, a miracle of alchemy, a miracle of cerebral technology, a miracle of love, she smiled and her eyes gazed at Dr. Tang as a child upon her mother. The light, the sparkle, the connection from one soul to another.

I resisted grabbing her hand and asking whether she recognized me. I didn't interfered with the witchdoctor's sorcery. The guards peeped into the farm to look at the ritual, but I reminded them to secure the barn and watch for agents.

When Dr. Tang took out the chestnut and handed it to Ingrid, she studied it and sniffed it. "I know you. Did I like you or did I hate you?"

"You certainly hated him, disgusted with his every breath, his every cell." Before I could embrace her, Dr. Tang moved his fingers down her left cheek until he held her chin.

She handed him a note, and while he read it, I peeped.

Dr. Tang didn't work on the Russian CP project.

"What else would you have gambled for love?" I said.

"I'm glad we won't know," Dr. Tang said.

I waited for him to hug her and kiss her but he didn't. If Ingrid had done the same for me, I would stand on a rooftop and proclaim my love for her. But, that's me.

"And you, you're still alive. But why did I want to kill you?" She raised her hand toward me but stopped with her fingers two inches from my face.

"Actually, I'm dead, if that'll make you happier. But don't worry, you didn't kill me. This body you see here... Well, anyway, whatever the reason, I'm glad you've forgotten it. And don't try to remember it." Some memories are best forgotten.

"I installed a seed, a trigger to help her regain her memory. Don't ask how I did it or where I got the equipment." Dr. Tang held her chin and kissed her.

I raised my fist to strike this mad scientist, but stopped in midair. I should thrash him for toying with Ingrid's mind, but he would have sold his soul to save her memory. Indeed, he might have. Despite the possible side effects, I would have done the same.

"Even though I'm already dead, I wouldn't forgive you if she doesn't recover. I want her to return to her former self. Sans the knowledge about me." A branch snapped in the distance as I lowered my fist. Yet, in the woods, no branch swayed.

"I weighted the risks and chose to go ahead. I'll take responsibility for what happens to her even though I feel now, more than ever, the limits of my courage and strength. No, no one ever has enough of them." He wiped his face with the hand towel.

"How can we destroy this technology?"

"We don't know whom Dolly has sold the technology to or how many rogue agents have gotten hold of the data. At least, the Russian Intelligence Agency probably didn't make any copies. And Rick's version is no better than PC and SP. Still, at this point, the laws of propagation would take over. Geometric growth. So, in the end, I've failed to destroy the data."

Ingrid handed me a note. She had asked Dr. Tang to place a trigger in her mind so he could recover her memory. She even signed the statement.

"I couldn't refuse her request. Her only request."

Ingrid handed me another note. She had informed her contact that Agent Rick is a Russian double agent. No wonder she had to meet those agents. Though buried under the barn, they probably had already sent the intelligence to headquarter to implicate *Groucho*. After eliminating Rick, the Agency would have to put together another team to go after Dr. Tang. By that time, surveillance satellites and video cameras wouldn't be able to locate the fugitive anymore and the Agency might have enough data on CP to ignore him. I could only admire Ingrid's courage, determination, and trust born of love. If only they lived in a different world, even if Francisco's wasteland. Beyond the treetops, more clouds twirled above the flaming cabin's plume of smoke. More fog and perhaps rain to smother this nightmare.

"No, you couldn't." Neither could I. Unlike Francisco, who would seize the glory for himself, I would allow Ingrid to sacrifice herself and she would fulfill her destiny and become the heroine.

I might not see Ingrid again, so I studied the color of her eyes, the curvatures of her lips, and the lock of hair against her ear. Of course, she is Alpha's sister. She had tried but failed to save him, and she stabbed me to avenge her brother, to try to eliminate this sadist, this psychopath. At the hospital, she had poisoned me. And later with the spaghetti. I would have died more than once if I hadn't already died. I should have died to escape from the past, the pain, and the nightmares. Anyway, she succeeded when the Agency took away her memory. She must never remember my crime. She should just dwell in a hillside cabin as if she had never known me, as if she had never had a brother. She shouldn't have wasted her youth on me, a psychopath, a sadist, a murderer. Now, rather than waste more years on the past, she would stroll across the moonlit meadow with Dr. Tang and delight in their shadows merging under the shifting light.

Still, I would like her to recognize me and hate me. A selfish desire.

While Ingrid cleaned her face, Dr. Tang said, "She was close to her brother and the grief continued through the years. Her time as a rebel sharpened the pain rather than relieved it. I tried to persuade her not to take revenge, but I failed. And she refused to mention the killer, probably didn't want me to stop her."

She would soon see the sun. She should focus on the future and forget the past, the opposite of what I had pursued.

Unlike Dr. Tang, I couldn't forgive myself, and I could afford not to. I would carry the pain of murdering her brother throughout my life, centuries given this body. Even taking on her pain, her grief, her suffering. The pain would remind me how I had wounded her. Guilty, forever. Condemned, forever. Without mercy, without pardon, without redemption. Long live eternal judgment and damnation.

While Dr. Tang and I cleaned our faces, a boom shook the woods, and a gust carried dust and dirt and splinters into the barn. The cabin's debris still burned, but farther down the road, probably where we had parked our vehicles, another plume of smoke rose above the trees. Either the rebels had hunted down Agent Rick or they had met their ends.

The sounds I had heard in the woods bothered me. I might not be able to defend Ingrid and Dr. Tang against the agents.

I pulled them deeper into the barn as the two rebels charged out, either seeking or fleeing from the enemies. Two pops as if someone opened champagne bottles, and the rebels fell and twitched on the ground.

The branches didn't move. No twigs snapped. The sniper must be aiming his rifle at us. I could probably parry his bullet but might not be able to protect Ingrid and Dr. Tang.

Agent Rick might have contacted other rogue agents to help him finish his job. If so, even if the intelligence agents should come, they would only find our bullet-filled bodies. I had a chance to be a hero, but unlike Francisco, I didn't want to. How could I dream of such a hyena? How could he dream of such a mouse?

"They're after me for the CP data. Won't kill me. I can bargain with them for Ingrid's safety." Dr. Tang held Ingrid's hand. "Or, if you prefer. Take Ingrid with you. You can protect her. In that case, I'll surrender and let you have a chance to escape."

Sure, I could wave my arms and walk away, and let those agents surround and seize them. Not my problem. Not when I had died, not when I cared about nada. Not when I was no hero. But his words ignited a feeling, a hope and a vision. I pulled out the pistol, not sure why the hell I didn't just rely on my superhuman power. Even without a body, even with just a brain, I cared about them, those sensations evoked from my memory. They had to walk toward the sunset holding hands. They had to walk into a new tomorrow, one that I wouldn't have a part in. Hope and happiness had to continue in them even as these moods dissipated in me. The inscription on my tombstone: not the sadist who had killed Alpha, but the amnesiac who sacrificed himself to save Ingrid and Dr. Tang.

"What's the best strategy for escape?" I hid behind a pile of hay and peeked through the window. If Agent Rick had returned with his thugs, he probably had his henchmen at the tunnel's other end. So the sniper, discovering we were gone, would bring his colleagues into the tunnel and trap us inside. Rick wouldn't harm Dr. Tang or me, but he didn't need Ingrid and would eliminate her.

When Dr. Tang grasped my arm, I said, "Glad we agree that's the best plan to escape. You don't have to like it. And don't underestimate me." I looked forward to carrying out the plan. For the first time since waking up in the fake prison, I found myself and glimpsed at my future. I had to live, to relish my choice and my action, even if just for minutes. To freedom. To life.

They would hide in the tunnel and I would impersonate Dr. Tang and emerge from the barn, luring away and hunting down the hunters. Agent Rick would have to gather his thugs from the tunnel's other end to chase after me. Meanwhile, Dr. Tang would guard the tunnel and surprise any thug who tried to get in. After the thugs had chased after me, he and Ingrid would leave the barn and escape in his car.

Dr. Tang couldn't disagree. I could deal with the sniper and he had to take care of Ingrid. I would be the hero even if I didn't want to.

"Send me pictures of pines and spruces, of the valley and lake, and of the mountain ridges thrusting into the clouds." I didn't let him protest. No one could stop me, not even he.

I stepped out of the barn toward the two rebels. A single bullet penetrated each forehead. Perfect aim. Stooping down I took their rifles and grenades and returned to the barn. The sniper didn't try to scare me with a bullet.

I gave the rifles and grenades to Dr. Tang and asked him to take care of Ingrid. For her sake, he would play a coward. I took Dr. Tang's raincoat, shook his hand and said he was my friend. Kissed Ingrid on the cheek, a last farewell. I looked forward to sacrificing my life and helping them escape. I imagined charging on horseback and aiming my pistol at the agents' semiautomatic shotguns while sand swirled under the setting sun.

After they had stepped into the tunnel, I closed the trapdoor but kept it ajar with the whip. Then covered the trapdoor with hay, and put on the raincoat and the straw hat.

Behind the window, I aimed the pistol at the trees and pulled the trigger, then hid behind a barrel in the stall. The fire crackled and the leaves rustled. Several minutes later, I fired another shot through the window.

A branch cracked. The leaves swooshed. Footfalls among the trees. I waited for the agent to approach, mulling over whether to shoot him, but to my surprise, the footfalls receded. Maybe this agent was baiting me while the others aimed their weapons at my forehead and heart.

I didn't mind playing the game. I walked out of the barn, expecting eyes to lock onto my every step, and followed the footfalls while the bonfire warmed my back. When a breeze wafted through the woods, the smoke greeted me, a slap on my face. I inhaled fumes into my metal lungs and imagined Dr. Tang and Ingrid fleeing from the tunnel, the woods, the country, to a better land, a land of sunshine and breeze, of meadow and stream and of swallowtails circling lilacs. As for me, living a death like no other carcass. The air stuffy, the road slippery, the corpses stiff, through their woes, consoled me. Why would I want a face to feel the ash, a nose to smell the blood, and ears to listen to the whistling bullets?

The leaves swirled under a gust as I approached the elbow in the road. I seized a tree trunk with both hands and snapped it. Why would I want a body, to maintain, to suffer, to decay? I relished the freedom, a mind without a body, like alcohol without intoxication or love without breakups. This immortal realm.

Yet, my youth, like a specter hanging onto a soul, haunted me through the woods. I shouldn't have promised Dr. Tang not to destroy my brain, but maybe I could erase my memory again in Russia. Instead of just severing the link to it, I would wipe out that memory, deactivating the neurons. I stopped before the headstone and read the fading words *My Beloved Alpha*. My memory should have faded along with the inscription. I stabbed the dagger into the ground, its handle pointing at the headstone.

"If you want to impersonate Rainier, lose a few pounds."

The specter from my past walked up to the headstone, a rifle in hand.

Dolly. The same eyes as when she had played Molly, but now piercing into my mechanical heart. The same lips, but tightened as if about to spit.

"Was expecting Agent Rick. He wouldn't have known Dr. Tang like you do." I had kissed those lips and caressed that face, and through them learned about Molly, whom I loved, even as I despised the face before me. I imagined Molly taking notes as her master had when imitating her transient global amnesia. She had been Dolly all along and only my interpretation, born of ignorance or enlightenment, created fact or fiction. In the other illusion, I met Molly; in this one, Dolly; in still another...

"You should appreciate the manpower and effort to recover your memory. Wouldn't have done it for anyone else." Dolly stooped before the headstone and straightened it. For a second, her navy-blue cardigan and turquoise pants, and even the lock of blonde hair curving over her ear reminded me of Ingrid. "See, the truth is better for catharsis than whisky or scotch."

With Dolly's help, I had stored the CP data from the Moscow double agent into my mind using PC, SP, or CP. The password from the Guzman code unlocked the file in my head. However, the data is the memory I volunteered to erase. The memory of having killed Alpha in HYMN1 many years ago. The Russian researchers had stored the data in case I wanted it back. Dolly stole the file so she could return my memory, but she didn't program it into my mind so I would have to jump through the hoops to retrieve my memory. So I could claim the reward of my effort: the guilt and pain of my past atrocity. As for the research data on CP, she wasted no time in implementing and testing it.

"Should've checked with your comrades down the hallway. Then you would've known I'd died in the accident." I stooped down to pick up several withered white chrysanthemum petals. Had Francisco's brother killed their father here? My mind probably created the spot from repressed memories.

"These androids should be very lifelike. Feel pain just like me. Suffer just like me. And in some way, even more sensitive, with these refined sensors and neural networks. I hope so. I hope you enjoy your suffering as no one ever had. That'll give me pleasure." She swept away the foliages with the rifle butt and pulled out the thorns crawling up the headstone. She didn't seem happy; she wasn't enjoying my pain and suffering. A shame.

"Noble of you to take up an android's cause." I tossed the petals onto Alpha's headstone. "But Molly—"

"You killed him, my beloved Alpha." She caressed the headstone. "That night, we were going to make love under the stars to seal our love. We would've been so happy. But you, a sadistic psychopath, took that from us, from me."

"The shot in the head."

"Part of the plan."

"How could you kill her, your own clone, the same blood, the same flesh? You're a cold-blooded killer. You're a sadistic psychopath. Just like me." I drew out the dagger and pointed it at her abdomen. I should stab her and avenge Molly's death, but when she approached as if daring me, I tossed the blade into the stream.

The water splashed onto her hair and the dagger sank under the water as my memories into oblivion.

"She was only a clone. She existed to serve me." Dolly pushed the rifle barrel against my solar plexus. "Anyway, you never knew her; you were with me, not her, during that time. How could you have feelings for her? Don't be such a hypocrite."

"And how can you not have feelings for her?" I restrained myself from grabbing the barrel and pushing the butt against her gut, and just walked around the rifle. "Did that pedophile really rape her?"

"He did what a pedophile does. Just as you did what a psychopath does."

"How could you make love to me when you hated me so much?" The very thought nauseated me, a sadistic killer.

"You don't understand dedication and loyalty. You don't understand mission and purpose. Your don't understand pain and suffering. You don't understand hatred and love." She spat in my face. "How dare you compare yourself to me? My love for Alpha, my hatred toward you, the pain and suffering in my guts are stronger and mightier than your disgust."

She probably shot Molly in the temple, cleaned the revolver, and showered while her clone bled to death next door. I grieved for Molly. I pitied Dolly and myself for plunging into the abyss. I punched the tree trunk and thrust my fist though the wood, but couldn't vent those feelings.

"It seemed right to end everything here, where everything had started." She straightened up while the wind played with her hair.

"But not yet, one more thing—" I must give Dr. Tang and Ingrid more time to flee before ending what I had started twenty-two years ago. To show I cared about my friends.

"Thank you for helping Rainier and his girl escape." For a second, hatred and bitterness fled from her face and I glimpsed the girl in love with Alpha.

"Thank you for helping me help them." I understood why Dr. Tang had loved her. Even as I hated her, I could love her.

"That's why I'm here." She slammed the rifle into the ground, smashing a stone. "Why shouldn't I let him escape? Just wish I'm escaping with him."

"You had your chance five years ago, but let it go. You let happiness go." I handed her the meadow painting I had kept in my backpack with my laptop. I pitied her as I pitied myself. I despised her as I despised myself.

"No, you took away my chance twenty-two years ago." She took the painting, her hand shaking. "Just as you took away my painting."

"Should've given the painting to Dr. Tang, but no, you blew it. Now, there's only regret." I longed to hold onto Molly, but must confront the surfs without the lifesaver.

"Maybe, just maybe… I might've … I might really have… but that's in the past. I've given that up, in exchange for this, giving you enough pain to last a few lifetimes." She set the painting on fire with her lighter.

"You are piteous, giving up love for revenge, for my suffering, for this fire. What is my suffering compare to love? You've sacrificed in vain. You could've fled with Dr. Tang. But I'm glad Ingrid has replaced you. She, not you, deserves him."

The painting burned on the ground next to the headstone. She had burned it to raze her love and I would testify to her vow. After the fire had ended, only the ash remained with her, and me.

"Don't say you're sorry," she said, her breaths hot against my face. "We're beyond apologies and amends. Everything must play out to the end according to justice and natural laws. No redemption for you or me. Only the inferno."

"None expected. But first, we help Dr. Tang and Ingrid escape this hell. Then onto my hells." I walked toward the smoke and the parked van and trucks. "By the way, if goons who don't look like agents come with sub-machine guns, grenades and rockets, don't be alarmed. Only the Mexican client completing the deal. You'd probably introduced us, though I still can't remember him. Of course, since I don't have any data, they'd kill you and me."

"Don't you realize Pratt forged your handwriting?" Dolly kissed the headstone and scattered the ash. "And remember? When he lies, his eyelids twitch. You must've lost your common sense along with your memory. A bonus. Good for you." The corner of her mouth twitched and she almost grinned, probably from satisfaction. Almost, but not quite.

By then, I didn't care whether a customer would vent his frustration on me. Another team of goons coming after me might help me. Since the Mexican client didn't exist, he would miss the bash. Tough luck for him.

"How about my killing Pratt's son? Was that a lie also?"

"You showed Pratt you mean business. It worked. He was so scared afterward that he hid his face. That coward." She walked shoulder-to-shoulder with me.

So, I had murdered a boy without remorse to threaten Pratt. I hadn't changed and wouldn't change, a sadist and a psychopath, before, now and forever, as immutable as the fundamental constants of the universe. I should point a gun at my head and pull the trigger. I should kill this murderer, this monster. So, I belong in this world, with Dolly and Pratt and Rick and Beta and Gamma, my comrades in bloodshed.

"Come on, let's go. You'll have time to relish killing an innocent boy."

When we reached the vehicles, the van was burning and several charred figures reclined against the seats. The leader and two rebels lay on the ground and leaves had gathered around them, the swishing a dirge to mourn the departed souls and escort them to the void. "You should deactivate the other bombs. In case Dr. Tang decides to take the truck instead of his car." I bent down to check the rebel leader's pulse to confirm she was dead. Her right hand was reaching for a locket three feet away. I picked it up and after finding her son's photo inside, put it in her hand. Did she think about her last moments when she gutted Pratt?

Would she have spared him the pain and suffering? Maybe the fighting and the sabotages and the bloodshed had wiped away her humanity and she lived for a moment when she tortured her ex-husband. Maybe, she also belonged in this world.

While Dolly deactivated the bombs in the trucks, I recalled killing Alpha, a film rewinding again and again in my mind. I plunged the knife into his abdomen. He groaned. His muscles convulsed. His blood squirted onto my wrist.

Memory like a wormhole linked that moment with the present and revived Alpha, who now seemed to stand beside me, next to Dr. Tang's car. Not only the boy but also my younger self, who winked as if sealing a deal, a covenant between fiends. Though time separated me from this other self through the years and pain and regret, memories and emotions integrated us along a different dimension. Through our camaraderie in this other dimension, his flesh and blood united with my switches and circuits, his excitement with my disgust, as mystics with their gods through meditation and contemplation. But my consciousness refused to bow down to spatial-temporal or biological laws. Refused to embrace the excitement and disgust as if they were diamonds amid coal and ash. Not only that, the linkage had induced pain sharp enough to oppose time's erosion, to bloom into a mature and lasting suffering, to remind the future I how this present self opposed that past ego. Memory, like an obsession, refused to die without a struggle against the will. The struggle, for a moment, delivered me from the woods into a sea of dunes and sweat poured down my forehead and back, the heat burning my head and my torso. I wouldn't bow to the other self, this sadist and demon, this stranger trying to claim my mind and heart.

Dr. Tang has a *thick*, subjective present with a fruitful past and potential futures. But I would relinquish my past through cerebral programming, and thus nip off possible futures and live a *thin*, dimensionless present. I would rather live without past and future than with that phantom trailing my every step.

After Dolly had deactivated the two bombs, we walked down a dirt road deep into the woods where a warbler welcomed us with its trill. About fifty yards into the trail, we reached her car. We would pretend to be Dr. Tang and Ingrid and lure away the agents. Inside the car, the seatbelt strapped a dummy in the backseat.

"That's you," Dolly said, after getting into the car.

"Very thoughtful."

She charted her course and followed the steps to the last details. With her helping Dr. Tang and Ingrid escape, I could sit back and watch the show. What *Last Supper* could she have prepared me?

She drove onto the main path where the van still burned, and after we left the maple woods and passed the HYMN1 sign, the car skirted the forest. The fog had dispersed but the clouds lingered and a southern breeze lifted leaves into the air as if to welcome my end. In the distance, several jeeps and trucks parked near a bush and men and women in black suits and pants guarded a shack. Agent Rick was talking on the phone.

"The other end of the tunnel. Ricky's waiting for Rainier and his girl." Dolly shoved her rifle onto my lap as three trucks came toward the shack from the other side of the road.

I held the rifle and aimed the telescope at Agent Rick.

"We came to help Rainier escape. Save your itchy fingers for the amusement park. Just get their attention." She stopped the car and pointed at the incoming trucks.

I aimed and shot a truck's tire and it swirled to the side and flipped sideways against a tree. Then waved to the thugs as they pointed their guns at us. Dolly turned the car around and retraced our path. Several booms echoed behind us but sounded as if they were shooting into the air. When I turned around, five sedans and the two trucks chased after us. No one had stayed around the shack. They must have spotted the dummy.

"It worked."

"Of course, I planned it."

Soon, we left the dirt path and reached the local road where hills brown and rocky rose on the left. Once in a while, we passed horses, cows, and sheep beside barns and windmills, but more often, only the ecru meeting the gray at the horizon. Behind us, the goon squad kicked up a dust trail that turned the sky sallow.

"Glad I could help Dr. Tang and Ingrid escape." I put the rifle on the backseat.

"I'm, too. Would've been happier if it weren't for you."

I forgave Dolly for recovering my memory, but couldn't forgive her for killing Molly. Of course, my thrusting the dagger into Alpha and taking his life had turned her into the sadist who murdered her clone. My hand might as well have pulled the trigger and killed the woman whom I learned to care about only after her death. In my mind's eyes, the bullet entered Molly's head and I had to shake my head to toss away the image.

"Where're we going?"

"I planned a surprise."

"For them or for me?"

"Both."

I looked forward to my *Last Supper* and leaned back to view the occasional shrubs in the fog. On the roadside, vultures feasted on a dead deer beside a withering tree. Beside me, Dolly rushed to her banquet. About three hours later, the sky darkened, but the plume of dust still tailed us. After passing several farms, she pointed at the tavern ahead and said, "Here we are."

I would soon find out where is *here*, so I didn't ask. With Dr. Tang and Ingrid out of the country, I could strut into hell. With Dolly, I expected hell to the nth power. We got off the road and parked next to the tavern, two dozen cactuses growing around it. For all I cared, I could be walking among palms or pines. After we got off the car, she hid the dummy in the trunk and took the rifle.

At the entrance, a sign displayed the words THE END OF THE ROAD. Behind the sign, the cherry wooded tavern evoked the sense of majestic decay. The metal eaves and the shingles on the slanting roof had discolored and almost faded into the silver sky. The front door was ajar and the opening seemed to invite me into the engulfing darkness.

"Everything will end here." Dolly knocked on the sign several times with the rifle. "I wouldn't disappoint you, I promise."

She wouldn't. Dusk had arrived and I wished Dr. Tang and Ingrid happiness in a new land. If the doctor didn't lie about the sun, it would shine on them tomorrow though I wouldn't be enjoying it. Still, I would like to see it. In the distance, the dust trail like an apparition raced toward us and I caressed the sign, my epitaph. Only in the end did I see the vultures feasting on the deer. If wisdom had visited me sooner I wouldn't have wasted my time recovering my memory, looking for my past. I inhaled the evening air and treaded to the front door and opening it entered the tavern. I wouldn't come out.

I descended a flight of stairs to another door, two torches lighting the entry. What happened to electric or oil lamps? I didn't linger at the entrance, just opened the door and entered. Light from the torches along the left and right walls smeared flickering shadows onto the floor. At the other end of the room, where the altar stood, Agent Rick the Priest was offering a lamb. I had returned to the Underground Temple's sanctuary. Yes, everything began here and would end here, also.

CHAPTER 54 - FRANCISCO

October 29, 2011

Holy Dostoevsky. Never expected the amnesiac to meet his doom in the Underground Temple. For that matter, never expected the Temple to appear in my dream. And imagine that, Agent Rick, who looked like the chief lunatic, was indeed the Priest. Not quite. It was Nick. After helping the amnesiac escape, *Skippy* stayed long enough in the Intelligence Agency to help his friend (not the amnesiac) dodge the agents. Then took the job as a priest-in-training. Meager pay but benefits included meals and lodging in addition to three weeks of vacation, one week of sick leave, and fifteen holidays, not to mention health insurance. I certainly didn't have such benefits as the Underground Temple Prophet. That's why I quitted.

Anyway, *Skippy* waved to Descartes, while tending his lamb. The aroma of burnt fat wafting through the air.

Dolly followed Descartes into the sanctuary and locked the door. "Don't waste time trying to break it down. It's titanium." She knocked on the door twice with her rifle butt. "So, just wait for the surprise ending. By the way, an *old friend* is waiting."

Descartes put the straw hat on the stone table beside the altar and waved to Nick.

Before old Fyodor's portraits, he shut his eyes and hoped to wake up in an alternate universe where he weaves baskets to make a living and travels with Ingrid or Molly to the Pacific Islands, but when he opened his eyes, he remained in the Underground Temple. I wouldn't dream a different dream. My dreams had converged into his plight, so he should swallow the fate I'd served him. He should've never crossed good old Francisco. He should've known I'd always win.

"Watching you fall for *Molly* and expecting you to suffer alleviated some pain," Dolly said, "Of course, I didn't hate you any less." About a year ago, she'd persuaded Descartes, a third-rated agent, to earn his deserved retirement rather than just receive government handouts, the pittance they called salary and pension. She recruited him to hide the CP data that she should've handed to the Intelligence Agency. Of course, she was only luring the dunce into a trap. She'd planned her revenge since joining the Agency and she met Dr. Tang to learn about CP. Just didn't expect to fall in love and care about the doctor. Well, she did. Another fool.

Instead of punching her for killing Molly, Descartes smashed the stand next to the altar. The loser.

"Don't expect me to pity you." She kicked aside the broken stand and took off her coat and after handing it to Nick, she loaded her rifle. "At least you can look forward to my surprise."

"The CP data could've helped you retire. But you abandoned it for revenge, just as you had sacrificed love for hate." Descartes considered torturing her and forcing her to enter the front door's access code, but the coward hesitated. Again.

"It IS valuable. It WILL help me retire. I don't make mistakes."

"I should congratulate you for recovering my memory with the CP technology." As the aroma of grilled lamb tickled his nose, Descartes yearned to taste freedom, to sail across the Pacific, to trek into the Himalayas, to pass a winter at the North Pole. To live life. Which drifted beyond his reach as the smoke thickened. When he woke up in that abandoned school, he should've taken Ingrid to the Usual Café for a slice of durian pie, then eloped with her. Now, he could only dream.

"Maybe Rainier would've learned CP in such a short time, not anyone else. Certainly not me. So sorry, you didn't get to be my guinea pig. Only used SP. Now though, after six months, that's a different story. As you'll see."

"I'm still waiting for your surprise. And that *friend* you mentioned." Descartes took the leg-of-lamb and bit into it. At last, a gutsy move. Of course, I would've taken the offering meant for Fyodor as soon as I'd entered the hall, not that I cared much about lamb. As I'd said, I prefer beef. He searched the sanctuary for a door that Dolly and Beta might've

missed. He yearned to inhale the outside air again and regretted not having subdued Dolly before entering the sanctuary. More regrets.

"Don't think about leaving the sanctuary." She tapped the rifle on the
floor. "Death will be heaven and you don't deserve it. I have something
better."

As Descartes munched on the lamb and tried to savor the juice
flowing inside his synthetic mouth, he had to agree. He wished for
cheesecake and Merlot. He wished for sunshine. Well, just wishes. After
finishing the lamb, he returned the bone to Nick and thanked him for the
offering.

"After the accident, you tried to recover your memory. Didn't you?
Well, you got what you need, not what you want, that grisly incident in
gory details. Nothing else. Should thank me." Dolly took the bone from
Nick and said, "I'll need it later."

"Yes, I must thank you for recovering my nightmare and returning
those sleepless nights. How should I express my gratitude?" Descartes
ripped off a corner of the stone table and squeezed his fist and fragments
fell onto the floor. "Before going to Moscow, I used to relive that incident every night." I tried to calm him so he could plan his escape, but
somehow couldn't control his emotions, damn it. I might need more
practice to direct my dreams. Then again, he might be the problem.

"But how could I be a psychopath if the memory continues to bother
me?"

"Believe me, you're a psychopath, through and through." Dolly
jabbed the bone into the amnesiac's solar plexus.

Dr. Tang doesn't think so. And I'm sure Ingrid doesn't either.

He rejoiced in his friends not considering him a monster, but he was
a psychopath. As they say, once a psychopath, always a psychopath. You
know, fate and destiny and all that crap.

After directing Nick to watch the amnesiac, Dolly went to fetch the
old friend. When she'd left, the priest skipped down the altar steps and
whispered, "Well, old chap. This is a trap. You'll never get out alive. If
you want to escape, I can take you to the escape tunnel. Otherwise, I'll
get you one last drink. They've got neat drinks here, better than the muck
in that fake hospital." Damn it, the abandoned school. *Skippy* couldn't
even get his realities straight. Another feeble mind.

Descartes thanked Nick and followed him across the sanctuary to a
side door under a Dostoevsky portrait, but neither of them could open it.
Titanium door. Nick led Descartes to the back of the altar and stepped
into the temple's holy ground. They passed the Prophet Office to the

service elevator, but when *Skippy* entered the access code, the loud speaker on the wall announced he needed a new one. Dolly had changed it to prevent the amnesiac from escaping.

Descartes patted Nick on the shoulder and urged him to stay in the Priest Office and avoid the crossfire and bloodshed in the sanctuary.

"But Doc asked me to do what I can," Nick said. "How else could he get the info?" So, Nick had been channeling info to Dr. Tang even after leaving the Intelligence Agency. If Ricky found out, he would remove Nick's hippocampus.

While the priest searched for a hidden exit, in the Prophet Office, my office, Descartes typed his last entry into his laptop. He emailed his journal to Dr. Tang and Mrs. McCoy, hoping they'd publicize the testimony of a self without a past, a mind without a body, an android without a soul. Then hid the laptop in my drawer.

Nick returned with a map and pointed at a mark. "An old exit that we don't use anymore. At the farther side of the sanctuary. I didn't even know it exists. Should be locked but it's old, so I guess it's wood, not titanium." The door through which I'd first entered the Underground Temple. Would he come into my world through that door? Would I face him, my dream self?

At that moment, Descartes lusted for freedom and he took the map and urged the priest to lead the way. Nick was tiptoeing through the sanctuary when Gamma, in an army uniform, stepped through a side door twirling a serrated whip.

"So, all good things do come to an end." He approached them and tapped the amnesiac's nose with the whip. "By the way, you're wrong. I'm not Gamma. I'm Beta. You should've spotted the difference with your super-vision."

"As I said, same ugly face."

Though I created and directed this scene, I couldn't distinguish the two clones. Maybe, I had confused this dream with another one, another reality for Descartes.

"Do you know why Dolly loved Alpha?"

"Should I know the intricacies of the heart? I'm only an android with a synthetic heart, the beats synchronized to a cesium clock." Descartes seized the whip and threw it into the fire. The fool tried to amuse me but I didn't laugh. The timing was off, as usual. If he'd known the clone's secret, he'd shove the whip down the creep's throat. Then again, maybe not. No guts, you know.

"My friend, playing the fool to entertain me won't help." Beta dusted his uniform and sighed, as if pitying the amnesiac, but he looked forward to the finale, to removing the brain from the android.

"When have you become my friend?" Descartes was about to subdue the clone and head toward the back door when his left leg stiffened and he couldn't lift it. Just as in Pratt's apartment. He thought Dolly or Beta had shut down his circuitry.

Well, a fool is a fool is a fool, or some crap like that.

"I give you permission to try to leave, but not permission to leave. Hope your amnesia hasn't nixed your reasoning." Beta walked to the altar and fetched a bottle of whiskey and three glasses from the compartment below. Then leaned against the stone table and poured a glass.

"You're forgetting one thing," Descartes said.

"You want a quick death? Sorry, no can do. I wish I could, but that's beyond my power. Bureaucracy and red tapes, as usual. You'd have to petition my superior's superior for permission." Beta asked Nick to bring in three chairs. "Of course, you'd have to wait a while since our head-quarter was destroyed. Anyway, red tapes take time, you can understand." He offered Descartes the glass.

Instead of accepting the glass, Descartes took the watch from Beta's pocket before the clone could stop him. "How much bonus did you get for destroying the IAB?"

"Be a nice android and give me back my watch." The clone drank the whiskey. "If you want one, I'll get you another. That's been mine since I was created."

"No, this isn't your watch. But Dr. Tang's gift to Gamma." He flipped open the cover to reveal the word *Tang*.

Holy Dostoevsky, Dr. Tang is sneaky. Somehow I couldn't penetrate his mind, though I created him. Did he use CP to shield his thoughts from me? Did he use CP on me? I also didn't realize Gamma was Beta in disguise. Am I losing my touch because of what happened to Faith?

"Answer one question." Descartes took out Gamma's watch, which Dr. Tang had given him, and put it on the stone table. "How did you co-ordinate bombing the building when you were inside killing the agents?" He grasped his left leg and shook it but it wouldn't respond.

The clone finished the whiskey and smiled, as if daring him to smash the watch.

Descartes swung the watch on its chain in front of Beta's nose and said, "You mean this is Gamma's and not yours? In that case, goodbye watch." He tightened his fist.

"Like any good manager, he delegated the bombing to his subordinates." Dolly emerged from a side door, rifle in right hand and the bone in left. "Now, be a good android and give him back the watch."

"Of course, my sidekick took control while I sneaked out of the building and ordered it destroyed. I was giving the command while you slept in the alley with spaghetti dangling out of your mouth. Well, you can see I'm alive and well. Now, if you don't mind, that's mine." Beta, a.k.a. Gamma, grabbed his pocket watch. He checked the cover and polished the surface with a handkerchief before pocketing it. "I had to blow up the IAB to create the publicity and the fear, to promote my cause, to get me elected to the Senate. Part of the election campaign." He took out a durian pie from the compartment under the altar. "I cleaned the dungeon shelves. And prepared a spot for your brain, with a forest view, not that you'd care. But the visitors could observe your brain. You know, like Lenin."

"What will your cronies shoot me with? Armor-piercing bullets?" Descartes dusted the stone table with his handkerchief and knocked on the tabletop several times and he karate-chopped another corner off the stone table and wiped his palms.

Nick was carrying three folding chairs into the sanctuary when the slab fell onto the floor. He dropped the chairs and the clangs echoed throughout the hall, the rumble shaking dust off the pillars and beams. Beta backed away until his back hit the wall and knocked down a torch. The durian pie dropped onto the floor. What a waste. If I were Beta, I would've eaten the pie before backing to the wall.

Descartes tried to limp toward the back door but he couldn't lift his right leg, standing still as he had in Pratt's apartment. He turned to Dolly and waited for her to sneer and reveal her remote controller.

She raised the rifle and said, "Have a few more drinks. I'm in the mood for brandy, to celebrate this occasion. And here's to Alpha. May he rest in peace." She shot down a portrait on the left wall and waved the lamb shank. "Anyway, this bone's not for you." Like the amnesiac, she was a psychopath through and through, and they belonged together in their cesspool of a world. I wanted nothing to do with them. I tried to wake up from the dream, but somehow, I couldn't. Damn it. Fyodor, bring fire and brimstones on them.

Outside the hall, men shouted. Ricky and his troop had arrived. Descartes couldn't remember ever living. He had to taste life, even if just for a few months, or a few days. He'd trek across the Swiss Alps, scale the

Himalayas, and swim in the Arctic. He had to escape the Underground Temple and travel to Moscow, to have his memory removed, once again.

"Never mind the agents." Dolly picked up a chair and unfolded it. "Since you now regret your crime, I won't allow anyone to destroy you. You'll live for many years. I promise. At least a century."

Beta took out a whistle and said, "This trick will impress you."

Descartes grasped his left leg and stepped forward and did the same with his right. His mechanical pump thumped as he realized he could escape and breathe the outside air. He might even see the sun. "If you aren't going to arrest me, I'm leaving. I don't care for Agent Rick's face." He turned to Nick and said, "Of course, I don't mind yours." He limped toward the backdoor, but only after three steps, the front door flew toward him and he had to duck

Ricky stepped into the sanctuary. Two agents in black suits followed him into the hall and he motioned for one to get a folding chair, then pointed at Nick, who cowered behind the amnesiac. "Get out."

Descartes glanced at the entrance thinking about the cloudy sky outside, dreaming of tomorrow's sun, but when he tried to run for the entrance, his legs betrayed him.

"Where's Tang?" Ricky sat on the chair keeping his hands inside the coat pockets. "Don't try to escape. I have the place surrounded."

"With you three?" Beta swung the whistle by its cord. "By the way, we know you're a Russian double-agent and there's a reward on your head. Yeah, bad news travels fast. Anyway, I look forward to the reward for my Christmas vacation in the Bahamas. Thanks in advance."

"I don't have time for bullshit," Ricky said. "And you won't need any vacations where you're going."

While the two men bickered, Descartes whispered to Nick to get two five-foot lead pipes. After *Skippy* had left the sanctuary, the amnesiac licked his lips trying to taste freedom. Gathering saliva in his mouth. And preparing to attack.

"Oh, your men. They're probably resting in peace. In a much better place than you're, I must say." Dolly tapped the chair's leg with the bone as if sending a Morse code. "Do you know cactuses can maim and even kill?"

Ricky pulled out a remote controller and pressed a button before the amnesiac could grab a piece of the stone table. Descartes couldn't move his right arm.

"Tang, I want him," Ricky said.

Descartes pointed at the straw hat on the table and Dolly picked up Dr. Tang's coat and said, "Isn't that a nice coat? That's Rainier's favorite raincoat. But this outfit here, my own."

Ricky pointed the device at Descartes. "I'll snip every wire in your body."

As Descartes reached for a piece of the table, Beta blew the whistle and a figure leaped out of a side entrance and charged at the angry agent. Before Ricky could dodge, it bit his wrist and he dropped the remote controller. The two henchmen pulled out their guns but before they could shoot the beast, six pistols pointed at their heads.

Six cactuses behind the henchmen held the pistols.

Beta waved his hand and the cactuses took the two henchmen out of the sanctuary.

Meanwhile, Ricky wrestled with the jaw to get those teeth off his wrist, but the beast with an inmate's uniform refused to let go. They rolled over and over and hit the altar. Ricky kicked the beast several times in the butt, but it still wouldn't let go. Well, he didn't know how to kick butts.

"Say please." Beta stood akimbo and watched the struggle. When Ricky begged for mercy, the clone blew the whistle and the beast retreated.

During the dogfight, Descartes picked up his legs one at a time with his left hand and moved toward the remote controller, but when he realized Mr. Smith was biting Ricky, he stumbled and fell onto the floor. He crawled toward the controller but Dolly picked it up, pressed a button and said, "Actually, we brought the dog for you, not for that angry bird."

Descartes could move his legs. He leaped up, prepared to escape the nightmare, but he still had to help Mr. Smith, the poor man. He bent his knees to hop toward Dolly but she pressed a button, and again he couldn't control his legs. He bent down and picked up a slab, smoothing it into a stone ball. The show-off.

Beta handcuffed Ricky and took his badge and wallet, then called a cactus to take him away.

"We wanted Pratt for the show," Dolly said, "but he got himself gutted. So we have to find a replacement. Lucky he's also an *old friend* of yours."

Descartes would've preferred Pratt there so he could spit in his face for the lies the ruffian had vomited out to foul up his life. As he recalled the ruffian wobbling down the stairs and falling onto the sidewalk, he realized he'd never partnered with the man. Pratt had tried to steal the data from Dolly, so the amnesiac, to scare him away, killed his son. He thought the rogue agent had tried to trick him into giving up the CP data, but of course, he erred again.

Mr. Smith growled and bore his teeth, but when Beta blew the whistle, he stooped and hung his hands in front of his chest.

"Down, boy. Be nice to this android." Beta blew twice and Mr. Smith barked. "A cheap trick. But works on weak minds." He blew three times and Mr. Smith stuck out his tongue and panted. A cheap trick, Beta got that right.

When Mr. Smith rolled over, Descartes imagined a legion of man-dogs lined up in columns waiting for the whistle to set them after their prey. Of course, this mind-control impressed me and I intended to learn it. I'd always believed in career training. For example, I'd learned to open a safe from a client in just a week.

"This is not SP or PC but CP, the next great thing in training agents and civilians. He's test subject Aleph." Beta patted Mr. Smith on the head.

"And you blamed Pratt for fleeing after that accident," Dolly said. "He was running from the agents to save his ass. Of course, he did pretend to be your partner in crime. On the other hand, I forgave him though he tried to kill me. No, that's nothing compared to what you did." She threw Mr. Smith the bone. "He's so happy now. Not a thing to worry about. And Pratt would've been happy too if he hadn't gotten himself killed."

She pressed a button on the controller and Descartes dropped his right arm. He gathered saliva in his mouth and vowed to escape from them.

Even if he had to kill again.

He didn't want to snuff out another life, but he refused to surrender and live out the rest of his long life in a dungeon. Of course, he couldn't escape anymore than Pratt could breathe again.

As he prepared to spit at Dolly's hand, Nick returned to the sanctuary with the lead pipes. To distract the evil duo, Descartes swallowed his saliva and said, "You don't even have an iota of decency or an atom of humanity. Destroying their pasts and their lives? And for what? Revenge?"

He preached and preached as if in front of a pulpit. As the Prophet, I didn't even proselytized, not that I had to, to brainwash my troops. No wonder I despised the amnesiac.

"If you're a decent person, you would've destroyed the data and found another way for revenge."

"Well, when Pratt tried to kill her and steal the data, we had to reeducate him," Beta said. "He was lucky enough to get gutted. Of all the aspirations, he wanted to retire to the Bahamas. What a silly idea. He should've aspired to fight the rebel to the end."

"And Smith," Dolly said, "the nosy body. He took Molly from me. Lucky for him I didn't torture him."

"There's a line that we don't cross, that we can't cross." Descartes watched Nick set the pipes against the wall.

"Well, you'd crossed that line and eliminated mine when you killed Alpha. No more lines. Total freedom, free for all. Remember, all's fair in love and war." She pointed the remote controller and said, "Well, here's to your end."

Nick rushed up to Dolly and grabbed the controller before she could press the button. He retreated behind the altar as she tried to retake the device and he pointed it searching for the right button.

Beta blew the whistle and Mr. Smith barked and sprinted toward *Skippy*.

Nick pressed a button. Turned around. And entered the holy ground and shut the door as Mr. Smith smashed his shoulder into it.

Descartes felt his arms and legs. Clenched his fists. His heart pumped and his body heated up. Well, surprise, he rose above his stupor. Still, since his life as an android would end soon, he might as well blaze through his last few minutes. Go for it.

He smashed the stone table into several pieces and ran for Mr. Smith.

Nice move. Toward his end, he imitated my spunk, my grace, and my verve. Well, almost. Maybe, I did create him in my image, though I didn't intend it. Death can either make or break a guy, and in his case, he'd unleashed his potential. Bravo.

"Go ahead, kill that dog." Dolly opened the compartment below the altar and took out a bottle of Champagne, then poured a glass and drank a draft.

Descartes reached the door. Grabbed Mr. Smith. Tossed him across the sanctuary. The *dog* flew toward Beta, who ducked while sipping his whiskey, and crashed into a folding chair. Descartes ignored them. Turned toward Dolly.

She sipped the Champagne and said, "Do you feel the joy of torturing again? Let it engulf and consume you. Come, you want to take your revenge. Kill me and feel the excitement again. You're a psychopath and will always be."

He and Ingrid had lost their memories. Thousands of soldiers would march into fires, bombs, and radioactive bunkers and millions of citizens would chant slogans and hand over dissenters. Visions of this utopia prevented him from recalling a world he'd known, my world, and from remembering the streets of New York. He'd lost everything, not only his memories, when he woke up in that hospital/prison/school. His end had budded on that morning and blossomed as he faced his fate. For one thing, I, Francisco Guzman, who values freedom more than life, would never tolerate such a world. Never.

Descartes picked up the stone slab and smashed it against the altar, the concrete breaking into a dozen pieces as the altar collapsed and cracked in two. He dashed for the side entrance, not caring whether they'd shoot him. He wanted to breathe the outside air. He wanted to visit Dr. Tang and Ingrid. He wanted to escape Fyodor's gaze.

He left the altar. One step. Two steps. Passing Dolly. Three steps. Four steps. Stepping down the platform and marching toward the back door. The wind outside was calling him, the sun beckoning him to step into tomorrow's morning air. He'd shake Dr. Tang's hand and embrace Ingrid. He passed Mr. Smith, who'd fainted, and Beta, who backed away. Seventeen steps...

His legs froze. His arms froze. He turned his head and body and he froze as if posing for a centerfold. Dolly drank the Champagne and behind her, the door opened and Jack Conman entered and handed her the remote controller. The amnesiac should've done away with the crook when he had the chance, but he never planned ahead, just stumbling into his future, or lack of. Like a puppeteer, I tried to pull the amnesia's strings and will him into motion, but I couldn't. Damn this dream.

Dolly finished her drink and threw the glass into the altar. "And now, you suffer for all eternity." She approached and kicked his butt, and the poor soul collapsed onto the floor.

I tried to reach out and help him escape, but somehow, I lost control of this dream. I was there, observing, but couldn't even move a speck of damn dust. If only the amnesiac's misery would end sooner. If only I could end the dream, wake up, and return to my life...

***

I found myself above an operating theater on the third floor of the new Intelligence Agency Building, the room reeking of disinfectant and two strobes glaring at the operating table. With nanobots and computer-aided equipment, Dr. Jack Conman, now with a goatee and a glass eye, detached Descartes' brain from the artificial body while Dolly and Beta sipped coffee and watched the operation from the observation deck. As the neurosurgeon imitator removed the brain, the agent nodded in approval but Dolly only stared at the gray matter. I tried but couldn't sense her emotions or touch her thoughts as if she'd learned to shield her inner life from me, her creator.

After Conman confirmed the brain was alive, he put it in a jar with saline solution and connected tubes and wires to it. When the doctor had accessed the right and left insula through nanobots, Beta uploaded the video of the operation into the brain so it could *see* its last minutes in a body.

"We'll load his connectome into the computer for storage," Dolly said, "and very soon we'll upload everything into an artificial brain. That way, his memory wouldn't decay and he could remember every detail forever. We certainly don't want him to forget that he's a murderer and a sadist, a psychopath of the first degree."

The poor soul, who could've become me, had to endure his life imprisonment in a dungeon, everyday reliving the morning he'd killed Alpha. All the while remorseful. Until one day dementia would relieve his pain and suffering. No, of course not, with his connectome downloaded into an artificial brain, he'd savor his crime forever. Not the way I'd want to live. Of course, everyday he'd still dream of being me, Francisco, living in paradise, making love, eating durian pies, breaking into corporate databases, and earning certificates and trophies until I must build a gallery to house them. Lovely.

Glad I'm Francisco, not Descartes.

April 1, 2012

This morning, the sun peeped through the window between two skyscrapers while Virginia E. Boss showered and hummed a jingle. Next to the window, I admired the *horn concerto* below while the yellow roses I'd bought my neighbor yesterday bloomed on her windowsill. She'd been going to physical therapy for about half a year but still needed her wheelchair. I'd drive her to the clinic before going to the office and pick her up for lunch, and I looked forward to this ritual, sometimes even more than my work.

Yesterday, from an investment bank database I retrieved the deleted emails that confirmed a fund mismanager promoted subjunk-graded mortgage derivatives. While selling several hundred million dollars of financially engineered junk to his favorite clients, he'd hedged against them and earned almost a billion dollars, a respectable profit for a scam. The government had been onto the mismanager and the firm after the derivatives lost ninety percent of their values and two clients committed suicides, one leaping out of a Manhattan skyscraper and another overdosing on sleeping pills. After sending the emails to the government official, I'd called Ms. Boss to celebrate. Champagne and *pate de foie gras*.

I hadn't gone mad even after six months without dreams. In fact, I was flying above the clouds and swimming in the ocean. Must've been getting my REM sleep elsewhere. Last night, after making love with Ms. Boss, I finished Proust's *In Search of Lost Time*, six volumes and five thousand pages. Not that I cared much about M. de Charlus's many adventures or the infatuations of Swann, St. Loop and Marcel. Been enjoying steak, Merlot and sauna more than ever. Guess what, I even painted landscapes and composed piano concertos. Without having to dream of Descartes, my brain was on turbo.

Of course, if I'd dreamed of being the amnesiac, he'd have no legs to walk, no eyes to see, and no lips to kiss. Only his brain vegetating in a display, or maybe on a lab table, probes tickling the gray matter. So why bother? In the dream, he couldn't see or hear or do anything, except to recall killing Alpha in the woods, and of course to dream of my adventures in this world. But why'd I bother entering the dream's dream, and returning here and now? Why should I waste my mental energy? I might as well do nothing and stay here, awake. Logical, right?

I'd tried to find Ganesh and Faith but they seemed to have vanished, as if they'd never existed. Couldn't find a word on them even in the CIA or Interpol databases. If the nerd is my Guardian, he should hang around and shape my memories. I'd like warm memories with Faith. I'd like to forget Holly and the diamond lover. Of course, I could do these and more without him. Sure enough, he left so I wouldn't depend on him, so I could soar into the sky. So I vowed to succeed and not disappoint Fernando.

***

After breakfast, Ms. Boss left for LaGuardia Airport. Had to spy on an Alabama Congressman promoting family value while having an affair with a college student. Typical politician. Her client, a political rival, would pay five thousands dollars for pictures of the lovers in bed. She could've sent the Messenger, a.k.a. Agent Z, but had to get hands-on once in a while. She'd promised to share the pictures if I invited her for dinner. Not surprisingly, she enjoyed my cooking, medium-rare steak with sauté mushrooms and onions. Who wouldn't?

After putting the plates in the dishwasher, I took out a slice of durian pie. I was reviewing my journal and eating the pie, which had lost its zing since my last dream, when the doorbell rang. Had Ms. Boss forgotten her camera or returned for another kiss? When I opened the door, Holly walked into the living room with two glasses and a bottle of champagne. Kicking aside the socks and underwear to open a path to the sofa and sweeping my T-shirts and shorts from the sofa onto the floor. I hadn't seen her since the Guardian's demise but she looked as if she'd won a million bucks.

She closed my laptop with her elbow, put the bottle and glasses on top and said, "Don't waste time on the fiction you called your diary. You were never imaginative anyway."

"Why did you harm your ex-boyfriend? He was a nice man. But then, there's my neighbor and Suzie. You killed her, the innocent girl. And Faith, what you did to her." I kicked aside a T-shirt and shut the door. Couldn't forgive her for giving Faith's address to Clint. I considered torturing her to avenge Faith, but now, the pain paralyzed me. What'd happened to Fransuccesco?

"Faith surprised me. Didn't expect her to have the cunning to steal the old book from me." She poured two glasses of champagne and stared at the bubbles as if contemplating the mystery of life or the universe.

A while back I called Faith but her phone had been disconnected. I checked the government databases and tapped into the underground network, but couldn't trace her. Even the lunatics and my beggar associates couldn't locate her. Without her picture, I could only rely on the memory that I trust less and less each day to recall her smile and her voice.

"Would've liked to give you the book. You would've learned something."

"Would've preferred Faith kept her book. Would've also preferred Clint didn't harm her." I did learn from the underground man, as she'd soon find out.

"Well, those submissive types, when they get a chance, would erupt and vent their hatred. He surprised me. But anyway, Clint got what he deserved. And so will you. That's justice."

I secured the laptop. Didn't want to share my thoughts and feelings with her, not anymore. How could I have loved her and considered her my friend, even my best friend after Fernando? If only I were Descartes, the sadist. I couldn't even recall the tortures I'd prepared for Clint.

"I have something especially planned for the end. Something different from the mind trick." She handed me a glass of champagne.

"I would've preferred something more dramatic, like massacring a town, than just killing my father. I know. I know. Lies must have enough truth to make it stick. Some damn fool's wisdom."

"That diamond lover turned out to be a second-rated hypnotist. Disappointing. But you, you kicked butts and solved the puzzle. Even when you had no idea what was going on. Really, you're quite amazing."

"Too bad you couldn't collect your winnings and treat me to dinner. Should've asked him to transfer the money to your offshore bank account before he released his last breath."

"I believe in you, not like that creep who couldn't even hypnotize right. I believe you can battle against the winds of suffering. In fact, pain propels you through your pain. Like a positive feedback. So I had the Guardian give you a somewhat painful memory to test your resilience." She raised the glass and toasted to my triumph over pain. "Because your heart isn't flesh and blood. And your nerve, well, your nerve—"

"You shouldn't have dragged in Fernando's name. I would've found the password whether or not he created the file."

My neighbor was eating oatmeal and drinking orange juice next to her kitchen window. I should join her and take her for a stroll in Central Park. Maybe we'd go for chilidogs after her therapy session.

Holly finished the champagne, got my laundry basket from the bathroom and gathered the socks and underwear strewn throughout the living room.

"I preferred to have killed the old man. Should've let me keep that fake memory. And you're right about my heart, pure granite." Still, I drew strength from Fernando having killed the old man. At a cost though. I'd lost my appetite for durian pies. "Do you hate me or are you just sadistic? At least, Dolly schemed and murdered out of hatred and vengeance. That, I can understand and even respect. But you, I don't."

"I love you."

"I hate you."

"No, you don't. You can't love and you can't hate."

"I must admit, you're quite ingenious to use the code-word to unleash that dream in the woods. Then use the same dream to wipe out the fake memory." I got a napkin from the kitchen. Time to impress her with a trick. "But the dream popped up several times before I entered the password. So that charlatan's hypnosis really sucks."

"That quack, he resisted my idea. Maybe next time—"

"Not likely, as you'll soon find out. But you're right, this is the end." I didn't care when the diamond lover had broken into my house and hypnotized me. What did it matter? I turned my right palm upward and placed the napkin over it. "Steak or lobster?"

"Steak."

I pulled away the napkin and handed her the plate of medium-rare filet mignon with sauté mushroom and onion. I'd learned to do that trick yesterday, but still didn't understand how it worked. The steak appeared as if I could change matter and energy and warp space and time. Had I become God? I hope not.

"By the way, I wrote that story about the boy killing another boy. Last summer while in psychotherapy. Don't need to worry about it. Gone from your mind. Won't dream of it again. That is, if the diamond lover didn't mess up your brain." She accepted the plate and cleaned her hands, then pinched a piece of onion and tossed it into her mouth.

"Not just that dream," I said. "A nice touch changing my diary entries. But what's up with those dry scenes? Should've spiced them up with nasty villains and pretty women. Then, I wouldn't suspect they'd been tampered with." Thanks to her, I no longer could distinguish between real and fake entries. But, no harm done. "See, I know something about fiction."

"That creep claimed to be the *Guardian of Memory*. But, he knew zilch about you. Not even your egotism and narcissism."

"Do you despise my egotism and narcissism? They're some of my best qualities." For the past months, I came to despise these traits. I thanked Fernando for giving me the chance to care for Suzie and I thanked Suzie for giving me the honor to talk to her. I'd treasure those moments more than my statuettes and certificates.

"But I love you." Holly opened the locket hanging from her neck to reveal my picture and she kissed it.

"What do you mean?"

"I know you inside out. I know you as much as I know myself."

I handed her the fork and knife wrapped in a napkin. The Priest would've offered her to old Fyodor if the police hadn't arrested him for killing Clint. Even now, while on bail awaiting trial, he was looking for the burnt offering and would thank me if I gave him the chance to earn another life sentence. But I had other plans for her.

"Can you guess what I've planned?" She sat on the sofa and sniffed the steak.

"How do you want to end our story?"

"There's a reason why I love you so much. No mush. No sentimental drivel. Just plain old Francisco Guzman." She stabbed the mushroom with the fork and put it into her mouth. "You deserve a special ending."

She cut out a cube of steak and turned the fork to inspect it and she raised her thumb to approve the cuisine. I expected nothing less. Even Ms. Boss, the connoisseur, praised my cooking. If only I could cook for Faith, my beloved.

Still, even if I could create a more fascinating world, I wouldn't trade my experience. The sun warmed my face as I finished the champagne. A sparrow landed on the ledge below the window and sang to the new day. Yes, the brain in the cellar was dreaming of my adventures. Let Descartes dream since he couldn't do anything else. Let me, Francisco, live what the brain could only yearn and dream.

"Can you imagine that diamond lover looking down at you? I would've killed him myself if you hadn't. So you'd know how much I admire you, how much I love you."

I believe her. She would kill. Her calm, but sad eyes reminded me of Ingrid in my dream. If I forgot everything she'd done, if I only looked into her eyes, I would've believed she loved me. But she'd harmed everyone I cared about. She'd even defiled Fernando's name. So what did she mean by love?

"Wish I could take credit for it." I admired Fernando for having the foresight to get rid of the diamond lover. Each evening, even when dead tired, I'd glance at his framed picture and favorite baseball card on the nightstand before sleeping. I'd visited his and Suzie's graves every month since my last dream, and even begun to write letters to him, confessing how much I miss him, how much I love Faith, and how I helped the government track down a Ponzi schemer and recover six-billion dollars from his Cayman Islands account. Taking those letters to his grave and reading them while I listened to my voice mingle with the wind's whispers. Sometimes, I wouldn't want to come back to the apartment.

Holly put the steak into her mouth and drank champagne to wash down the food. Looked out the window and followed a sparrow's path until it disappeared beyond the Empire State Building. She threw the glass across the living room, spilling the champagne and cracking the glass into thousand fragments on the kitchen counter. "You still don't get it. I love you."

"You're right. I don't get it." I recalled Faith lying on the floor after she'd been tortured, her leg sticking out of the blanket. Again feeling her fragile body. After finishing the champagne, I also threw the glass into the kitchen.

"I did everything for you. Not for the money, but for you. I could've taken on several more cases and earned a few million dollars, but I didn't. I planned. I coordinated everything. I convinced that creep to go along with the idea. Don't you see? All my effort, all for you." She put the plate on the coffee table and again opened the locket to reveal my picture.

"I don't get it." I leaned against the wall, my legs struggling to support my body. I should to sleep and dream of being Descartes' brain. I'd failed time and again and Faith and my neighbor had suffered and Suzie had died. Even after cracking the code, even after eliminating Clint, I couldn't protect them. Above all, I couldn't understand Holly. Ganesh should've come and unravel her nonsense with his twisted logic.

"When I looked for you after getting the job offer, I only wanted to celebrate my success. Nothing more."

"We celebrated." That night's shapes and colors still flashed in my mind, but its details didn't warm my heart anymore. I avoided her face as I shunned her thoughts and feelings. I no longer knew her likes and dislikes, as I no longer knew my mind and heart.

"But something happened along the way. I grew and matured. Saw part of me in you and part of you in me. You and me, different but rounding out each other, like yin and yang. Incomplete without the other. After we'd broken up and dated others, I realized you're the only man I could ever love." She grabbed the champagne bottle and swigged several drafts. "None of your lovemaking meant an iota of love. Even if you made love to that girl Faith, you'd dump her sooner or later. You can't change your DNA. Well, I love you just as you are."

"I don't get it." I couldn't compose her words into a picture or a story, the syllables bouncing off my eardrums like random notes. As if my brain had fired me. As if she had spoken in Latin.

"Haven't you realized through all this how much I love you? No, not to possess you, not to control you, but just to love you." She picked up the fork and rotated the steak on the plate. "But somehow, your brain is missing something. You couldn't understand. Or maybe you don't want to understand. And you still couldn't understand how much I love you."

"What do you mean by love?" No, I didn't understand what the hell she was saying. The loony virus must've attacked my brain cells. Or maybe the government had programmed my mind.

"Do you know what love is? Have you ever loved anyone? Have you ever loved even yourself?" She pushed away the plate and paced between the sofa and the window. She was desperate. She was suffering. "No, no, no, you couldn't even love yourself."

"Did you enjoy the thrill of the bet? Like when you won a thousand dollars in Las Vegas. And even at your job, you thrived from the thrill of gambling on your strategies and tactics. You love winning. You're addicted to it." Did I love Faith? Yes, I did and still do. I'd destroy Ganesh to win her over. Never giving her up like the loser handing Ingrid to Dr. Tang. Never, I'd fight to the end for love even though I don't have superpower.

"Wasn't sure you'd suffer. Didn't believe you would. But it seems you had. Then, how could you not feel my love? How could you not understand love?" She caressed my cheek, her eyes shining bizarre warmth. "You poor lost soul. I'd tried to redeem you. To help you find that missing piece. No, nothing can fill that void, I know that now. I don't blame you. It's your brain that's the problem."

"Thank you for your help. Wish that could compensate for everything. But since you led Clint to Faith, what should I do to you?" I'd suffered. More than she could imagine. More than I'd expected. After Fernando had passed away, I didn't believe I could suffer for anyone else. But I suffered, and experienced pain and love and regret when my neighbor went into a coma, when Faith groaned in pain, when Suzie departed.

At that moment, light beyond the galaxy shone in my mind and a whisper in the silence touched my heart. Satori. I understood the secret behind my magic trick. I could've resurrected Suzy. I regretted the wisdom and the enlightenment. I regretted the knowledge of good and evil. If only I were real. If only I could proclaim, "Cogito ergo sum." I cursed Descartes for creating Holly, such a monster, a sadist, a psychopath. Sure, he was one, so he created one in his own image. But no, I created her. I created the monster.

"You can begin by kissing me. Then we can improvise as we move along." She took off her dress. And wrapped her hands around my neck. "We belong together. We're so alike."

"So I'm sadistic also?" I could love and hate, that much I knew. Sure, I'd hurt my enemies. And would I. But not to enjoy their pain and suffering. Anyway, nothing mattered anymore.

I didn't want the adventures to end, but all heroes, even the Almighty Fransuccesco, must depart to a better world. Some crap like that.

I grabbed her. I kissed her. She stabbed me. She twisted the blade's handle. I continued to kiss her until her hand released the knife, the blade deep in my abdomen. She stabbed me just as Ingrid had the amnesiac.

"Such a cheap blade. I expected something more fancy. Now, I'm really disappointed." I yanked out the knife and, to impress her, slashed my wrist with it. And behold, no blood. Holly backed away until she tripped over the sofa and stumbled into its bosom.

No, wrong guess, I'm not an android. No way I'd be that amnesiac.

"As I said, the end. Hope you had fun." I waved my hand. Day turned into night. The steak turned into lobster. The coffee table turned into a dinning table. And Holly turned into Faith. Lovely.

I held her. I kissed her. I am Descartes and I am the Alpha and the Omega.

###

ABOUT THE AUTHOR

Leonard Seet is the author of the novel *Meditation On Space-Time* and *Magnolias in Paradise.* His short stories have appeared in the Duende Literary Journal, *Quarterly Literary Review Singapore*, and *Pilcrow & Dagger.* The story "Black-Naped Oriole in Hokkaido Snow" was a podcast winner at Pilcrow & Daggar and he received honorable mention in the Writers of the Future Competition for "Don't Be Afraid of the Black Rain."

Visit the author's blog:

http://leonardseet.blogspot.com